THE SILENT LISTENER

A searing psychological thriller that will have you gripped from the first page

LYN YEOWART

JOFFE BOOKS

Joffe Books, London
www.joffebooks.com

First published by Penguin Random House
Australia Pty Ltd

First published in Great Britain in 2021

This book is a work of fiction. Names, characters, businesses, organisations, places and events are either the product of the author's imagination or are used fictitiously. Any resemblance to actual persons, living or dead, events or locales is entirely coincidental. The spelling used is Australian English except where fidelity to the author's rendering of accent or dialect supersedes this.

Cover art by Adam Laszczuk

ISBN: 978-1-78931-778-7

For every child denied the love, security, and peace that a home should provide, especially John and Ken.

PROLOGUE

JOY AND GEORGE

1983

The moment he dies, the room explodes with life.

I am up, pulling open drawers and dragging out underpants, singlets and socks with ugly, trawling fingers.

I'm probably in too much of a hurry, but there you go . . .

I don't care.

I wonder why I didn't do this sooner, why I waited until the end.

I can't find it.

I want to ring Mark (but of course I can't) and scream, 'He's dead. He's dead. Do you know where it is?'

He'd say, 'On the nail.' I'd say, 'Nail? What nail?'

'In the wardrobe.'

I yank open the single door of the old wardrobe and stare at the clothes hanging there. Thirteen sets of clothes he hung with obsessive care and put on so many times they took on his shape. Thirteen images of my father.

One by one, I pull them out and toss them on the floor.

Dad the longest-standing Elder. Dad in the vegetable garden.

Dad trying to impress the bank manager. Dad playing bowls.

Dad fishing.

Dad fixing fences.

Dad killing Ruths. I stop. All those chooks over all those years, each one called Ruth, each one beheaded by him on the chopping block. I throw 'Dad killing Ruths' to the floor and continue.

Dad praying with Mr and Mrs Boscombe after Wendy disappeared. Poor Wendy Boscombe. Ruth was right when she said they'd never find her or her missing doll.

Dad playing in the band.

Dad at Hall Committee meetings. Dad at Bible Study.

Dad milking cows.

Dad goal-umpiring. White trousers, white shirt, long white coat. Like a modern-day angel. (Right at the back, I notice.)

I stick my hand into the darkness, and my palm hits something sharp. I peer in. And there it is. A solitary nail hammered into wood. And hanging on the nail is a belt.

One belt. And ten thousand magenta screams.

I see my father pushing back his disguises and reaching in for that belt, oblivious to the old screams in there. Then, later, hanging it up delicately, obsessively. Oblivious to the new screams.

I unhook it and hold it in my hand.

It's a simple farmer's belt. Wait — allow me to clarify. Not the belt of a simple farmer, but a simple belt that belongs to a farmer. Correction: belonged. Past tense, which tastes delicious on my tongue.

The belt is made of plain black leather, and has a silver buckle with a silver tongue.

That's how they'd describe it in, say, a criminal trial. But that's only its outward appearance. More accurate for the defence counsel to say, with much emphasising and heavy pauses and gesticulating, 'Yes, members of the jury, just an ordinary, simple farmer's belt. But allow me to tell you what you can't see when you look at this belt. This belt is thirty-five years long and two children wide, and old blood leaks out of every hole. Children's blood. Run your fingers down it, and feel not leather, but pain. Hold it up to your nose and smell not leather, but fear. Bend it, and hear not leather creaking, but children screaming.'

The people in the gallery would gasp, and the jury members would shake their heads, appalled.

If it ever got to trial.

This is the first time I've held it. Of course, I've seen it before, and heard it, hundreds of times . . . dividing the air above me. And felt it, exactly the same number of times. Now I am the one holding it and he is the one on the bed, quiet and afraid.

Surely he is afraid? Now that his time has come?

I lift it towards my face. The defence counsel was right. The smell of fear burns your nostrils.

I walk over to the bed. His face is yellow-grey.

I look at the mess on the old bedside table: empty pill bottles, the thin blue face-washer with some mucus and blood sitting on it, the infant's cup he couldn't even hold to his mouth towards the end, the almost empty bottle of Passiona I got for him because he asked for it because it reminded him of Christmas and summer, and because he hated how his tongue yucked from the roof of his mouth, dry and sticky.

I made a special trip into town and bought eight bottles of it, filthy sinner though I am.

At the end of the bed is the local paper I bought for him, too. He's been reading the same page over and over for days now, his demented mind sinking into misery each time, as he recognises the names of people who died last week. Well, to be accurate, I've been reading them to him. 'Dad, I've just picked up the local paper. How about I read you the death notices?'

I pull back the orange blankets and look at the thin body lying there, frail and lonely, but protected, dignified by blue pyjamas. I was never so lucky.

Now is the time for revenge.

I hold the pointed tail of the belt in my right hand, and raise my arm, with the belt hanging down behind me, the buckle annoying the top of my thigh. But that won't work, so I pull the tail with my left hand until the buckle is halfway down my back. That's better. With my eyes wide open, I sweep an arc with my arm and bring the belt down — counting, just like he always did.

'*One* — believe me — *two* — this hurts — *three* — me — *four* — more than it — *five* — hurts you — *six*.' He doesn't scream 'Stop, stop, please stop' because it's forbidden to say anything.

I count to fifteen, punctuating the numbers with the words I still know off by heart.

At the end, I collapse onto the chair beside the bed. Who'd have guessed it was so exhausting?

I stare at the death notices thrashed almost into pulp. Every last name, every first name, every 'beloved husband/wife/son/ daughter/mother/father of' is now in ribbons, but his silent, immobile body is intact. I was so sure I'd be able to inflict on his dead body what he'd inflicted on our living ones, but there you go. He was right after all — I'm useless.

On the upside, there'll be plenty of death notices for me to read in the next edition. All beginning with HENDERSON, George.

I'll put my own in every newspaper in Australia, so Mark will surely see one of them, and come to the funeral. So we can be reunited.

The belt, I notice, is still dangling from my hand.

* * *

At eight on the dot, I walk out of my bedroom into the kitchen, where Ruth will be waiting for me, like she always is. When I tell her that he's dead, that will be it for her. She'll leave. I knew she was only going to hang around while he was still alive.

But she's not there.

I frown, remind myself to stay calm, and walk into the good room to make the necessary telephone calls. Over at the phone, I slide the letter-finder on the old wooden tele-index down to H. The hospital says I have to ring his doctor.

I close the tele-index and slide the letter-finder up to D. There she is: Dr Cooper, Vicki. She says she will leave straight away, so she'll be here about nine. I want to say 'No rush' but instead I say 'Thanks' through grief-stricken tears.

Down to H again for Henderson. His brother's widow sobs. I want to say, *Don't cry, Aunty Rose, this is the happiest day of my life.* She says she will come tomorrow. But I say, 'No, don't worry, I'll take care of it all, I'll let you know when the funeral is. Yes, I found him this morning when I got up, not half an hour ago. No, I'm sure he wasn't in pain . . . he was on very good painkillers, you know. Bye, Aunty Rose, yes I will, I promise, bye.'

Up to B, for *Blackhunt Gazette*. I compose HENDERSON, George's first death notice over the phone. Derek on the other end makes a suggestion. I say, 'No, thank you.' He makes another suggestion. I am silent for a second, then I say, 'No, I know what I'm doing, okay?' He grimaces and rolls his eyes. I know he does. After he reads it back to me, he says, 'Right,' (a little too slowly for my liking, the 't' coming out like the ting of a triangle) 'that's nearly two lines, and it's two dollars twenty-one per line or part thereof, so that's four forty-two, and payment is due within twenty-eight days. You're just in time for tomorrow's edition. Thank you, Miss Henderson, and my sincere sympathy.'

Yeah, right.

When Vicki arrives, she puts on a sombre face and says she's sorry. Unlike Derek, she's at least perfected the art of sounding sincere. Steps over the shredded newspaper, raises her eyebrows slightly, and puts a finger to his cold wrist before pronouncing my father dead.

You need a degree for that?

Back in the kitchen, we sit at the old table while she asks me some questions and writes my answers in the top half of a form on a clipboard. Then she looks straight at me and says, 'Righteo,' in her merry-as-a-lemon-meringue-pie voice.

I think she's about to ask me to give her the leftover pills, so I mentally say to Ruth, 'I told you!' But instead Vicki says, 'Will Mark and Ruth be able to help you with all of this?'

Surprised by this question, I spit out, 'Well, not Ruth. She's left, hasn't she? I haven't seen her all morning.' As soon as the words come out, I know I shouldn't have said that. It's just going to complicate everything. And then I cry. I am, after all, a grieving daughter and an equally annoyed and worried sister.

'Righteo,' Vicki says again, but this time in a not-so-merry voice. I try to sneak a look at what she's written down, but can't make out a word. 'Not sure if you know the drill, but since he died . . . let's just say, unexpectedly . . . in his own home, and because your sister has left . . . unexpectedly . . . we have to notify the police. I'll call them if you like.'

I know she means 'whether you like it or not', so I gesture towards the good room where the phone is. While she makes the call, I sit in the kitchen and wonder what the hell's going on with Ruth. She didn't have to leave straight away, for God's sake.

Vicki comes out of the good room and plops down beside me. 'Local cop's on his way. Nice guy. Alex Shepherd. Been here forever apparently.'

I nod as if the name means nothing to me. But I'm thrown a little bit off balance if I'm honest.

'I took the liberty of calling Dunnes as well,' continues Vicki. 'Definitely the best undertakers for miles. Only ones, too.' She grins at her joke, and I offer a small smile in return. She keeps talking. 'So while we're waiting for Shepherd, best you call a minister, love.'

Back at the tele-index, I slide the letter-finder to B (no luck), then to R, where I find Braithwaite Alistair (Rev). I propose Tuesday afternoon, followed by tea and scones. Maybe a lemon slice or two. He says Tuesday is too soon, there'll be so many people, and the CWA will definitely need more time, even if it is just tea and scones. And lemon slices, I remind him.

He launches into a one-sided discussion about psalms and prayers for the service, but all I can think about is *there'll be so many people*, because we both know that about two thousand, give or take, are going to be there. Yep, that's right, hundreds of people are going to fill the church right up to its holy seams, and overflow into the hall where I used to go to Sunday School with Felicity.

Then, as if he can read my mind, Braithwaite Alistair (Rev) says that he'll install speakers and a television screen so people in the hall can watch, and that the CWA will serve the tea and scones — and lemon slice — in the same hall. And now I'm picturing how, one by one, all those people will grasp my hand and tell me they're grief-stricken and so, so sorry for my terrible, terrible loss.

But I bet not one of them will even mention Mark. Or Ruth. Eventually we hang up and I can focus again. The police will be here soon, so I've got to stay in control. And that means I need to curb my imagination. *Curb.* What a sensational word. The instant I think of it, its image of a soft, pliable orange sphere with a section sliced off it at an angle bursts into my mind. I give in to the bliss of the moment, then refocus. My control these days, as I will remind Ruth later, is excellent. Then I remember she's gone.

While we're waiting for the police to arrive, I make a pot of tea, and keep telling myself it will all be over soon, I've just got to get through the next few days, and after that . . . peace. I'll never have to talk to Ruth or look at her in that chair again. I'll get on with my life — for real this time — and never return to this decrepit storehouse of memories.

As I pour the tea, Vicki prattles on about some patient's problems, which I assume is meant to distract me from my grief. At appropriate intervals I frown and shake my head, all the time thinking that the undertaker from Dunnes will undertake to take my father away and bury him six feet under. As I picture the hearse (although I'm not actually sure if 'hearse' is the correct word at this point in proceedings) making its sombre way up the driveway, I decide on a cremation. In preparation for my father's next and final destination.

And while Vicki prattles on, in between dunking Mrs Larsen's shortbread into the tea and taking great slurps from the cup, I think about the conversation I'm going to have with Mr Dunne in a few days.

'Mr Dunne,' I rehearse in my mind, 'I have something to go in my father's coffin.' I lift up the hessian bag and hold it over the desk between us. He stares at it.

'Please,' I say in my grieving-daughter voice. 'It meant a lot to my father.' With the back of my left hand, I wipe away a tear from my left eye and then my right eye.

'But,' he says, 'it's too late. Everything is ready. And this is most . . . unconventional.'

Huh! He thinks I'm a pushover. A compliant little girl-woman who needs to be put in her place. He probably knew my father. Hell, they probably played bowls together, or prayed together. Or both.

The old Joy would have apologised and quietly retreated with the bag concealing her father's belt. Because the old Joy always let my father and people like Mr Dunne tell her what to do and keep her small and obedient, while the eels writhed in her stomach, getting fatter and blacker and slimier by the second.

But the old Joy, the silent listener, is gone, and the new Joy looks right back at him and says, 'All you have to do is lift up the lid and put it in. Less than thirty seconds. So it would only be too late if he was already cremated, wouldn't it?' And she smiles as she puts the bag on his desk.

He snatches it up and shakes it as if he's calculating the excess baggage fee he'll have to pay to St Peter. Or Cerberus.

'Yes. Well, of course. Whatever you want for your beloved father.' I can see drops of white sarcasm dripping from his mouth, but I don't care. 'And now,' he says as he stands up, 'if you'll excuse me, Miss Henderson, I have several things that require my attention.' He holds the bag away from his body as if it's full of hissing ferrets. 'And this is the first of them.' He turns towards the door behind him.

'Just a minute, Mr Dunne. There's one more thing.'

He turns around slowly, a smile positively chiselled into his face. 'Yes?'

'This goes in too.' I put my hand in my pocket, lean forward and place it on his leather-edged blotter.

'What is it?' he asks.

I look surprised, as if he should know. 'This . . . is the last nail in his coffin.'

PART ONE

1

GEORGE AND GWEN

June 1942

He walked straight up to her before the first dance of the night, while Gwen and her friends were fidgeting with their belts and gloves and hats. 'Excuse me, ladies,' he said, as he made a beeline for her.

They looked up at him, giggled, and huddled a little closer like chooks, heads angled and eyes agog.

He smiled at Gwen and bowed his head a fraction. 'George Henderson. May I have the pleasure of this dance?'

'But . . . they haven't started playing yet,' said Gwen, pointing at the band setting up on stage.

'When they do?' George broadened his smile and held her eyes with his.

'Well, yes, you may.' She couldn't help but return his smile. 'Thank you.' He nodded, still smiling, and took a step back.

'Ladies.' And he bowed his head slightly to them before returning to his chair a few feet away from them.

The girls watched him, giggled again, and whispered, '"May I have the pleasure of this dance?" "When they do?"'

Gwen hissed 'Shhh,' giggling herself, but pleased he had chosen her.

'He's a looker,' said Jean. Gwen nodded, glancing at the stylish wave of thick black hair swept upwards from his forehead, his strong eyes and well-proportioned features. Plus, he was at least six foot, and reasonably well dressed despite rations. She wondered why he wasn't serving, but then again she could wonder that about all the men in the hall.

When the band began, he returned, smiling, took her hand and led her onto the dancefloor, her heart fluttering.

And from the minute they began dancing, it was clear that the smiling George Henderson had decided they were to marry.

2

JOY AND RUTH

December 1960

God decorated the dirt track that ran between Wishart Road and Kingfisher Primary School with thistles, snakes and bull ants. Then He added rain and mud. Almost made you want to get home quickly.

This was the last time Joy would walk along that track. Next year, in just a few weeks, after Christmas and January had been and gone, when the long terrible holidays were finally over, she'd be catching the bus with Mark to high school. Travelling forty-eight miles every morning and evening, leaving home a lot earlier and coming home a lot later.

Saying goodbye to Mr Plummer and the thirteen other students had made her a little sad, especially because she was walking home by herself today. Usually she walked with Wendy Boscombe. Wendy was only nine so they weren't really friends, but they walked down the track together every afternoon until they got to Wishart Road. Wendy's mother was always waiting with a big smile and a hug for her daughter, and sometimes a warm treat just out of the oven, like a jam biscuit or a coconut drop. Then Wendy and her mother would drive down Wishart Road to their farm three miles away, while Joy crossed the road and walked along the tractor lane to her family's farm in Bullock Road.

But Mrs Boscombe had been waiting for Wendy at school this afternoon because it was the last day of term and they were going into town for a chocolate milkshake, and from there they were going to Lakes Entrance for a holiday at the beach. Wendy had boasted about the holiday for the whole of the last week of term, and every time she'd mentioned it, Joy had felt the eels bite her stomach. As Wendy got into the car, the eels in Joy's stomach grew fatter and angrier. Even when Wendy rolled down her window and waved to Joy, smiling and calling out, 'Goodbye, Joy. I'll miss you next year,' the eels wouldn't leave her alone.

Walking along the track in the grey drizzle, Joy concentrated on enjoying the image of pale dusty-blue bubbles the word *nostalgia* created in her mind. What a wonderful word. She had only discovered it two nights ago in the little green dictionary Aunty Rose had sent her last Christmas, and the image of the powder-blue bubbles was already one of her favourites.

Even though she wasn't having a milkshake in town with her mother, and there were seven-and-a-half long weeks of holidays stretching ahead of her, she wasn't going to let that ruin anything. Because after that, everything was going to be different.

She'd be in Form 1 and Mark would be one of just sixteen students in Form 5. Most children left school as soon as they turned fifteen, but the school had written to their parents late last year recommending Mark stay because he was 'excelling academically' and made 'an invaluable contribution to the school's sporting successes'. Their father carried that letter with him everywhere, pulling it out to show people how clever and talented his son was. He'd even agreed to let Mark play for the local football club that winter and had goal-umpired at every match. Joy had enjoyed the Saturday afternoons with her father and Mark gone. Her mother often let her finish her chores quickly so she could sit in her room, where she and Ruth talked and read together.

Mark had told her there were over 200 students at Blackhunt High School, so Joy knew for sure that, unlike primary school, there would be other girls her age, and that she would make Friends — with a capital F. She also knew that the library took up an entire room, not just five shelves in a lonely bookcase next to the cricket equipment.

Yes, next year was thick with possibilities, like an ever-fattening cow about to have her first calf.

Joy's schoolbooks for next year were already stacked on the table in the good room. They had been there for three weeks now, stoically waiting for the grocery bill to be low enough that her mother could afford some plastic covering. That way, they'd stay clean and could be sold to a Form 1 student next year. Joy loved how crisp and promising they were and wanted them to remain this pristine forever. *Pristine* was another of her favourite words, and its image of a roll of silver silk unfurling into infinity was also one of her favourites.

But the price of groceries just kept growing like the thistles around the dam, thanks to the government and the endless grey rain, while the price her father got for milk just kept going down, thanks to the government and the greedy butter factory. So Joy knew that the books would probably never be covered and would grow sad and dirty and curl up at the corners. She would try, she would honestly try, to keep them clean . . . to keep them happy . . . to keep her father happy.

But every time her father looked at her, when his eyes swept over her ugly face that betrayed her as a 'filthy sinner', she knew she could never try hard enough.

When she got to the back door, she saw the tiny figures of her parents on their way to the dam. She squinted to get a closer look, and saw that her father was rolling the 44-gallon drum they'd kept chook pellets in. He'd discovered a small hole in it, which meant the mice and rats had been eating more pellets than the chooks. Although her family burnt most of their rubbish in the tank in the front paddock only twenty feet or so from the house, the dam was the final resting place for anything that was too big for the tank or wouldn't burn, like rusted rabbit traps and broken plough-blades her mother found when she was digging a new flowerbed. Her father certainly wasn't going to waste petrol going to the tip on the other side of town, let alone pay the fees to dump rubbish there.

Sometimes, if they had a large item like an old tractor tyre, they would leave it lying on the dam's bank, as if the effort to carry or push it through three paddocks was enough for one day. Then, a few days later, when someone was picking waterlilies from the dam, they might — or might not — decide to roll the rotting item into the water.

Joy never did, though, because the dam was, as her father often said, 'One foot deep for one foot, then fifty feet deep forever.' Even though she could swim, the infinite depth and darkness of the dam frightened her, and she knew that if she ever slipped over the one-foot-wide ledge, the hundreds of eels that lived in the dam would wrap themselves around her and pull her down to the bottom, and that would be that.

Joy could just make out that her mother was carrying the Dutch hoe they used as protection against snakes, as well as to pick waterlilies. Her father always lectured them about the snakes hiding in the grass and the dam. 'You never go to the dam without a long stick, d'you hear? You get bit by a snake around here, you're dead. Snakes love water.' And just in case that didn't frighten them into submission, he always added, 'And children.'

Joy knew her parents wouldn't return from the dam for at least twenty minutes, more if they were going to pick waterlilies, and that the bus wouldn't drop Mark off for another hour, so she walked straight through the kitchen, right past her bedroom door, pretending Ruth wasn't sitting in there in her chair . . . waiting for her . . . like she was every single day.

Then, with black corrugated fear sidling up her nostrils and down her throat, she crept into the good room. They weren't allowed in this room without one of their parents, and they weren't allowed in their parents' room at all, but she wanted to feel again the crisp, clean promises rippling out from the schoolbooks. Just looking at them made her mouth water.

The title of the book third from the top on Mark's pile had caught her attention when they'd unpacked them three weeks ago. 'Pride' she knew all about because it was one of the Seven Deadly Sins, but 'prejudice' was a new word. That night she'd looked it up in Aunty Rose's dictionary. 'An illogical dislike for a person or persons because of certain attributes, such as race or skin colour. An illogical belief that a person or persons with such attributes are of lesser value or are unable to perform at a particular level. Origin: Old French, from Latin *praejudicium* (*prae* "in advance" + *judicium* "judgement").'

Even though the image that appeared in her mind when she read the word was thrilling {a green winged dragon with black talons and glittering scales}, prejudice had to be a sin because God commanded us to love all His children.

She removed the books sitting on top of it, picked it up, opened it to the first page, and started reading. 'It is a truth universally acknowl—'

She slammed the book shut and put it back, terrified that somehow her parents would return impossibly quickly and catch her in this room. But even as she took a step away, the cover caught her attention. The author's name was written in swirling letters that made Joy picture a tangled vine covering the sun-drenched wall of a large garden that concealed a secret gate that opened on to a winding pathway that led to a turreted castle where there was an old woman with long wild black hair wearing a purple gown made of velvet, and in the very top room of the tallest turret there were hundreds of boxes of all shapes and colours and sizes, chaotically scattered in the room like petals fallen from camellia bushes, and made of every material known to man, like marble and silk and porcelain and mahogany and hand-woven grasses and cinnamon-smelling bark and embossed tin and painted glass, and each box came from a different part of the world and a different time, and contained magic the old woman had trapped in there centuries ago, and if you were brave enough to visit her, she would circle her long spindly finger over them all, finally nodding and saying, 'Yes, this one is for you,' and she would place it in your trembling hands, and when you lifted the lid—

She heard her bedroom door being opened, and her mother calling out, 'Joy! Where are you?'

The wizened woman and her mysterious boxes crumbled as Joy whirled around.

She put her hand on her stomach to calm the eels. They were always there. Her father caught eels in the dam and her mother chopped them up to make stews. It was a cheap meal and he said they should be grateful they even had food because millions of people all over the world were starving and they'd be grateful for a stew with or without eels. Joy chewed each mouthful more than the required sixteen chews, trying to be grateful, trying not to gag, but when she was eight and had the most terrible pains in her stomach and Dr Merriweather couldn't find anything wrong with her, she knew that all the pieces of eel she'd eaten had somehow grown into new eels in her stomach. At first, they were skinny and didn't hurt her very often, but they'd grown thick and angry and slimy. Five of them, each as fat as the rolls of butter her mother made on Saturdays.

And now, Joy felt them writhing and hissing.

'What are you doing in here?' Joy's mother was standing at the door of the good room, looking at Joy holding *Pride and Prejudice*. 'You're lucky your father didn't catch you.' She nodded towards the kitchen. 'You start getting tea ready. I've got wreaths to do.'

As her mother headed to the workroom where she made funeral wreaths and wedding bouquets, Joy felt her shoulders relax, though she was cross with herself that she hadn't thought of an excuse for being in the good room. She could have said she was dusting, or wanted to read her schoolbooks to be ahead. But whenever she was nervous or in trouble, her tongue sat on the roof of her mouth, her lips clamped together, her father's words keeping her silent. *Be quiet. Don't answer back. Did I say you could talk?*

She tried so hard to be good so she wouldn't end up like Mark. Their father often had to punish him for all the terrible things he did. On holidays and weekends, and after school, Mark had to help their father get the cows up to the dairy, bang in fence posts, mend barbed wire, wash cow muck out of the dairy, fix the windmill, scrub out the troughs, clean and sharpen tools, wash the tractor and the van, carry bales of hay to the cows, load the full milk cans onto the trolley and push it out to the road where the tanker collected the cans and returned the empty ones. And these were just the jobs Joy knew of. She thanked God every day that she only had to cook and clean under her mother's supervision. And pick flowers — being careful not to bruise them, of course.

Colin from the farm next door helped their father, too. Everyone liked Colin, even her father. Colin wasn't very good at reading or writing, but he could do anything and everything on a farm. Once, Joy had seen him accidentally tip over a full can of milk right in front of her father, and the eels in her stomach had reared up because her father's anger was like knives. She watched him lift his arm to smash Colin's face, but instead it landed gently on Colin's shoulder and her father said, 'Never mind, Colin. Grab the hose and we'll clean it up. No good crying over spilt milk, eh?' And as they hosed and swept it away, her father patted him on the shoulder and said, 'Good job, Colin, that's the way. I don't know what I'd do without you.' And Colin had, as was his way, repeated the words, 'Good job, Colin.'

Her father never punished Ruth either, but of course she never did anything wrong. Never had, never would. Oh no, their father was never angry with Ruth. All because of the accident. Once, on her tenth birthday, Joy had heard her father praying in his bedroom, asking God to take special care of Ruth. The familiar white jealousy had tingled at the back of her neck . . . even when it was her birthday, her father wasn't praying for her, was he?

Now, peeling the potatoes, she pushed her red barbed-wire annoyance with Ruth down into her stomach where the eels were, and tried to imagine how different things would be if there had been no terrible accident.

Poor Ruth, she told herself for the millionth time, trapped in her chair because of the terrible accident. Poor Ruth, trapped in the house, never able to go to school or work or even Church because of the terrible accident. Whenever Joy went into their room, whether she'd finished her chores or had just got home from school or Church, there was Ruth sitting in her chair. Always smiling, always eager to know what Joy had been doing, even if she'd just gone to collect the eggs. Always offering her opinion. And even though Joy was sorry for her big sister, she often wished that once, just once, she could walk into the bedroom and not see Ruth's smiling face or have to answer her questions or listen to her advice.

She covered the potatoes with water and got the meat and peas from the fridge. She heard Mark walk into his room to change out of his school uniform, then head outside to help their father.

As she put the potatoes on, unwrapped the chops and shelled the peas, she thought about *Pride and Prejudice*, and the old woman in the house with the magic boxes.

The potatoes had just started to boil when she heard the back door open and Mark walk into his bedroom. The eels reared up like cobras, their angry heads pushing and hissing.

She stood and watched the big bubbles {pink camellias} explode in the water above the potatoes, waiting for her father's footsteps. Just as the potatoes were starting to soften, she heard the back door being wrenched open. He stomped through the kitchen, ignoring Joy, and walked through the good room into his bedroom. She kept her head down, concentrating on the boiling water and staying quiet. He stomped back through the kitchen, and into Mark's room.

The screams came not even a minute later. As the water bubbled and the potatoes became softer and softer, she closed her eyes and saw her father chopping off Mark's limbs, blood spurting out like water from the fountain she had seen in *Rome: The World's Most Beautiful City*, her favourite geography book in the bookshelf at the little primary school.

She knew Mark's limbs were not being cut off, but the images were so vivid that she could smell the blood and feel how thick it was.

Her father came into the kitchen again. Joy kept perfectly still, her back to him, her tongue pressed to the roof of her mouth, watching the bubbles and feeling the eels getting fatter.

Please God, please help me to be good. Please don't let me get into trouble.

He stomped through the kitchen to his bedroom.

For thine is the kingdom, the power and the glory, For . . .

He stomped back through the kitchen and went outside, as Joy breathed out and drained the potatoes.

. . . ever and ever, Amen.

Later, when Joy and her mother were dishing up the chops and peas and mashed potato, Mark limped in and slowly sat down on his chair at the table. Her mother carried the plates to the table, while Joy got the salt and pepper and tomato sauce. Mark was looking down at the tablecloth in front of him. He could have been offering up peaceful thanks to God, his head bent, hands under the table, his body perfectly still. He said a quiet 'thank you' to their mother when she put his plate in front of him. His father directed one word to him: 'Grace.' It was a shard of ice. Mark recited grace, and the meal began. They ate in silence.

Swallowing a mouthful of mashed potato, Joy read the sing-song words roughly embroidered onto a dark-blue piece of velvet that hung on the wall behind Mark. The sole ornament in their home, it had been there all of Joy's life.

Christ is the head of this house
The Unseen Guest at every meal
The Silent Listener to every conversation

She remembered how, when she was younger, she had thought the unseen guest actually hovered over their kitchen table at mealtimes, stroking his beard and holding up his robes so they wouldn't dangle in the soup or mashed potato, watching to see if one of them gagged when they swallowed the tough meat, or didn't say please or thank you or excuse me, or used too much tomato sauce or salt, or ate too quickly, or too slowly, or squashed their peas, or drank too much milk or not enough, or pushed the food around their plate, or let their elbows touch the table, or put down a knife or fork too loudly, or chewed too loudly, or didn't chew enough, or . . . the list was endless. One Saturday, after Joy had finished her chores, Ruth suggested she write down all the meal-time rules they could think of. She stopped after she filled two pages of her maths exercise book. Not because she'd run out of rules, but because, as Ruth had said, that was enough.

If the hovering Christ saw one of them break a rule, He floated down to whisper in their father's ear, and then it would start. The thump on the table, the scraping of the chair on the lino as it was pushed back, the screams of eternal hell and damnation, his hot red face not ten inches away from the sinner's.

'You're an ugly, filthy sinner. What are you?'

'An ugly, filthy sinner.'

'A lazy, good-for-nothing sinner. Say it.'

'A lazy, good-for-nothing sinner.'

'Ask for forgiveness like the filthy sinner you are.'

'Please forgive me, Dad.'

'*Ssss*. You're useless.'

If he was screaming at Mark, Joy sat straight and still as a fence post, just like her mother, while the squirm of eels in her stomach grew. If he stopped shouting to take a mouthful of food or milk, she would quietly push a small amount of food onto her fork, carefully lift it to her slightly opened mouth, and chew sixteen times before silently swallowing. Inevitably, he would begin shouting again. Eventually the final word would be shouted as he thumped his fist on the table, or the wall, or Mark's plate, whichever was closest: 'Room.' His children would scramble up from their chairs and go to their bedrooms, mustard-coloured fear curling up from Mark's shoulders, while their mother would go to her workroom. Then there was the waiting — the terrible waiting. Ruth and Joy sat in their bedroom, not knowing what Mark was doing in his. They would hear their father go into his own room, come back and stomp into Mark's room.

And then there would be the screams.

No wonder Jesus had said, '*Suffer* the little children to come unto me.'

It was only a couple of years ago that Joy had realised Christ wasn't actually in the room, so she no longer worried about whether the unseen guest hovering above the table was wearing underpants under His robes, or whether His blood would drip onto her food from where the nails had been banged in.

But even though it was only His spirit hovering in the kitchen, Joy wished that the unseen guest would go away. Surely Jesus could be keeping an eye on sinners worse than her and Mark? Then she quickly prayed for forgiveness for having such terrible thoughts.

Looking away from the wall-hanging, she finished eating, then she and her mother took away the empty plates and dished up preserved pears and a large spoonful of cream from the top of the bucket of Maisie's milk that Colin brought up from the dairy every morning. When her father was halfway through his dessert, Joy or her mother put the kettle on so he wouldn't have to wait for his cup of tea and sultana biscuits.

But tonight, before he started drinking his tea, he suddenly pushed back his chair, making it scrape on the lino so fiercely that they all jumped, wondering who was in trouble now. He marched over to one of the kitchen cupboards, reached in and pulled out a small dark brown bottle.

He came back with the bottle clenched in his hand and shook it in front of Mark's face. 'See these? I have to take these because of you.' Going to the fridge, he pulled out his Passiona, which no one else was allowed to drink, threw two blue capsules into his mouth, and washed them down with the fizzy yellow liquid straight from the bottle.

He turned around, and Joy looked down at her bowl, not daring to move, her spoon frozen in a half pear. She heard him shut the fridge, put the pills back in the cupboard and return to the table. When she heard him pick up his cup of tea, she thought it was safe to start eating again. As she lifted her spoon, she looked up and saw him staring straight at her. 'Don't you go thinking you're better than he is, sneaking around in the good room like a filthy sinner.' The muscles in her neck stiffened and the eels squirmed. 'Because your time will come, believe me. Your time will come.'

And that was the moment when Joy realised that one day she was going to do something so bad — so sinful and so terrible — that he would shout the word *room* at her. And when that day came, he would chop off her limbs too, and she would die smelling her own thick blood.

3

JOY AND GEORGE

1 February 1983

'Hello! I'm Dr Cooper,' she says in an infuriatingly sweet voice, leading me into the consulting room. 'But call me Vicki, love. Vicki with an i.' She sticks out a sweaty hand for me to shake. It's plump, hot and wet. Disgusting. 'We spoke last week on the phone.'

'Yes.' I try to be inconspicuous when I wipe my hand on my jeans.

'It's so good of you to come all this way to nurse your poor old dad.' Vicki collapses into a chair behind her desk. 'Sit, sit,' and she waves at one of the chairs on the other side. I dutifully sit while Vicki, far from inconspicuously, looks at her watch. 'I'm sorry, but I haven't got long because I need to duck out and see poor old Clarice Johnson. She's got warts all *over* her feet. Had them for years, and now they're spreading up her legs.'

I have no idea how she expects me to react to this.

'She lives out west of the town on Johnson's Road, named after her dead husband's family. Not a neighbour for miles, so that's why I make a point of going to see her.'

Why the hell is she telling me this? I nod. I mean, I have to do something.

'Mind you, I did say to her, "I'm sorry, Clarice, but I might be late tomorrow. George Henderson has *family* arriving, and I've arranged to meet his daughter at the clinic at noon precisely." She was so upset to learn that George . . . your father is ill.'

Yes, of course she was.

Vicki sighs, then instantly cheers up and keeps talking. 'Anyway, I'm sure you haven't come to hear about Clarice's warts.'

I smile at her, and Vicki with an i lowers her voice.

'Now . . . your father. He's a little . . . delusional. It's the painkillers. Combined with his slow decline. And the muscle relaxants and anti-depressants. And his blood pressure tablets. And the anti-diarrhoea tablets. And the anti-constipation tablets. You know,' and her voice becomes merry again, 'modern medicine is marvellous. If it weren't for the painkillers, he'd be in the most terrible agony. I saw him this morning, and your neighbours said they'd drop in about eleven to make sure he was okay. They were relieved to know you were arriving, means they can focus on their own worries. Not that you heard that from me, love.'

I hold up a palm and shake my head, as if sworn to secrecy.

Does the woman ever shut up? 'Which neighbours?' I ask.

'Barbara Larsen, love.'

'Really?' Why would that old battleaxe check up on him?

'She's a good stick, isn't she? Anyway, as I told Clarice, and Barbara too, for that matter, your poor old dad should be in hospital, but you know what some people are like — well, mostly men, of course — and I told them, if he's going to be looked after, if his *family* are going to be here, then, I said, why *shouldn't* he be allowed to die in his own bed in his own house? It's what we all want, isn't it? And that's why I said yes to him, provided someone from your *family* is here to look after you.' She smiles and reveals teeth so white and perfect they have to be false. 'And . . . here you are. Family.' She lowers her voice again and laces it with sympathy. 'He must be so pleased.'

I nod and smile, wondering why she feels she has to change volume and tone every thirty seconds . . . and why my father would be pleased to see me.

'So, I'll just run through everything. First, you'll need to get these scripts filled, so you can give him the tablets he needs.' She opens a manila folder on her desk and pulls out some prescription sheets.

I look at them with horror. 'No, no, no. I can't give him his medication. I don't know anything about that sort of thing.'

'There's nothing to know, love. Well, nothing for *you* to know. I've done all the hard work.' And, pushing the scripts towards me, Vicki grins as if she's just shoplifted a couple of Cherry Ripes for us. 'Everything you need to do is right here.' She slaps a pile of papers that were underneath the prescriptions in the manila folder. 'You'll be fine.'

She hands me the sheets of paper, each labelled with a different day of the week. 'My own invention,' she says. Down the far-left column she's written the name of each medication and its required dose, while the other columns have times in the day. She's put a large red dot in various cells to indicate when I have to give him which medication. 'It's so easy. You just give him the right amount at the required time, and cross it off. Da-da! You can't go wrong.'

'But don't you have to do that? Or a nurse or somebody?'

'Sorry, love, I can't go way out there every time he needs a tablet. By the time I got back into town, I'd have to turn around and drive out again. Besides, there are people like Clarice Johnson who don't have family to look after them. And it's not as if you have to give him injections or anything.'

Grinning yet again, Vicki with an i picks up a bottle containing blue pills and shakes it like she's shaking Caribbean maracas. 'Best of all, I have a free sample of the painkillers for you.' Her voice becomes serious. 'He needs two of these every four hours.'

She walks around to my side of the desk, sits in the chair beside me and plonks the bottle right in front of me. And then she puts one of her large sweaty hands on my wrist, which was sitting on my leg doing absolutely nothing that warranted such attention. 'I've given you enough for a week, but . . .' She sighs, a little melodramatically, if you ask me. 'I'm afraid you'll have to come back for more if he . . . well, we don't know how long it will be until . . .' She looks heavenward for a moment, then — merry voice again — says, 'Anyway, these painkillers are strong as hell. You'll be fine. Just remember to make sure he gets them on time, otherwise he'll be in excruciating pain.'

I nod, having taken careful note of what Vicki has just said: *otherwise he'll be in excruciating pain.*

'Now, your father's told me all about you, of course.'

'Really?' Another surprise.

'Oh, yes. And your brother and sister. I've only been in Blackhunt a few months, so I don't know anything about anybody, but he told me he'd had three children,' she exclaims happily. 'You, Mark and Ruth. Mind you, he couldn't remember any of your phone numbers, but I found *you* in the White Pages,' she clicks her fingers, 'just like that.'

I study the sheets of paper because I don't want to look at her. I can't imagine what my father told her about me, let alone Mark and Ruth, so I play it safe and just nod.

'Between you and me, love, not that it's my place to pry, but I think your dad would have been very surprised to see either of them.'

'Well, you know how families are.' I stand up — I have to get away from this woman.

'Oh yes. Then I went looking for Ruth's number, thinking she might be interstate, and—'

'Is there anything else? I'd hate you to keep Mrs Johnson waiting.'

Vicki looks at her watch again and grabs her doctor's bag. 'No, I don't think so. I'll walk out with you.'

I can hardly object, so off we go as if we're long-lost pals. At least she doesn't charge me for the consultation. While we're walking through the waiting room, she suddenly says, 'I guess you knew Wendy Boscombe then, living so close?'

'What?' How does she know about Wendy?

'Such a sad story. I saw Mrs B the other day. First time she's been a patient of mine so I was reading her record before she came in, and it's just . . . so, so tragic.' Vicki shakes her head slowly. 'The suffering they must have gone through. I know it wouldn't matter what day it was, but to disappear just two days after Christmas.' She lets out a heavy sigh.

The fact is, I've never been able to come to terms with what happened to Wendy. The whole thing distressed me so much. I quickly sniff, scared that I might actually cry in front of Vicki. 'I know,' I say, hardly able to get the words out.

'Can you imagine never knowing what happened to your daughter? Poor woman. She said that's the worst part . . . not *knowing*. "If only we *knew*, Vicki," she said. Over and over again. "If only we knew what happened to her, then we could get some peace, our ordeal would be over." I was lost for words, I really was.'

I shake my head with empathy, although I'm sure that Vicki is never lost for words. Unexpectedly, pity washes over me like a nostril-burning cow-drench — if I'm honest, whenever I think about Wendy, I think about how upset I was, not how upset her parents must have been all these years.

We stop outside the chemist shop and my stomach lurches with guilt. But then I see from the sign on the door that it has different owners, so I've escaped what could have been an awkward situation.

'Okay, thanks, Vicki,' I say. 'I'll stay in touch,' and I walk inside.

After the chemist has filled all the prescriptions, I casually ask her if she knows the previous owner.

'Oh yes, I worked here with him for ages, and then we bought the business after he died.'

'Died?' I can feel the thick slimy blackness of eels in my stomach. 'What happened?'

Just as she starts talking, a woman in the shop yells, 'Filthy sinner,' and I turn to see her slapping a little girl's face, as a packet of jellybeans and a doll fall from the girl's hands to the floor. I'm like Pavlov's dogs — even after all these years. I can't move and all I can hear is the girl screaming while the woman, who is presumably her mother, grabs hold of her. 'Stop it, Belinda,' and she twists the girl's wrist. 'Stop it, y'hear?' But Belinda wails more loudly.

My eyes are frozen, my back is like a fence post. The woman bends down to pick up the jellybeans, dumps them back on the counter, hits the girl's bottom with force, and screams, 'Stealing's a sin, a filthy sin, y'hear? Now stop crying or I'll have to hit you again.' The doll's lying about a foot away from me, and its eyes are staring up at me from its porcelain head. My torso is a cold solid lump, and my tongue is pressed up against the roof of my mouth.

I blink when I realise the chemist is still talking to me. 'Did you know them?'

'A long time ago,' I say. 'I'll take a packet of jellybeans too. Is the rest of the family still here?'

'No,' she says. 'They moved to Antwerp, of all places. Very odd.'

I am ashamed. Of my childhood, of my family, and of my adult self for never contacting Felicity or her family — not one letter or phone call. Not even to let them know I was coming back. I promise myself that when this is all over and I've found Mark, we'll go to Belgium and find them.

I bought the jellybeans for Belinda, but I know the mother will scream at me too, so I stuff them in with the medication. I'm pathetic.

But I do pick up the doll. The mother snatches it out of my hand and shakes it in the girl's face. 'If you can't look after this, you won't have it, y'hear?' She jams it into her bag head-first and glares at me. 'What are you looking at?'

My heart is racing. There is so much I want to say, but the words are impossible. I stand there hating myself, and then I remember Felicity putting jellybeans in my hand a long time ago. I stick my hand back into my bag, pull out the packet and hand it over to the girl. 'These are for you, Belinda.'

She doesn't know what to say, so the mother screams, 'What d'you say, you ungrateful sinner?'

Belinda mutters, 'Thank you,' as her mother drags her back out into the heat.

I get in the car, trembling. Seriously, what kind of religious nutter speaks to their kids like that these days? I throw the pills and Vicki's medication sheets onto the passenger seat and reverse out. Vicki's on the footpath, smiling and waving.

'Good riddance,' I say, with a friendly wave, knowing she can't hear me. 'With a bit of luck, he'll be dead in a couple of days, and I'll never have to see you again.'

4

GEORGE AND GWEN

June 1942

While they danced, George smiled at Gwen and complimented her on her hat and her eyes and her dancing. He talked quietly, calmly, confidently. Gwen liked that.

He told her that he worked on his family's sugar beet farm, that his older brother, Bill, had returned from the war with two missing legs. Gwen shuddered involuntarily and wondered whether his hand on her back had felt her disgust. But he just smiled and kept on talking. He and his brother had a car. Well, not a car, but a little van that he loaded up with sugar beet twice a week to take to market, and not many young men could boast that in 1942. His father had died six months ago, his mother many years before when George was seven. After George and Bill got their inheritance, they were going to sell the farm. With the proceeds of the sale Bill was going to buy a small house in town, and George was going to buy a sugar beet farm — and a van — of his own. You couldn't go wrong with sugar beet, George explained, because sugar would always be in demand.

Gwen listened, aware of how different their lives were. True, both of them had lost their parents, but there the similarities ended. She was working in a factory to support the war effort, and on Saturdays she was allowed to work for Stan Forsythe, the local florist. Gwen had been lucky to get the job and her friends were envious of her day away from the factory. Stan made wreaths to go on the coffins of the dead, including those of soldiers who returned home to die, and the empty coffins of the soldiers who didn't return, and, more often than Gwen liked, the coffins of the parents who died of grief. Those were the saddest wreaths. (She wondered how George's mother had died, and if his father had died of grief after Bill had returned from the war without his legs.) She stuck camellia leaves into the bases of the sad wreaths, wired the dahlias and camellias that Stan then arranged above the leaves, and sprayed water on the finished wreaths to keep them looking fresh.

It sounded like George hadn't and wasn't going to serve. He didn't mention any training or postings, and she didn't want to ask. Maybe you were exempt if you were an orphan with a crippled brother? Or perhaps the sugar beet farm was deemed an essential service. She glanced at his face, and, now that hers was just inches away, she could see he was a lot older than she was. Probably not too old for the war, but too old for me, she told herself.

Just when she had decided that she would politely refuse him if he asked her for the next dance, his large hand on her back moved to where he could feel her bra through her thin dress. Embarrassed, she made a misstep and looked down at her feet to concentrate. But the more she concentrated, the more mistakes she made and the hotter her back became. And the more George smiled at her and complimented her on her dancing.

So it seemed impolite to say 'No, thank you' three minutes later.

During the weeks that followed, George persistently swept her off her feet with smiles and kind words, and

Gwen became more and more pleased that she had not said 'No, thank you.' And her friends became more and more impressed with this good-looking, kind, smiling man.

One Saturday evening, as he was walking her home from Stan's shop (where he was always waiting for her now at 5.30 on the dot), a small child came running towards them crying. His mother was at least twenty yards away, calling out 'Kenny, Kenny!' as she pushed a pram with one hand and held a howling baby over her shoulder with the other.

'Whoa, young man,' called George, kneeling down on one knee. 'What's the rush?' But when the boy was only about five feet from George and Gwen, he veered off the path and onto the road. A blur of George flew towards the road, and Gwen heard the blast of a car horn just as George caught the boy's leg above the ankle, somehow wrapped an arm around the boy's waist, and pulled with all his might. Before Gwen had even worked out what was happening, George and the boy were both lying on the nature strip. The boy was still crying, and there was blood on his face. His mother had thrown the baby into the pram and was racing towards them.

George climbed to his feet, pulled out his handkerchief and wiped his blood from the boy's face before pressing it against his own temple, which was bleeding badly.

When Kenny and the baby had finally stopped crying, the woman shook George's hand, confused thanks tumbling out of her. Then George took Kenny to one side, knelt down so their heads were level, and told him firmly but gently that he had to stay with his mother, even if he was angry with his baby brother for crying all the time, and that he would soon be a man and would have to protect his mother and brother. Kenny, obviously still shocked, nodded miserably.

As the mother grabbed both of Gwen's hands in hers, she noticed the small engagement ring on Gwen's wedding finger. 'Oh,' she said, 'what a lucky woman you are to have found such a kind, brave man.'

'Yes,' said Gwen, smiling. 'I am.' And her heart swelled with pride.

5

JOY AND RUTH

December 1960

Just as the image of her father cutting off her limbs and the smell of her own blood was filling her head, the lino screeched once more as her father pushed back his chair for the second time that night, this time to leave the room. It was only then that Joy felt time begin again.

Instantly, the rest of the family began the nightly routine. Dishes were carried to the sink, the sauce was put in the cupboard, the tablecloth was shaken and folded and put in the third drawer, the salt and pepper shakers were placed in the middle of the table ready for tomorrow's breakfast, the dishes were washed, dried and put away, and the floor was swept.

When her mother was rattling the metal soap shaker in the sink, she said, as if one of them had asked the question, 'He's fine. Absolutely fine. He gets migraines. So we all need to be kind to him.' It was Friday night so Joy knew that in a few minutes her father would reappear in the kitchen dressed for his Elders Session, walk through the room and leave. Monday and Thursday nights he had committee meetings, Tuesday nights was band rehearsal, and Saturday nights he either played guitar in the band or MC'd at engagements and wedding anniversaries held in Blackhunt Hall.

The dishes were nearly done when he came back into the kitchen with his Elders briefcase and left without a word.

After the chores were finished, they went to the bathroom, one by one, from youngest to oldest every night, to brush their teeth and then go to their bedrooms. On school nights, she and Mark were expected to do an hour's homework before going to sleep. They both had a makeshift desk in their rooms so that they didn't make a mess in the kitchen. Joy's desk was made from an old door her father had removed from the pump room in the dairy, then sanded, and sat on two wooden crates.

When it was holidays, their parents didn't care what they did in their room, as long as they were quiet.

In bed, Joy pulled out the little dictionary from under her pillow and opened it randomly. Each night she learnt a new word, enjoying the word's image as it burst into her head. This was the only time she could let the images take over, the only time she didn't have to first and foremost concentrate on the meaning or spelling of the word. When she managed to concentrate properly, she could read reasonably well, but if there was a word with a particularly vibrant or horrific image, like the bloodied axe that had burst into her head when she discovered the word *camisado*, she couldn't see anything but the image and could do nothing but sit, mute like an imbecile, while the image overpowered her brain. No wonder adults got frustrated with her when she was reading, and other children laughed at her. But she couldn't stop the images, any more than she could stop seeing Mark's limbs being chopped off when he was being punished, or stop the stories, like the one about the woman with the magic boxes, from wrenching her away from the here and now.

Ruth, of course, was right. She had to grow up and stop this ridiculous {a blue giraffe} nonsense.

Opening the dictionary, Joy decided to look up the new word her mother had used. When she found *migraine*, she allowed the image of a hot, throbbing multi-coloured bolt of lightning to fill her head. It was a strong word with its two bullet-like syllables, and it had an equally strong image.

'Joy!' Ruth's voice was silky smooth and beautiful. 'Put the dictionary away. Go to sleep.'

Reluctantly Joy closed the dictionary and pushed it back under her pillow. She didn't like to argue with Ruth because Ruth always won. It was as if she sat in that chair all day working out how to win every argument they would ever have. Joy looked at her sister, sitting on her bed, brushing her hair.

Ruth had the most beautiful hair Joy had ever seen. It was the colour of the shiny brown-red diamond on Maisie's white forehead. It was Maisie's milk that Colin brought up in the bucket each morning because Joy's mother said Maisie's milk was the best. Watching Ruth brushing her Maisie-coloured hair, Joy thought for the thousandth time that it wasn't just Ruth's hair that was beautiful. She had soft features and evenly set blue eyes like their father's, with a small nose dotted with brown freckles as if their mother had shaken some nutmeg across it. She would have been perfect if it hadn't been for the accident . . . and the purple birthmark that covered the left side of her face. But, Joy reminded herself, if you just looked at the right side, you'd think Ruth was an angel {a scrunched-up ball of clear cellophane crackling as it gently unscrunches itself}. Yes, Ruth was like an angel from Heaven — except for the accident and the left side of her face.

'Ruth, do you think Dad's sick and that's why he's taking pills?'

Ruth stopped brushing her hair. 'People don't take pills unless they're sick. But I don't know about migraines. He's probably got . . . what's that word you found a few weeks ago — the thing that grows in people's stomachs when they're angry?'

'Ulcer,' said Joy. The word's image was spectacular — an enormous red-brown toadstool exploding into thick brown liquid. She'd noticed that lots of words that contained the letter U had particularly disturbing images. It was very odd, but then again the letter U was a particularly abrupt letter, hard like a bullet. 'Do you think he's right, and Mark makes him sick?'

'You mean, do you and Mark make him sick?'

Joy grimaced. Ruth was right. She thought of how their father often said that he was 'pained' that he would be the only sad person in Heaven because Mark and Joy would be in Hell. So she knew she was going to end up with all the Catholics, Jews and heathen savages burning, screaming and bleeding for eternity. But whenever he said that, he seemed to forget that beautiful perfect Ruth would be in Heaven, so he wouldn't be alone. Joy knew that he would be angry if she said, 'But what about Ruth?' so her tongue stayed at the roof of her mouth.

Joy sent a quick prayer to God. She meant to say *Dear God, please make my father better so he doesn't need pills anymore,* but somehow it came out wrong. *Dear God, please make my father die.*

'Joy!' Ruth's whisper was as sharp and swift as a newly cleaned axe-head, cutting the words in half and making them fall to the floor so they couldn't escape through the ceiling and fly to Heaven.

'It was a mistake. I meant to say "*Don't* let my father die."' Ruth raised her eyebrows and stared at Joy.

'It's time to sleep.'

Silently, Joy walked to the door and turned off the light, felt her way back to bed and climbed in. The eels were pulsating in time with her heart.

'Goodnight, Joy.'

'Goodnight, Ruth.'

She pushed her hand under the pillow to feel the cover of her dictionary. Little black letters slid off the pages and shimmied over the back of her hand. The ink was soft and furry like the white velvet collar Mrs Larsen had sewn on Joy's Sunday School dress, and the letters made a tiny tinkling sound as they danced on her fingers. Joy's heart slowed. Words and letters were her best friends.

Apart from God, of course. And Ruth.

How could she possibly have such terrible thoughts about her father? She shivered and prayed for God's forgiveness. She would try harder. Her father was right. She was an ugly, filthy sinner and would certainly go to Hell with the Catholics and savages.

It was just as he had said. *Your time will come.*

6

JOY AND GEORGE

February 1983

When I turn into the gravel driveway, I'm surprised to see it's still lined with the forty-two camellia trees my mother planted before I was born. They look haggard, sick of life. The heat and the drought have almost destroyed them, but I figure a good downpour and a dose of fertiliser would resurrect them. Just in time for his funeral. Not that Mum will be making any of his wreaths.

I take my foot off the accelerator so the car slows down as it makes its way to the house. Just like my feet did when I walked up this driveway after school. I peer at the flower beds surrounding the house, most of them now exploding with red poppies. I grimace, thinking how the hundreds of flowers in bloom all through the year so colourfully disguised the kind of family we were.

The car stops just short of the path to the back door, and I look around, seeing everything through adult eyes for the first time. Paddocks as far as the eye can see, the bank of the dam rising in the distance, dilapidated sheds, the gardens now full of dead plants and sticky weed (except for the poppies), the chook shed with its sagging wire, the dairy to one side of it, the old wooden house itself. There they all are. On display for me, like some cheap, cruel museum.

The pills on the passenger seat are moaning. Jesus. I thought I was over that stuff. I sit there for a bit, with the engine running. I could turn around and go back home. Right now. Because I'm only doing this out of the goodness of my heart. When Vicki rang, I said 'of course' as if we were playing that stupid card game Happy Families. Collect the father, mother, son and daughter from the same family, and, hey presto, you have a happy family.

I'm definitely not here to play Happy Families.

I get out of the car and squint through the heat at the 'view'. Whenever I tell people I grew up here, they always say how lucky I am, how beautiful it must have been living among green hills in a dream countryside, blah blah blah. As if they'd actually enjoy trampling in the rain through mud-filled paddocks every day, and living fifty miles from the nearest town in a cold, rundown farmhouse with floors and walls that hide lies and terrible secrets. Those 'lovely green hills' reek of chores, mud and misery. And they're not green now — just yellow, rain-starved paddocks that roll up and away in every direction, dotted with black-and-white cows.

I can smell the disgusting stench that curls out of the old rubbish tank in the front paddock, a trail of smoke coming from it. How it burns, day in and day out, is beyond me, but even from this distance the ash and smoke are singeing my nostrils and throat.

Aren't there fire restrictions, for God's sake? I don't bother knocking.

The tall cupboard is the first thing anyone sees in the back porch. That's where we kept our coats, rubber boots, and a few gardening tools that Mum could grab without going over to the big shed. I fling open its doors and everything's still there, even the hooded plastic raincoat I was wearing the day I read half of the first line of *Pride and Prejudice.*

When I see the Dutch hoe we picked waterlilies with, I feel like something has punched me in the stomach. I push one hand against the coats so I don't fall. Honestly, if this farm was a theme park, they'd call it FearWorld.

I put my other hand on my stomach, swallow and lift my head. I'm here for one reason and one reason only, so a little bit of fear — okay, a tidal wave of fear and memories — isn't going to get in the way.

I walk past the laundry, where we plucked dead Ruths and stored layers of waxed winter eggs, and take a breath as I push open the kitchen door. The blinds are pulled down over the south-facing windows so it's dark and unexpectedly cold. I stand still so my eyes can adjust to the darkness.

Who am I kidding? I'm standing still because I'm not sure I can do this. Not sure if I can go through the good room, into his bedroom and up to his bed where he must be lying.

Then I hear a crackly papery voice cutting through the dark air. 'Hello, Joy. You took your time. He's probably only got a couple of weeks left, you know. If that.'

I squint towards the voice. Ruth. She hasn't changed a bit. Tall and thin, with red-brown hair parted in the middle, long tapered fingers and smooth skin. My big sister. My perfect sister. If you ignore her birthmark. And the accident, of course.

The words come out before I can stop them. 'What are you doing here?' She's the last person I expected or wanted to see. But I'm just going to have to deal with it. I dump Vicki's forms and the bottles of pills on the Laminex table.

'And I'm pleased to see you, too,' she says. Even with the blinds still drawn, I can see the purple birthmark on the left side of her face pulsating as she talks. 'I have a plan.'

'I'm not interested,' I say, pulling up the blinds. Suddenly it's not that cold in the room after all, and I open the mustard-yellow fridge, which has been there all my life. The blast of cold air's a relief, and if I hold the door open I can't see Ruth.

'But you'll love it.' Now her voice is silky and silvery. It always took a few moments for it to change if she hadn't been talking for a while. Presumably an odd side-effect of the accident. 'I'm going to help you get the one thing you've always wanted, Joy.'

I pull out a bottle of Passiona. His favourite drink. The drink we were never allowed to have. There's not much left so I glug it straight from the bottle. It's a bit flat, but cold and wet.

'So we've both come back to nurse him,' continues Ruth. 'Such good daughters, aren't we?' She looks at the medications on the table. 'Are those his pills?'

Ignoring the question, I examine the meagre contents of the fridge, looking for something half-decent to eat. There's next to nothing and I'm cross that I didn't buy any food when I was in Blackhunt. Between Vicki with an i and Belinda's screaming mother, I wasn't thinking straight.

Ruth smiles and puts down the book she's reading. 'We've got a lot to talk about.'

'Have we?'

'Of course. But first you have to go and see him.'

I'm standing there with the empty Passiona bottle dangling from my hand. 'I don't want to.' I know I sound like a petulant child.

'It won't be as bad as you think,' says Ruth, gently.

I put the empty bottle on the kitchen bench. My hands are hot and trembling, and the eels in my stomach are hissing and writhing. I remind myself that he's old and sick. Practically dead, according to Vicki. What is there to be scared of?

'He can't hurt you, Joy.'

I run my hands over the scars on my shoulders and repeat once more what I said a thousand times on the drive from Melbourne.

Never forget, never forgive.

I have no intention of doing either.

7

GEORGE AND GWEN

August 1942

Walking down the aisle wearing a borrowed wedding dress, Gwen thought about how quickly the two months had gone by since her first dance with George. But everyone got married quickly these days, at least in Willshire, thanks to the wars and the Depression. Everything was precarious, except marriage, which was forever. Especially, she thought, marriage to George Henderson.

He had been so insistent, and Gwen had been overwhelmed with joy and pride when he said he'd booked the church even before he proposed to her.

Her boss, Stan Forsythe, gave her away in front of a congregation of fifteen, who later made their way to the reception of sandwiches and tea in the same hall where George and Gwen had first danced. Yet another example of how thoughtful and sentimental George was.

Despite her love for George, Gwen was horrified that his brother Bill came to the wedding in an ugly wheelchair with empty trouser legs folded under his stumps. She avoided looking at him, and even as she uttered 'I do' she was thinking that it would be much easier for everyone if people in wheelchairs just stayed at home, out of sight, so that no one would be offended.

Stan gave Gwen away because Gwen's father had died from tuberculosis before she was born — and before he had married her mother. For reasons that no one could explain to Gwen, her mother had refused to have her adopted, but after she left Gwen with her spinster aunt one day, saying she'd be back in two hours, she was never heard of again. Rumour had it that she'd flung herself off the riverbank behind the Mechanics' Institute, though her body was never found. The aunt kept her abandoned great-niece for eighteen years, but also kept her distance. Gwen frequently heard her informing anyone who would listen that children were like dogs — they had to be taught how to behave or they'd turn out to be wild creatures. So Gwen was always somewhat perplexed when she saw families laughing rowdily in shops or on their way to church, and oddly relieved when she returned home to the simmering unease in her great-aunt's house.

After Gwen said yes to George's proposal, she realised with pride (an unfamiliar sensation) that she was embarking on a journey that her parents had not even bought tickets for.

Although the wedding was small and unremarkable, Gwen's bouquet was not. She had picked and wired a mass of white roses and foliage from various neighbours' gardens, arranged them into the shape of an upside-down drop of water with a long curved tail, and covered the wires with a white ribbon she'd pulled out of an old dress. Everyone ooh-ed and aah-ed at the magnificent bouquet, and the following week the front page of Willshire's local paper had a photo of her and George standing outside the church, with the headline 'Wedding Bouquet "Rose" to Occasion'. Jean, who was Gwen's bridesmaid, proudly placed the newspaper cutting in her photo album so she could show Gwen when she came to visit. But it lay there, slowly yellowing, for decades until Jean died. When her son was throwing out her unwanted belongings, he momentarily wondered who the strangers were, before tossing it into the incinerator.

George and Bill had managed to sell their father's farm, and George had indeed bought another van and a small farm, paying the deposit with his half of the inheritance. But, as George explained to Gwen, the days of sugar beet were over. It seemed that sugar cane farmers up in sunny Queensland were killing the sugar beet industry in Victoria. It was time to give up that game, so he'd bought a dairy farm — and its cows. 'People will always want milk and cream and butter, Gwen. Believe me, I know what I'm talking about.'

After the wedding, Gwen and George got in George's little second-hand van and drove to Willshire's only hotel. They stayed just one night because the next day George was taking them straight to their new home. 'No need for an expensive honeymoon,' he'd said, smiling what Gwen thought of as his Cary Grant smile. 'Living on our own farm, setting things up for our new life, that will be honeymoon enough.' And Gwen was sure it would be.

The next morning, they drove to the great-aunt's to pick up Gwen's clothes and glory box. The elderly woman also gave them a metal box packed with food and ice. Gwen muttered her thanks but could not look her aunt in the eye; she was deeply embarrassed that George had pushed her white flannel nightie up to her neck the night before and removed her white underpants so he had access to her whole ashamed body.

As they drove away, Gwen felt her great-aunt's relief pierce her chest. It reminded Gwen of how she had pierced the calyx of each rose for her bouquet with the black florist's wire — it was both cruel and exhilarating.

The further they drove from Willshire, the more excited Gwen became about her new life. It wasn't that her old life was terrible, it was just that the phrase 'new life' promised so much. No more working in the factory, and no more feeling beholden to her great-aunt. And surely George wouldn't claim his spousal rights every night.

As the hours passed, the roads became rougher and narrower and the houses further and further apart. At 12.30 exactly, George pulled over and, sitting in the little van because of the rain, they ate the sandwiches left over from their reception. At 12.45 exactly, George started the engine again. When it was nearly two o'clock, they turned onto an uneven dirt road that was more like a mud track.

After another hour, when George turned into a gravel driveway, announcing that they were 'home', Gwen was lost.

8

JOY AND RUTH

December 1960

On Saturday, the first day of the school holidays, Joy's mother was up and gone early to collect a package of wire, ribbon and wreath bases that she regularly had freighted to Blackhunt's train station.

After doing her chores, Joy began preparing lunch for the rest of the family, occasionally glancing towards the good room, where she could see the schoolbooks piled up on the table. The pages of *Pride and Prejudice* were calling out to her. *Come and read me, come and read me.*

Her father was a long way away; the book was only seven steps away. So even though the eels were hissing warnings, Joy found herself lying on her bed with *Pride and Prejudice* in her hand. She would read just ten pages — no, five. No one would know. She would be very careful.

Just as Mr Plummer had instructed, the first thing she read was the blurb {a tall silver swing}. Then she opened the book — just enough so she wouldn't crease the spine — and began the little biography of Jane Austen on the soft cream pages.

'You'll get into trouble,' said Ruth. 'Terrible, terrible trouble.' Joy ignored her.

'I don't think you should do this,' said Ruth. 'It's too dangerous.'

'I'm just going to read five pages,' Joy said, knowing that she was being stubborn.

She turned to the next page, the publication details. She swallowed softly as she read the name of the publishing company, 'New World Library of Literature Incorporated', and an image burst into her mind. A magnificent building, with high-ceilinged hallways that opened on to room after room after room of authors wearing soft warm clothes that never got dirty from mud and cow muck, and writing on creamy sheets of paper with long-nibbed pens filled with rich indigo ink, or using typewriters, fingers and keys whirring as if the human and the machine had knitted into one, working and plotting together to create stories that would thrill and beguile children and adults alike (Joy smiled a little bit — that sounded like an advertisement for a circus). In other rooms, illustrators were creating intricate drawings to pepper the books' pages with fire-breathing dragons, dirty urchin-orphans pickpocketing in London's plague-ridden lanes, ancient wizards making bats disappear, and mischievous elves giggling uncontrollably. And when the illustrations and manuscripts were all finished, they were rushed to the enormous printing room, where wizened men painstakingly {the twisted hand of a dead child} fed frames full of metal letters and engravings into the clanking metal machine that stretched the entire length of the vast room. The Master Printer did a last-minute check, added a drop of oil into a minuscule hole, opened a little side door and peered inside before meticulously adjusting a set of knobs that clicked and clacked as he turned them this way and that.

Then he straightened his back, looked at the other printers gathered around him and, with a careful and decisive pull of a large yellow lever, started the machine, which clanked and heaved and hissed and sighed as the metal plates—

'They'll be back soon, you know.'

'I know, I know. I just want to read that universal truth.'

At the sound of the back door being opened, she jumped. If her father found her reading one of the books from the good room — one of Mark's books — before it had been covered . . . she shivered.

'Quickly,' whispered Ruth.

But it was too late. Her father had stomped into the room. 'You! Get out!'

She froze. Mark's book was sitting in her sinner's hands. Was it now? Had her time come now?

The eels were writhing and hissing.

He was in his boots, overalls and oily raincoat, the hood flung off his head, his face red, brows tense. 'The chooks are out. Get out here now.' He walked back into the kitchen.

Joy closed her eyes to quickly thank God, pushed the book under her pillow and followed him as fast as she could.

Her father hated the chooks, even though he ate two boiled eggs each morning with gusto. 'Should get rid of them,' he would spit, looking at the account the owners of the supply store handed over each month when they delivered the pellets. Her mother, however, loved them and much to her father's obvious annoyance called all of them Ruth. Joy, too, was annoyed that they were all named after her sister.

Now, as Joy scurried to the kitchen, her father's angry shout of 'Hurry up!' hit her like red jagged spears. As she followed him into the back porch, where they stored their raincoats and rubber boots, she heard their van coming down the driveway and had an idea that would make her father happy.

He pulled open the back door, and the cold air and rain burst into the back porch. Joy tipped her boots upside down and banged them on the floor to make sure there were no spiders lurking in them. 'Dad? You know how Mum can always get the chooks to come back? Now that she's back, why don't you get her to do that? Before we all get wet? Get her to bang on the feed bin and call them. They always come back when she does that.' It was such a good idea. It would save all that messing around and yelling in the paddock in the rain. Her father could return to the fencing and she could find out what that universal truth was.

Her father grabbed the neck of her jumper and hissed in her ear, 'I said, *get out there*, and that's what you'll do.' His hand moved up swiftly and slapped the side of her face. She fell on to her knees, her stinging cheek feeling as purple as Ruth's. 'Don't you tell me what to do, y'hear?'

He walked out of the door and she grabbed her plastic coat from the hook and followed him down the old cracked cement path. She pulled the hood over her head, but they were walking into the rain, and her face and neck were soon cold and wet. In her stomach, she felt the eels roll back and forth — and grow a little.

Why didn't her idea make him happy? She watched the van swing into the shed. Surely her mother could put off loading the wreath bases into her workroom and come and call the chooks? Joy sighed and followed her father.

Mark was already in the front paddock standing silently next to the chook shed, a vacant stare on his face, a long stick in his hand. Their father snatched the stick away from him.

Just like every other time that the chooks had escaped, he ordered Joy and Mark to different places in the paddock, while he stood near the gate of the pen, precisely where he wanted the chooks to come, and waved the stick, yelling commands and hissing at his children. 'Go left go right go back *ssss* move forward stand still *ssss* chase them this way not like that *ssssss*.'

When he wasn't shouting and hissing at Mark and Joy, he was shouting at the chooks. 'You're scaring the cows. Get back here, you stupid brutes.'

Scaring the cows? Unlikely. They were used to being rounded up each morning and night, used to being driven into the milking stalls with a stick to their rump, used to having their calves taken from them just minutes after they tottered on their wet stick-legs in the mud. They were hardly going to be scared by a dozen Ruths pecking in the paddock. Joy wondered if the chooks and cows were friends, like the ducks and cows and lambs and foals in children's picture books. They were strange books, full of lies with their mild sunshine and kind farmers who had soft plump wives cooking pound cakes (whatever they were) and making lemonade for the laughing children whose only care was whether an injured duckling was warm enough under the soft dolls' blankets in its little dolls' pram.

It was wrong that writers could lie like that. They should tell the truth about the mud and the rain and the chores and the cold and the bills and the government. Hadn't any of them been to Church and learnt that lying was a sin?

As Joy stood there, she imagined the cows nonchalantly {a duke lying on a couch} drawling, 'Isn't the grass delicious? But the rain, will it ever end?' The Ruths replied, '*Tchk*, yes, so good for us, so good for our eggs. But yes, *tchk*, when will it stop raining? There's so much mud everywhere.' And they'd scrape their yellow-white feet backwards, while their mottled beaks pecked around for a tasty insect or a—

A hot pain shot through her left shoulder, as the stick came down with a whack. 'What in blazes are you doing? Stop daydreaming and get over to the fence before they get into the bull paddock. *Ssss*. Now!'

The eels slithered over each other. She'd made him angry again. Twice, in less than half an hour.

Your time will come.

Every day it was getting closer. She had to try harder. She had to be good. She had to avoid the mistakes that Mark made.

Rubbing her shoulder, she trotted through the wet grass and mud to the fence, as slanted rain fell onto her cheeks and down her neck and collar.

After five more minutes of waving and hissing, her father called out, 'Gwen, Gwen. The chooks. Gwen!'

Mark and Joy were still running backwards and forwards trying to stop the chooks from getting into the bull paddock when her mother appeared and banged on the feed bin. She called out in a high, sing-song voice, 'Ruuuuth-RuthRuthRuthRuth', and the chooks turned and bustled back to the pen.

Her father stomped through the mud towards the back paddocks, and Mark followed him slowly. Through the rain's mist, Joy could see thick, dark-green hatred curling up from her brother's shoulders.

9

GEORGE AND GWEN

August 1942

As George's van trundled down the long driveway, Gwen saw a large corrugated-iron shed that was a rich red-brown. Totally rusted. She breathed in and smelt dilapidation and neglect.

They drove past paddocks littered with abandoned machinery — an old dray, a horse-drawn plough, iron wheels, other items Gwen could not identify. Like the shed, they were all rusty and ugly.

George pulled up beside a rundown wooden house with some crooked wooden sheds scattered around it.

A cracked cement path led from the driveway to concrete steps that were slippery from the rain. Gwen stood on the top step as George pushed open the back door, which was unlocked. Inside, the small house was dirty but appeared solid enough. It seemed that the owners (Gwen corrected herself: *previous* owners) had left behind all their furniture and household goods. She hadn't even thought about such things. Looking down at her neat cream pumps, she realised that, beyond the wedding, she hadn't thought about much at all. She glanced up at George, who was smiling at her. Reassured, she imagined how envious her great-aunt and Jean would be when she told them that her new home had an indoor laundry and toilet, thanks to a clever if crude extension on one side of the back porch, which enclosed what had been a little shed near the back door.

While George brought in their suitcases, she inspected the rooms. Near the back door there was a bathroom along with a bedroom that would be ideal for a boy. The kitchen was reasonably roomy and had a wooden table with six wooden chairs around it, and a brown couch in front of a fireplace. And a refrigerator. Fancy leaving a refrigerator behind. Gwen had only seen refrigerators in shops, so the previous owners must have been wealthy, despite the appearance of the house. She peeked into a bedroom that came off the kitchen (making it ideal for a girl), then walked into the good room that led to the front door. Beside the front door was the bedroom that, she guessed, would be theirs.

Later, with the four towels from her glory box in her arms, she opened what she thought was a closet next to the boy's bedroom, only to discover a tiny room about the size of the bathroom. There was a wooden bench running along one wall, which reminded her of Stan's workroom where she had stuck camellia leaves into the base of wreaths. And there was a cupboard in the opposite wall that would be perfect for towels and linen.

Or wreath bases impatiently waiting for people to die.

10

JOY AND RUTH

December 1960

That afternoon Joy was helping her mother make Christmas shortbreads and mince pies when there was a knock at the back door. Joy dusted the flour off her hands and went to answer it with a smile, because she knew that Mr Larsen would be on the other side with an even bigger smile on his face. Mr Larsen arrived every Wednesday and Saturday afternoon.

Mr Larsen was like an enormous friendly woodsman from a fairy tale. He had a big laugh, wore red check shirts that matched his red face and neck, had the largest hands Joy had ever seen, and often got words confused, which made Joy laugh — but only ever on the inside. Except for one day when she was eight, when she had walked all the way to his house to give him some mail that was in their letterbox by mistake. He insisted that she come inside and have some lemon water. Standing awkwardly in the kitchen and not knowing what to say, but knowing that her father would be angry if she wasn't polite, she said that it was a nice kitchen.

He grinned and said, 'It is indeed, lass.' Then he said that his cousin's house had burnt down not two months ago because of a fire that started in the kitchen. Joy said she hoped that would never happen to this house. Mr Larsen grinned even more widely and said, 'No fear of that, lass.' He walked over to a small red cylinder buckled to the wall next to the oven and patted it affectionately. 'I've just gone out and bought this magnificent fire distinguisher.' Joy laughed out loud, and then clapped her hand on her mouth in horror, but Mr Larsen didn't seem to mind and kept on talking.

Mrs Larsen was also like someone from a fairy tale — a horrible stepmother. She was skinny and mean, with a long crooked nose and long straight mousy-brown hair pulled back and held together with a rubber band at the base of her neck. She made extra money for her family by sewing and repairing dresses for women in the area. She talked over her husband, and always found fault with him. 'You're not leaving that mess there for me to clean up, are you?' she'd said that day when she walked in and saw Joy's empty glass on the sink next to the plastic juicer and lemon halves. Joy instinctively answered, 'Sorry, Mrs Larsen, no . . .' and started to walk to the sink.

'Not you. I'm talking to him,' she snapped. 'Well?' she said to her husband. Mr Larsen got up and winked at Joy, who swallowed and said she must go home, making sure to add, 'Thank you for the lemon water, Mr Larsen. Thank you too, Mrs Larsen.'

Colin was their fairy-tale son who was doomed to live a strange, sad life, although Joy liked to think he had magic deep inside him that no one knew about, not even Colin himself. Her mother had told Joy that he hadn't got enough oxygen at birth, although Joy didn't really know what that meant. He was around thirty, still lived at home, and when he wasn't helping her father on the farm, spent his time watching the Devil's box that Mr Larsen had bought for him the year the Olympic Games were in Melbourne. He didn't talk much. Joy's mother said that was because he was a good listener, and that when he did speak you should listen hard. Joy always thought that he looked like he was going to cry whenever their eyes met.

Even the Larsens' house belonged in a fairy tale. Not because it looked like a castle, but because it reminded Joy of a book of fairy tales that Aunty Rose had sent her for her fifth birthday. When you turned to the last page, a castle cleverly unfolded and stood up out of the page, and it was made so ingeniously {a maze in an old English garden} that you could even see inside, but only a little bit. That's how she felt about the Larsen house — that you weren't meant to see all of it. (Although when she thought about it, she realised her house was like that, too.) She had loved that book, but when she couldn't find it one day last year, her mother said her father had given it to the Church for the Christmas trash 'n' treasure sale.

So when Joy opened the back door to Mr Larsen every Saturday (and every Wednesday during school holidays), she thought about that book and the Larsens being from a fairy tale. Even so, she looked forward to Mr Larsen's visits.

'Hello, Mr Larsen,' she said. 'Come in.'

She stood back to let him lead the way into the kitchen. Her father always told her to let others go first because she was a girl, and a sinner. 'You never put yourself ahead of others, d'you hear? Always let others go first. Sinners like you go to the back. Pride cometh before a fall.'

'Afternoon, Robert. How are you?' her mother said, and gave Mr Larsen a big smile. Joy knew her mother enjoyed his visits too. 'I'm accelerant, Gwen, thank you very much.' Gwen's mother always threw a little glance in Joy's direction, as if to remind her not to correct Mr Larsen.

For as long as she could remember, after they'd exchanged these hellos, Mr Larsen whipped out a block of chocolate and placed it on the table. Then he walked into the good room, saying, 'Just going to make a quick trump call,' and jiggling the coins in his pocket to indicate that he was going to put money in the jar to pay for the call.

Also, for as long as she could remember, she'd giggled when he said 'trump call' instead of 'trunk call'.

Then, to 'give Mr Larsen some privacy', her mother would go into her workroom and Joy would be ordered outside.

Today, as Mr Larsen walked into the good room and Joy followed her mother out of the kitchen, a thought suddenly came rolling out of the dark crevices of her mind. 'Mum, why does Mr Larsen use our telephone when they have their own?'

'How should I know? You need to learn to mind your own business. Now off you go.'

Mr Larsen's tractor was, as always, sitting just the other side of their dividing fence, which had always led Joy to believe that he couldn't be bothered going all the way back to his house to make whatever call he suddenly needed to make. But now she realised they weren't spur-of-the-moment calls because they were always at the same time, and he always had the chocolate and coins ready.

Sitting at the table twenty minutes later, she smiled back at him as he tore open the chocolate.

'Chocolate, Gwen? Lass?'

He broke off a row and offered it to her mother, then broke off another row and held it out for Joy.

Mr Larsen's chocolate was the only chocolate she had ever eaten. And it was soft, milky and delicious. She placed her front teeth exactly between the second and third squares, bit gently and let the chocolate sit on her tongue and melt so it would last longer. Mr Larsen and her mother sipped their tea and talked about the rain and how 'conflation' was pushing the price of everything through the roof, so how any decent farmer was supposed to make a living was 'beyond comprehensive'. And today Mr Larsen told them how one of Kevin Stone's cows had drowned earlier in the week. Apparently it had fallen over when it was drinking from the dam and got stuck in the mud. Or it had got stuck in the mud and then fallen over. Whichever had happened first, Joy knew it was not the first cow in the area to have got stuck and died in a dam. Joy enjoyed these friendly chats because Mr Larsen was kind, and because her father was always working in the paddocks when Mr Larsen arrived. It was such a shame Mark was helping him, and didn't get to have any chocolate. But today she wasn't thinking about Mark — all she could think about was why Mr Larsen used their phone, and who he was calling. She wondered if he was doing something sinful like gambling on horse races or planning to rob a bank. She would talk to Ruth about it.

When they'd eaten all the chocolate, Mr Larsen stood up, looked at her mother squarely and said, 'Thanks, Gwen. Thank you very much.'

'You're welcome, Robert.' And her mother smiled at him, before nodding at Joy with a look that meant 'clean up'. Mr Larsen swept his big red hand across the table to grab the wrapper and foil and stuffed them into his trouser pocket, while Joy took everything else to the sink.

'I'll be seeing you, Gwen, on Wednesday,' Mr Larsen said before heading to the back door. 'And you too, lass, as you're on holidays.'

As always, Joy walked him out and when they got to the back door she said, 'Thank you for the chocolate, Mr Larsen.'

He gave her the same look he had just given her mother and said, 'It was my treasure. I'm glad you enjoyed it, lass.'

Joy watched him climb through the fence, get on his tractor, and trundle off.

She hurried back inside to continue helping her mother with the Christmas cooking, pleased that the sticky black eels were drowning in the soft brown chocolate, and excited that she would be having chocolate again on Wednesday.

11

JOY AND GEORGE

February 1983

His room smells like the orange blankets have licked up the dying odours from his body and are slowly releasing them into the air, and the semi-darkness reminds me of the day I hid in here and saw a snake on the bed, about to attack me. Here I am again, decades later, standing in the doorway, and I absolutely refuse to be scared. There's a tired fan in the corner pushing hot air around the room, and he's in bed, leaning against pillows staring at nothing.

'Uh, it's you. Took your time.' His voice is frail, but nothing else has changed.

'Sorry, I . . . I had to finish some stuff for work. I got here as quickly as I could.' Why on earth am I apologising to him?

'What day is it?'

'It's Tuesday, Dad.'

'Work on weekends, do you?'

'No. Well, kind of. I . . .'

That's it. I'm done. I can't stand him talking to me like this. I'm not a kid anymore. I'm going to go and stay at the

Blackhunt Motel till he dies. After I fill up with petrol from the 44-gallon drum in the shed.

'Water.' He starts coughing and waves his arm towards the little table where there's a bright-yellow infant's mug with two big plastic handles and a plastic lid with a drinking spout.

I suppose I can do that. That's not giving in. 'Okay, Dad.'

'Hurry up,' he hisses.

I hand him the cup, and notice that his hands are like a chicken's feet — thin bones and knobbled veins under near-transparent skin.

While he drinks, I wonder if he feels humiliated by how weak he is. Ruth was right, I don't need to be afraid of him anymore. But my heart can't stop drumming, and I can feel the eels waking up.

'I need painkillers, Gwen.'

Vicki was right, too. He's definitely delusional if he thinks I'm Mum.

What did Vicki say? *On time, otherwise he'll be in excruciating pain.* 'Not yet, Dad. You have to wait about an hour and a half.'

'What, are you a doctor now, Gwen? Give me some painkillers.'

'I'm Joy, Dad.'

'Just get the painkillers.'

Back in the kitchen, I check my watch and Vicki's sheets of paper. 'There's still about an hour to go,' I say to Ruth. 'What will we do?'

'Give them to him,' says Ruth, shrugging.

'But we'll already be breaking her rules. She only gave me enough for a week. What do we do when he's in pain again in three hours' time? Or less?'

'Jesus, Joy, we give him some more. If he's in pain, we give him some painkillers. How hard is that?'

'But the sheet says he doesn't need any more until two o'clock.'

'You want him to lie there in pain, moaning like that? Annoying the hell out of us?'

The groans from the bedroom are louder.

'Alright, alright,' I say, and roll out two of the blue tablets from the bottle, put an X in the med form for two o'clock and go back to the bedroom. I put the pills into his open hand and watch as he scrapes them from his palm into his mouth and takes a gulp from the cup.

That was easier than I thought it would be.

He motions to a copy of the *Blackhunt Gazette* lying on the floor. I pick it up and see it's a couple of weeks old.

'Read something to me.'

I open the paper to the death notices and spend the next five minutes reading to him. He shakes his head if he doesn't know the name I read out, and motions with his index finger when he recognises the name and wants me to read the deceased's notice. Sometimes he looks a little sad.

After I read out the last one, he says, 'Okay, go.'

I stand up, then realise I really am behaving like I'm twelve again. I'm not going to leave just because he's told me to. I have questions he needs to answer. About what he did to his children. And then, of course, there's the whole Wendy Boscombe thing that needs to be sorted out.

'Wait a minute. I've got some questions—'

'Ruth,' he says in a pleading voice, and although I'm annoyed that he's interrupted me, to be honest I'm also a bit flattered that he's confusing me with perfect Ruth. He points to the empty cup. 'Get me some Passiona.'

'Sorry, Dad, we don't have any.'

'Well, get some then.'

'I'll go into town in the morning, and get some decent food for us too.' Seems I'm staying after all.

'Don't be stupid. I want it now.'

It'll take nearly three hours to go into town, buy everything, and get back. There's no way I'm doing that. 'Dad, I just got—'

'I'm dying. Do you realise that? Dying.' I'm halfway to the door when he growls, 'Don't get that cheap imitation stuff, either.'

As I walk into the good room, I realise the bastard's pummelled me into a grey lump of wet cardboard.

Alright, I'll get his Passiona, but after that I'm not putting up with any more crap from him, and I'm not running away.

'Come and talk,' Ruth says calmly, patting the couch.

'I've got to go into town and get the bastard some Passiona. Plus we need food, and another fan. I'm going to melt if I stay here.'

Ruth's face, of course, doesn't have a drop of sweat on it — just that awful birthmark.

'I've been thinking,' she says. 'The medication. That's the answer. Vicki has delivered exactly what we need.'

The heat is unbearable. Unlike Ruth, I'm sweating all over, plus I don't know what she's talking about.

'You know what I'm talking about,' she says. God, I hate it when she does that, as if she can read my mind.

'Look, I just came to get some answers. And make him confess.'

'Confess?' cries Ruth, astonished. 'To what, exactly?'

'To . . . everything.'

'Fat chance,' says Ruth. She shakes her head and keeps talking, her silvery voice difficult to ignore. It was always like this. Ruth filling my head with ideas, me being the silent listener.

On the way out, I look in Mark's bedroom. I breathe in deeply, as if that could stop the emotions from overwhelming me, but there's nothing that suggests Mark ever lived here. This is where Ruth needs to sleep, at least while I'm here, so she doesn't whisper in my ear all night.

Then I look inside my mother's workroom. Always full of the colours and scents of flowers, now it just smells of dust and loneliness. There are still jam jars of wire sitting on the bench and spools of ribbon on the rod, looking neglected and forlorn, like a fairground after everyone's gone home. I bet if I opened the cupboard I'd see wreath bases in there. For the whole of my childhood, if she wasn't cooking or working in the garden, she was in here. It seemed that there were always people dying, so there were always wreaths to make. And she was always in here when our father was doling out his punishments.

It's no wonder that when I was a child, my mother was a pale, buff colour in my mind, like a manila folder — a neutral player who didn't know what to do except retreat into her workroom and make bouquets for pregnant teenagers and wreaths for dead people. It's odd that I didn't ever think about whether I loved her or not, or even whether she loved me. She was just there, in the background, physically and emotionally. Another silent listener. Especially to our screams.

Now, of course, I realise that she came here to escape. She even came in here the few times Uncle Bill and Aunty Rose visited us — she hated his ugly wheelchair and missing legs. As soon as they'd all had a cup of tea and our father had dragged out the photo album — presumably to help fill in the otherwise awkward silence — she'd stand up and excuse herself, saying she had wreaths to make. I always craned my neck to look at the three baby photos (one of each of us) when my father turned over to that page. There we were, each newborn, wrapped in hospital blankets, eyes closed. I used to think that Ruth and I looked the same, although I could never get a close look because my father would always turn the page quickly.

Now I realise my mother retreated to her workroom because she hated that photo album nearly as much as she hated wheelchairs.

* * *

On the way to town to get his treasured Passiona, I drive too fast, but it's Ruth's fault. I keep hearing her words over and over in my head. *He's going to die in a few days anyway, so we may as well overdose the bastard. No one will suspect a thing, and we'll finally get our revenge.*

12

GEORGE AND GWEN

August 1942

Gwen walked back to the dingy kitchen, alive to possibilities. A good scrub of everything would make the world of difference. And flowers on the kitchen table. Somewhere in that wild tangle of weeds around the house there must be some flowers. And she would plant more in the weeks ahead. The weeks and months and years ahead.

But before she had a chance to look for flowers, George suggested she unpack while he took a closer look at the sheds and paddocks and the 120 cows that were also now theirs. He glanced at his watch. 'We'll have a cup of tea at four-fifteen.'

As he walked out, she found herself sighing, her shoulders relaxing. Clearly she was tired from the excitement of the wedding and the long drive. She unpacked the food, then their eight wedding presents: three damask tablecloths, two sets of linen tea towels, two sets of salt and pepper shakers, and the present George had given her — six beautiful glasses that his parents had received for their wedding more than thirty years before. Made of delicate glass, each one had a gold rim and golden grapevines painted above a band of white frosting. Unable to imagine when they would ever use such special glasses, Gwen took great care placing them in two lines in the bureau in the good room. How George must love her to have given her these precious heirlooms.

After gently closing the bureau's door, she made their bed with the sheets and pillowcases from her glory box and the thin orange blankets the owners had left folded on the end of the bed. She hung George's trousers, shirts and jackets and her two other dresses and three cardigans in the old wooden wardrobe, then turned to the dressing table, where she would put their underwear, socks and jumpers. She shivered slightly in the cold house, and rubbed her hands up and down her arms. They would need those jumpers.

She thought that, like the fridge, this must have cost a fortune, with its six narrow drawers down one side and two wide drawers beneath a four-foot-wide mirror with a scalloped edge. But adjusting the angle of the mirror to look into it, she saw that it was grey and mottled, and distorted her image, which loomed out of a shadowy background seemingly miles deep. She shivered and looked away, deciding to sneak back to what she already thought of as her little workroom.

Sneak. How absurd. She could do whatever she wanted to in this house. Her house. Her home.

Yes, this room would be perfect for making wreaths and wedding bouquets. When she had cut and wired and taped and arranged for Stan, her fingers had come alive, and she had been able to forget about everything else going on in the world, like legless soldiers and missing mothers. Here, without rent to pay, she could charge much less than a town florist (wherever the nearest town was), especially if she grew her own flowers. She imagined the house surrounded by hydrangeas and camellias and roses and lily-of-the-valley and magnolias and stock and poppies.

And, of course, carnations, dahlias, chrysanthemums . . . the list was endless. She wiped down the workbench with some soap and a rag she'd found under the sink, and stood with her hands on her hips. Wouldn't George be proud of her?

She glanced at her watch. It was nearly twenty past four. For some reason, she gasped and walked quickly to the kitchen.

13

JOY AND RUTH

December 1960

After she closed the door behind Mr Larsen, Joy suddenly remembered that she'd pushed Pride and Prejudice under her pillow when her father had barged in. The eels started wriggling, and she desperately wanted to run and rescue the book. But it was another half-hour before her mother took off her apron and went into her workroom.

In five fast steps, Joy was in her bedroom and lifting her pillow, ignoring Ruth. The eels writhed angrily, their slippery skins rubbing against the inside of her stomach, as she saw with horror that a corner of the book's front cover was bent. The cover started sobbing and screaming, 'Look what she's done to me!' Joy glanced at the door (*please God, please don't let anyone come in*), frantically smoothed down the front cover with her palm and squeezed the book in both hands. Now it was growling harshly, 'She's a filthy sinner. She's ruined a perfectly good book.' Joy turned to Ruth in desperation, but her sister just shrugged and shook her head.

Surely her father would hear the screams and accusations.

Surely this would be the moment when everything changed. Surely now . . . her time had come.

But the kitchen door remained closed, so she crept back into the good room, silently pleading with the cover to stop moaning, and trying to ignore the twisting eels. Standing in front of the two piles of books, she rubbed the heel of her right palm up and down the crease, trying to erase it. She put the weeping book under the exercise books, and placed the thick Form 5 maths book on top of the pile. The heavy book muffled the novel's sobs and she felt her shoulders drop and a cupful of air escape from her lungs. She was about to let go of the maths book to see if the balancing act would work, when she heard the back door bang and her father walk into the kitchen.

She was trapped. The only way out of the good room was via the kitchen (impossible), through the front door (always locked, the key kept in one of the drawers of the bureau), or into her parents' room (totally forbidden).

She heard him push open her bedroom door.

'Joy?' The single syllable was like a tree crashing to the ground.

Her heart lurched as it hit her chest bone. He called more loudly, 'Where are you?'

She heard his boots walking on the kitchen floor toward the good room.

Please God, please.

She needed to get out of the good room. She lifted her hand off the pile of books, but the maths book wobbled, and she had to press down on it to stop the books from falling onto the floor.

She heard his boots stop.

This is it. He can hear me breathing. Or my heart thumping. The book screamed again, but it was still muffled: 'She's in here. She's in here. Where she shouldn't be. Squashing me. Help!'

She heard him start to walk again, and she knew this was it.

Her time had come.

She stood beside the pile of books, her left hand holding the maths book steady, her eyes on the door, black beads of fear leaking out of her pores and running down her arm and over the backs of her hands.

'George?' It was her mother's voice calling from the back porch. 'Robert needs a hand. His tractor's bogged.'

Her father grunted, and Joy heard him leave the kitchen. Sobbing, she adjusted the maths book so the pile was steady, while *Pride and Prejudice* let out a single, barely audible moan.

Thank you, God, thank you, Mr Larsen. Joy took two steps towards the kitchen then looked back with yearning. She wouldn't be reading *Pride and Prejudice* for a long time.

She took another step but stopped when she heard her mother in the kitchen. If she walked out now, her mother would certainly tell her father she'd been in the good room two days in a row.

'Joy? Are you in your room?'

Joy stood silently, willing her heart to stop beating so loudly.

She heard her mother open her bedroom door. 'Are you in here?'

Joy knew Ruth would not give her away. She was safe, because surely her mother would now look for her outside.

But the sudden ringing of the telephone made Joy's heart stop. It would take her mother less than ten seconds to walk into the good room to answer the phone. She had only one option. In just two long steps, and with a push of the door that was ajar, she was in her parents' bedroom. The one room in the house she had never been into. She gently eased the door back to where it had been, open only an inch or two.

Silently, she took another two steps in, as her mother picked up the telephone and reeled off their phone number, 'Three double-five.'

The heavy brown blinds in her parents' bedroom were pulled down, so Joy was standing in almost total darkness. There was a nauseating smell of ammonia mixed with old talcum powder and sadness, which made the eels squirm and climb over each other.

'Hello, Mrs Waddell. How are you?' She knew her mother was standing beside the little table where the smooth black telephone sat. Joy had always been intrigued by the phone's cold sleekness, which Mr Plummer had said was made of Bakelite {a taut muscled lynx, perfectly still, waiting to pounce}.

Beside the phone was a jar that her parents — and Mr Larsen — put coins into when they made a phone call, as well as a pile of old bills held together with a bulldog clip. Her mother wrote down orders for wreaths and bouquets on the blank sides of the bills, one order per sheet, so she could take the individual sheets into her workroom, and not waste money on notepads. The table also held a tele-index full of people's phone numbers. Joy heard the click-click-click as her mother idly moved the tele-index's slider up and down, as she always did when she wasn't writing down orders.

'Yes, I was sorry to read about his death too. That's right, the funeral is tomorrow. No, you're not too late. One ten-inch wreath with waterlilies. And the message on the card?'

Joy stood still with her eyes closed, listening to her mother, too scared to even look around this strange-smelling room. She couldn't move until her mother finished talking on the phone, but what would she do if her father came inside and walked into the bedroom? *Your time will come.*

He would kill her.

But 'dead' wouldn't be so bad. No more chores, no more mud, no more father.

She opened her eyes and looked around in the semi-darkness. Straight ahead on the opposite wall was a dressing table with two sets of drawers and a large mirror. Her parents' underpants would be in there. It horrified her that her parents had bottoms and wore underpants. As a terrible image began to fill her head, she squeezed her eyes shut and muttered some of her favourite words to let their images dominate. *Pristine, rainbow, filigree, catapult.*

'Yes, I've got that: "With heartfelt sympathy, the Waddell family." Very nice, Mrs Waddell.'

Joy opened her eyes when she heard her mother's voice again, and found herself looking in the mottled mirror. Even though it was dark in the room and the reflection in the mirror seemed to be in the distance, she made out the sad and pathetic shadow of an eleven-year-old girl who was thin and frightened. Of everything. She turned towards her parents' bed, and clamped a hand over her mouth to silence her gasp. Lying on the dark bedspread was a black snake coiled around itself. Its head shone even in the semi-darkness and she could even see the tip of its sharp silver tongue.

She knew that when it was cold and wet outside, snakes and spiders often crawled inside houses to find somewhere warm and dry, which is why you always gave a towel a good shake when you pulled it out of a cupboard, and never put your foot into a boot before banging it upside down.

The snake was lying still, preserving its energy, but Joy knew it could sense the ripple of fear heaving through her body. Now she was trapped between the snake's venom and her father's rage. Even if her mother went back to the kitchen right now, Joy knew she couldn't move, that her feet were stuck to the carpet as much as her eyes were stuck on the snake. Any second, it would attack and she would be killed in her parents' room. When she didn't turn up to peel potatoes for tea, they would search her bedroom and the sheds and paddocks, but they wouldn't find her. It would only be after tea, after her father had taken his pills and her mother had finished Mrs Waddell's wreath, that they would discover her there, dead, cold, and on her way to Hell.

They'd probably be relieved. One less mouth to feed, one less sinful child to be ashamed of.

Even so, she quickly closed her eyes and prayed that the snake was too cold to slither off the bed and attack her. But when she opened her eyes, she saw its tongue flicker. It had smelt her fear and was about to attack.

14

GEORGE AND GWEN

August 1942

George was already sitting at the top of the table, his arms crossed. 'Gwen, when I say four-fifteen, dear, that is exactly what I mean.'

'Sorry, dear. I got a bit distracted. Did you know that—'

'Can you please put the kettle on?' He smiled. 'And did your aunt pack any biscuits?'

Gwen smiled back. 'She did indeed, George. Some lemon slice and some Anzac biscuits.'

'I'll have lemon slice, dear.'

While she put the kettle on and rinsed out the china cups and the aluminium teapot, George went into their bedroom. He came back as the kettle began to whistle.

'I have pulled out the clothes and laid out the sets as they are to be hung. Trousers, shirt, jumper or jacket for each set on one coat hanger, as is the proper way. I suggest you do the same, dear. And I will have the drawers on the right side of the dressing table. You can have the two wide ones.' He smiled and patted her arm. 'It will be much easier for both of us that way.'

'Oh. Yes, alright.' Despite his smile and the gentle pat, she felt humiliated. But, she asked herself, what was she upset about? What did it matter if her clothes were here or there, in this drawer or that drawer? And maybe she had been a bit slapdash when she'd hung up his clothes, focusing more on her new workroom.

She made the pot of tea, slipped on a pink knitted tea-cosy she'd found in the third drawer, put two pieces of lemon slice on a plate, and carried the pot and the plate to the table. He picked up a slice and ate it while she returned to the bench to bring the milk and teacups to the table. After she poured the milk into both their cups, she took a breath and said lightly, 'George, you know that little room at the back?' She began pouring tea into his cup. 'There's a workbench in there and I thought—'

'It's not strong enough.'

'Pardon?'

He pointed to the teapot. 'It's too weak.'

'Oh, the tea.' With the strict rationing, she had placed just one-and-a-half caddies of tea leaves into the pot, but perhaps she hadn't let it brew long enough. She put the teapot down, spun it around a few times, counted to thirty silently, and spun it around again. Tentatively, she poured tea into the other cup and slid it over to him with a smile. He smiled back at her and took the other piece of lemon slice.

She fetched herself another slice from the tin and sat down again.

She took a bite and said, 'I was thinking . . .' But a piece of coconut got stuck in her throat and suddenly she couldn't talk. He watched her stand up, trot to the sink coughing, pull out a glass, fill it with water and drink.

As she swallowed the water, she thought with horror that she hadn't rinsed the glass and that there had probably been cockroaches running through the cupboards for months or however long the house had been empty.

With equal horror, she realised that not only did she have no idea how long the house had been empty, she didn't know anything about this farm, not even the address. She didn't know why the previous owners had moved out, nor why they had left everything behind, from the dressing table with its strange mirror to the revolting tea-cosy. She didn't even know if George could milk cows.

When she stopped coughing, she forced herself not to think about the cockroach eggs that might be sitting in her stomach and said, 'Do you know how to milk cows?'

'I will in about,' he looked at his watch, 'ten minutes. The next-door neighbour's coming down at five to show us.'

'Us?'

'Well, I can't do it by myself, Gwen.' He smiled at her. 'I'll need you to help me.'

'Oh.' She tried to sound light-hearted and happy. But it felt like black paint was dripping over her heart.

15

JOY AND RUTH

December 1960

Joy knew that snakes were fast and angry. Her only hope was that this one would decide to uncurl itself and slither down to the floor before striking, rather than spring from the bed and throw itself through the air to attack her throat. She calculated that she had two seconds if it sprang from the bed, three if it slithered to the floor.

Please God, I promise I'll never do anything bad again. I'll never read Pride and Prejudice, *I'll never even touch it. For thine is the kingdom, the power . . .*

Joy knew that to get out of the room she would have to jump quickly and pull the door behind her, or move so slowly that the snake would not detect her. She no longer cared if her mother, or even her father, saw her; no longer cared if her time had come. She had to get away from that snake.

While she kept her eyes fixed on it, she heard her mother say from somewhere a long way away, 'Thank you, Mrs Waddell. Yes, I might see you at the funeral,' even though she wouldn't because her mother hated funerals, despite the money the wreaths brought in. Then Joy heard the click of the handset being dropped back into the cradle, and she knew her mother was going to take the piece of paper with details of the order to her workroom. She also knew that in the seconds she'd been listening, the snake had decided to strike, punish her — kill her — for all her sins. She swallowed and held her breath. It was now or never. Without taking her eyes from the snake, she got ready to leap forward. Then, without stopping to think about it, she propelled herself towards the door. As she grabbed the handle and opened the door, she swung around to see whether the snake had reacted.

It was still lying there, motionless. Unnerved, Joy stopped. And as the light from the good room illuminated the bed, she realised that she had been unbelievably stupid. She had been petrified by nothing more than her father's belt neatly coiled on the bed.

Flooded with humiliation, she ran into the kitchen. Silently screaming, *calm down, calm down*, she walked to the cupboard where the potatoes were kept, pulled out a handful and reached for the peeling knife. Her hands were shaking and the eels were rolling over and over. She leant over the sink and vomited.

She was washing the yellow bile down the sink when the kitchen door opened and her mother shouted, 'Where in blazes have you been?' Joy turned, trying to look normal, her tongue stuck on the roof of her mouth. 'Your father's down at the chook shed. Get down there quick smart. We're having roast tonight.'

Joy scuttled past her mother and out the back door. She never understood how her mother claimed to love the chooks but let her father kill them.

He was walking from the shed to the chook pen, the grey hood of his jacket obscuring his face. He was holding the axe just below its head, so the long handle swung in time with his long strides. The axe-head was glistening and shiny — he must have just attached a new one.

He leant the axe against the dark blood-stained block of wood a few feet away from the wire gate and walked into the pen. Joy had to stand holding the gate closed, but not latched, ready to quickly open it to let him out, then just as quickly latch it without letting out any chooks.

As soon as her father went through the open gate, all twelve Ruths raced to the far corner of the muddy yard, jostling each other and trying to fly. But their wings had been clipped the day they had arrived at the farm as chicks, small enough to be held in one of her father's red hands. Before they even knew they had wings.

He stepped forward quickly and grabbed one of the Ruths with both hands, fingers splayed to stop the beating of the flightless wings. It was so easy. The others tutted and cackled, spreading out in the yard again. Her father and the seized Ruth came through the gate that Joy quickly opened and shut.

Then Joy had to stand in the drizzle and wait. She closed her eyes at the moment of impact.

While he walked to the shed with the bloodied axe, Joy carried the dead Ruth up to the laundry, holding her feet and the handle of the bucket by the same hand so Ruth's blood dripped from her headless neck onto her lifeless head at the bottom of the bucket. Her mother came into the laundry, chopped off Ruth's feet with the secateurs once used to clip her wings, threw the feet in the bucket with the head, then swung the body into the cold cement trough. The dead Ruth lay awkwardly in the trough while Joy's mother yanked out feathers, and let the cold water run over her quick hands and the dead bird to wash away the blood and grit. The wet, dead-Ruth feathers stuck to her hands, to the trough's grey cement, to the floor. They got stuck in the plughole, along with the kidney and heart and giblet and intestines, the pure white quills sharp against the pink guts.

The smell made Joy's stomach pinch in on itself.

Her mother took the plucked Ruth into the kitchen, and left the guts and feathers in the trough for Joy, who pulled out the feathers and carried them to the compost pile. Then she scooped up the guts and giblet and put them into the bucket with Ruth's feet and head. With the grey rain still falling, Joy carried the bucket back down to the chook pen and tossed its contents over the fence into the mud, watching as the remaining eleven Ruths came trotting down to see what treats had come their way. And although she thought she should look away, she put down the bucket, hooked her fingers through the sagging bird wire, and watched while they pecked and fought as they gobbled and swallowed their sister's remains. Then she unhooked her red fingers, rinsed out the bucket, poured the pink water into the chook trough and returned the bucket to the shed. Her father was in there on an old stool, polishing the new axe-head with a soft blue cloth that he kept in a small plastic case. She placed the bucket upside down on an angle against the shed's inner wall so it would dry, and made her way back to the house.

Dead Ruth was already in the oven, and there were potatoes sitting on the bench for Joy to peel and add to the roasting dish.

As she peeled, she thought about her father's swift single downward stroke of the axe with its gleaming new head. She pictured herself at the chopping block, holding down the squawking squirming Ruth with one boot, just like her father did. She raised the axe, just like her father did, and brought it down with one swift action, just like her father did.

But the head she chopped off was his.

16

JOY AND GEORGE

February 1983

I wake up with his moans penetrating my dreams. For crying out loud, it's two in the morning. Then it hits me — if he needs painkillers every four hours, that means during the night as well.

I'm glad I left the doors open so I can hear him because he's obviously distressed.

Well, he can lie there in pain for all I care.

While I wait to see how long I can put up with his carrying-on, I think about the dream I've just had. I haven't had one like it since the last time I slept in here. I shiver, remembering how real it was. They always were. It's Ruth's fault, of course — her and her ideas for revenge.

It occurs to me that I could be a murderer dreaming that I'm a normal person, rather than a normal person dreaming I'm a murderer. But if I can hear him moaning and calling out now, it must have been a dream.

I'm wide awake and I won't be able to get back to sleep if he keeps on like this.

When I turn on his light, the orange hills of blankets are moving up and down rapidly in time with his breathing and moaning, and his face is grey, his eyes betraying his fright.

'Dad.' I race to his bed. 'Are you alright?'

Now he's gasping, and his face is changing from grey to pink. I tip out pills from the bottle in my hand, and pass him the infant's drinking cup, now full of Passiona. 'Take these. Quickly. You'll feel better soon.'

He takes the tablets while I try to calm down, and realise I thought he was going to die. Actually die. Right in front of me. Jesus, I was terrified. Obviously, some rogue neuron kicked in without my permission.

He begins to breathe more normally. So either a placebo effect has occurred remarkably quickly, or he was just checking that I'd come running like a good little girl made of wet cardboard. I sit on the chair beside the bedside table, and watch him as he closes his eyes and seems to begin sleeping peacefully. At some point I sleep too, and when I wake up to more of his moaning, it's six on the dot. I get the tablets into him quick smart and stagger back to my room. My neck is sore as hell.

When I go out to the kitchen, Ruth's sitting in her chair, staring into the empty fireplace.

'I've worked it all out,' she says, watching me make a pot of tea. 'Mmm, aren't you the perfect daughter? Passiona yesterday, pills in the middle of the night, pot of tea in the morning. No one will ever suspect a thing when you kill him.'

'I'm not going to kill him.' I pour the boiling water into the old tin teapot and put the pink tea-cosy on it. My hands are trembling. Old habits die hard. 'Vicki was right when she said he's delusional, and he's obviously in a lot of pain. That's enough revenge for me. I just want the truth, and justice.'

I look at Vicki's form for Wednesday, and tip out blue painkillers, a white one from another bottle, and a small pink one from a foil pack. I draw a large X in three corresponding cells.

'The justice you want *is* revenge, Joy,' says Ruth, picking up her book which, I notice with considerable annoyance, is *Pride and Prejudice*. 'Look, we have two options, basically. Option one, we give him extra pills. Just one or two more, maybe sometimes three, every time he's due for some, until he's gone. He won't know how many he's had, or when he's had them because,' she mimics what I just said, '*He's delusional and obviously in a lot of pain*.' She turns the page. 'Then we get on with our lives. The sooner the better.'

'Oh, sure. And you think Vicki won't ask for her pills back when he's dead, and not notice that half of them are missing? That in thirty-six hours he's had fifty instead of sixteen? She'd be smiling that infuriating smile all the way to court.'

'Good point. Amendment to option one: we call Vicki and tell her he's in a lot of pain and she'll *tell* us to give him painkillers more often. She won't suspect his dutiful daughters are doing anything but acting out of love and concern. In fact, she'll probably suggest we up the dose. Three tablets instead of two, and every three hours instead of every four. Problem solved.'

'And option two?'

'Option two,' she turns another page, 'we don't give him the painkillers . . .' She trails off.

'What?'

'Well, Vicki did say he'll be in excruciating pain if he doesn't get them on time.' She sighs melodramatically. 'And what a shame that would be.' She turns another page of the book, then slowly whispers, 'It wouldn't be the first time you've done that, would it? Remember the bicarb of soda?'

I don't reply, but I can't pretend I haven't heard her dark suggestions.

Later, when I'm back in his room, he grunts as he watches me put the concoction of tablets on the bedside table.

'Have you told that nurse that I need more painkillers?' His voice is frail.

'Vicki's your doctor, Dad.'

'I don't like her.'

I laugh. Something we agree on.

I turn on the fan, and it blasts out cold air straight away. 'It's too cold, Gwen. Too cold.'

'You need to stay cool, Dad.'

'She's trying to kill me, you know.'

'Who?'

'That nurse.' His voice is warming up, like Ruth's does. 'Did you bring tea?'

'I'll get you a cup in a minute. But first, you need to take these. Painkillers and' — I don't know which tablets are for what, except that the blue ones are painkillers — 'your blood pressure ones.'

'She's trying to kill me, I tell you.'

'Dad, no one's trying to kill you.' I stay and watch while he reluctantly swallows the tablets I pour into his hand.

He suddenly says, 'Your mother left me. Like everyone else. Her. Mark. Joy. Ruth. They all left me.'

'Dad, you're getting confused. Mum died. I'm here, and Ruth—'

'You need to go to the cemetery.'

'Yes, I know.' God, I'm sick of him telling me what to do. 'To visit Mum.'

'Ruth, too.'

'Yes, yes.' As if Ruth's going to stay here while I go to the cemetery.

Suddenly, he buckles over with pain and lets out a wail. I should comfort him. Pat his back. Or offer the cup with Passiona.

I stand and watch him.

'Painkillers.' His voice is croaky again.

'Dad, you just had some. They'll kick in soon.'

'Trying to kill me. You and that nurse.'

He reaches out and grabs the top of my arm, right where my scars are. 'Gimme pills.' He squeezes and twists his hand, and my scars burn. I can't believe how strong he is.

'Sorry, Dad, sorry.'

And I can't believe how weak I am.

He lets go of my arm and I half-stumble out of the room. When I get to the kitchen, there's a small blue and white cardboard box beside the bottle of tablets. Bicarbonate of soda.

Ruth watches me carefully. 'Excellent,' she says quietly. 'Justice and revenge.'

17

GEORGE AND GWEN

August 1942

At five minutes to five o'clock, Gwen walked down to the dairy as he had told her to. She wondered if she should have started tea. She had no idea how long it would take to milk 120 cows. One minute a cow? Ten minutes a cow? Half an hour a cow? She should definitely have put tea on.

When she met their neighbour, Robert Larsen, she was surprised at how old he was. At least old enough to be her father. Tall, solid and with skin that looked like it was sunburnt, he chatted incessantly, laughed at his own jokes and got lots of words confused. He told them he was married to Barbara and had a son, Colin, who was fifteen and would come and help them milk if they wanted, because he didn't have a job but could do anything that needed doing on a farm. Gwen wondered why Colin didn't have a job.

'Doesn't he need to help you, Robert?'

'Milking's not for me, Gwen. Not after twenty-six years. One day I woke up and my self-conscious must have been working overtime while I was asleep because I just opened my eyes and said, "Your milking days are over, Robert Larsen!" I had to milk them that morning, but I sold every singular one that very day. Came back with some calves that I never let a bull get within a bull's roar of. So they never had their own calves and never needed to be milked. Buy 'em, grow 'em, 'n' sell 'em, I say. That was a good eight years ago, and I've never looked back.'

George was as friendly as pie to Robert, smiling and laughing at his jokes and stories. Watching him, Gwen decided that he had snapped at her earlier because he was as nervous as she was about their new life. He even winked and smiled at her when Robert said, 'All we have to do now is clean everything with some disinsectant.'

Yes, George was a kind man who was nervous about having a new wife and a new farm and a new life.

But when they went back to the house and tea was not ready, his face became dark and thick. 'I can't milk every morning and night and not come back to a cooked meal.'

'No. Of course not,' she said, 'I'm sorry, dear.'

She was relieved to see her apology rewarded with one of his smiles.

18

JOY AND RUTH

December 1960

Walking into Church the next day (Joy always gave the noun a capital C in her mind), she knew everyone was inwardly laughing or frowning at her. It wasn't just her ugly face; it was her socks as well. Her white school socks sticking out from her church shoes and folded over to look like church socks.

She wanted cream tights like all the older girls. The socks had been fine while she'd been a little girl, but she was about to go to high school, after all. And have Friends. Friends who wouldn't wear socks to Church, let alone folded-over school socks.

Of course, she had church shoes, but that was only because you could never pretend that school shoes were church shoes. They had been last year's Christmas present, but she wouldn't get another pair this year because she was only now fitting into these ones properly. Her mother was clever that way, buying them a size too big so they would last for two years.

To keep their church shoes clean and shiny, they wore their rubber boots to the van, then put on their shoes, and did the reverse when they arrived home.

She also had a church dress, with a white bodice, white velvet collar, pale-yellow puffed sleeves, a skirt that was pale yellow, too, but made of a different material, and a sewn-in tulle petticoat that scratched the backs of her thighs. Joy was nine when her mother had paid Mrs Larsen to make her dress out of remnants of dresses she'd made for other children. That's why the petticoat scratched so much — there were lots of seams where odd scraps had been sewn together. The dress was so tight now that Joy was sure she would get a new one this Christmas, because it was important to dress properly for Church.

She felt that God would want a capital C for his holy buildings, and wondered why He wasn't more direct about things like capital letters for important words like Church, even if, according to *English for Grades 5 & 6*, it was not a proper noun. He could, after all, make it a proper noun. Not that she knew how God would actually do that, but He did make everyone give His personal pronouns a capital letter, so it couldn't be that hard. Maybe He could issue another Ten Commandments, because there were so many new things these days that hadn't existed when God gave Moses the first Ten Commandments. Take Devil's boxes, for example. The Hendersons didn't have one, of course, even though lots of people had bought one to watch the Olympic Games. According to her father, they filled people's minds with the Devil's rubbish. So one of the new Commandments could be 'Thou shalt not own or watch a television.' And 'Thou shalt spell Church with a capital C.' And, of course, 'Thou shalt be a Presbyterian, and not worship the pope, or be a Catholic, or Jew, or heathen, nor follow any other false religion.'

But this was confusing because Jesus was a Jew. The problem was that the Jews didn't think He was the Son of God. But why else did God send Him to Earth, and how could He perform all those miracles if He wasn't the Son of God? Her father was right — the Jews and Catholics and everyone else were wrong.

Walking through the rain to the Church's entrance, she prayed to God to do something to prove that He existed. To burst through the clouds and boom at everyone, or send down another son (although she knew that was a big ask). He had to do something — anything — so that everyone knew He existed and that you could only go to Heaven if you were a Presbyterian.

Anglicans, Baptists and Methodists who lived good lives would, thanks to our Lord's infinite mercy, probably go to Heaven, because they were Protestants. Though then again, since they worshipped and prayed all wrong, there was a good chance they wouldn't.

Catholics, of course, had everything wrong and were going to Hell. Forever and ever, Amen.

Savages were going to Hell, too. Joy was sad that the Africans and Aborigines who had never even heard of Jesus or God were going to Hell. But then again, they did kill and eat each other, so God was hardly going to let them into Heaven.

Poor Ruth couldn't come to Church because of her accident. And Joy's mother didn't come because of Ruth. So Joy and Mark sat either side of their father in the front pew on the right, directly in front of Reverend Braithwaite, following his instructions. They stood, sat, hung their heads in prayer, sang hymns, listened to the choir, listened to the sermon and echoed or responded to the Reverend's words perfectly correctly.

Today's sermon was about the sin of lying. The sinful act of deceiving, falsifying, of being treacherous, duplicitous, untrustworthy, perfidious. What a magnificent array of words for one sin. She repeated the last one in her head over and over . . . perfidious, per-fid-ious, per . . . fid . . . i . . . ous {fingers tinkling up and down a piano}. Joy liked how Reverend Braithwaite often used multiple words for the same thing. He was like a talking thesaurus {a buzzing beehive}. And what a wonderful day it had been when she had discovered the thesaurus on Mr Plummer's desk.

Reverend Braithwaite said that we all lie, and even if it's sometimes to save ourselves or someone else from harm, we are all lying sinners, caught in the eternal struggle between obeying our Lord and giving in to the Devil's temptations {red-gloved fingers curling, one by one, to lure you closer and closer}.

Joy definitely gave Devil a capital D, to remind her of His extreme Evil. Even though she was surprised that God gave the Devil's personal pronouns a capital letter, she was not at all surprised that the word *Devil* had the word *evil* sitting right inside it. Nor that the letters of *evil* could be rearranged to make *vile* and *veil* . . . which was exactly what the vile Devil was trying to put over God's holy words. Nor was she surprised that spelling *evil* backwards gave you *live*, as if being evil was the backwards way of living the way our Lord wanted us to.

It was interesting how some images matched their word's meaning, like Devil {the red horned beast Himself ruling Hell}. And how others, like bland {a wall painted a washed-out yellow} were hardly worth it. But most of the images were magnificent. Like puzzle {a herd of zebras}. And rose {a dark velvet cushion}. And syllable {mashed banana}, which also came with the smell, taste and feel of mashed bananas. Some absolutely remarkable words left her overcome with emotion, such as butterfly {the feeling you get when you understand that one day you are actually going to die}.

She loved words so much.

But, wonderful as their images and sensations were, Joy wasn't sure that everyone else enjoyed them as much, so she had asked her mother, it seemed like a hundred years ago, if everyone had the same pictures for the same words. Her mother frowned, her answer both sharp and blunt. 'Words are words. Just concentrate on getting those potatoes done.'

When Joy was learning to read in Prep, the pictures had danced about in her head totally out of control, and she'd found it hard to concentrate on their letters. One day when she was copying down a spelling list from the blackboard,

Mr Plummer had asked her (thank goodness) what the problem was. 'I can't see the words because of the pictures, Mr Plummer. It's like they're smashing into one another, isn't it?'

Despite his odd look, Joy continued, 'Do we all see the same pictures, Mr Plummer?' It was so hard, especially because she had to say 'Mr Plummer' a hundred times a day, and every time she did, an image of a peacock burst into her head.

'Are you trying to be funny?' His voice was hard and bumpy, which was how he spoke to the Keane twins when they were throwing sticks at each other. 'Copy the spelling list, please, Joy, without asking any more ridiculous questions.' Joy blushed, and she was confused. Was her question ridiculous because everyone *did* have the same pictures or because everyone had *different* pictures? If her mother and Mr Plummer weren't going to tell her, she knew no one was, so she didn't mention the images in her head to anyone else. She'd already learnt that there are lots of things you never talk about. Like how pepper {fireworks} tastes, or how snapdragons {a cow's tongue} feel, or how you have to be careful of your father's anger {a red ball covered with sharp metal spikes}.

And Ruth's accident. She just added word images to the list.

She had also learnt that when she absolutely had to concentrate on a meaning of a word, not its picture, she could force herself to pull across a huge curtain to separate the picture from the word's meaning. The curtain was made of a thin oily white fabric, so Joy could see the shape and sometimes even the colour of an image as it pushed and twisted to break through the membrane {egg white sitting in a glass bowl}. She'd been so pleased when she'd discovered the word 'membrane' in the dictionary. Whenever an unwanted image was forcing its way through the membrane, her heart sped up and her eyes burnt as she fought to send it back to wherever it came from. But sometimes it would push its way through, no matter how hard she concentrated. It would erupt into her sore brain, filling it with colour, movement, shapes, and sometimes sounds, smells and textures. Maybe the Devil was worming His way into her soul {a spiral of light brown smoke}. She closed her eyes and moved her head around in a circle to see if she could feel any of His red tendrils sneaking around in her brain.

Without warning, her upper left arm became hot and sore. She opened her eyes, and realised her father was slowly pinching and twisting her skin with his left hand. She had no idea what Reverend Braithwaite had just said, but she knew she had pained her father by moving her head in Church like a drunken clown. She bit her bottom lip, because to make a sound would be unforgivable, and concentrated again on the Reverend's sermon on lying.

Joy felt her most recent lie wrap around her like the wings of a huge black bat. 'No, Dad, no, I promise I didn't drop any eggs. It must have been one of the chooks. I remember seeing some shell on the ground.' Sometimes the chooks did push an egg out of the pen, but not yesterday.

Straight away, she'd sent up two prayers to God simultaneously. First, there was the 'real prayer', asking for forgiveness. 'Please God, forgive me for dropping the egg and covering it up. For thine is the Kingdom, the Power and the Glory, for ever and ever, Amen.' Then there was the 'selfish prayer'. 'Please God, don't let my father find out. I promise I will worship you for ever and ever, Amen.'

'For the Lord did say,' continued the Reverend, '"I am the way, the truth, and the life." All sinners, yes, all sinners, shall be cast into eternal misery {a wreath of thorns}, into the place of weeping and gnashing of teeth from which there shall be no release. Today I beseech you to ask the Almighty to forgive you for your sins, so that you may never know the fires of Hell, but only the love of our Lord. Please stand.'

Everyone stood, bowed their heads and closed their eyes. While Reverend Braithwaite prayed, Joy couldn't stop wondering why, if God was omniscient {a perfect pale-blue sphere floating in space} and omnipotent {a perfect silver oily sphere floating in space} and omnipresent {a perfect dark-blue sphere floating in space}, He would let anyone be cast into eternal misery. Why didn't He make sure everyone knew what they had to do to go to Heaven instead of Hell?

'For ever and ever . . .'

'Amen,' chorused everyone.

When the organist started playing 'How Great Thou Art', the children squeezed past adults to make their way to Sunday School. As Joy walked up the outside aisle {a long maroon ribbon}, she pictured Christ and our Almighty Father in Heaven wearing large billowing smocks over their holy robes and each dabbing at a painting on a golden easel. But their great art filled her with horror. They had painted black savages, Chinese people, liars, cheats and Catholics falling into a large black crack in the ground with orange flames leaping up to a dark sky full of large ominous clouds. Doomed to Hell and eternal misery, they were screaming for mercy, their hands clasped under their chins in prayer, while red demons laughed at all the sinners who had never even heard of our Lor—

Joy tripped on the step leading into the hall, and the paintings disintegrated. But the image of the sinners screaming as they fell into Hell would be burnt into her mind for all of eternity.

19

GEORGE AND GWEN

August 1942

At 10.30 in the morning on their second day on the farm, Robert knocked on the back door. Barbara was with him, and she handed Gwen a paper bag of warm scones for morning tea. Gwen was excited and grateful. She and Barbara would no doubt become friends, though their houses — and their ages — were so far apart.

But when Barbara asked for the paper bag back as she left, her face was as hard as her scones had been. It had not helped that all Gwen had for the scones was butter because her great-aunt had not packed any jam. While Robert and George talked about the weather and the mud and the cows as if they'd known each other for years, she and Barbara exchanged polite questions and answers. Barbara kept her lips pursed and Gwen was sure she had quickly worked out that Gwen knew nothing about farming.

After the couple left, George sat at the kitchen table writing on a sheet of paper while Gwen washed the dishes.

'Don't ever embarrass yourself like that again.' He handed her the sheet of paper. 'Tomorrow, when I go into town to talk to the bank manager, you can come with me and buy the items on this list.' He smiled. 'You will notice that at the top of the list is "jam ingredients" — whatever they are.'

'Oh,' said Gwen, feeling as if he had slapped her, and struggling to smile back. 'A trip to town will be lovely.' She took the list and read the items on it. Her stomach lurched because she knew that their ration coupons would not entitle them to enough sugar for jam and the two teaspoons of sugar George liked in every cup of tea.

As he left the kitchen to continue checking the fences, she realised she had still not told him about her plans for the workroom. The next morning, it took them nearly an hour to drive to a town Gwen had never heard of before. When they drove past a sign that said 'Welcome to Blackhunt. Population 627', the paddocks gave way to weatherboard houses on rectangular blocks of land. Half a mile on there was a sprinkling of shops. When Gwen saw a handful of people, she felt buoyed. George would relax and be his kind self when they were with other people.

He parked in front of a shop with large bold letters on the window that read 'Arnold's Grocery'. He pulled out his wallet and said, 'Here are our ration coupons, and money to buy food for a week. Did you bring the list?'

'Yes, George.' It was strange taking money from him.

'I will be back here in exactly thirty minutes.'

She checked her watch, put the coupons and money in her purse and walked into the grocery.

Arnold was as old as Robert, with glasses that sat half-way down his nose, and a way of smiling that made Gwen think he was running a very successful business. When he had everything on the list piled on the counter, including half the sugar she wanted (rations were rations), he asked her if she had just moved to Blackhunt.

'Yes. No. Well, not exactly. My husband and I have bought a farm. Out of Blackhunt.'

'Really? Which one?' he asked, punching the cost of each item into his till.

'Which one?' she repeated dumbly. 'Um, it's quite a long way out.' And she pointed in the direction they'd come from. 'We were driving for nearly an hour just to get here.'

'Is it the one the Dalgleishes got rid of?'

What could she say — 'I don't know'? She blushed. 'Yes, that's the one.'

'Well, you've got your work cut out then, haven't you? It's a rundown place if ever there was one. That'll be three pound, sixpence, thanks, ma'am.'

Gwen looked at the money in her purse. George had given her three one-pound notes, and not a penny more. As she looked up at Arnold with dread in her eyes, she realised she was a fool. She didn't know where Blackhunt was, she didn't know where she was living, and she didn't have enough money to pay for the supplies on the counter. Her head felt light, as if she was teetering on the edge of a cliff and staring at the dark sea below.

She smiled feebly at Arnold. 'Oh dear. I only have three pound. It seems I didn't get quite enough before I left home. Can you . . . put back two of the sausages?' And she handed over the three notes.

'Tell you what,' he said, smiling the smile that made him popular with his customers. 'I'll let you have the two sausages for nought, and you agree to stay away from the competition down the street.' She wanted to protest, but the doorbell tinkled and George walked in. He came straight up to the counter, hand outstretched, with the same smile and gaze that had charmed Gwen at the dance. 'George Henderson. And you must be Mr Arnold?'

The grocer laughed and shook George's hand. 'Yes, I am, Mr Henderson, but Arnold's my Christian name, and that's what everyone calls me.' George laughed with him.

'And I'm George. You've met my wife, Gwen. I hope you've got everything on our list, dear.' He took her hand and wrapped it around the crook of his arm. Gwen smiled back at him and nodded. This is what married life is, she thought — smiling with her arm hooked around her husband's while they chatted with friendly shopkeepers.

'I hear you've bought the old Dalgleish farm?'

'No,' said George. 'I bought the Wentworth farm. Out on Bullock Road.'

'The Wentworth farm?' said Arnold, surprised. Gwen stared at the floorboards, her other hand gripping the handle of her purse. 'I thought you'd . . . ah, well, I must have got it wrong somehow. I'll see you next week, then, Mrs Henderson?'

Gwen couldn't look at him. 'Yes, of course. Thank you, Arnold.'

Before George started the van's engine, he held out his hand and asked Gwen for the change.

'Oh dear. I'm sorry, George, there wasn't any.' She opened her purse to show him that it was empty, and wondered why she was apologising.

'Are you saying it came to exactly three pound?'

'Yes . . . well, no.' She felt her voice getting smaller. Could she lie to him? 'It was actually a little more than three pound, so I asked him to give us less minced beef.' What was wrong with her? Why not just tell him that Arnold had given them two sausages for free in exchange for Gwen's loyal custom?

George drove off without saying anything. After a while, Gwen asked casually, 'How was your visit to the bank?'

He watched the road ahead and said in a friendly voice, 'You don't need to worry about that. I'll take care of the bank, and you take care of the house. That's the way it works, dear.'

Relieved that he was being friendly again, she readily agreed, and mirrored his affection. 'Yes, dear, thank you.'

'The bank manager asked me if you had any money.' He kept his eyes on the road. 'I told him that you were an excellent saver. He was very pleased and said we should put it into the mortgage. It makes sense, he said.'

'Oh.' Gwen wasn't sure if this was normal or not, but if that's what the bank manager said . . .

'When we come back next week, bring your bank book and we'll transfer your savings to the mortgage.'

'How much?'

'Well . . . the whole lot, dear. That's what the bank manager said.' He smiled at her, and took one hand off the steering wheel to pat her two hands that were sitting, fingers entwined, on her lap. Later that night, as they were going to bed, George pointed out that she had folded his socks and singlets and underpants incorrectly. He made her copy him as he folded one of each 'correctly'. As Gwen followed his movements, her face was burning with humiliation, and she felt again that he had slapped her. Twice in one day.

Months later, she couldn't remember when the first actual slap occurred. Or what she had done to deserve it.

20

JOY AND RUTH

December 1960

'Good morning, everyone.' Mr Jones was using his sugary voice, his hand resting on the shoulder of a girl Joy had never seen before. 'Please welcome Felicity to Sunday School and make her feel part of our Lord's family. Joy, move over so Felicity can sit next to me.'

All the students who were more than ten years old were sitting cross-legged in a circle on the hard floor of the hall. Joy was the oldest child in this group and Mr Jones made her sit next to his chair. Shuffling over to make room for Felicity, Joy couldn't help but stare. As well as having the fanciest name, Felicity was wearing cream tights and a blue skirt with a matching jacket that made her look about seventeen. Joy pulled her church dress over her knees to hide her socks.

Twirled on top of her head, Felicity also had the biggest bun Joy had ever seen, with a thin white ribbon wrapped around its base and curly tendrils hanging down to the collar of her jacket. Soft wavy wisps of hair hung either side of her face. Joy ran a hand over her own lank brown hair and wished her mother was a hairdresser instead of a florist who made wreaths for dead people.

Felicity didn't cross her legs on the floor like everyone else, but bent both legs to the left, placed her left hand on her left ankle and leant on her right hand, taking up more space than she needed to. A gold bracelet dangled on her right wrist and a delicate gold watch was wrapped around her left one.

Joy's eyes moved from the top of Felicity's huge perfect bun to the shoes that were exactly the same blue as her skirt and jacket. 'Stop staring,' Mr Jones snapped, and Joy went bright red before she realised that he was talking to everyone. He coughed, and began the lesson: 'Now, what was Reverend Braithwaite's sermon about this morning?'

For the whole half-hour, Joy was both fascinated and frustrated by Fancy Felicity who sat with her legs tucked beside her like she was a duchess {an enormous pile of soft yellow tissue paper} and didn't answer any of Mr Jones's questions. When they were colouring in Christ accepting Peter back into the fold, they were allowed to talk, so Joy asked Felicity questions as casually as she could.

'Are you twelve yet?' she said, colouring Christ's face pink. Felicity answered her with a single nod, as she coloured the grass orange. Joy moved on to Christ's hands. Hardly anyone stayed at Sunday School after turning twelve because their sinful parents let them stay home instead. Joy would keep coming until she was fifteen, just as Mark had, then stay in Church with Mark and her father for the whole service. She coloured Christ's hands and feet pink. 'Are your parents in Church?' Another single nod. Christ's robe had to be pale blue, except for the strip around the edge. Joy stopped colouring, looked at Mr Jones, who had wandered away to talk to one of the other teachers, then lowered her voice, hardly believing the words slithering out of her mouth. 'See that girl in the gingham dress in the group with the really old teacher? That's Marion Becker and her parents don't go to Church. They drop her off and pick her up afterwards. Same with Philip MacIntosh, the boy with red hair in our group.

His father's our vet, but he doesn't come to Church either. And usually Wendy Boscombe is in that group too, but she's on holidays at the beach . . . they're rich so they won't go to Heaven.' Felicity stared at Marion, then at Philip. Joy coloured the trim on Christ's robe yellow to match the gold in the picture in the Bible. 'Are you going to Blackhunt High School next year?'

Felicity shook her head.

Joy picked up a brown pencil to colour in Peter's robe. How could Felicity not be going to high school if she was twelve? Maybe she wasn't very smart and had been kept down.

'Why not?' Ha! — she couldn't answer that with a shake or a nod. But Felicity shrugged, picked up the green pencil and began colouring in the sky, leaving Christ and Peter blank. Joy was about to tell Felicity that the sky had to be blue when Mr Jones's voice interrupted her thoughts. 'Joy! Will you please concentrate on *your* picture, not Felicity's?' Joy's face burnt with shame. The eels wriggled inside her, and two silent prayers slipped out together.

Please God,
forgive me for not paying attention.
Please don't let him tell my father.
For ever and ever,
Amen.

She picked up the yellow pencil again to colour in Christ's halo. Felicity had given Christ a purple halo and orange lips.

'Alright, pencils back in the bucket.' Mr Jones walked around the circle. His voice wasn't sugary any more. 'Then everyone stand for the closing prayer.'

They all stood up, and Joy held Paula Sanderson's dry hand on one side and Fancy Felicity's smooth one on the other. The only good thing about Fancy Felicity arriving at Sunday School was that Joy didn't have to hold hands with

Mr Jones, who was now droning 'May the grace of our Lord Jesus Christ . . .'

Joy tilted her bowed head to one side and opened her right eye a smidgen {a squashed ant} to look at Felicity, only to see her staring straight at her. Was she thinking how ugly Joy's face was, she wondered, but then Felicity grinned at her and Joy opened both eyes in shock, before remembering to quickly close them and bow her head before Mr Jones finished.

'. . . the Holy Spirit be with you all.'

'Amen,' said everyone.

On their way out, Felicity pulled Joy to the back of the group and whispered, 'You didn't have your eyes shut during the prayer.' She looked pleased that she had caught Joy peeking, and Joy knew Felicity was going to tell her father.

'I was just . . .' said Joy, then she stopped. 'Well, you didn't either.'

Felicity let out a high-pitched laugh. 'Yep, you got me there!'

'Why didn't you?'

'So I could see what everyone was doing. It's much more interesting. Anyway, God doesn't say you *have* to close your eyes when you pray.'

Joy thought for a second. Felicity was right. 'Why aren't you going to high school?'

'Of course I'm going to go to high school, just not yours.'

'Where, then?'

'Stupid old St Anne's.'

'*Saint* Anne's? Is that Catholic?' Joy was dumbstruck.

'Anglican.'

'But aren't you Presbyterian?'

'I don't know,' said Felicity. 'Mum and Dad say it doesn't matter which church you go to, just so long as you pray with your heart and you're kind to everyone.'

While Joy waited for Mark under the large triangular porch that jutted out of the Church like an afterthought, she watched Felicity greet her family. Her parents were dark and striking, and she had an older brother as well. Felicity showed them her colouring-in and the four of them laughed out loud, and her father kissed her forehead. Then Felicity's parents introduced her to the adults they'd been talking to, and Felicity talked and laughed with them as if she was a grown-up too. Every time she laughed she pushed the wisps of her hair behind one ear, just like her mother. Mrs Felicity had thick black hair that was smooth and fell to her shoulders, the ends curling inwards a touch, and she wasn't wearing a hat. Every other woman at Church had a short perm and wore a white wide-brimmed hat adorned with plastic flowers. When Mark came out, they got in their van to wait for their father, Joy in the back seat, Mark in the front. Their father was always the last person to leave Church, except for Reverend Braithwaite. The Reverend stood in the narthex to thank and farewell each person as they walked out, and their father, who was the Church's longest-serving Elder, stood beside him, greeting and shaking hands as if the Reverend couldn't do it without him. Today, from the van, Joy saw Reverend Braithwaite and her father come out of the Church and walk straight up to the new family.

'What a show-off,' said Mark.

Joy let out a small grunt of agreement.

'Look at him,' Mark continued. 'All friendly because they're new and obviously rich. I bet he's telling them that he's the longest-serving Elder, that he's on eighty-seven committees, and knows everyone.'

'Hello, I'm George Henderson,' Joy said in a deep voice. 'I'm on eighty-seven committees and I'm the longest-serving Elder in the Church, and the most devout Christian in the world.'

Mark was laughing as he turned around to look at her. 'That's exactly like him,' he said. 'When did you learn to do that?'

'What do you mean?' she said in the same deep voice. 'I'm George Henderson and I'm perfect. I'm going to Heaven one day, but my children will be burning in H—'

'Shhh, here he comes.'

Joy's tongue instantly flew to the roof of her mouth. She looked out her window and saw the Felicities walking towards a big shiny car. *They are rich*, thought Joy, ashamed that she had told Felicity that Wendy Boscombe's rich parents wouldn't go to Heaven. *Well, that Felicity is just too big and fancy for her own boots anyway.*

Felicity opened her car door, then turned around and waved enthusiastically at Joy, a huge smile on her face. Confused but pleased, Joy waved back equally enthusiastically.

At lunch that afternoon, her father couldn't stop talking about the Felicities. He never talked this much at home unless they had visitors. When Joy came into the kitchen after changing out of her church dress, he was already telling her mother all about them. 'They've brought two farms next to one another the other side of town, on Pepperell and Boots Road,' he said, obviously impressed.

As she sat down, the eels in Joy's stomach rolled over — why couldn't her father ever get *brought* and *bought* right?

'Two farms?' asked her mother.

Her husband continued as if she hadn't said anything. 'They're from the city, so they won't last long. And they also brought the chemist shop in Blackhunt and the one in Kongarra, but he's no more a chemist than he is a farmer. Beats me,' her father added, as if anticipating his wife's next question. 'Robert said they're probably investors.'

His children stared at each other with mutual questions in their eyes. How much money must they have? What's an investor? Why would they move *here*?

'Also, I've enrolled the two of you,' he pointed at Mark then Joy with his knife, 'in Bible Study for the holidays. Tuesday and Thursday mornings. Better than making a nuisance of yourselves here every day.'

They both said 'Yes, Dad' politely and loudly enough that he couldn't find anything to be angry about.

That night, while Ruth brushed her hair, Joy told Ruth all about Fancy Felicity's clothes and hair and mother. 'You should have seen Mrs Felicity's hair. It's so smooth and beautiful.'

They sat in silence for a little while.

'I wish you could come to Sunday School with me, Ruth,' said Joy.

'You know I can't,' said Ruth. And her voice was not silky, but sharp like a ferret's teeth.

Joy knew she should feel sorry for Ruth, but the truth was she felt a familiar white tremor of jealousy. Starting at the base of her neck, it spread down through her body and up into her scalp. Rather than get into a fight with Ruth, she turned to face the bedroom wall and pulled out her little dictionary to find tonight's new word. But she could feel Ruth's ice-blue anger piercing her shoulder blades.

Like father, like daughter, she thought.

21

JOY AND GEORGE

February 1983

There are things I need to attend to so I can leave as soon as it's all over. Like the chooks eating time in the pen behind the back garden. What on earth has he been doing with the eggs? Not making sponges or meringues, that's for sure. Maybe boiled eggs on toast. Had he learnt to boil and toast? Even that seems impossible.

Standing outside the pen, I watch the chooks while the sun heats up my scars, and am not entirely surprised when my mother walks out from behind the back of the pen and starts 'tuk-tuking' to them. She lifts up one of them, tucks it under her arm and pats it. 'Gooood girl,' she says calmly. 'Gooood Ruth.'

No wonder I was jealous of Ruth. My mother never ever named a single chook Joy.

I force myself to ignore her and walk into the wooden pen. Inside the nest, broken eggshells and small eggs with thin blotched shells compete for space. The broken eggshells mean the chooks have started to eat their own eggs, which means no one's fed them or collected their eggs for ages.

Their water trough is empty, despite the black polypropylene pipes that run underground from the dam to all of the troughs on the farm. Polypropylene. A word I loved to say almost as much as I loved its image of a tap dancer in a tuxedo.

Looking at the trough, it dawns on me that the dam must have dried up. And that means everything sitting at the bottom of the dam must be on display for anyone to see.

I pour water into the trough from a bucket I fill in the laundry, wondering how much water is in the tank that supplies the house. Then I fill the feed bin with pellets. A last supper. As the Ruths bustle and bump with excitement, I count them. And there's Mum, watching me, shaking her head because I'm wasting time counting when she knows how many there are. She's standing in the corner, wondering how she could possibly have a daughter so unlike her. Of course, there are twelve Ruths, just as there always were. Until one of them became a roast.

In the good room, I slide the tele-index slider to C for Chooks. Jinny Pollard asks me how many there are, and for a second I think about saying eleven, because maybe we could have a roast tonight. But the thought of getting the axe and beheading one of them makes me feel ill. A round dozen, I say. When she asks me if they're still laying, I say, 'Absolutely, I made us an omelette this morning.' She says she'll come and look, no promises.

She arrives on time with a covered trailer behind her car, which she backs up close to the pen.

'They're still layin', then?' she asks again, pushing open the gate to the pen. I'm offended by her suspicious tone.

'Yes, yes.'

'So why don' you want them no more?' She picks up one of the chooks.

'Oh. Well, they're not mine. They were my father's.'

‘I didn’t know your father died. When was that, then?’ She’s squinting into the sun, and I’m annoyed that she noticed the past tense I’ve just used.

‘Oh. No, he’s still alive. But . . . he’s dying.’ She has me flustered. ‘I mean, he’s going to die soon.’

She stops patting the chook under her arm. ‘What?’

‘That’s what the doctor told me.’ I know I’m being too defensive. ‘I’m looking after him.’ *I’m doing the right thing,* I want to add. ‘Okay.’ She puts the chook in the trailer, and turns to me again.

‘So, why don’ you take them?’

‘I live in Darwin.’ Why did I say that? What is it about this place that makes me lie so often?

‘Uh-huh,’ she says.

When all twelve of them are in the trailer (faster than my father ever retrieved just one and chopped off its head with his glistening axe), we duly exchange money, and Jinny and the twelve Ruths disappear down the driveway.

For the first time in at least forty years, the pen is empty. Except for my mother, standing in the back corner sadly waving goodbye to the last of the Ruths. Or maybe to me. I can’t tell.

I look at my watch. I need to see if the dam’s dried up, then give my father some more tablets.

22

GEORGE AND GWEN

November 1942

While she was clearing up the breakfast dishes on the Friday that marked exactly three months of living on the farm, Gwen realised her life had settled into a routine that would have stunned her great-aunt and Jean — and her previous self. Up at 4.45 to cook George's breakfast before he milked the cows (what a blessing Colin was, otherwise she would have to help with the milking), clean up after breakfast, wash yesterday's clothes in the copper boiler, sweep and mop the kitchen floor, make scones or sultana biscuits for George's morning tea, push the clothes through the wringer and hang them on the line, cook lunch and clean up afterwards, sweep and mop the bathroom and toilet, prepare George's afternoon tea and clean up afterwards, bring in the clothes, get tea ready, clean up, go to bed at 8.30, roll on her back for him. Repeat it all the next day.

For ever and ever, Amen.

The only break in the routine was Sunday morning church, and Monday morning grocery shopping. There was no money or time for dances or lipstick because there was always fencing or troughs or tools or pumps or machinery to be repaired or bought, and endless bills and mortgage payments.

Just last night, George had sat at his place at the head of the kitchen table and written figures in his blue accounting book, slammed the book shut, rubbed his forehead and groaned. Gwen asked if she could do anything to help, but George muttered she had enough to do with all the cooking and housework. Then smiled his wide generous smile that always overwhelmed her — these days mainly with relief.

She didn't know how much George owed on the farm or how much he had left over from his inheritance. All she knew was that on the first day of each month, they received a cheque from the butter factory based on the total amount of milk George and Colin had wheeled out to the road each morning and night in the previous month, and that every week there were more and more expenses. Gwen was nervous. What if they had children? She hoped they would, and assumed George did too, as he'd bought a house with three bedrooms. But if they couldn't afford to live properly now, how would they manage when there were extra mouths to feed?

She knew George was nervous about the money too because now he gave her only two pound, ten shillings for housekeeping on Monday mornings, and scoured the derelict sheds for coils of old fencing wire, nails and other equipment to avoid buying anything new. She knew that she had to try harder to be economical, have tea ready on time, keep the house clean and be presentable at church and in town. When she let him down, she felt inadequate and tried harder because she didn't want to make him angry.

Still, shaking the soap-cage in the hot water in the sink, she was strangely satisfied at how she had succumbed to the routine of this new life, bending to it like a willow. She smiled wryly, then winced as a shot of pain flew from her tongue to her right eye: she'd bitten her tongue as her head was flung to her left shoulder after she'd made him angry that morning by overcooking the toast *and* the eggs when he'd been a few minutes late coming up from the dairy. As the first dish went into the soapy water, she realised she really didn't know how to be a wife, at least not a *good-enough* wife. Because the thing was, she was the only person who made George angry. He was already widely respected and admired in the community: he was friendly and helpful; he helped all their neighbours with their fencing and their stuck calves and their water pumps and their broken tractors and windmills; and none of them ever made him angry. She was the only one. She and she alone. She pursed her lips and sucked to produce extra saliva to soothe her tongue. She just wasn't up to scratch in the wife department. No, not at all. And she knew it was because she'd never lived in a house where there had been a wife and a husband, a normal family.

George certainly worked hard, there was no doubt about that. And was a fervent Christian. In the last couple of weeks he had joined two local committees and a local band as their guitarist. When she raised her eyebrows in surprise when he told her, he patted her hand and said, 'We have to become part of the community, dear. We have to do our bit.' But when she said she might join the local crocheting group that a woman at church had mentioned. George's hand stopped patting hers as he thought for a second, screwed up his mouth and shook his head slowly. 'Do you really want to spend your valuable time *crocheting*' — he said the word with such contempt — 'when you're struggling to get everything done here?' Of course he was right, but she did miss the company of other women, of her friends. Even her great-aunt.

Looking out of the kitchen window, she saw him repairing a fence, and remembered with a mixture of relief and pride that, despite this morning's breakfast, she rarely made him angry at mealtimes now that she understood his preferences. Roast or mashed potato . . . peas and carrots, no other vegetables . . . any meat, but no offal . . . vegetable soup, not tomato . . . lemon meringue pie, blancmange or stewed fruit, no other dessert.

When they'd first moved in, mealtimes were full of talk about fencing and paddocks and cows and the dam and electricity bills and the weather and the outrageous vet bills. Gwen had loved that they were so immersed in their new farming life, but when she suggested they put in a new gate between the bull paddock and the dam paddock to save time, he said there wasn't enough money. And when she suggested they milk the cows earlier in the afternoon so they could have an early tea and go to the cinema, he said there was a reason they milked at five o'clock and she should have worked that out by now, and there certainly wasn't enough money for trifles like movies.

He was right, of course. What did she know about farming? Or anything, for that matter? Except floristry, perhaps. It was no wonder she made him angry when she disappointed him so much. She just had to change how she did some things, learn what he wanted and provide it for him, just as she had with the meals. Then everything would be fine.

Wiping down the table, she looked up at the wall-hanging opposite her. After they'd been at the farm for just three weeks, George told her they needed something on the kitchen wall. Gwen had pictured a painting of red roses or yellow daisies. But George had something different in mind.

The following Monday he instructed her to buy a small square of blue velvet and a skein of white embroidery thread from Arnold in exchange for a little less meat for herself. Over the next few days she embroidered the lines of verse he wanted while the potatoes were boiling. Working in Stan's shop, her fingers had always got on like a house on fire, so it was annoying how they argued with each other while she was embroidering. Each night, when it was time to drain the potatoes, she sighed at the crooked letters. On the sixth day, she wanted to throw it in the bin and start again, but that would be a terrible waste of money.

George did not seem to notice or care about the awkwardness of her work as he fed a thin piece of wood through the top hem followed by a length of fence wire, and hung the ugly thing on a nail he hammered in the wall above the kitchen table. And now whenever Gwen sat at the table, or chopped vegetables at the bench, she was facing the wall-hanging, and it was impossible not to look at it. She wondered if that was what George had wanted all along.

23

JOY AND RUTH

December 1960

The next day, Joy turned twelve. She lay in bed for a few minutes, enjoying the tingle of being a year older.

'Happy birthday, Joy,' said Ruth, a big smile creasing her birthmark.

Joy walked into the kitchen, where there was a brown-paper parcel at her place on the table. Her mother said, 'Happy birthday, Joy. Open your present.' She came over and kissed her on the forehead, and gave her a quick hug. As she pulled her arms from Joy, she said, 'I will always remember the day you were born,' and wiped a tear from her face. She said that every year, and Joy was never sure whether the tear was because she was happy or sad. Or both.

Mark teased her. 'Twelve? You're such a baby.'

Joy smiled, unconcerned. Breakfasts were the best meal of the day because their father was usually still in the dairy with Colin, milking and cleaning up the muck.

As she turned the parcel over to undo the knot in the string, Mark said, 'It's a jumper.'

She held up the new thick jumper, which was the same mustard colour as the fridge and Mark's fear. Even though she'd wanted a new church dress to impress Felicity, she was happy with the jumper — she hadn't had a new one for two years and her father said it was going to be another cold, wet year. It had rained incessantly for weeks and there was mud everywhere. Before December, everyone had complained that summer was coming and that meant droughts and bushfires, but it hadn't stopped pouring, and now everyone was complaining about the wet because they couldn't cut hay. And if they couldn't cut hay, there would be no winter food for the cows . . . which meant the cows would produce less milk . . . which meant less money, even though the price of everything else would go up faster than the water in the rain gauge.

Joy's father blamed the government. None of those smarmy lawyer types had ever done a real day's work in their entire life. None of them knew what it was like to round up cows in the mud, make your living with your hands and muscles, and fight the weather every single day of your life.

Joy knew they would never be able to afford plastic for the new schoolbooks.

She put her birthday jumper in the third drawer of her chest of drawers, on top of the green jumper she'd received two years ago, then started on her chores.

The chore she hated the most was emptying the rubbish bin into the tall corrugated-iron tank in the pump paddock. Anything and everything that fitted into the tank ended up there when they no longer needed it — empty cans and bottles, eel heads, rags, dead rats and mice that had eaten the Ratsak her father sprinkled everywhere, flat batteries, broken plates that couldn't be glued together, old fence wire, buckets with holes in them, newspapers, and anything else broken or old and useless. Whenever something was thrown in there, it was followed by a twisted taper of newspaper, lit with a match. And, despite the constant rain, there was always a fire in there, slowly burning, smoke rising from it. The stench made Joy gag.

She climbed up the wooden steps beside the tank. There was no handrail so she climbed with one hand pushed against the waves of the corrugated iron, while the other pulled the kitchen bin behind her. Standing on the final step, she lifted the bin above her head, angled it over the rim, and banged it so the rubbish would fall in, always terrified that she would lose her grip and the whole bin would drop in, or that she would break it by banging too hard. She knew that the tank sat atop a crack in the earth that led to Hell, which explained why the fire never went out, and why it smelt so putrid.

In the afternoon, she went into town with her mother. Her mother shopped every Monday, because that was when the prices were lowest and the local newspaper came out.

When they pulled up at the newsagent's, Joy ran in. Back in the van, she handed the paper to her mother who, red pen at the ready, briskly turned the pages to the personal notices, saying just as briskly, 'Let's hope there's a good one today.'

But it was not the notices announcing celebrations such as births and wedding anniversaries that interested her mother. No, it was the death notices Joy's mother turned to. And a 'good one' was a funeral that would attract lots of people. The funeral of someone widely admired, like a primary school teacher, or someone with power, like a local councillor. Or a child. The more tragic the death, the more orders she'd receive. 'There isn't a farmer around who thinks it's worth paying extra to the town florist for a wreath that's thrown away the same day it's made. And plenty of townsfolk agree.' A couple of years ago, Joy had seen her mother lick her lips when there had been over forty death notices for the granddaughter of the butter factory's manager, who had died when she was just hours old.

Joy wondered if baby Stephanie had gone straight to Heaven to be with Christ who was sitting on the right hand of God the Father Almighty. Even though Joy knew that the people who had written the Bible meant the right-hand *side* of God the Father Almighty, she always pictured God's right hand being squashed by Christ's bottom. Then immediately prayed for forgiveness. Sometimes she imagined God yanking His right hand out from under Jesus's bottom when it got sore, shaking it up and down because it was numb and tingly, and saying to Christ, 'For crying out loud, Son, stop sitting on my right hand. I can't issue holy orders with you sitting on it all the time.' Christ would say, 'Sorry, Dad, but I did tell everyone that I'd be sitting on your right hand for eternity. You wouldn't want to make a liar of me, would you?' And they would roll around laughing in their pristine robes, and God would forget what command He'd wanted to issue. Joy thought it must be then that bad things happened in the world.

She wondered if people got older in Heaven, because what would babies like Stephanie *do* in Heaven all day, let alone all of eternity?

Roman Catholics, however, believed in Purgatory — a place where you had to wait until enough people back on Earth prayed long and hard for you to be allowed into Heaven. Joy imagined Purgatory was like a waiting room at a small desolate railway station. The waiting room was cold, and full of shuffling sinners with thin brown coats, thin dirty scarves and thin grey eyes. When the door opened, the bitter wind blew in, paper serviettes would flutter off the Laminex tables and someone would kick the drinks machine, and the rusty tin sign outside would clank and rattle. Next to the platform was a single railway line that went forever in both directions. Heaven to the right, Hell to the left. Or maybe the other way around. Nobody knew. Whenever a rusty train scraped to a halt, everyone avoided looking up in case it was taking passengers to Hell. But that didn't save you. If you were going to Hell, you had only yourself to blame. And your Catholic relatives who didn't pray enough.

Joy's mother put her pen back into her bag and threw the paper into the back seat. 'No good ones,' she said. 'Just a poor old woman in her eighties. Might get two wreaths if I'm lucky.'

In the supermarket, Joy pushed the trolley while her mother compared pennies per ounce or fluid ounce, and wrote down what she bought and how much she paid for it on the back of an old bill.

At one end of the supermarket, there was a long counter where customers could ask for precise quantities of items, such as ten ounces of sultanas or two cups of custard powder, instead of buying the packages on the shelves. Joy loved the large maroon tins that held the dry items — the black writing on the front made her think they came from a lost civilisation of gypsies. You could also buy 'seconds' there. Joy's mother asked for half a pound of broken Teddy Bear biscuits because Joy's father liked them and the broken biscuits tasted just the same but were nearly half the price.

As they went up and down the aisles, her mother recorded all the prices, and kept a running balance of the total. Every time Joy came shopping with her, she explained why she did this — so Joy would know how to manage her own housekeeping one day. 'You only get so much housekeeping each week, and you can't go over it. Imagine how embarrassing it would be not having enough money.'

Joy also knew that her mother had to show her list of purchases to her father each Monday night. When they had placed half a pound of plain flour into the trolley ('It's a waste to pay the extra for self-raising when all you need to do is add some bicarb'), her mother calculated the final balance. 'We're nine pence over. Something has to go back.'

Joy suggested the broken biscuits.

'Mmmph,' her mother snorted. 'You can't. They say they don't know what you've done to them — sneezed in the bag or poured rat poison on them. Looks like we're putting back the sugar or the rice. Come on.'

As they walked towards the shelves of sugar, Joy's mother told her that a long time ago, before there were supermarkets, there had been a grocer in town. 'It was owned by a man called Arnold,' she said. 'We were friends. Kind of.' She swapped the bag of sugar for a smaller one and recalculated the balance. 'But when the supermarket came, that was the end of Arnold's shop. I wanted to keep buying from him, but your father insisted that we go to the supermarket because it was so much cheaper. And he was right.'

She sighed and continued. 'One day I came into town after I'd just done a big wedding and I decided to go to Arnold's, and hang the expense. I'd made nearly two pounds of profit on that wedding, and back then my entire housekeeping for a week was only two pounds, ten shillings. It was four months after the supermarket opened and I wanted to buy a whole week's worth of groceries from him, and explain why I was going to the supermarket. But when I got there, the shop was closed and there was a sign in the window thanking all his customers.' She gave Joy the bag of rice, and pointed to the smaller one on the shelf. 'I don't know why he wrote thank you. He certainly wasn't thanking us for shopping at the supermarket.'

Two doors down, the butcher knew the drill. He weighed each item, told Joy's mother the cost, and waited for her to tell him to remove some sausages, replace some of the chops with smaller ones, pick out a smaller corned beef, and take out some of the pork offcuts because she could always bulk up a pork casserole with potatoes and carrots.

After they'd left the butcher's, to Joy's surprise her mother smiled and led her back to the supermarket. She walked straight to the stationery section and Joy knew they were going to buy some plastic to cover the schoolbooks. She could see it on one of the lower shelves.

But her mother didn't reach down to pick it up. Instead, she picked up a roll of what looked like thick white wax paper, which had a label shouting 'New! Self-adhesive contact!' She put it in the trolley, bent down, looked at the price of the plastic on the lower shelf, unfolded her piece of paper and wrote 'Plastic for books — 1s 6p'. Joy looked at the price of the contact: 3s 9p.

'Mum, you've written—'

'This,' she interrupted, pointing to the opaque roll in the trolley, 'is what we're going to cover your schoolbooks with.

It's like plastic cover, but it sticks to books like . . . rabbit skin sticks to rabbits. It's expensive, but at the end of the year we'll sell your books for much more money, so it's worth it.'

'But you wrote down the wrong price.'

'I don't think so. I never write down the wrong price,' said her mother, and headed towards the counter.

When they drove past the sign that read 'Thank you for visiting Blackhunt. Come back soon!' Joy's mother turned to her. 'The contact . . . we're not telling your father how much it cost, alright? It's a secret birthday present for you.'

Joy nodded.

'So, you and I will be eating those small chops, and a sausage less. Your father and Mark need to keep up their strength to work on the farm. But you can't say anything about the chops being smaller, or anything. Understand?'

Joy nodded again, pleased.

It wasn't until they crossed over Kookaburra Creek, a mile from home, that she realised with dark-green horror that her mother was going to lie to her father, that she was a sinner, doomed to the fire and brimstone of Hell. She would end up screaming every day for all of eternity because of her lie — and because it was too hot to grow flowers down there.

What if her mother died right now in a terrible crash before she had time to pray for forgiveness? What if a milk truck came screeching around the corner, driven by one of Satan's devil-angels ordered to find as many sinners' souls as quickly as possible, and slammed into the van before her mother had a chance to pray and swerve? Or before she had time to say to Joy 'I love you'?

'But isn't it a sin?' Joy burst out.

'Isn't what a sin?'

'Writing down the wrong price? And not telling him?'

'It's a white lie. That's all. We spent a bit more on one item, and a bit less on others, but the total cost is correct. Just a little white lie that doesn't hurt anyone.'

Instead of answering, Joy prayed silently. *Please God, don't let a milk truck smash into us. For thine is . . .*

'Plus, if I don't tell him, then it's not lying. And I'm not telling him, because if he knew he'd be upset. And I don't want to upset him. Do you want to upset him?'

'No.'

So it was alright to 'not-tell' something so people wouldn't get upset? Joy wondered if Reverend Braithwaite would agree, but she pushed that thought right out of her head because it made perfect sense to 'not-tell' so people wouldn't get upset, especially her father.

That night, when her father was at a committee meeting, they covered the new schoolbooks with the contact. The work was finicky {rabbits' whiskers}, and there were lots of bubbles and creases on the books' covers, but as they were gathering up the leftover bits for Mark to throw in the rubbish tank, Joy felt that she had never had as much fun with her family before, even though she'd only been able to look at *Pride and Prejudice* with a deep pink yearning, and still didn't know the universal truth that was revealed on the very first page.

Later, Joy talked to Ruth about what their mother had done. Ruth didn't seem surprised. 'Well, everyone lies, Joy. Even Mum.' She paused, and added, 'There's a universal truth if ever there was one.'

In the middle of the night, Joy woke up suddenly and violently. Her dream was still swirling in her mind. She and her mother were driving home with a secret on the back seat when the road in front of them opened up, showing them the inside of Hell, and the van jolted to a stop. Suddenly her father was on the road, pointing at the secret and roaring, 'Your time has come.' But instead of running away or cowering, Joy got out and walked towards him. She was fifty feet tall, and as her father was shouting 'Your time has come,' she picked him up by his collar and threw him into the orange flames of Hell. After his body burnt to a black lump, the crack closed over, leaving a few black tendrils of smoke to escape into the air. Joy wiped her hands like Pontius Pilate and shouted, 'No, *your* time has come.'

Trembling, Joy told Ruth she was scared their father would find out about the contact and be upset. It was a few seconds before Joy heard Ruth's papery whisper. 'But it's not really so he won't be upset, is it?'

'Yes, it is. That's what Mum said. We don't want him to be upset.'

'Well, that's true. You're "not-telling" so he won't be upset. But it isn't *him* you're protecting.' Her voice was silky smooth now. 'You're "not-telling" to protect yourself.'

Joy stayed silent.

'Well, I'm glad we got that sorted out,' whispered Ruth. She paused and said in her silkiest voice, 'Because you can lie — or "not-lie" — to others, but not to yourself, Joy.'

24

GEORGE AND GWEN

November 1942

'Busy day, Arnold.' Gwen had been waiting in line for twenty minutes.

He rubbed the top of his bald head as another customer came in, and grinned. 'Sure is. Price of milk gone up, has it, Gwen?'

Gwen had no idea if the butter factory was giving them more money for their milk or not, so she smiled and handed over her list, ration coupons and housekeeping money.

'Gwen, while I get this for you, could you pop down to the florist and grab a bunch of flowers for me? It's my wife's birthday.' He held out one of the pound notes she'd just given him. 'A big bunch.'

Gwen jumped at the word *florist*. She had not ventured down the street, and was surprised to learn there even was a florist. Not to mention a Mrs Arnold. 'Of course. What would she like?'

Without looking up from scooping flour into a bag on the scales, he said, 'Whatever you think.'

In the florist shop, she wandered around the buckets of cut flowers, clutching the pound note, nervous about choosing for a woman she'd never met, and amazed at the exorbitant prices written on the little tickets stuck into each bucket. Finally, she picked up a bunch of orange roses, a bunch of white lilies and a pot of maidenhair fern.

'Would you mind wrapping them separately? And I'll have a yard and a half of white ribbon and of orange ribbon, please.'

As the florist measured and cut the white ribbon, Gwen summoned the courage to ask how business was.

'Best it's ever been. Everyone who can is getting married, and brides want big bouquets brimming with white roses and lily-of-the-valley. And seems like anyone not getting married is arranging memorials for their lads and ordering huge wreaths brimming with white lilies.'

'Oh.' Smiling, she asked him the cost of a 10-inch wreath and a 12-inch wreath, and nodded as if his answer was very reasonable. Then, as if it were an afterthought, she said, 'And how much for a wedding bouquet with twelve white roses?'

He glanced at her wedding ring. 'Planning to kill your husband then marry your boyfriend?' he said with a wink.

Gwen laughed nervously. 'No, no. We've just moved here.'

The florist cocked his head, before cutting the orange ribbon with a quick snap.

When Gwen returned to Arnold's, he looked up, opened his eyes with surprise, and nodded when she asked if she could go into his back room. She emerged ten minutes later holding an enormous posy, the roses and lilies arranged into the shape of a dome but evenly spaced and angled so that each one seemed to float. Delicate sprigs of maidenhair fern trembled above the flowers and circled the entire posy. The paper the florist had used was wrapped around the posy at an angle, and Gwen had added a sheet of tissue paper from Arnold's back room at a different angle. The whole arrangement had a gentle sense of wildness. As a final touch, Gwen had tied the orange and white ribbon in a criss-cross pattern around the paper covering the stems, and had created a large multi-layered, two-toned bow that trailed five long thin tendrils.

'Is this alright, Arnold?'

Arnold paused to look up, cleaver raised to cut a piece of cheese.

'Alright? Marilyn's going to love it. How much do I owe you?'

'You don't owe me anything. I bought it all with your money.' Laughing, she put the change beside the till. And wondered when she had last laughed.

'Yes, but . . .' Arnold couldn't stop looking at the posy. 'Gwen, you're a magician.'

The woman waiting for Arnold to cut her cheese was staring too. 'Do you work at the florist's?'

Arnold answered for her. 'No, she and her husband moved into Wentworth's old farm a few months ago.'

'Oh. So do you work out of there?'

Before Gwen could reply, Arnold answered, 'Yes, she does.' He lowered his voice. 'And she doesn't charge as much as down the road.' He winked at the customer. 'No rent to pay, you see.'

'Wonderful,' said the woman, holding out a gloved hand. 'I'm Iris Waddell. We need eight table arrangements for our Rotary Club Christmas dinner next month.' She looked at Arnold. 'You'll be coming, won't you, Arnold? The mayor will be there.' She turned back to Gwen. 'I want them all like that. Give me your telephone number and I'll call you to finalise details and get a price.'

'I'm sorry,' said Gwen, 'I don't . . .'

Arnold interrupted. 'They don't have a phone, Iris, so come back next Monday. You're always here at ten-thirty on Mondays, aren't you, Gwen?'

Gwen nodded as Iris said, 'Wonderful. I'll see you next week, then.'

Now Gwen would have to tell George about her idea for the workroom. And the thought terrified her.

25

JOY AND RUTH

December 1960

Getting ready for the first Bible Study class, Joy kept thinking about her dream. Her father's screams as the road closed over his burnt dead body on its way to Hell were so loud and insistent she almost forgot to pack her Bible into her old school bag.

As she and Mark walked down the driveway, she hoped Mr Jones wouldn't be taking the class. Surely he had a job on weekdays? 'I don't see why we have to go to stupid Bible Study,' said Mark suddenly, and he spat onto the gravel.

'At least we get three hours away from home.'

'Yeah.' He looked at Joy as the bus pulled up. 'I want to run away. Go to Darwin, where it's sunny and you can swim all year round and not go to bloody Bible Study.' He picked up his bag and spat onto the gravel again. 'And not have to put up with him.' Joy followed him up the steps, scared that their father would somehow find out that Mark had sworn, but more scared that he would indeed go to Darwin, leaving her and Ruth and their mother behind, with the mud and the eels and the headless Ruths.

And their father.

When they got to Church, Reverend Braithwaite told Joy to go into the hall with Mr Jones, and Mark to go into the Church to join the 'Young Adult Christian Congregation', which the Reverend would lead. Joy walked to the hall, wishing that she could go with Mark, and dreading the thought of spending more time with Mr Jones.

Inside the hall were two trestle tables, and sitting at one of them was Felicity. She smiled and called out, 'Hey, Joy, come and sit next to me.'

Mr Jones obviously found it awkward that Joy and Felicity were the only students in the class. He told them to open their Bibles and begin reading Genesis. He had 'something important to do' and would return in half an hour to question them about what they had read.

Joy and Felicity worked quietly for a while, then began whispering about how mean and lazy Mr Jones was, then fell into talking about school and their families. While Felicity rattled off stories about funny events and big celebrations, Joy stuck to safe topics like the flowers her mother grew, Colin and Mr Larsen, and the letter from the high school about how clever and sporty Mark was. She would never tell Felicity — or anyone — about Ruth's accident, her father's temper, or the eels in her stomach.

When Mr Jones returned, there were only about five minutes to go, and Felicity, who seemed to already know a lot about the Bible, said that she and Joy had read about how God had made the earth and mankind in His image, and the tragedy of the Garden of Eden.

'Alright, that's enough. Let us pray,' said Mr Jones, before delivering a quick benediction, running the words together as he did when he was angry. 'MaytheLordblesstheeandkeepthee.'

'Amen,' the girls chorused with him.

Felicity's father picked up Felicity in a different but equally big and shiny car, while Joy and Mark ran to the bus stop, scared that they would miss their bus and get into trouble.

When they were walking up their driveway, Mark said, 'God, that was the worst hour of my life.'

'Worse than being here?'

'I meant apart from all the ones spent in this hellhole. And, yes, I know I shouldn't swear, but I don't care. I can't wait to get out of here.' He looked at her. 'I'll do Form Six first. Then I'm going to Darwin. And university, if they have one there. Hell, even if they don't.'

The eels squirmed. 'Can I come with you? I'll be fourteen by then.'

Mark let out a small laugh. 'Sure. We'll all go. Mum, too. Leave him to suffer by himself.'

Ruth was waiting for Joy in the bedroom, but instead of asking her how Bible Study had been, she said, 'I've been thinking about Mr Larsen, and I think he's a spy.'

'A spy? Who for?'

Ruth thought for a moment. 'The Russians. Or Mr Guglielmo — that Italian who moved into old Mr Twigg's place after he died. I mean, he's a foreigner.'

'Why would Mr Larsen spy for him?'

Ruth thought. 'Maybe he's Japanese. Or German.'

'Mr Guglielmo?'

'No — Mr Larsen. Alright, he's probably not Japanese. But maybe he's working for the Japanese, or the Germans. Or both. That's why he doesn't have to milk cows and can afford to buy all that chocolate.'

'It doesn't explain why he uses our phone.'

Ruth thought again. 'Because,' she said triumphantly, 'Mrs Larsen doesn't know. And if the government suspects him, they'd be listening to phone calls he makes from his house.'

Both of those made sense. And if Mr Larsen was a spy, someone needed to stop him. It would be the end of the Saturday chocolate, but spies were dangerous and had to be caught.

'The thing is,' said Ruth, 'we need to be sure. So I have a plan.'

26

JOY AND GEORGE

February 1983

I stand inside the wide opening of the shed, out of the burning sun, while terrifying memories strike me. Hessian bags and hay twine hang from bent nails; faded spray cans lie in an old tub like dead soldiers in a trench; a dirty tarpaulin half-covers a pile of old buckets and hoses; garden tools lean against a wall, their crisscrossed handles reminding me of awkward teenagers at a dance; a pile of traps sits beside the old rabbit cage; rusted hand tools stick out of equally rusted tins at the back of the big wooden workbench. And the padlocked metal chest beside the bench — like everything else — is covered with grime and murky neglect.

The only thing not filthy is the axe-head glinting at the back of the shed. I can't help but shudder. Has he really kept polishing it all these years?

I step into the hot, musty shed, and let the name that has been suspended in my brain ever since I left this place land with a thud.

Wendy Boscombe. Poor Wendy. Never to be found. Alive or dead. With or without her doll.

After Wendy disappeared, my father visited the Boscombes every day for more than a month to pray with them, and then about once a week, then once a fortnight. Even after that, not a month went by when he didn't drop in to pray. Always showing his pious, caring Dr Jekyll side. I suppose they appreciated what he did. Not that their prayers were answered, any more than mine were. I wonder if they ever wanted him to stop coming around and just let them get on with their empty lives. All these years of not knowing. How do they sleep at night?

I turn to the chest. My father always told us that it was full of 'good' tools that belonged to his father, a carpenter. A 'wizard with wood' he said whenever he talked about his father. He would frown at this point — at us, I always assumed. But now I wonder if his father also owned a belt dripping with children's blood. If it's even the same belt. Of course, talking about his past always ended in a lecture. 'You wouldn't whinge if you'd lived through the Depression and the war.' As if we ever dared whinge about anything. 'You wouldn't turn up your nose at good food if you had to chew on a stick of dried sugar beet when you were hungry.' As if we ever dared turn up our noses at anything. 'You wouldn't even know how lucky you are, you filthy sinners.' As if we dared forget we were filthy sinners.

Even though his father's tools were 'better than anything you can buy these days', he never used them, or even unlocked the chest. He claimed they were 'worth a fortune, more than an arm and a leg' and that's why he'd never sell them. Which is completely illogical. I mean, if they were worth *nothing*, that would make sense, but if they were worth a fortune, why *not* sell them, for crying out loud? We could have lived well, if only for a week or two.

One day, a long time ago, I dared to unlock the chest, and to my surprise, it *was* full of tools, and they did look valuable. So I'm sure as hell not about to let some shifty second-hand dealer 'reluctantly' pay $20 to take them away. I pull down the bunch of keys hanging on a nail at the back of the shed and I pick out the smallest. I know it's the right one, but it won't even go into the padlock, let alone turn. I need some WD-40.

I walk over to the tub of spray cans and screw up my face — there are cobwebs all over it. I can't see the WD-40, so I kick over the tub, and as the cans roll out, a fat redback scuttles out as well. A swarm of baby spiders follows and starts to spread out on the concrete floor. I stamp on them frantically, taking careful aim to kill the engorged mother and squash it completely. It makes a satisfying crunch and squish. After I've killed them all, I find the WD-40 and go back to the chest.

I spray the key and the padlock furiously, until they're both dripping with white bubbles, then try the key again. The heat and memories and that nest of redbacks are making my pores sweat and my heart race. I turn the key and it protests a little, so I wiggle it back and forth gently before trying again. The shackle jolts out of one hole with a pleasing click. I pull down the body of the padlock, twist it and pull the open end of the shackle through the chest's eyelets. Just as I did all those years ago.

I'm about to lift the lid, when I wonder if the police ever looked for Wendy in this chest. It's big enough to hold a nine-year-old's body, that's for sure, but did they ever really seriously think that my father had killed Wendy? I doubt it. George Henderson was one of the Elders in the church Sergeant Bell went to.

My hand is on the lid, unwilling. The memories come flooding back. Wendy, Wendy, Wendy. Those nightmares I had after she disappeared . . . her wave as she and her mother drove off to buy their chocolate milkshakes on that last day of school . . . the last words she said to me.

'Do you want to play, Joy?'

I spin my head quickly to look at the driveway where the voice has come from.

Wendy is standing there, holding a doll, smiling at me. 'Let's play hidey,' she says.

Her face is the grainy black-and-white image that was on the front page of the local newspaper after she disappeared. After a couple of weeks it was on page 3, and then it was nowhere to be seen until the anniversary of her disappearance, when it was on page 5. That's what a local newspaper does, of course. You're only front-page news once.

I cover my face with my hands — I can't stand how images of dead people keep popping into my head. When I take my hands away, the driveway is empty, and I turn back to the chest.

Decisively, quickly, I lift the lid, throwing it back all the way, so it clangs against the metal edge of the workbench. The tools are lying there, neatly laid out, just like they were when I opened it the first time, all those years ago. Planes, hand drills, spirit levels, chisels, rasps, and other tools I'll never know the names of. They're clean and smooth, and perhaps they are worth a fortune. So maybe I will sell them when this is all over.

There's a calico bag in one corner. I remember it contains hand-made dowel plugs. And poking out from under it is something else, smooth and white, which wasn't here the first time I opened this chest. I lean forward and swallow, and my heart thumps faster than that fat redback's did just before I stomped on her.

I pull back the calico bag slowly, and I'm looking straight into the smiling face of Wendy Boscombe's missing doll.

27

GEORGE AND GWEN

November 1942

Gwen stared at the sign in Arnold's window.

> *Order Your Bouquets and Wreaths HERE!*
> *Top Quality, Excellent Prices*

He was grinning on the other side of the glass and waving her inside.

'I have a plan, Gwen.'

Arnold explained that he would take orders for her and in exchange keep 10 per cent of the cost of each one.

'But Arnold, I only come into town on Mondays. What if someone wants something on a different day? And I don't have any equipment. Nothing. Not even wire.' She wanted to add, 'And I haven't told George.'

She had planned to tell him at tea last Monday night after she'd met Iris, then the following night, then the following one. But every evening there was something in the way. The newborn calf that had died, the outrageous vet bill, the smaller cheque from the butter factory, the broken pump, the useless windmill, the endless rain. And George's endless anger, sometimes simmering behind smiling eyes. A whole week, and there just hadn't been a right time to tell him.

'I have it all worked out,' said Arnold. 'The butter factory collects your milk every day. Your driver, John, is Marilyn's nephew. He'll pick up your arrangements with your cans of milk, and deliver them to me. And I'll give him any new orders to give to George the next morning.'

'But . . .' Gwen hesitated. 'I haven't told George, Arnold. I don't think he'll want me to work.'

'Gwen, together we can make a fortune. Well, probably not a fortune, but a bit of pocket money. Tell George tonight. He's going to say yes. He's a good man, Gwen.'

She knew Arnold was right. George was a good man.

He smiled at her. 'I hear he's going to become an Elder in the Church.'

This was news to Gwen. It seemed they both had secrets.

28

JOY AND RUTH

December 1960

There were only four days to Christmas and Joy's mother wanted to have forty-eight mince pies and twelve rounds of shortbread made by the end of the day.

Of course, the family would never eat all that food, but every year in the days leading up to Christmas and for the week or so afterwards, her father took paper plates of mince pies and shortbread everywhere he went. To bowls, to Elders meetings, to the Hall Committee meetings, to Reverend Braithwaite, to all the town's businesses, and other people Joy didn't know. Even the vet got one.

As well, there was always a flurry of visitors dropping in to 'say hello before Christmas and give you a little something'. Invariably, these presents were jars of nuts, plastic trays of dried sugary fruit, or tins of biscuits with large sugar crystals on top. Joy's parents reciprocated by giving each visitor a gift from the homemade shortbreads and mince pies wrapped in florist's cellophane and tied with florist's ribbon, or one of last year's gifts that they hadn't eaten.

Her father also insisted the guests have some Passiona in the 'good glasses' that were kept in the bureau of the good room. Terrified that she would break one of the precious glasses, Joy served all of these visitors with trembling hands, and politely sat and listened to the conversations about milk prices, mud, rain, bills, dead calves, and the guest's latest physical ailment.

That morning, as Joy and her mother rolled the shortbread dough and cut it into triangles, Joy was nervous. She and Ruth had agreed that Joy would put Ruth's plan into action, so they could find out if Mr Larsen was a spy or not.

'Are you sure I'll be able to hear him?' Joy asked.

'I don't know,' Ruth admitted, 'but it's the best idea I have.'

In between her chores, Joy collected the items she would need and hid them in the little shed where the briquette hot-water heater was.

Now, while helping her mother with the Christmas shortbreads again, she waited nervously for Mr Larsen's knock, and tried to stay calm as she let him in.

The second he put the chocolate on the table and before he had time to say, 'Just making a quick trump call,' Joy started heading outside, excited and scared, as the eels squirmed in her stomach.

'Joy!' Her mother's cry made her breath stop. 'Get Mr Larsen half a dozen eggs.'

She walked into the laundry and put six of the waxed winter eggs into a carton.

As she handed them to him, he said, 'Thank you, lass. Mrs Larsen will make a fine lemming meringue pie with these.' And he winked at her.

'You're welcome, Mr Larsen.' Joy smiled back, suddenly suspicious about all his silly word blunders. Were they just a cover so no one would ever suspect that he was really a very clever spy?

She walked around to the little shed, reached behind the spare bag of briquettes, and retrieved her tiny torch and a stick before taking five quick steps to the small access door set in the side of the house at ground level.

With legs that felt like the blancmange her mother had made last week, she slipped back the latch and pulled the door towards her. It got stuck in the wet grass but she kept yanking, and eventually it opened enough for her to squeeze through. She collected the torch and the stick, pushed them through the open door, and crawled in after them.

Even though it was just after three o'clock, it was dark under the house, so it was good that Ruth had thought of the torch. Now all she had to do was pull herself along in the dirt until she was right under Mr Larsen so she could hear him talking to the other spy.

She turned on the torch and swung it from side to side to get a view of this dark place, filled with rubbish that hadn't made it to the tank or the dam. Everything was covered with cobwebs and dirt and smelt thick and brown. She dragged her legs up beside her stomach and pulled the little door shut behind her, making it completely dark under the house. Quickly switching on the torch, she wriggled around so she could make her way to where she could hear Mr Larsen. She reached around for the stick, but realised how difficult it would be to move if she was holding both the stick and the torch.

But she couldn't leave the stick behind. There were spiders everywhere. And there would be rats keeping dry and warm under here. And snakes, too, awake and angry after their winter hibernation. What if she disturbed a writhing mass of them, throbbing with rage and venom? What if there were baby snakes that could slither up her sleeves and down the neck of her jumper? She knew that at this time of the year baby snakes were everywhere and that baby snakes were more dangerous than adult ones. Ruth hadn't thought of this, had she? Because she wasn't the one crawling under the house where there were spiders and rats and snakes, was she?

She wriggled towards the good room, manoeuvring around the rubbish and trying not to breathe in the dust she was stirring up, until she could hear Mr Larsen's voice directly above her.

Lying there, with one hand tightly clapped over her mouth to suppress any coughs, she listened intently.

'Yes. Yes, dear.'

He called the other spy 'dear'? That was ridiculous.

'Yes, I will. It will all be over soon. Now that Colin is . . . yes, I know. Very soon. Yes, I promise, my dear. On Sunday.'

He was obviously talking in code. It sounded like he had completed his mission and was going to sell the government's secrets to Germany or Japan on Sunday. Maybe the spies disguised themselves as Christians and met at Church. That would be the perfect cover. But what did Colin have to do with anything?

'Yes, I love you. Always remember that, no matter what.'

I love you? More code — and clearly for something important, such as 'I have the diagrams for the weapons.'

'Yes . . . yes, dear.'

There was a pause while the other spy said something. Then laughter. A big laugh.

'Yes. Of course.'

Another pause. More laughter.

'Yes, yes, yes. You're absolutely right.' Pause.

'Yes. Alright, dear, I must go. It's so good of Gwen.'

Joy was dumbfounded. Did her mother know that Mr Larsen was a spy? Surely not. Surely she thought he was just making a phone call to . . . But for the first time in her life, Joy's imagination could not fill in the blank.

'Goodbye, Beryl, my dear.'

He was about to hang up. She had to get out of there and into the backyard. Releasing her hand from her mouth, she dug one elbow into the dirt and wriggled frantically towards the light coming through the door. Behind her, she heard a hiss and knew it was a rat, with its segmented metallic tail, spiteful eyes and teeth that could chew through anything, including human flesh.

Shaking, she tried to pull the stick out from under her arm, and her elbow hit a joist above her. Pain shot to her hand and her neck, but she muffled a scream, terrified that she would be heard. She dug into the dirt to pull herself along more quickly towards the sliver of light coming from the door, wondering how long it would be before anyone came looking for her if she didn't get out before the rat attacked her. It could feed off her for weeks. And if they did ever find her remains, her parents would put two and two together and realise their filthy sinner of a daughter had been eavesdropping on Mr Larsen. They would never tell anyone, though, because her father would not want people to know what a dreadful sinner she was. His reputation meant everything to him.

At least her mother would make a beautiful casket spray.

Finally Joy reached the door and pushed hard against it, but the wet grass on the other side was unrelenting and her body was exhausted. She twisted around so she could push the door with her legs. With each kick, she was sure someone would come running, but she no longer cared. She kicked and kicked until the door was open wide enough for her to wriggle through, and stood up in the grey drizzle.

She sat in the wet grass to kick it shut again, before ramming home the latch.

When she got to the back door, she pulled off her shoes then tiptoed to the bathroom. She looked in the mirror and saw that her face was brown and grey with dust, and her hair full of dirt and cobwebs. She brushed her hair vigorously, wiped her face with the face-washer, pulled off her jumper and threw it into the shower that no one ever used, and dragged the dry plastic curtain across to hide it. She would have to get it later. She rubbed the face-washer over the legs of her pants and threw it in the shower with her jumper.

When she walked into the kitchen, the pot of tea was sitting on the table in front of Mr Larsen.

'What have you been doing?' Her mother looked annoyed. 'Your face is filthy and so are your clothes. You look like you've been rolling in the chook yard.'

She tried to say something, but no words came out. 'Go wash. And hurry up.'

When she returned, the tea was poured and the chocolate open.

'Show me,' her mother ordered.

As Joy held out her hands to be inspected, Mr Larsen said, 'Ah, Gwen, she's just a young lass. No harm in playing in a bit of dirt. I'm sure she wasn't up to no good, were you, lass?'

Joy couldn't look at Mr Larsen as she shook her head and sat down at the table.

'Help yourself,' he said with his familiar smile.

Suddenly she was dripping with shame. She could feel rotten yellow beads of it oozing out of her pores. Here was Mr Larsen, with his smiles and his chocolate and his eyes that she liked, and his laughter and generosity . . . And she had crawled under the house to eavesdrop on him.

She looked at the wall-hanging as the eels bit the inside of her stomach. 'The silent listener to every conversation.' Yes, she had been a silent, sinful listener to Mr Larsen's conversation. A filthy sinner, prying into his personal, private life.

Personal, private life. He was no spy. Mr Larsen had been talking to a woman, telling her he loved her. Who was she? She had never heard her mother or father mention a Beryl. But as his calls were 'trump' calls, she must live a long way away.

Joy knew it was wrong for him to love Beryl when he was married to Mrs Larsen. He was breaking the Sixth Commandment. And the Tenth Commandment if Beryl was married.

Now she knew why Mr Larsen didn't make his phone calls from his house. He was committing a dreadful sin. And he knew it. Otherwise why wouldn't he make the phone calls from his own house, and why would he bring chocolate?

She looked at his smile and the torn purple and silver wrapper. The chocolate. It was a payment. He told Beryl, whoever she was, that he loved her, and then he gave Joy's mother chocolate.

She looked at his broad red face as he talked to her mother.

Maybe he was Satan, tricking them into sinning.

'Here you go, lass,' he said, and he slid the block towards her, just like Satan would if He was tempting her soul. 'I brought something different today.' He pointed to the wrapping that read 'Dark Strawberry Cream', and smiled and winked at her.

Joy looked at the chocolate, which was so dark it was nearly black, two rows already gone. She looked at Mr Larsen . . . Satan in disguise. *Please God, lead us not into temptation, but deliver us from evil.*

'Go on, lass. It's delicious, trust me.'

Trust me. Just what Satan would say when He was leading you into temptation, delivering you straight to evil. And she had all but taken His hand and merrily skipped down the path with Him. But she wasn't alone. There was her mother. And Beryl. And maybe others, too.

He probably had another block of chocolate to give to Mrs Larsen. Joy imagined him walking through their back door and pulling it from his top pocket, like a magician with an endless supply of chocolate blocks instead of coloured handkerchiefs. 'Here you are, love,' Satan the evil magician said to Mrs Larsen, touching His forehead quickly to make sure His horns were still safely concealed. 'It's delicious, trust me.' Mrs Larsen took a bite of the chocolate and suddenly Mr Larsen's horns were protruding from His forehead, and His red forked tongue was slithering in and out of His mouth. He stood up, grabbed up the fire 'distinguisher', and pointed it at Mrs Larsen. But instead of foam coming out of it, flames flew out, and—

'Joy!' Her mother's voice was hard and loud.

She looked at the chocolate sitting on the table, the silver foil glistening, the dark purple wrapper rich and luxurious, the chocolate shiny and smooth.

Please God, lead us not into temptation, but deliver us from evil.

He was right. The Dark Strawberry Cream chocolate was delicious, with its extra dark outside and its bright-red creamy centre. As she let the chocolate melt on her tongue, she watched Mr Larsen and her mother sipping tea, chewing chocolate, talking and laughing. She only ever saw her mother this relaxed with the two Larsen men.

Mr Larsen caught her looking at him and gave her another wink. His eyes twinkled. Satan's eyes would definitely not twinkle. Satan's eyes would burn red and be hollow and dark. Wouldn't they?

Mr Larsen laughed again, and her mother poured him some more tea.

When the talk of rain and vets was over, and the purple wrapper was in Mr Larsen's trouser pocket, Joy walked him to the back door, as always, but today observing him with a great deal more interest.

He turned and caught her staring at him, and the black eels in her stomach squirmed. Did he know? Was he about to reveal himself as the Devil?

'I've never seen anyone eat chocolate like you do,' he said, laughing. 'Bye, lass.'

She wiped her mouth in case there was Dark Strawberry Cream all over it, but when she looked, her hand was clean.

Suddenly she couldn't wait until his next visit. Let him make the phone calls, love Beryl, share his chocolate. And make her mother laugh. If God thought that was a sin then Joy Henderson didn't want to know about it.

29

JOY AND GEORGE

February 1983

I slam shut the lid of the chest, hiding the doll's head again, march up to his room and stand beside the bed. It's time for justice. He looks at me without saying anything, but I can read guilt in his eyes. His face is beginning to look like a chook's, too, the nose and eyes becoming more prominent.

I'm thinking about the first night he thrashed my naked body, and all the other nights he belted me or Mark. If he'd ever kept going when he was whipping our flesh into pink froth, instead of stopping after counting to fifteen, he would have thrashed one of us to death, for sure.

Not for the first time, I think that lots of people must have known what he was doing to us, but never did anything to stop him. Not the neighbours, not the oh-so-holy Reverend Braithwaite, not even the Felicities.

Or our mother. I don't know how to explain that. I don't know what hold he had over her, or why she didn't throw herself between him and whichever of us he was about to belt.

Maybe she thought he would kill her and still thrash us anyway. Maybe Ruth's accident was never far from her mind.

But that's all in the past, and now it's time for justice.

'Dad . . .' I take a breath, because otherwise the words are going to explode from me, and because I can't get that doll's head out of my mind. 'Did you . . .' I'm not sure I can do this. But I have to. I've been wanting to ask him this for years. I swallow and start again. 'You killed her, didn't you?'

'Who?'

'You know who!' I scream, enraged by his show of innocence.

His eyes open wide and he sucks in air as the muscles in his neck protrude, making him look even more like a chook. 'Need,' he takes another laboured breath, 'painkillers.'

I shake the bottle like Vicki did a couple of days ago. 'After you answer me.'

I want him to confess. I want him to say out loud that he's a murderer.

He opens his mouth, but instead of saying anything, he slowly closes his eyes. And out of his mouth comes a small puff of air, followed by a single, small rattle from his throat.

I frown and lean forward. He's not breathing, his face is grey, and his skin is looking strangely soft. So, just like that, without any warning, the bastard is dead? Quietly, calmly . . . dead? For ever and ever, Amen?

An explosion of rage surges through me. How dare he die without suffering for what he did, just when I get the courage to confront him? I've spent my whole life wishing he was dead, and now, the first time in my life I want him alive, he ups and dies.

I sit down and feel the vile yellow substance float out of my mouth like it did when Vicki rang with her 'sad news'.

So now it really is over. No more pills. But no justice either.

More than ever I want to ring Mark and shout, 'He's dead, he's dead, come home.'

But I can't, so I sit there. Exhausted. Angry. His soft dead grey face mocking me.

Then his eyes jerk open, he sucks in a lungful of air, and whispers a single word: 'Pain.'

I stand up, lean over his face and whisper back in a marble-white voice, '*Answer me.* You killed her, didn't you?'

He stares back at me. His breath is milky yellow, like the whites of his eyes. I don't even know if he can see me, or knows who I am, or knows what I'm asking him.

He takes another shallow, rattled breath, and his eyes close again, but I won't be fooled a second time. I purse my lips and wait.

When he speaks, his voice is like a piece of hard cracked parchment that's been buried in sand for thousands of years.

'Yes,' he says.

PART TWO

30

GEORGE AND GWEN

December 1942

'George . . .'

He had just slammed shut the blue accounting book and groaned loudly.

She placed a hand on each of her cheeks in case he became angry.

'What?'

As Gwen talked, he sat with his head in his hands, leaving her to wonder if he was even listening.

She could charge less than the town florist, she said, because she wouldn't have to pay rent, and if they grew their own flowers, they could make a lot more profit.

She put an extra caddy of tea in the pot she got up to make for him, and laid out three sultana biscuits.

'I can plant roses, camellias, stock, poppies. Everything I'll need.' She knew she was prattling, but couldn't help it. 'And ferns under the eaves on the east side of the house. And hydrangeas, and gypsophila and chrysanthemums. And Stan will put me in touch with suppliers.'

George chewed one of the sultana biscuits.

Gwen took a breath and continued. 'I met a woman at Arnold's, and she wants me to do some table centres for an event the mayor's going to. I can charge one pound for each one.'

'One pound? How many does she want?'

'Eight.'

He put down his cup and said, 'This won't interfere with your household duties.'

It was a statement, not a question, but she shook her head. 'I'll give you ten pounds out of the bank, and you have two months to make it work. If you can't give me back the ten pounds plus profit, this stops. And you'll have to go without until you've made up the difference.'

Gwen didn't know what she would 'go without'. All she ever bought was food. So if this didn't work, she would eat even less than she did now. It didn't matter. Her mind was racing, and her heart felt on fire. She was going to have her own floristry business. Everything would be alright.

31

JOY AND RUTH

December 1960

'Come back to my place for lunch,' said Felicity.

Mr Jones had let them out of Bible Study fifteen minutes early, and, not wanting to wait in the rain, Felicity and Joy were sitting in the cloakroom near the front door of the hall.

Joy was annoyed with Mr Jones because he hadn't liked her explanation of what they had read that day. As she and Felicity sat down, she mimicked his voice. 'NoJoyI'mverydisappointedwiththatanswer.' Felicity laughed and said, 'That's exactly how he talks. Keep going.' So for the whole fifteen minutes, Joy entertained Felicity with her impersonations of his mannerisms, his walk, his gestures and his general meanness.

'Even your facial expressions are spot on,' said Felicity, laughing so loudly Joy was scared they'd be overheard. But part of her didn't care, because she enjoyed walking around the little room licking the left corner of her mouth every so often and adopting his most annoying quirk {a kitten chasing a red rubber ball} of disregarding the beginnings and ends of sentences.

'Please give me your completely undivided attention [*lick*]please yes that includes you Philip this morning if you would be so kind as to [*lick*] stop nattering and fidgeting thank you well good morning Mr Stewart I'm *so* pleased you could find the time to attend our [*lick*] gathering I do hope it hasn't interfered *too* much with your social calendar although it appears your mother was unable to make a similar appointment with the [*lick*] iron this morning I suppose I should be grateful for small mercies and praise the Lord that you have arrived *just* in time to [*lick*] answer my first question.'

As Felicity laughed, Joy knew that she was the best Friend she would ever have. She also knew she couldn't go to Felicity's for lunch.

'Why not?' Felicity said when Joy told her. 'You can come back with us now, and Dad will drive you home later. It's easy.'

Joy's father had driven her and Mark to Bible Study that morning because he was going to see the bank manager, and they were to wait for him under the Church porch, no matter how long he took.

'My father won't let me. I've . . . never been to anyone's house before.' She waited for Felicity to laugh at her, but she just smiled and said, 'I'll get my dad to ask yours. You know he won't say no.'

Felicity was right. They both understood how these things worked.

Joy told Mark when he came out of the Church, and he nodded, impressed. When the Felicities arrived, Felicity ran to ask her parents, then turned around and called out, 'They said yes.'

Joy was stunned that Felicity thought it was perfectly alright to call out in the church car park. When her father pulled up behind the Felicities' car, both men got out and shook hands.

'Good to see you, Victor.'

'George. Good to see you too. Lovely day, isn't it?'

It was a horrible day, grey and overcast, but at least it had stopped raining.

'Now, I'm sure you're in a hurry,' Mr Felicity continued, 'but my Felicity here is adamant that your young Joy joins us for lunch.' Joy's father opened his mouth to say something, but Mr Felicity just kept talking, a broad smile on his face. 'I'll drive her back home, of course, at shall we say, four o'clock? That will give the girls time for a horse-ride or a run in the yard, or whatever it is that girls their age do nowadays. Genevieve and I would be very honoured if you'd say yes.'

Genevieve.

Joy could feel her father's dark-blue hesitation.

'Of course.' His reply was light and friendly as he smiled at Mr Felicity. 'If you're sure it's no trouble.'

'Not at all. Well, we'll see you at four, then. Alright, Joy. Give your father a kiss and we'll be off.'

Joy's heart stopped. *Give your father a kiss?* She turned to Mark, who gave an almost imperceptible shrug as his eyes opened wide. She turned towards her father, her legs heavy, the eels rolling around furiously.

'Ah, Reverend,' called out her father, as the Reverend came out of the Church. Her father turned back to Mr Felicity. 'Excuse me, Victor. I must talk to the Reverend about the new hymn books. I'll see you at four, then.' Joy doubted he even heard her say 'Thank you' as he walked over to the Reverend.

The drive to the Felicities' home was chaotic. Joy sat in the back seat between Felicity and her older brother, Barry, who didn't go to Bible Study but had come for the ride, and it seemed to Joy that everyone talked simultaneously the whole time. As soon as the car started, Felicity pulled her hair out of her perfect bun, handing the pins over one by one to her mother, who put them into her handbag. Joy had never seen anything like Felicity's hair before — it was unbelievably thick and reached her waist. Barry saw her staring at it and said, 'Yeah, her hair's Spanish — blame Mum.'

The Felicities laughed, but Joy wasn't sure why. Did it mean Mrs Felicity was — or was not — Spanish?

Mrs Felicity turned around and said, 'Not like Joy's lovely hair,' and Joy blushed because she knew she was ugly, that the rat tails she kept draped over her face were thin and straggly, and that Mrs Felicity was just being kind. But then Mrs Felicity said, 'See, Felicity? You could get a nice cut like that and it wouldn't take you so long to wash your hair every day.'

Every day?

The Felicities laughed again.

Mr and Mrs Felicity and Barry bombarded Joy with questions while Felicity twisted her Spanish hair into two long shiny plaits that stayed put even without rubber bands at the ends, and told them very loudly — at least three times — that Joy was quiet, not like them, and probably didn't want to answer these questions, but they laughed and Mrs Felicity said, 'Nonsense. I don't believe it. She's lying, isn't she, Joy darling?'

Joy was relieved that no one seemed to expect her to answer that particular question (especially as she was shell-shocked that Mrs Felicity, practically a complete stranger, had called her darling), but the questions kept coming. Do you like horse riding? What do you mean you've never ridden a horse? Well, we'll have to do something about that! Do you like risotto? Because that's what we're having for lunch. Joy wondered if 'risotto' was Spanish for roast, and politely said yes, it was her favourite. 'It is not,' screamed Felicity. 'I can tell by how you said yes. What is your favourite, really? Because that's what we'll have next time you come.'

More questions. Do you like cooking? What's your best subject at school? And your worst? What do you think you'll get for Christmas? What's your brother like? Would he like to come next time? We can bring both cars so there's room for everyone. 'Girls in one car, boys in the other,' said Mrs Felicity, throwing her head around and passing over a small paper bag to her daughter, while Joy wondered again how rich they must be to have two cars. 'That would be fun, wouldn't it?'

Without thinking, Joy said, 'Yes, that would be lovely, Mrs Felicity . . . I mean . . . sorry, I'm sorry!'

'Oh, that's priceless!' Mr Felicity roared. 'What do you think about that, *Mrs* Felicity?'

'I think it's lovely, *Mr* Felicity.' And they all laughed. Joy's face was burning, but Felicity looked very pleased and said, 'That's what you've *got* to call them for ever and ever.'

'Amen,' chorused the other Felicities and they laughed some more, while Felicity pulled open Joy's astonished hand and filled it with black jellybeans.

When they arrived at the Felicities' farm, Barry got out and opened the gate. They had a long curving driveway made of cream gravel cemented in place, and it was lined with white wooden fencing. Mr Felicity drove through the open gate and actually waited for Barry to get back in the car before taking off again.

The house was like the driveway — grand and seemingly endless. They even had a library that Felicity showed her, saying this was where her father worked and her parents read after tea, which they called dinner. 'What kind of work?' asked Joy.

Felicity didn't know. 'He writes stuff.'

'Books?'

'Yeah, and things called papers, which makes no sense at all!'

Felicity picked up a hard cover from a hexagonal-shaped table next to a huge white armchair, and handed it to Joy. 'He wrote this.'

Joy took the book carefully. It was called *Australia's Literary Giants 1901–1950*.The author was Victor Armstrong, so now she knew their real surname. On the front cover was a photo of a man reading in a magnificent upholstered armchair in front of an enormous fire. He was facing away from the photographer, but Joy was sure it was Mr Felicity. She turned it over and read the comments printed on the back cover:

The most comprehensive study to date of Australia's post-Federation literature and its authors.

A compelling combination of biography, literary criticism and anecdote, along with well-curated photographs of the selected authors at work and attending literary functions.

Generously peppered with accounts of the personal struggles the author endured during his period of research.

Scholarly, but eminently readable.

* * *

While Joy was wondering what struggles Mr Felicity could possibly have endured, he stuck his head in and said, 'Lunch is ready, your majesties.'

For the whole of lunch, Joy remained bewildered. To start with, there was no dishing up of food on the kitchen bench. Instead, everyone carried one or two large serving dishes from the kitchen to the centre of the table in the dining room (dining room!), talking continuously as they did so. There was the strange risotto, which was like porridge made from rice; also piles of roast vegetables and other food Joy couldn't identify. The enormous dining room table was made of thick shiny wood with round legs so large they reminded Joy of an elephant's. The chairs were of the same shiny wood and every seat was upholstered, not just Mr Felicity's. None of the plates or bowls were cracked and they all matched.

When everyone was seated, Mr Felicity said grace. Joy was caught unawares and found herself staring at him. 'Dear Lord, We thank thee for this wonderful food [at which point he opened his eyes, looked at Mrs Felicity and blew her a silent kiss], and we ask you to bless and provide for those who don't have as much as we do, Lord. And today especially, Lord, we thank you for the pleasure of the company of Joy [Joy froze, but it was too late, he was looking at her squarely with neither a joke nor a reprimand in his eyes, and then winked at her] and hope that she graces our table many more times.' He closed his eyes and bowed his head. 'For all of this, and so much more, we thank you, Lord. Amen.'

Everyone echoed his Amen, then the car-trip chaos erupted again. Joy wondered how four people could make so much noise. She accepted the platters passed to her, taking a tiny portion each time. Barry laughed and said, 'Good grief, no wonder you're so thin.'

The Felicities talked about their beloved horses and their funny next-door neighbours, the garden's bountiful supply of roses ('I'll give you some to take home to your mother, Joy darling'), and what Barry was reading. He was about to start Form 6 and one of his subjects was Literature. The book he was currently reading was called *The Strange Case of Dr Jekyll and Mr Hyde*.

'It's a wonderful book,' said Mrs Felicity. 'We did enjoy it, didn't we, Vic?' She put her hand over her mouth with a mock look of horror, and said, 'I mean, *Mr Felicity*.'

They all laughed, and Joy smiled as she put a forkful of the risotto into her mouth.

Barry wobbled his head a little and said, 'Well, I haven't made up my mind yet.'

Mr Felicity exclaimed with surprise, some rice and pumpkin coming out of his mouth. 'It's a classic, Barrington, an absolute classic.' He caught the food on his upturned fork and pushed it back into his mouth. 'It says so much about the human condition.' He paused for half a second, leant in and stabbed a roast parsnip on one of the platters. 'But I'm interested to see what you'll say when you've finished it. You know I like a good debate.' The parsnip disappeared into his mouth, and he reached for another.

Then they talked about how much food Felicity and Mrs Felicity were going to prepare for the men coming to build the new stables in January, and Mrs Felicity talked about how a neighbour ('Mrs Somebody') was giving her two dozen beautiful eggs each week. Laughing, she said,

'I've forgotten her name. How awful of me.' But her family laughed again as if it wasn't awful at all, and then Mrs Felicity added, 'Anyway, I've used eight of them in today's dessert!' It seemed to Joy that every sentence each of them uttered ended with an exclamation mark. 'Well, dessert has to *look* good, as well as taste good, so eight eggs it was!' But Mrs Felicity wouldn't tell them what dessert was.

Mrs Felicity pretended to be offended that Joy didn't like her cooking, which she didn't. The risotto's creamy lumpy texture reminded her of vomit, the salad had a strange oil poured over it that made the lettuce slippery, the roast vegetables had spiky green leaves scattered all over them, and the slices of hot crusty bread covered with melted butter and tiny white lumps left a strong aftertaste in her mouth. But when Mrs Felicity asked her if she liked it all, Joy, as instructed by her father whenever they had afternoon tea at another Elder's house, meekly said that everything was lovely. She hoped that her sentence sounded as if it ended in an exclamation mark too. Mrs Felicity said, 'It's alright, Joy, you can tell me if you don't like something,' but the others exploded with laughter again as if to dismiss the idea that anyone would not like the food laid out before them.

Joy laughed too, but was relieved when Mrs Felicity came back from the kitchen carrying a lemon meringue pie that she could honestly gush over. It had an absurdly high meringue (eight eggs!), and the crisp sharpness of the lemon curd was breathtaking. Joy wondered if her mother used a different recipe because her pies were never this lemony — or meringuey! — at home. As Mrs Felicity cut slices for everyone, Joy noticed that her hands were as white and smooth as the meringue — and quickly pushed her own under the table, suddenly ashamed of her stained nails and rough skin.

After Joy had finished a second helping, which Mrs Felicity insisted she have, Mr Felicity said, 'No need for you two to help clear or wash — the dishwasher will take care of everything.' Dishwasher? This was incredible. Barry said, 'Excellent,' and got up with the girls, but Mr Felicity grabbed him by the collar (Joy froze) and said, 'Hi-ho, Barrington, tell Joy what brand of dishwasher we have.' Barry laughed and said, 'It's me. Well, today it is, anyway.'

For the next two hours, Joy and Felicity sat in Felicity's bedroom, talking and laughing. They could be as loud as they wanted to be, and Joy's imitations of Mr Jones were so much better when she didn't have to be quiet and could strut around, exaggerating his arm and leg movements, as well as his voice and facial expressions. When Felicity left the room, saying, 'I'll be back in a sec,' Joy pondered this strange and wonderful life. The Felicities had horses for pleasure, but also presumably cows for milking. She liked Felicity and her family, but she envied everything Felicity had — her looks, her clothes, her hair, her easy laugh, her family. And it was red, stinging, lying-awake-at-night envy. Enough envy that if you spread it evenly throughout the whole congregation like a snake weaving in and out of every person's soul, they'd all go to Hell, no matter what else they did in life. She sighed. *Please God, please make me stop being envious.* She squeezed her eyes shut and prayed again, even harder. But the envy was as slippery and evil as the eels in her stomach, and as smooth and tempting as Dark Strawberry Cream chocolate. She was definitely going to Hell.

She wondered if the Felicities would go to Hell too, because as Joy knew all too well, it was harder for a rich man to enter the Kingdom of Heaven than it was for a camel to pass through the eye of a needle, no matter how hard they prayed or how much they thanked the Lord for their wonderful food.

When Felicity came in with a large plate covered with lots of different little cakes and pastries, Joy opened her eyes wide, and Felicity said, 'I didn't know which ones you'd like, so I got two of each.' Pushing her envy to the bottom of her stomach, where it could roll around with the eels, Joy repeated Felicity's words in Mr Jones's voice and they both laughed again. Mrs Felicity followed Felicity with a glass jug of chocolate milk and two tall glasses that looked like they had bubbles trapped in the bottom of them. Joy wrapped both her hands around her glass so she wouldn't drop it.

'Mum, you should see what Joy can do. She can mimic Mr Jones! Show her, Joy.'

With an unexpected rush of enthusiasm and bravery that surprised her, Joy put down her milk, and instead of mimicking Mr Jones, mimicked Mr Felicity. 'It's a classic, Barrington, an absolute classic,' she said, pretending to catch food falling out of her mouth.

Felicity and her mother screamed with delight, and Joy kept going until, in between laughs, Mrs Felicity said, 'Stop. No more. My stomach's hurting.'

Later, Joy asked Felicity who was going to milk the cows today if Mr Felicity was driving her home at four o'clock. Felicity reached for another pastry and said, 'We don't have any cows. There's an old dairy but it's horrible.' Joy couldn't understand how they could make money if they didn't have cows, and then remembered the two chemist shops. But who on earth would live on a farm for fun?

When they'd eaten the cakes, Joy wondered what time it was. She was scared that the Felicities wouldn't worry about what time they took her home, and she'd get into trouble for being late, but she couldn't possibly say anything; she just had to wait for Mr Felicity to remember.

Luckily, a few minutes later, while Joy was looking through a slide viewer and laughing at old photos of Felicity's parents, Mr Felicity poked his head around the door. 'Time to go, young Joy. Felicity, you stay home, dear, I don't want you to get another cold.'

On the way out, Mrs Felicity gave Joy a large bunch of red roses for her mother. She thrust it into Joy's arms then held her face and kissed her on the forehead. 'Thank you so much for coming over, dear. I'm already looking forward to the next time.'

Felicity exclaimed, 'She can come again on your birthday.' She turned to Joy. 'You've got to come. We always do something special on birthdays.'

Joy, still worrying about how she could tell Mrs Felicity that her mother had more than fifty rose bushes, managed to mutter 'Alright', even though she was sure that her father would say no.

In the car, Mr Felicity asked her about school and her favourite subjects, and didn't tell her to stop mumbling and speak up or mind her manners or even remind her that she was a sinner.

When they were driving down Bullock Road, she began to feel embarrassed about their dirty little house, and anxious that Mr Felicity would be horrified by it. But when they got to the bottom of the hill and she said, 'This is our driveway here,' Mr Felicity made a point of checking his watch, before saying, 'Sorry, young Joy, I lost track of time, so I can't come in and have a cuppa with your parents. I'll just pull up here, if that's alright. Please apologise to your parents, and do tell them that you were a delight to have in our home.'

'Thank you, Mr Arm—'

He swung his head around in mock horror. 'Mr Felicity.'

He laughed and waved as she got out of the car with the roses.

When Joy reached the back door, her father walked out and said, 'I hope you remembered your manners.'

In the kitchen, she handed the flowers to her mother and told her they were from Felicity's mother.

'Oh. Well. I'll be able to use them on Mr Cutler's wreaths tomorrow.'

Joy wanted her to put them in a gleaming glass vase in the middle of a big polished table in a dining room.

She waited for her mother to ask her if she'd enjoyed herself, or at least behaved herself, but all she said was, 'Maisie's having trouble with her calf.'

At tea, Joy knew not to ask for the salt or more milk, and was extra careful not to make any noise with her cutlery. Maisie's calf had died, the vet had charged her father six pounds, the rain had started again, and the lamb-chop stew — which was mostly carrot — was tough and dry.

No one asked her about her lunch at the Felicities.

32

JOY AND GEORGE

February 1983

I can't believe he's confessed. Just like that. I want to shake him, but I'm scared it will kill him, that his body will disintegrate into millions of fragments of dry skin and bone. And I'm not going to let him die that easily. Now I know the truth — that it's not just my suspicions — I've decided that he needs to suffer.

I think of the doll's head in the chest. And I start putting the pieces together. Slowly, but surely.

He groans, and there's another rattle coming from his throat.

I rub a hand across my mouth. I've got to think fast. Before he dies. Get the wheels of justice turning.

From each of the yellow eyes sunken in his grey, shrinking chook-face, a single tear slips out.

He's pathetic. More pathetic than I ever was. 'It was an accident.'

I roll my eyes. An accident? Like all the times he belted Mark and me? This man never does anything by accident. Look at how he hangs up his clothes, for crying out loud.

'I'm sorry,' he whispers.

'Sorry?' My voice is jagged and hot. 'I . . . I was angry.'

Well, that doesn't exactly surprise me.

'Everything was . . . wrong.' He pulls in a long gasp of air. 'Before I knew it . . . my hands were—' He closes his eyes, takes another long breath, and I wait, my face solid as the grey cement trough in the laundry. 'She fell . . . and . . .' He turns his head away from me. I think I hear, 'And then it was too late.'

'And she died, didn't she?' I spit out the words, the Ts and Ds as sharp as the barbs of a shiny new roll of fencing wire. 'It wasn't an accident. You're a murderer. Aren't you?'

'Everything was out of control, Gwen.' He rubs two bony fingers across his forehead.

'I'm Joy,' I say, disgusted. 'And everything's out of your control again, because I'm going to make you pay for this.'

'Ruth, Ruth,' he says, looking at me, but I'm so over his delusions, and the lies and the fear and the thrashings I lived with for sixteen years, that I feel like spitting on him. Then, as smugly as a vet who's just pulled a living calf out of its mother, he adds, 'After . . . she died . . . I prayed to God to forgive me. And He did. God forgave me.'

That's the last straw. Does he really believe God forgave him? For murder? I walk away — I can't stand to look at him anymore. Even if they arrest him, he'll never get to court. They'll give him the best care money can buy, and he'll slip away peacefully, pain-free, in air-conditioned comfort. Not exactly what I'd call justice or revenge.

I turn off the fan.

'Ruth!' He's trying to call out, but his voice is scratchy. 'Listen to me! I didn't . . . I didn't mean to kill her.'

He hasn't called me Joy once since I've been back. If the courts aren't going to dispense justice, then I will. I go back to the bed and pour some pills out of the bottle.

He takes another long, shallow intake of air, and it's obvious it hurts. Then he coughs, and an eruption of phlegm and blood lands on his chin and the sheet. I feel like leaving it there, letting him soak in the putrid muck, but I'm not an animal, so I wipe it up with the face-washer, dry retching. I drop it onto the newspaper on the floor, then tip the pills into his hand.

He opens his eyes wide. 'Four?'

'Yes, four. Vicki said if you're in this much pain this often, you need more.'

I'm sick of the moaning and I don't think four will kill him. I just need him to sleep while I think.

He puts all four tablets in his mouth. I hold the spout of the mug up to his mouth and tip. He lets the yellow fizzy drink fill his mouth, then swallows.

He takes another deep rattling breath and I see fear sweep into his eyes. Good.

'Give me all of them.' His voice is like an old thorn. 'Too much pain. Want to die.'

'Not yet,' I say, picking up the face-washer. 'Leave them for me,' he croaks.

I walk out, wondering if the act of dying is, in itself, painful. If you die in your sleep, for example, are those last one, two or three seconds painful simply because you're dying and your whole body is shutting down? I hope Wendy wasn't in pain when she died.

So at last I have the confession I wanted. I really wish I'd been brave enough to confront him about this years ago. I'm sure that once I show the police the doll's head in the chest, they'll work out that he killed Wendy, but I know from lonely nights watching crime shows on TV that fingerprints are the clincher. Would there still be fingerprints on the doll's head? I have no idea how long they last.

I walk out to the shed and throw back the lid of the chest. The doll's face is still staring up at me, and it's unnerving to say the least. But I've got to do this. I pick it up, holding it in my palm like it's Yorick's skull, then shake my head. I can't believe how stupid I was. I'm going to have to wipe off my own fingerprints first.

I look around and see the axe leaning against the wall, and its small plastic case sitting on the strut behind it. I open the case, spray copious amounts of the cleaning fluid on the doll's head and rub it furiously with the soft blue cloth. The hair gets tangled, but that doesn't matter. Then, just to be sure, I repeat the whole process, making sure every millimetre of porcelain is thoroughly sprayed and wiped.

With the head wrapped up in the cloth, I carry it inside and tell Ruth the plan. She nods and says, 'Justice *and* revenge.'

He's asleep, his bird-hands resting on the sheet where the phlegm and blood were. Those pills have knocked him out.

'Dad,' I say in a loud voice. He doesn't move. I say it again, a lot louder, but he still doesn't move.

Gently, I turn over his right hand, and place the doll's head in it, making sure I don't touch the head with anything but the cloth. Then I close his thumb and fingers around it and move the head around and press his fingers onto it again and turn it back and forth a little bit. It can't be a single clean, neatly arranged set. I turn the doll upside down and repeat the process, and do the same with his left hand. He doesn't even moan.

I stick my little finger, covered with the cloth, up the opening of the doll's neck and go back out to the shed. I put the doll's head back in the chest, pull out my finger, and sprinkle some dirt from the bottom of the chest over the head. I put the calico bag over it completely, then pull it back so the whole of the head is revealed and the bag sits scrunched up at the doll's neck. I drop the lid with a loud bang, as if I've just made the horrific discovery, and leave it unlocked. After neatly folding the cloth — just as my father always did — I put it and the cleaning fluid back in the plastic case and return it to the strut.

My heart lurches as I realise that my prints are all over the chest and the padlock, but of course it doesn't matter. *Dad always said there were valuable tools in there, Detective, so I thought I'd sell them. And then when I pulled back the calico bag . . . I still can't believe it. Do you think there'll be fingerprints on it?*

The wheels of justice are finally turning.

33

GEORGE AND GWEN

December 1942–February 1943

Two months to make a profit wasn't long, certainly not enough time to grow flowers. But there were wild ferns around the house, and some scraggly roses and unkempt woody plants that Gwen couldn't identify. Weeding furiously in between chores, she found dahlia and hydrangea bushes planted near the front door, and camellia bushes down near the chook pen. She dug vegetable peelings into the ground surrounding them all and cut them back so they would sprout more vigorously.

She used Arnold's telephone to ring Stan's suppliers, ordering small quantities of everything she needed, disappointed she didn't have enough money to make the cheaper bulk purchases. When she held out one of her precious pounds to Arnold to pay for the calls, he shook his head.

She ordered the flowers for Iris's Rotary Club dinner from the local florist. He looked a bit suspicious, but Gwen smiled and complimented him on the shop and two of his rose arrangements she noticed needed more balance and less ribbon.

Back in the little room, she spread out her florist's wire, tape, cutters, ribbon and paper on the bench and stacked the wreath bases in the cupboard. On the evening of the Rotary dinner, John picked up the finished arrangements with the milk cans, placing them gently on the floor of the truck's cabin. Iris paid Arnold the next day, who paid Gwen (less his commission and John's fee) the following Monday, who paid George not two minutes after she got home.

After that, more orders came. Lots of them.

George wrote down everything in another accounting book with the word 'Gwen' scrawled on the front cover. In it, he made her detail everything — the cost of flowers, how many pieces of wire she used, and how much florist tape and ribbon.

After two months she had made a profit of three shillings. It was hardly worth it, but George kept his word, and she used the three shillings to buy seedlings of five different types of perennials that would flower through winter.

34

JOY AND RUTH

Christmas Day 1960

Christmas Day was like any other day, except there were two presents for each child (one from their parents and one from Aunty Rose) under the pine tree in the corner of the kitchen. The other difference was that Joy's mother came to Church. But not Ruth, of course.

At Church, Joy felt very mature wearing the new church dress her parents had given her (thank goodness it didn't have puffy sleeves) and the cream tights Aunty Rose had sent. She couldn't wait to see Felicity. When she and Mark walked out of the Church, the Felicities were waiting in the porch and said with big smiles, 'Merry Christmas, Joy. Merry Christmas, Mark.' Felicity said, 'Sorry, we have to go. We're racing to Melbourne for a big family dinner,' then exclaimed, 'We have matching tights!' as she waggled a leg at Joy.

Joy said, 'Merry Christmas to you, too,' and watched the Felicities race through the rain to their car laughing.

Even the rain seemed to make them laugh.

That night, as Joy lay stiff and tight in bed waiting for the screams to come from Mark's room (he had not cleaned out the muck in the dairy properly), she wondered why her father even had children. Then she wondered why God had a son if He knew that one day someone was going to bang nails into His hands and feet and let Him die hanging and bleeding in the sun. It was worse than what her father did to Mark.

As the first of Mark's screams ruptured the night's silence, she remembered her father's words again. *Your time will come.* And she knew that time was soon.

35

JOY AND GEORGE

February 1983

'Are you going to kill him now?' Ruth's voice is laced with what I think is a little too much enthusiasm. 'Now that he's confessed?'

I take a swig of Passiona, cross that I'm shaking. 'I'm going to make him suffer.'

I walk to the table to grab the pile of pills, and hear Ruth open her mouth to tell me what she thinks I should do, like she always does. And suddenly I don't want to hear it.

'You know what?' I don't wait for a reply. 'I'm sick of listening to you. I had to listen to you — and him — until I got away from this god-forsaken place, and I'm over it. This is *my* idea, and *I'm* going to do it the way *I* want to.' I pull the table away from the wall, making the old lino squeal in protest, walk around to the other side, and yank down the wall-hanging that I hate almost as much as I hate my father. 'I'm not going to be a silent listener ever again.'

As I grab a box of matches from the cupboard near the back door, I can hear Ruth's voice. 'What do you mean? What are you going to do?'

I stomp down to the rubbish tank and climb the wooden steps. I can feel the heat that's always emanated from this portal to Hell — even more scorching than I remember — and hold my breath so I don't have to inhale the stench. I light a match and hold it to one corner of the old velvet rectangle. It catches fire really quickly and 'Christ' is gone almost immediately. I watch for a couple of seconds as the small flames spread much faster than I thought they would. Scared that it will burn my fingers, or that I'll drop it onto the dry grass below, I throw it over the rim, and let out a sigh.

'You can all go to Hell,' I shout.

When I'm back in the kitchen, which now seems hotter than it is outside, Ruth's purple birthmark is quivering. But I'm not sorry for what I said, and I haven't finished yet.

'I'm sick of you, Ruth. Sitting in your chair, never doing anything, always telling me what to do.' I take a breath and collapse onto the couch. 'I don't even know why you're here.'

She doesn't say anything, so I keep going, hardly knowing where the words are coming from. 'You think I don't know the truth about you and your accident?'

I turn around and stomp outside again, pretending not to hear her whispered reply: 'No, Joy, you don't know the truth.'

Out of habit, I walk down to the empty chook shed as if I'm going to collect eggs, and realise I still haven't gone to the dam to see if it really is empty. It's so hot, I can't see how any water can possibly be left in it, but I'm cross I haven't been over there, and now I'm too exhausted. All this plotting and arguing, and the stifling endless heat, have drained me.

I make tea in silence, ignoring Ruth, who reads *Pride and Prejudice* as if I'm not there. After tea, I grab all the pills and the forms and go back to my father's room. He's stirring, but very sluggish.

I put the tablets on the bedside table. After all, he did ask me to leave them for him so he could kill himself. So there they are behind the cup and the bottle of Passiona.

Just out of his reach.

'Dad,' I whisper. He manages to open his eyes, and I lean in. 'I'm going to tell the police that you killed Wendy Boscombe.'

He opens his eyes wide and shakes his head as hard as he can. 'No,' he whispers.

'Yes,' I answer back. 'I want everyone to know the kind of person you really are. They might not care about what you did to your children, but they'll care about this. And not one person will want to have anything to do with you when they find out.'

He looks terrified. At last.

'I'm going to ring the police, and I'm going to tell them I found Wendy's missing doll.'

He shakes his head in disbelief.

'Yes, I found Wendy's doll in the chest. Well, her head, to be precise.'

He's confused, of course. He'd assume I didn't know where the key was to unlock the chest.

'But . . .'

His raspy voice is annoying me. I put my hand over his mouth so he can't talk. For the first time in his life, *he's* going to be the silent listener.

'The police will take the doll's head and they'll find your fingerprints on it, and they'll arrest you. I haven't figured out everything yet, but I will. And when I do, they're going to find where you hid poor Wendy. You might be a murderer, but you're not as smart as me.'

I take my hand away from his mouth, and he takes in big gulps of air. 'No. No. You can't . . .' He begins to cough. 'Drink,' he pleads.

I hold the cup up to his lips. He doesn't have long now, so I can't waste any more time.

I walk out, ignoring his frightened little raspy voice. 'Why, why? I told you, it was an accident.'

When I come back to the kitchen, Ruth has found her voice again. 'The reason I'm here,' she says as if I'm twelve, and as if we were still in the middle of the conversation, 'is to help you.'

I roll my eyes and say nothing.

I watch her horrible birthmark move up and down as she talks, her voice like rotten grapefruit. 'You're weak, Joy. "No more silent listener"? What a load of crap. That's all you are, that's all you've ever been. I thought you were going to do something at last, kill him. But no, you won't even do that. You're a nobody, a waste of space. Like you have been all your life.'

'Me? What about you? All you've ever done is boss me around and put ideas in my head, drop poisonous whispers in my ear to take revenge on him. And ever since I've been back, all you've had to say is, "Kill him," "Make him suffer," "Make sure the police know he killed Wendy." But, I told you, I'm not going to be a silent listener anymore. Not his, not yours.'

'You don't know what you're talking about. If it hadn't been for me, you'd never have done any of those things. You'd have stayed timid, docile little Joy. If it hadn't been for me, you'd never have known how delicious revenge is. I helped you more than you'll ever realise.'

'Helped me? Well, I've got news for you. I was perfectly fine without you.'

'Really?' says Ruth, and I can see white sarcasm dripping down her chin. 'Got a steady job, have you? A bevy of friends? A boyfriend to take care of you?'

She's gone too far.

'It's not my fault,' I scream back. 'It's his fault!'

I sit down at the table, sweating and completely exhausted. Ruth opens her mouth and I interrupt her again. 'I don't need you, Ruth. Do you understand? I don't need you.' I get up to walk to my bedroom.

'Oh, you need me, Joy,' she says in her silver voice. 'Especially if you kill him.'

'I'm not going to kill him,' I say quietly, and close the door. But it doesn't block out her final scream.

'Well, if you won't kill him, I will!'

36

GEORGE AND GWEN

November 1943

'You need to cut costs or increase your prices,' George said one Monday night, after Gwen handed him the money she'd collected from Arnold that day. 'Or both.'

'We need a telephone, George.'

'You think we have money to spare?' His face was red. He pushed back his chair and picked up the accounting book in front of him. 'Do you?'

'No, dear. I just mean that we wouldn't have to pay Arn—' The book's blue cover was smashed into her cheek.

The next morning, when Gwen heard a knock at the door, she dragged herself off the bed in the back bedroom where she'd been lying, and pushed the bucket to one side. She had to get to a doctor to find out why she was sick every morning now.

She held up a hand to cover her left cheek and the corner of her mouth, and opened the back door to see Robert.

'Hello, Gwen. I thought I'd let you know that . . . Oh goodness, what happened?'

‘Oh, this . . .’ She lifted her hand from her face. ‘Nothing. I was weeding yesterday and didn’t see a tree branch.’

‘Tree branches,’ he said, nodding. ‘Always hiding where you least inspect them.’

She couldn’t help but laugh.

Later, George arrived for morning tea a good half-hour before he normally did, and banged a large bucket on the kitchen bench.

‘You want a telephone? Here’s your telephone.’

She looked in the bucket. Two long, thick black eels were wriggling angrily in a foot of water.

‘They’re from the dam. Good in stews, apparently. Two free meals a week. Get out your sharpest knife.’

Gwen gagged. She opened the second drawer, pulled out a knife, and turned to her husband. ‘Where are you going to kill them?’

‘You want a telephone, you kill them,’ and he walked out.

She looked at the knife, shook her head, and put it back in the drawer. Then she leant down, pulled open the third drawer and took out the cleaver. Holding a tea towel, she reached for one of the eels, but when it wriggled angrily and let out a horrifying groan, she screamed and pulled her hand out of the bucket.

Caught up in the tea towel, the eels thrashed harder and emitted guttural rumbles. Gwen snatched up another tea towel and this time pushed both hands into the water and grabbed one of the eels. She dragged it out of the bucket, threw it onto the chopping board, its long body thrashing wildly against the side of the bucket, its groan getting louder and more horrifying. Holding it tightly with her left hand, she picked up the cleaver with the other and smashed the blade on to the base of its head. Blood spurted out, and she let out a gasp of disgust and relief.

But the head remained attached to the body, which was still whipping back and forth. Letting out a loud groan herself, she brought down the cleaver with increased force, relieved to hear the thud of the blade against the board. She threw the head and the body into the sink, and without letting herself stop to think, pulled out the second eel, threw it onto the chopping board and, ignoring its growl, brought down the cleaver with as much force as she could. She only needed one cut this time. She threw the second eel into the sink and ran water over both bodies until the water was clear.

One at a time, she put them back on the chopping board, cut the fins off, slit the underside of each eel from the neck to the tail, and opened it out flat. Inside, there were bright-red entrails and a long, narrow backbone. Gagging again, she used her fingers to scrape out the tendrils, some pink, some black, and pull the bone away from the flesh. She threw the fins, entrails and bones into the sink with the heads, and ran her bare fingers up and down the bodies again and again until she was sure that she'd removed everything. She grabbed the blue and white box of bicarbonate of soda, threw some over the chopping board, and rubbed it furiously with the tea towel, which she then used to wrap up the heads and entrails. As she made her way to the rubbish tank, she regretted using the tea towels that Jean had given her for their wedding. Still, a telephone was more important. She could use any old rag as a tea towel — and buy new ones with the extra money she would make.

Back in the kitchen, she cut the bodies into one-inch slices and threw them into a large saucepan with butter, onions and carrots. Then salt and water mixed with cornflour. While it simmered, she peeled and chopped the potatoes, and hoped that the eels would be edible.

When George came in after milking, she dished up the grey sludge and mashed potatoes with some pride. 'One telephone for tea tonight, Mr Henderson.'

George smiled and patted her hand, and she felt relief wash over her. They would be alright; things were going to get better. The eels were tough and grainy so Gwen knew she had to wash them more thoroughly the next time, and maybe cook them more slowly and for longer. After his first mouthful, George asked her to get the tomato sauce, and reached for the salt-shaker again.

But he did not complain.

In fact, he suddenly started talking. He had other ideas for saving money. They would get chooks for the chook pen at the bottom of the cracked path, and he'd catch rabbits with the rabbit traps he'd found in the shed, or maybe get ferrets to catch them for him. Two rabbits and two eels a week would be good for four meals. The eggs from the chooks would save them more money, and he could kill one every now and then for a roast. A real treat. Gwen could make butter from the cream from the milk. How silly they'd been to use their coupons to buy butter when it was just cream and salt. She could make bread as well. They would eat like kings and have a phone and Gwen would make wedding bouquets and funeral wreaths, and George would not have to beg the bank for more money or more time, and soon they would own the farm.

'How soon, George?'

He pushed another piece of sauce-soaked eel onto his fork, and smiled his charming smile. 'Twenty-four years, dear.'

Longer than she'd been alive.

37

JOY AND RUTH

Boxing Day 1960

Not far from the house was an old tank stand. The tank was long gone, but the unsmoothed posts were still solid in the ground. Wrapped around the posts was netted wire that made two enclosures Joy's family called rooms. The first room had just enough space to stand in with your arms spread out. The second room was much larger and the previous owners had kept budgerigars in there. Happy birds that chirped and whistled, flying around like little shooting rainbows. Joy didn't know how she knew that they had kept budgerigars. Maybe she'd even made it up.

Joy's family kept four ferrets in there.

To get to the ferrets, you had to open a wire gate into the first room, close it, then open the next gate to get into the second room. If you didn't close the first gate before you opened the second one, the ferrets could whip around your feet and escape. Everyone knew that. Everyone always closed the first gate before they opened the second gate.

Joy hated the ferrets and the way they looked at her. They had wild rat faces, matted and mottled fur that reminded her of vomit, and four curved, pointed fangs at the front of their mouths. Fangs that could, she knew, kill.

Every week or so, Mark and her father went into the cage, wearing rubber boots so the ferrets couldn't bite their feet or ankles, and after some chasing and yelling, caught them and somehow stuffed them into a hessian bag. When all four were squirming in the bag, hissing and rasping, her father would twist the top and hold it tightly. Then he and Mark would head off to the bull paddock, her father holding the wriggling bag and Mark carrying an empty one.

After a couple of hours, they returned with both bags squirming. According to Mark, when they got to the paddock they let the ferrets out one by one, each near a rabbit burrow. Each ferret would pick up rabbit scent, fly down a hole, the rabbits would fly out of another one, and her father or Mark would somehow catch them. Joy could not imagine how. And then they caught the ferrets again. There were big voids in Joy's mind about how all this could work, but she was just glad she did not have to go with them.

They put the rabbits in a small cage in the shed, where they ate scraps from the kitchen until they appeared in a stew. Joy was not sure why or how they died. Maybe from ferret bites. Maybe from sadness.

But rabbit stew was cheap and filling, and the meat not as tough or disgusting as eel.

On Boxing Day, Joy was peeling potatoes when Mark carried in a bucket with two dead rabbits in it. He put the bucket on the kitchen floor and said to their mother, 'Dad says I have to clean the tractor and Joy has to do the ferrets.'

Their mother nodded, and Joy felt sick.

While her mother cleaved off the heads and feet, then skinned and gutted the rabbits, Joy peeled and chopped potatoes, onions and carrots and added them to the lard in the pot. The whole time, the eels squirmed and hissed in her stomach.

'Okay, off you go,' her mother said when she'd added the chopped up rabbits to the vegetables.

Joy didn't want to look inside the bucket, but it was impossible not to. Skin, fur, two heads, intestines and other unidentifiable innards. White bits. Red bits. Rabbits. She knew they were vermin that ate vegetables and ruined paddocks. According to the Bible, chooks and rabbits and eels didn't have souls, so it didn't matter how they died or that people ate them.

When she reached the cage, the ferrets were climbing over one another along one side watching her, wiry and frenetic {little red explosions of fire}. Joy knew they could smell the dead rabbit bits, knew they were thirsty for blood. She would push everything through the wire. But when she looked at it, she realised that she might be able to poke the red and pink bits through, but definitely not the skin and heads. She'd have to go right inside to the second room.

She felt sick. The ferrets were revolting, but it wasn't just the ferrets. Or the rabbit guts and fur and heads. It was the wet muddy farm. Her father's anger. Her brother's despair. Her envy of other people. All the killing and death: eels, chooks, spiders, snakes, rabbits, unborn calves, drowned cows. Jesus hovering and whispering. And God taking her father's side.

It seemed like everything made her feel sick, so she thought hard about what made her happy. There were the Felicities (she would definitely ask Mark if he wanted to come with her next time). And high school wasn't that far away, where she would make more Friends and read wonderful books like *The Strange Case of Dr Jekyll and Mr Hyde.*

She looked in the bucket again. She would have to do this. She unlatched the outer gate to the cage and stood inside the first room, her stomach lurching. She gagged and spat out some bile, surprised to see that it wasn't black and sticky like the eels. She took another breath, then opened the second gate and closed her eyes as she tossed out the bucket's contents.

The ferrets flew past her, a blur of sharp teeth and fur.

In horror, she watched them disappear beyond the flowerbeds into the bushes between the cage and the bull paddock. She dropped the bucket and started to follow them, but she hadn't taken three steps when she stopped. Even if she could see them, she would never catch them.

She ran to the shed where Mark was cleaning the tractor. He looked up and saw her white face. 'What?'

'The ferrets.' She pointed to the cage and Mark saw the open gate. He covered his mouth with his hand, then took it away and looked at her. He spoke quietly. 'It's okay. It will be okay.' But his face was white, too.

Just at that moment, their father walked into the shed. Mark twisted the cloth he was using to clean the tractor. 'Dad,' he said. 'The ferrets . . .'

'What about them?'

Joy stared at her brother. She couldn't believe that Mark was going to dob her in. She needed to stop him, but she knew it wouldn't make any difference. One way or the other, her father was going to find out, and that would be that. She breathed in and opened her mouth to confess, as cold fear spiralled up her chest to her head.

But Mark beat her to it. 'I let them escape. By mistake. It was an accident.'

'You what?' His voice was quiet. Too quiet.

'I let them . . .'

'No, no, he's lying,' sobbed Joy. 'I did it. Not Mark, me.' The black silence stretched to the end of the universe. They all knew.

Her time had come.

38

JOY AND GEORGE

6 February 1983

I look at the pills in my hand, the morning's intense heat already leaking their blue colouring onto my palm.

Everything will be fine.

I jiggle the pills, and the blue stain spreads. There are globules of sweat erupting all over my forehead and hands, and underneath my shirt.

Today is the day. Justice and revenge.

I'm at his bedroom door. I always leave it open so I can hear his moans of pain and calls for help. And that's what I'll tell the police. If they ask. Even if they don't, I'll make sure I say, 'I always left the door open so I could hear him moaning or calling out for help.' I won't add, 'and ignore him.'

Where the hell is Ruth? She's always here. Not that she's actually trapped in that chair. Oh no. I know the truth about her.

From the doorway, I can see the clothes lying all over the floor. I check the orange lumps of his body under the blanket. They're not moving.

I put the glass on the floor hastily, and it falls over. I know the bright-yellow soft drink will stain the carpet. Five steps to the side of the bed. The sheet's pulled up to his bottom lip. He looks like he's praying. Eyes closed, contemplating Heaven. Or Hell. Always with a capital H.

I stretch out my hand to touch his forehead.

It is — there's really no other way to describe it — deathly cold.

It really is over. No more Passiona, no more blue pills, no more eels.

I'm still gripping the melting pills in my blue-stained palm. *I was taking him his pills, Detective.*

I pick up the empty glass I dropped a minute ago and rub my foot back and forth on the spilt liquid. *I could tell he wasn't breathing, and I dropped his glass of Passiona. Right here. It's his favourite drink. I mean, it was his favourite drink.*

There's no need to lie.

* * *

In the kitchen, there's still no Ruth.

In the back porch, which Blackhunt Real Estate will soon dub 'a cosy entrance way', I push open Mark's bedroom door. The room is empty, the bed neatly made. I open the wardrobe door. It's empty, too.

Outside, the heat is brutal; I feel sick. My sleeves are sticking to my arms.

'Ruth?' My cracked shout is sucked up by the heat. 'I'm sorry I said I didn't need you.'

It's so hot I'm wishing it was wet and miserable like it was all through my childhood, when I could pretend that if the endless grey curtain of rain and mist lifted, I'd see another house. And in that house, there'd be a family who, now that the rain had stopped and the mist had rolled away, would finally see me, their long-lost daughter hidden for years by the grey curtain, and reclaim me. We'd move to Darwin with

Mark and I'd live happily ever after, wrapped up in apple-green love and sunshine.

I looked so hard for that home and that family, but all I could ever see were boundless muddy hills, fenced-in animals, the rubbish tank and the dam with its drowned cows and rusted junk.

Now the hills are dry and yellow, dotted with knobby skeletons of trees holding their withered limbs up to the hot sky. Pleading with God for relief.

I let out a long, pent-up scream. The neighbours are so far away that, as I well know, they can't hear screams, even in the dead of night.

Although sometimes I wondered. Wondered if Barbara or Robert or Colin (the closest of our faraway neighbours) ever woke up and cocked their heads, and thought, *What's that noise?* before drifting back to sleep. Or if the Boscombes, in their sleepless anguish, thought the screams were Wendy's?

I walk down the cracked cement path to the chook yard, eyeing off the chopping block stained with chook blood. And standing in the quiet of the empty yard, I know Ruth's left for good, that I'll never see her again.

To avoid the vicious heat, I keep to the shade as I walk back to the house, but my hands have become heavy and swollen.

Swollen.

Like my father's dead lips.

I walk quickly now, not stopping until I'm back in the bedroom. Nothing's changed, but everything has changed. The sheet's still sitting against the cold chin, the fan's still whirring, the heat's still suffocating. But I have to do this first.

I take the five steps to the side of the bed again. I breathe in slowly, deeply, and then grab the corner of the sheet hanging off the side of the bed. The eels in my stomach are writhing. I just want it all to be over. So I can leave this place once and for all.

I pull back the sheet and blankets in one sweep. My stomach buckles and yellow grainy vomit forces its way into my mouth.

My father is dead alright. And around his neck, pulled as tight as possible, is his belt.

39

GEORGE AND GWEN

August 1944

It had been six months since he had hit her, with or without the blue accounting book.

'I'm so happy,' she told Barbara, who had appeared at the back door not thirty minutes after she and George arrived home from hospital with the baby.

Ever since their first meeting, Barbara walked the mile and a half to the Henderson farm, uninvited, for a cup of tea and whatever Gwen had baked. There was no pattern to when she arrived, and no set time, so Gwen always felt that Barbara was judging her, as a mother-in-law might. Had she baked that morning, was the kitchen clean, were the sheets on the line every Monday?

'I have something for the baby.' Barbara held out a package, and with a pang of guilt Gwen remembered the day she'd told Barbara she was pregnant. 'When I was expecting Colin . . .' Barbara had begun. 'Were you excited?' Gwen interrupted, then immediately regretted the question: according to Arnold, Colin had 'brain problems', because he had been deprived of oxygen during his birth.

When Gwen had first met Colin, she'd found him a little disconcerting. The boy was handsome, strong, and blessed with a lovely nature, but hardly ever made eye contact, and he turned his head this way and that way, as if he could hear things that others couldn't. Though he was hardly a boy, she'd reminded herself — he was only three years younger than her. And Gwen was eternally grateful to Colin because he was so much better than she would ever be at milking and cleaning up cow muck, and all of the other endless farm chores.

He was also an excellent listener. On the first morning of his unpaid work helping George, he brought up the half-bucket of milk they drank each day, and Gwen automatically asked him if he would like a cup of tea. He nodded and smiled, and sat down at the head of the table, where George always sat. As they drank, she started talking, and suddenly she was telling him about how much she had enjoyed working for Stan at Willshire, and how guilty and inadequate she had felt her whole life living with her great-aunt, uninvited and unwelcomed. Each morning, Colin brought up the milk, sat down for a cup of tea and listened and nodded, often repeating her words so she knew he was listening. He never complained about how strong or weak the tea was, and ate her sultana biscuits enthusiastically. As the days and weeks went by, she found she enjoyed his company and his polite, but touching, repetitions of her words.

'Excited?' Barbara had said in answer to Gwen's question back then. 'I suppose.' She'd looked out of the window. 'But after the baby's born . . .' She'd taken another bite from a sultana biscuit, and stared hard at Gwen. 'It's no bed of roses, you know. You spend months getting fatter and heavier while you're carrying around . . . a parasite. Then there's the birth itself, which is surely God's way of punishing women, and when you get home, you have a thousand more jobs to do.'

Gwen had picked up their empty cups and carried them to the sink. *God's way of punishing women*? Of course it was hard work having a baby, especially one like Colin, but surely there was much joy to be had — as well as a life-long friend? She'd touched her slightly swollen stomach.

'I still have some maternity dresses,' Barbara said, looking her up and down. 'You're a lot bigger than me, but it's better than buying new.'

She couldn't possibly accept. What if she ended up with a child like Colin, and Barbara's bitterness? Besides, if Colin was eighteen, the dresses were nineteen years old. Why on earth had Barbara kept them?

She rehearsed a line as she rinsed out the cups. *Thank you, Barbara, but a friend who had a baby last year has promised me hers*. Friend? What friend? She didn't have friends anymore. Apart from the smiling Arnold and, ironically, Colin. She felt self-loathing coil around her heart. How dare she refuse Barbara's offer?

So wear them she had, throughout the pregnancy — and she had one on now because her dark rippled stomach was still enlarged and grotesque.

She opened the large paper bag Barbara had put on the table.

It was full of baby clothes.

'They were Colin's,' said Barbara. 'They're a bit old, but it's better than buying new.'

After Barbara left, she lay down with Mark on the single bed in his bedroom, wrapped her arms around him, and let the tears flow.

40

JOY AND RUTH

Boxing Day 1960

For the rest of the afternoon, Joy's fear was mingled with a burning hope that the ferrets would return to the cage by themselves, hungry for easy food. *Please God, please God.* She prayed all afternoon, but God did not answer her prayers.

As she cleaned the bath and basin, hung out the washing, and slowly swept and mopped the back porch and the laundry and the toilet and the bathroom, she prayed constantly, while the shiny black eels in her stomach grew fatter and slimier and angrier.

When she finished her chores, she went to find Mark. He was in the shed doing something to the lawn mower. He looked at her and shook his head.

She went to her room and lay on her bed. It was nearly teatime and she would have to set the table and help her mother dish up. Ruth did not say anything. Even she knew that Joy's time had come.

Joy could smell the rabbit stew. She didn't know how she could eat it, but knew she would have to. Her whole body felt hollow and somewhere else.

She hauled herself from her bed, and walked into the kitchen. Her mother had already dished up plates of the stew and peas and carried them to the table. Mark was sitting silently; their father was pouring tomato sauce onto his stew. There was an empty plate at Joy's place.

'You.' He pointed to her chair. 'Sit down, don't say a thing. You're not eating tonight, y'hear? We're going to have to buy more ferrets, so maybe you'll learn the value of things if you go without. Sit down, and get ready to say grace, because they're the only words coming out of your mouth tonight.'

When her mother sat down, her father looked at Joy and said tightly and coldly, 'Grace.'

Joy's voice was barely audible. 'For what we are—'

'Speak up, you ungrateful sinner.'

She swallowed and opened her mouth and tried to speak normally. 'For what we are about to receive, may the Lord make us truly grateful. Amen.'

Everyone echoed the Amen.

While the others ate, Joy sat with her head down, looking at the empty plate, her hands clenched together on her lap. The black eels rolled into a large, writhing mass in her stomach, before little eels the size of tadpoles floated out of the mass and burrowed into her veins. She sat still as they drank her blood, getting fatter and fatter.

After the rest of the family had eaten their stew, Joy had to give them each a bowl of rhubarb pie with cream scooped from the top of the bucket, then sit back down at her place. The unseen guest and silent listener of the wall-hanging looked down on them, but Joy's fear of Him was nothing compared to how much she feared her father that night.

When their mother had taken away the bowls, her father broke the silence. 'Next time, you'll think before you act, and appreciate how hard it is to put food on the table.'

Then the familiar words. 'What are you?'

Even though she was terrified, her brain detoured for a second and wondered how Mark had learnt the right answers, the ones she had grown up hearing.

'A filthy sinner.'

'A lazy, good-for-nothing sinner. Say it.'

'A lazy, good-for-nothing sinner.'

'Ask for forgiveness like the filthy sinner you are.'

'Please forgive me, Dad.'

'*Ssss*. You're useless.'

He thumped the table and pushed back his chair, making the lino screech. And then he uttered, from a deep dark place, the single word she knew was coming.

'Room.'

PART THREE

41

GEORGE AND GWEN

October–December 1945

Gwen often told herself how lucky she was. The war was over, she had a son who was healthy and would hopefully never have to go to war, her floristry was helping them keep their bills under control (and allowed her to buy a little foundation for her face, which George had agreed to), and her husband was one of the most admired men in the district. Of course, she had to deal with his anger and occasional outbursts of violence, which had begun again when Mark was a few months old, but whenever he smiled at her, whenever she pleased him, she knew she was on the right path. If she could just get better at pleasing him, life would be fine.

So Gwen worked hard at not making George angry. It was simply a matter of thinking ahead, anticipating his needs and wants — meals ready on time, tins full of his favourite biscuits and slices, the house clean, the shillings from her bouquets and wreaths handed over each week, nods and smiles at whatever he said. It wasn't that difficult, really.

When she slipped up, she avoided seeing other people until the bruising subsided. But Barbara still dropped in unannounced, Colin still brought up the milk each morning, and customers who lived nearby preferred to pick up their bouquets and wreaths from the farm instead of Arnold's. So she learnt to apply her foundation liberally.

The one part of their life she couldn't control was Mark. She couldn't stop him crying if he was sick or hurt, she couldn't stop him making a mess with his food, she couldn't stop him being a baby. Yet whenever he was noisy or messy, George yelled at Gwen, 'Why can't you control him? There must be something wrong with you.'

'Sorry, dear, I'll pop him in his bedroom,' Gwen would say gaily. And she would sit there with him, quietly rocking him and singing lullabies until he went to sleep. It meant she had less time to do her chores and make the ever-increasing number of bouquets and wreaths that people kept ordering, but she learnt to work faster and harder and cut corners. And as she managed to meet all of George's demands, she became more and more exhausted.

Gwen lived for the time after tea when Mark was asleep and George was out (which was most nights) being a good community member at one meeting or another, because she could do her chores or floristry without being interrupted. When George wasn't out, he practised his guitar in their bedroom. When they were courting, she had told him that her favourite song was 'You Are My Sunshine', so now he always played that first, and often last. On cold nights, he practised in front of the kitchen fire or they listened to the wireless together, Gwen silently praying that Mark would stay asleep and not upset George.

Each Monday, she and Mark arrived at Arnold's before he opened so they could settle their finances. Even though most people now rang Gwen directly, Arnold still had his sign in the window and took in a few orders, for which Gwen continued to give him 10 per cent. One day, Arnold suggested that she pay him a flat fee instead. 'You don't really need me anymore, Gwen, and it isn't fair that I take ten per cent when I'm only passing on messages. Besides, when people come in here to place an order, they always buy something from me as well, so I already get my cut.'

At the end of the first week of her new arrangement with Arnold, Gwen forgot to tell George about it, so the calculations in his accounting book showed the 10 per cent to be paid to Arnold, instead of the flat fee. When he asked Gwen for the profit he'd calculated, she handed it over and later softly exclaimed at the extra money in her cash box.

Strangely, she forgot again the next week. And the next.

But she did remember to buy some extra items — just a few little things that a growing toddler needed, and a slightly more expensive foundation that worked like a treat on bruises.

42

JOY AND RUTH

December 1960

The morning after the ferrets escaped — the morning after her father had screamed 'Room' at her — Joy's mother told her to go to the dam and pick twenty-five waterlilies for wreaths. She was to be 'quick smart', and make sure she didn't bruise any of them. Mark was down in the dairy replacing the fan belt in the pump room, and her father was repairing fences at the back of the farm. He wouldn't return until late in the afternoon, having taken sandwiches and a thermos of tea with him.

Wincing with pain, Joy walked over to the dam slowly, banging the ground ahead of her with the Dutch hoe to frighten away snakes, knowing that she could never tell anyone what had happened the previous night. She would always be angry with herself for being so stupid.

She was grateful that Bible Study wasn't being held that week because of Christmas. She didn't know how she would have sat on the bus for the long ride into town. Or looked at Felicity without bursting into tears.

Although it hurt to walk, Joy was glad she was going to the dam by herself — for the first time ever — because it meant she could cry without anyone hearing her.

As she'd pulled out the Dutch hoe from the cupboard in the back porch, her mother had warned her about the ledge. 'And don't dare stand on the ledge, alright? It's—'

'I know,' Joy said, nodding miserably and repeating her father's words: 'One foot deep for one foot: fifty feet deep forever.'

When she got back, she cleaned the Dutch hoe, put it in the cupboard and took the waterlilies to her mother in her workroom. Then she washed her blood-stained sheets and pyjamas in the old copper, wound them through the wringer and hung them on the line. She was ashamed and scared.

She had never been so scared in her life. She was going to have to be more careful from now on. Forever. A lot more careful than she had been yesterday when she'd walked into the now-empty ferret cage. She would have to be smart, too. Very smart and very careful.

Lunch was relatively calm since her father was eating sandwiches miles away. Joy relaxed a little.

She helped her mother wire and stick camellia leaves into the wreath bases. The funeral was 'a good one', so they had to prepare forty-three bases, then make 129 white bows out of the stiff florist ribbon. That way all her mother had to do the next morning was wire and attach flowers for the top layer of each wreath, and jab the ribbons into place. While they worked, the squirming, hissing eels and the pain in her body reminded Joy that she had to be smart and careful forever.

Especially when she heard her father come inside and throw something into the trough. Joy knew he had beheaded a Ruth, because they were having a roast that night.

Finally, with the wreath bases and ribbons stacked in piles against one wall, her mother said it was time to make tea.

While Joy's mother plucked the dead Ruth in the laundry, Joy peeled and cut the potatoes and carrots that would go in the baking pan with the chook. When her mother came into the kitchen, Joy knew to take the innards out to the chooks.

As she was walking down to the chook yard, Mark lifted his arm to wave to her with a wet soapy cloth he was using to wash the van. Joy raised a hand a little bit and waved it tentatively, noticing her father sitting behind Mark, polishing the axe-head he'd just used to chop off Ruth's head.

As she was walking up the cracked cement path with the now-empty bucket, she saw Mark inside the back of the van, washing down the walls. Their father was a stickler for Cleanliness, sitting as it did right next to Godliness.

Tea was almost ready when the phone rang, and her mother groaned as she wiped her hands on her apron and walked into the good room to answer it, leaving the door wide open. Joy knew she hated it when people rang with last-minute orders for wreaths. 'Three double-five, Gwen Henderson . . . Hello, Barbara. How are you?'

Joy heard the click-click-click of the tele-index's slider as her mother listened to Mrs Larsen. Then the clicking stopped abruptly. 'What? No, no. I'm sure she'll be fine.' Silence while Mrs Larsen spoke again.

Joy stopped stirring the gravy and listened intently. Were they talking about her? Did Mrs Larsen know what had happened? She felt the pain in her legs and back, and the red-hot shame in her head, and thought, *I will never be fine again.*

'Of course, Barbara, although I doubt they will have. I still can't believe it. Thank you for letting us know. Goodbye, Barbara.' Her mother banged the phone down and walked quickly back into the kitchen, a hand clapped over her mouth.

'What?' asked Joy, terrified of what her mother was going to say.

'I'm going to make a start on those wreaths or they won't get done in time,' her mother said, frowning. 'Finish making tea and call me when it's ready.' But Joy heard her walk outside, not into her workroom.

After her father said grace at the table, he took a mouthful of roast Ruth then nodded quickly at her mother, who cleared her throat and spoke. Joy jumped. Her father was always the first one to talk during a meal. If anyone spoke at all.

'The most terrible thing has happened.'

Joy tightened her grip on her knife and fork, both jammed into a potato.

'Wendy Boscombe has . . . disappeared.'

Her mother gave them the details. Nine-year-old Wendy had been playing outside with her dolls while her mother was in the kitchen and her father was fixing a broken pipe in a paddock a long way from the house. When Mrs Boscombe went looking for her, she found some of Wendy's dolls and her dolls' pram two hundred yards down their driveway. The dolls were in a row, face down in the mud, and the dolls' pram was on its side next to them.

So that's what Mrs Larsen had told her mother on the phone. 'The police say that Wendy probably just wandered away and perhaps fell over somewhere, but poor Mrs Boscombe is sure Wendy would never do that. When the police asked her if there was anything of Wendy's missing, she nodded and said she thought some dolls might be missing, but she couldn't be sure how many.'

Joy wondered exactly how many dolls Wendy had. So many that Mrs Boscombe didn't even know how many. Joy imagined the line of beautiful dolls in the mud, with their creamy lace dresses and shiny black shoes.

'I thought they were away?' said her father.

'Viola and Wendy were. They went to help Viola's sister. Poor Viola told me they could barely afford the petrol to drive there, but her sister was very ill. Anyway, they came back yesterday because Viola's sister went into hospital.'

Barely afford the petrol? Weren't the Boscombes rich, with all their milkshakes and dolls and holidays? It didn't sound like Wendy had been to the beach at all. But before Joy could untangle all of this, her mother continued. 'The police have searched the whole farm. And now they're going to interview everyone. In case someone saw something. Or heard something.' She stopped, waiting for one of them to say, 'Yes, I heard something,' but there was silence.

Her father swallowed a mouthful of potato, then said, 'For goodness sake, you can't even hear a truck drive past on the road, it's so far away. There could be someone down in the dairy right now, or in the dam drowning, screaming for help, and we wouldn't hear a thing.'

More silence. Her father picked up one of roast Ruth's legs in his hand and began pulling the meat off with his teeth.

'Barbara said Viola is scared someone drove on to the farm and . . . stole Wendy.'

Joy could see Wendy Boscombe playing with her dolls on the driveway in the rain, while a car with sinister intent slowly, silently, came down the driveway, and stopped behind her. The driver was wearing black gloves and had a black face. Not like an Aboriginal face, but totally black, without eyes or a nose or a mouth — just a flat, black oval. A non-person. Silently he got out, pulled Wendy off the ground, kicked over her pram, and quickly tied her up with black rope. She screamed, but her parents were too far away to hear.

The man with the black face threw Wendy into the back seat, like Joy had seen her father throw calves into a cattle-truck, and, just as slowly and quietly, he reversed up the driveway.

Joy's heart was thumping as she remembered Wendy waving to her from her mother's car, calling out, 'I'll miss you next year.' As if they were Friends.

'But . . . people don't steal children,' she said. That black, faceless man was only in Joy's imagination, after all.

No one said anything, so she added, 'Do they?'

Her parents looked at one another, and her mother turned to Joy to say something when there was a knock at the back door. Everyone, even Joy's father, jumped. He motioned with his head that his wife was to answer the door.

Joy's mother looked scared, but she got up while the others sat still, straining their ears. When she returned, two police officers were behind her.

Her father leapt up immediately, a broad smile on his face, his hand outstretched. Sergeant Ronald Bell from Blackhunt Police Station introduced himself, even though he went to their Church, then introduced his offsider, Constable Alex Shepherd, 'the new kid on the block'. Despite her thumping heart, Joy couldn't help wondering if all police officers had surnames that were common nouns.

Her father gave a small nod to her mother, who walked over to the sink and put the kettle on, but with a shake of his head and a friendly smile, Sergeant Bell declined a cup of tea.

Her father invited them to sit on the brown couch in front of the fire, but Sergeant Bell declined that also, saying they just had a few questions, that it wouldn't take long. Her father remained standing too, his hands resting on the back of his chair. Joy's mother stood behind the kitchen bench, even after the kettle had boiled. The children sat, stunned, as their roast Ruth and potatoes went cold, and the gravy turned into a glutinous mass.

Although Sergeant Bell was trying to be official and impartial {a flat white sheet of paper}, he and Joy's father had known each other for years, and Joy thought that it was as if they were chatting in the street. Shepherd, on the other hand, hardly said anything, but watched carefully, occasionally looking around the room and writing in a small notebook.

Her father answered Ron's questions for all of them. Yes, they had only just heard the dreadful news. No, they hadn't seen anything unusual today, or heard anything. 'Goodness, Ron, someone could be screaming in the dairy or drowning in the dam and we wouldn't hear it from here.' (Joy thought it odd that he repeated to Sergeant Bell what he'd just told his family.) No, they didn't know anyone who didn't like the Boscombes.

Joy noticed that Shepherd was reading the wall-hanging above Mark and grimacing. Maybe he wasn't a Christian. He had a very ordinary face, she thought, nowhere near as interesting as Sergeant Bell's older, friendlier face. In fact, she thought it was nondescript {a lump of mashed potato}, and was pleased to be using another recently discovered word.

Her thoughts were interrupted by Sergeant Bell suddenly being brisk and saying, 'Right. So, where were you all this afternoon?'

Her father quickly said, 'We were here,' rolling his hands back and forth on the top of his chair.

But from behind the kitchen bench, her mother said, 'Except when you—'

He looked towards her quickly, frowning.

'What I mean is,' and her mother smiled, 'you might have seen something . . .' Her voice became smaller as her husband stared at her. 'Or heard something,' and it grew even smaller. 'Or maybe . . .' Her voice trailed away altogether.

He turned to the officers, smiling. 'We were all on the farm. I was on the farm. All day. We were all here.'

Bell smiled reassuringly and said nothing, while Shepherd kept writing.

Joy could see the white silence throbbing. Did they think her father had something to do with Wendy's disappearance?

'Yes, well,' her father said, breaking the silence, 'when I said I was on the farm all day, I . . . um . . . actually drove around to the back of the farm, and up the tractor lane to the back fences.'

'Ah, excellent,' said Bell. He turned to Shepherd and explained that most adjoining farms in the area had T-shaped tractor lanes running between property borders to give farmers easy access to their back paddocks. The south-west corner of the Henderson farm met the north-east corner of the Boscombe farm, and the tractor lane ran off Wishart Road between the Boscombe and the Wallace farms.

'So, George,' Bell continued, 'any cars driving down Wishart Road? Cars, trucks, anything at all?' Joy could guess why Bell was asking that question. He was thinking that whoever had stolen Wendy might have driven right past her father. With Wendy screaming in the boot. 'And you were on your tractor, George?'

Bell must be asking that because of course he didn't think George Henderson had stolen Wendy. Apart from anything else, no one could steal a nine-year-old girl on a tractor. There was nowhere to hide anything on a tractor, let alone a nine-year-old girl, and tractors didn't move much faster than a centipede.

'That's right, Ron. Sergeant.'

'I thought you took the van, dear.'

Her father's smile didn't change. Not one iota. 'I might have said I was going to take the van, but I ended up taking the tractor. The van isn't durable enough on that old lane.'

Her father knew the word *durable*?

'When was this, Mr Henderson?' This was from Shepherd.

'Um, about ten-thirty.'

'And when did you return?'

'About three-thirty.' He looked at his wife to confirm this. 'In the after—'

Joy's mother interrupted, nodding, and said a little too brightly, 'Yes, that's right. In plenty of time to do the milking. After you killed . . .' her hand fluttered to her mouth before she laughed nervously, 'a chook for tea.' And she waved her arm at the table where her children were seated in front of roast Ruth.

'I see.' Sergeant Bell looked at Shepherd to make sure he'd written this down. Shepherd gave a quick upward nod. 'And you didn't see anything suspicious? A stranger? A vehicle you didn't recognise? Anything at all?'

'That's right. I mean, no, I didn't.' Her father frowned, looked up at the blue wall-hanging and then quickly looked back at Sergeant Bell. 'Wait a minute. I did. I saw a blue car. Well, a dark car, driving away from the Boscombes towards town. But I don't know if it came out of their driveway or not.'

Her father couldn't give them any more details about the car. He didn't know if there had been anyone beside the driver and he hadn't noticed the registration number.

'Not even the first letter, George?'

'Sorry, Ron.' He shook his head. 'I didn't expect anyone to be asking me about it.'

'Righteo, then, let's just take a look at your tractor. Purely for elimination purposes. And I want to have a quick chat with you outside, George, just the two of us.'

'Of course, of course.' Her father smiled and pushed in his chair, making it scream on the lino. The rest of his family, including Joy's mother, jumped.

The eels began squirming in Joy's stomach. Surely Sergeant Bell didn't think her father had stolen Wendy? Maybe Bell thought that her father had seen something, but didn't want to say so in front of his family? That was a distinct possibility. But surely if he'd seen anything, he'd have come thundering in quick smart and rung the police.

She wondered if Bell was looking around the shed for clues, and she remembered the axe-head her father had been cleaning earlier in the day. *This looks newly cleaned, George. Why is that?* And then, Joy thought with a thud, there was the van that Mark had washed, inside and out. But that had nothing to do with anything because her father said he'd taken the tractor.

She pictured Bell and Shepherd scouring the shed looking for clues. And stopping in front of the chest where her father kept his father's tools — the chest that was, Joy realised with a terrible shudder, easily big enough to hold the body of a nine-year-old girl. Joy couldn't get rid of the idea that Sergeant Bell thought her father had stolen Wendy. That he was going to accuse her father of having driven his newly washed van (not his tractor, as he'd said) down the Boscombe driveway (not the tractor lane, as he'd said) and seen Wendy doing something sinful, lost his temper with her, and chopped off her head with his glistening axe (newly cleaned after he'd used it to kill the Ruth they were eating). Or that he'd tied up Wendy and dumped her in the dairy, where, as he himself had pointed out — twice in less than five minutes — she could be screaming in vain.

But that was ridiculous. Bell knew that her father would never do any of those things; that if he'd gone to visit the Boscombes and seen Wendy playing with her oh-so-many dolls, he would have pulled over, certainly, but only to smile and say something kind that would make her giggle. That was the man Sergeant Bell knew.

Nervously, she pushed her hands under her thighs, the thighs that until last night were soft and smooth. Her face burnt with shame as she wondered exactly how angry her father would have to be to kill a child.

'Joy!' her mother's voice cut in. 'Detective Shepherd asked you a question.'

Her tongue slapped against the roof of her mouth.

'Actually, Mrs Henderson, I'm not a detec— Ah, never mind.' He looked at Joy and smiled. 'Now, you must know Wendy from school. Can you tell me about her?'

'She lives near here. Um . . . She had a half-sister who has a baby.'

Why on earth had she said that? Wendy's half-sister and her baby had nothing to do with anything.

He nodded. 'Oh. I see.' Now he paused. '"Had", you say?'

'Pardon?'

'You said Wendy *had* a half-sister? Why past tense?'

'I . . . I don't know.'

Shepherd stopped writing in his little police notebook and looked at her. And Joy saw the silence throbbing again, but this time it was bright pink. 'I guess because I don't go to that school anymore.'

What were her father and Sergeant Bell talking about? And why *had* she used the past tense? She just couldn't think straight while Bell was outside with her father.

'And did you play with her at school?'

'Kind of. There were only five girls at school. He's not arresting my father, is he?'

Joy had no idea how people were arrested, except for what she'd read in adventure books, where on the last page dozens of police suddenly arrived to take away the smugglers or jewel thieves who'd been tricked by the children. And while they were bundled into police vans, the children were praised and given scones piled high with strawberry jam and lashings of whipped cream.

'No, no. You don't need to worry about that,' Shepherd said, but kept writing.

Joy knew that he thought she was stupid. He didn't ask her any more questions, but went into the good room, and they all looked at one another as they heard him go into her parents' room. When he came back, he poked his head into Joy and Ruth's room, then walked through the kitchen towards the back door. Joy's mother began wiping the bench furiously as if, thought Joy, she was cleaning off drops of Wendy's blood. The children watched, exchanging scared glances.

They heard Shepherd go into Mark's room, then her mother's workroom, the bathroom, the laundry, and even the toilet. Joy heard him pull back the plastic shower curtain in the bathroom, open the cupboard filled with wreath bases in the workroom, and open the cupboard in the laundry, where they kept the layers of waxed eggs covered with oats.

He was being ridiculous if he thought her father had hidden Wendy in any of those places. Besides, her father had not stolen or killed Wendy. He was well known for being an upright pillar of the community, as well as the longest-standing Elder of the Church.

Finally, the kitchen door opened and the three men came back in. Joy looked up quickly. So her father had not been dragged away to jail.

'Right, thanks, George,' said Bell, smiling. 'I'll see you at Church on Sunday.'

'Yes,' said Joy's father. 'I'll just finish my tea, then I'll go round to Neil and Vi's to pray with them.'

Bell nodded his farewell to Joy's mother. 'Mrs Henderson. Don't worry, I'm sure we'll find Wendy safe and sound.' He turned to the table. 'And you children be careful.'

Her father walked Bell and Shepherd out to their car. When he sat back down at the table, he said, 'We must pray for Wendy and her parents.'

Joy nodded. She had already prayed for Wendy at least twenty times.

No one said anything, and they finished their meal, including the cold masses of gravy, in silence.

Joy watched her father carefully as he walked out of the kitchen with his Bible in hand, on his way to the Boscombes. He looked unsettled, troubled.

When Joy and Ruth were talking about it later, in the dark of the night, Ruth whispered, 'Do you want to know what I think? I think he's responsible for what happened to Wendy.' And, slowly and miserably, Joy nodded in agreement.

In the middle of the night, her dream woke her up, frightening her with its sense of dread. Wendy's dolls had been lying in the driveway, the moon shining down on the backs of their heads. Then, in unison, they rolled over in the mud, so their faces were looking into the sky, then, still in unison, they opened their eyes in their porcelain faces, sat up straight and held out their arms. As plastic tears rolled out of their plastic eyes, one of them started singing 'Wendeeeee, Wendeeeee, where are you? Come back,' then one by one they joined in, singing it as a round, each one starting after the previous one had sung 'Wendeeeee', their thin plastic voices disappearing into the grey rain.

But Wendy did not answer. She did not run down the driveway, scoop them into her arms, wipe away their plastic tears and tut-tut at the mud on their beautiful dresses and porcelain faces. And when the last one finished singing 'Come back', they closed their eyes, lay back and rolled over so they were once more lying face down in the cold muddy gravel of the driveway where Wendy's mother had found them.

Joy was shivering. She reached under her pillow to let the dictionary's black velvet words tickle her fingers. But the words that slid out were *death*, *mud* and *murder*, and they pricked her fingers like hot needles. She pulled her hand out quickly, closed it into a fist and pressed it against her cheek.

'Poor Wendy,' whispered Ruth in her ear. 'We need to pray for her.'

Joy closed her eyes and prayed harder than she ever had in her life. But she was still miserable and afraid.

43

JOY AND SHEPHERD

February 1983

> HENDERSON, George. Loved brother of Bill (dec.), brother-in-law of Rose, loving uncle to Sarah and James. We shall always remember the laughs we had together, the songs you sang for us, the joys we shared. 'Surely goodness and mercy shall follow me all the days of my life: and I will dwell in the house of the Lord forever.'

I wipe my damp forehead. The heat in the kitchen is stifling, and the eels haven't let up. I have to stay in control and concentrate. Concentrate.

Constable Shepherd (or whatever the hell he is these days) has been to the bedroom, seen my dead father, and is now taking notes while I explain, in a distraught voice, what happened.

'I was taking him his painkillers, Detective.' I hold out my blue-stained palm.

'Senior Constable, actually.'

As if I care. As if I'm going to make a mental note to carefully address him by his proper rank.

'I could tell he wasn't breathing, and I think I dropped his glass of Passiona. He loves Passiona, Detective.' I take in a huge gasp of air. 'Sorry. *Loved.*'

There's no need to tell him I went looking for Ruth, so I say that when I noticed the swollen lips, I pulled back the blankets, and . . . I sob again. 'I ran out of the bedroom because I was going to vomit.'

Shepherd is scribbling frantically. 'And after you ran out of the bedroom?'

'I rang Vicki. No, I rang the hospital, *then* I rang Vicki.'

We're sitting at the kitchen table. Shepherd is at the head, where my father always sat, while Vicki and I are next to each other, across from where the wall-hanging was. Vicki has one of her big sweating hands clasped over mine on the tabletop. It's like my hands are buried under a pile of warm eel stew.

Anyway, she nods in agreement with me. 'She did indeed.'

'You didn't ring the police? Because of . . . the belt.' His voice is so deliberately neutral that I can taste buff-coloured manila folders. He's focusing on his notebook, so I take a closer look at him. Early forties, I'm guessing. Nondescript. Hair slightly receding, shirt slightly tight across his lower stomach.

He hasn't said so, of course, but I can tell he's got me in his sights. 'I suppose I should have, but . . . I don't know. My father was dead, so I thought I was supposed to ring a doctor. But that doesn't make sense, does it?'

'Oh, but it does, love. Of course it does.' Vicki smiles and her free hand pats our mess of sweaty ones on the table. As a wave of nausea sweeps over me I throw her a grateful look and pull out one hand to wipe away a tear.

'Well,' says Shepherd, 'it's hard to know what to do in such circumstances.'

Is he trying to lull me into a false sense of complacency? As I lower my hand from my tear-streaked cheek, Vicki grabs at it and pulls it back down to the table. Trapped again.

'I always left the door open so I could hear him moaning or calling out for help.' It isn't perhaps the right time to say this, but it's done now. And at least he's got the picture that I'm a caring and responsible person, as well as understandably confused.

'There's a missing sister, too,' says Vicki with deep concern in her voice.

'What?' says Shepherd quickly.

Oh Jesus. Now I have to explain about Ruth. I should never have mentioned her to Vicki.

'When I arrived,' Vicki continues, conveniently forgetting that I'm the one being questioned, 'poor Joy said she hadn't seen her sister Ruth all morning. She's disappeared, gone.'

'Your sister was here but you haven't seen her all morning?'

I decide to just nod my head. It's too difficult, too messy, too strange. My father confessed to murder and now he's dead, Wendy's doll's head is waiting impatiently in the chest, and Ruth's gone. I can't possibly explain everything to them. Especially when it's so stinking hot. I have to think. I have to make sure I do everything properly if there's to be any justice.

'Don't worry, love,' Vicki says in the voice I suspect she uses when she tells someone they're terminally ill. 'I'm sure she'll be fine.'

Shepherd ignores her. 'Tell me about your sister's relationship with your father.' He's speaking gently, to make me feel comfortable.

I pause. This is a delicate balancing act.

'Well, I haven't been here for years. I've been overseas.'

'Yes, she has,' says Vicki, like a faithful Irish setter.

Shepherd opens his eyes wide in Vicki's direction and holds up his left hand in a stop signal. Vicki beams at him. He looks back at me and waits. I know this strategy. But I'm not playing his games. I've got my own to play.

The silence continues for a few seconds. 'What about when you were children?' he says. Round one to me, then.

'Well, my father . . . loved Ruth.' That's enough for now.

Eventually I'll have to tell him the whole story.

But not yet.

44

GEORGE AND GWEN

June 1948

Mark was almost four before Gwen was sure that she was expecting again. Marilyn, Arnold's wife, asked her if she was seeing Dr Merriweather, the new doctor, who was excellent. When Gwen told her that she hadn't seen any doctor, Marilyn gently explained that these days some people thought expectant mothers were irresponsible if they didn't. Doctors had learnt so much about how to keep mothers and babies alive if something went wrong. Arnold added, 'My bet is that you've got a beautiful baby girl in there. So you wouldn't want anything to go wrong, would you?'

'Nothing's going to go wrong, Arnold,' Gwen smiled, but all she could think about was how much a doctor would charge. The vet's bills were bad enough. And she was nervous that George would find out the truth about the poppy seedlings she'd bought. Poppies were the only flowers she hadn't got around to planting until last week. The wholesale nursery had said this particular variety was very robust, and she'd planted seedlings in every bed to find out which soil, sunlight and shade they preferred. She was looking forward to them exploding with colour about a month before the baby was due. At ten shillings per punnet, buying fifty had far exceeded what she normally spent on flowers and plants each month, but she'd written in her accounting book that she'd bought twenty, each one costing just five shillings.

These days George let Gwen manage her own accounts because he was no longer interested in the details of all the orders and the different prices of bases and wire and ribbon and all the other equipment a modern florist needed. Instead, Gwen had to show him the accounting book at the end of each month, and hand over half her profit. She had already worked out how she was going to cover up her — there was only one word for it — lie about the poppy seedlings in the accounting book, so he would never find out if he ever checked her records.

As she entered some slightly adjusted figures for other costs and income, she frowned at her trembling hand. Even if he did discover her lie (which was unlikely), she'd survived his slaps and kicks and punches, even the bangings of her head into the fridge, so she didn't know why she was trembling. The *papaver rhoeas* (she'd started using the botanical names printed on the order forms) would be so vibrant in so many arrangements that she would be able to charge customers a little extra. But not until they flowered. So right now they definitely couldn't afford a doctor.

At tea that night she told George she was expecting again and he stopped chewing on his eel stew. 'We can't afford another baby, Gwen.'

She wanted to explain that she'd charge more for wreaths and other arrangements once the poppies flowered (she never used the botanical names with George) and that because they self-propagated she would never need to buy poppy seedlings again. But somehow the words didn't make it out of her head.

Instead, she told Mark, who was sitting in the chair beside her, that he was going to have a little brother or sister. He cried. These days he cried all the time.

'Shut up. I can't stand it!' yelled George.

Mark jerked his head back at the loud noise and cried more loudly.

'I said. Shut. Up.'

'Mummy!'

George screamed at Gwen, 'Make him shut up, for goodness sake!'

'I can't,' Gwen yelled back. Her heart stopped.

George pushed back his chair and the lino screeched. He grabbed both her wrists and pulled her to her feet, as her cutlery clattered onto the lino.

'George, please, I'm sorry. I'm tired, we're all tired. Mark can't help—'

He let go of one wrist and slapped her face. 'Mummy, Mummy!'

George pushed Gwen away from him and she fell onto the lino. Instinctively, she put a hand to her swollen stomach.

'Don't you dare talk to me like that.' He turned back to Mark and raised his arm. Gwen grabbed one of his legs above his ankle and screamed, 'No, leave him alone!'

Without looking at her, he wrenched his leg out of Gwen's grasp, kicked backwards, and smacked the heel of his shoe into her throat. She fell onto the floor clutching her neck, gasping for breath.

George looked down at her, his chin raised, and in a single chilling moment she realised that her husband chose to exercise control through violence. And that he knew exactly what he was doing.

45

JOY AND RUTH

December 1960

The next day, Bell and Shepherd returned. With a fingerprint kit.

In an official voice, Sergeant Bell informed the family that Wendy had not turned up safe and sound, and there were now 'grave fears for her safety'.

'This is terrible,' Joy's father said. 'But why are you here, Ron?' Joy recognised her father's 'I'm the longest-standing Elder of the Church' voice.

'Purely for elimination purposes, George. Totally routine, I can assure you,' Sergeant Bell said, smiling at her father. But as on the previous night, he declined her mother's offer of tea.

'Are there fingerprints on the dolls? Or the pram?' Mark asked.

'I'm afraid I'm not at liberty to give out any information like that, son,' said Sergeant Bell.

'So you don't have any idea who could have done this, Ron?' Joy's father asked. He had returned to the Boscombes that morning to continue praying with them, and at lunchtime announced to his family that the police were fingerprinting the Boscombes' doors and windows, the letterbox, everything in Wendy's room, and of course the dolls and pram found in the driveway. Joy sensed that he was enjoying the drama of it all, especially his role as the Boscombes' spiritual guide, praying with them to give them strength and courage until Wendy was found.

'If we had any idea who did this, we'd be locking them up, George,' Sergeant Bell said, in such a monotonous {grey corrugated-iron fence} voice that her father just said, 'I see,' and swallowed. Shepherd stepped forward, pointing to the ink pad he'd set up on the table. 'If you could just start with your right hand, please, sir.'

One by one, from oldest to youngest, they each pushed their ten fingers into the inkpad, rolled them onto the corresponding grids on the paper, and gave their 'correct and full name and date of birth', which Shepherd wrote above their fingerprints.

When it was her turn, Joy's hands were trembling. Shepherd held her hand firmly as he rolled it back and forth so the full print was properly transferred onto the paper.

While Shepherd placed the sheets of inked paper into a folder, Sergeant Bell thanked them for their cooperation, and assured them that although there was concern for Wendy's safety, the police were still confident she would be found safe and sound. 'Which,' he added, 'will be more than you'll be able to say about that . . .' he pushed his lips together and glanced at the children, 'that villain, if I ever get my hands on him.'

Villain. What a wonderful word, thought Joy, as an image of a sparkling new roll of barbed wire burst into her head.

Her father nodded vigorously at Bell's words. A little too vigorously, thought Joy.

46

JOY AND SHEPHERD

February 1983

> HENDERSON, George. To our respected and second longest-standing Elder whose dedication and strong conviction showed us how to be true Christians. We will miss your pious voice on Sundays, and your endless devotion to our church and our Lord. Your fellow Elders at Blackhunt Presbyterian Church.

Senior Constable Alex Shepherd could feel the cogs turning in his mind as he assessed the situation. One dead father, strangled with what was probably his own damn belt, one missing daughter, and one allegedly distraught daughter — who put a little too much emphasis on the word 'Ruth' when she said, 'My father loved Ruth.'

He went through the most probable scenarios.

Scenario one: Ruth had strangled her father, then fled, leaving Joy to deal with the fallout.

Scenario two: Joy had strangled her father then killed Ruth, and had got rid of Ruth's body, to make it look like scenario one.

Scenario three (which refused to be ignored): a person or persons unknown had driven to this rundown farm in the middle of the night, abducted one daughter, left the other one sleeping peacefully, and killed a man who, according to Vicki, was going to die within days from a concoction of fatal diseases.

Implausible though it was, scenario three unnerved him. Wendy Boscombe had disappeared not far from here in 1960, and Shepherd remembered that he and Ron had visited scores of farmhouses during the search for her. They'd all been the same — isolated, run down, surrounded by mud, and inhabited by poverty-stricken farmers and their families. Of course, the Hendersons' would have been one of those farmhouses. Back then, twenty-one and cocky, Shepherd was convinced that he and Ron would find Wendy alive and well within hours. When night had closed in, he'd been sure they would find her the following morning. Then the next day. Then the next one, until his cockiness was replaced by despair. More than twenty years later, Wendy had never been found, dead or alive, and no arrest had ever been made.

Shepherd still harboured a thin thread of hope that one day he'd solve Wendy's disappearance, maybe even find her body (because surely there was no hope of finding her alive). But if anyone pulled that thread, they'd discover it was short and brittle. Sometimes he thought Wendy Boscombe's disappearance would be the death of him unless he got out of this god-forsaken place. Just as, he was sure, it had killed Ron eighteen years ago. Ron, first his superior, then his mentor and friend. The friend Shepherd had made a promise to as the machines kept him alive those few days between strokes. A promise to find Wendy Boscombe's murderer. A promise he'd not yet kept.

The station was lonely without Ron. Even after all these years, Shepherd missed him pushing open the door at 8.40 with a grin on his face, or phoning at 8.10 with another damn excuse for being late.

Ron's death had left Blackhunt a one-officer town, and the powers-that-be in faraway Melbourne had decided to leave it like that. The letter Shepherd had received after requesting additional manpower had cited a tight budget and Blackhunt's low crime rate that 'indicates a superior level of community-centred policing of which you and the late Sergeant Bell were rightly proud, but which unfortunately means it is not currently possible to justify . . .' Blah blah blah. Not even a phone call, let alone a visit from the regional office.

And now here he was alone, not far from Wendy's home, faced with George Henderson's murder. He was going to make damn sure he didn't have two unsolved homicides on his record.

There were two important things to note from his preliminary search of the farmhouse. Firstly, there were clothes littered all over the floor of George's bedroom. Had the murderer been looking for something important or valuable, at least to them? Secondly, Ruth — or the person responsible for her disappearance — had gone to great lengths to remove everything she owned. Even her damn toothbrush was gone. What criminal makes a mess of one victim's room, but carefully tidies the room of another one, Shepherd wondered. Unless he — or she — wants to confuse the police. Or unless two people came into the house last night.

Statistically, of course, it was more likely that George Henderson had been murdered by a member of his family. And all Shepherd's instincts brought him back to Joy. Or Ruth. Or both of them.

Nonetheless, he shouldn't and couldn't rule out scenario three. Like everyone around here, the Hendersons never locked their back door, so anyone could have come into the house last night, killed George, killed or abducted Ruth and fled.

But why? The cogs felt like they were in thick black mud.

Driving out here had reminded him of being at the Boscombes the day Wendy disappeared, and how difficult it had been to hear Ron ask them questions that, though aimed at eliminating them as suspects, added to their distress.

Shepherd looked at Joy and knew he would be asking her similar questions. First, he would start with the scene of the crime and work outwards. That meant asking Joy about the clothes lying on the floor in George's room.

'Did you go looking for anything in his room? Before — or after — you realised he died? Was there anything of value in there, that would explain why it looks like someone ransacked it?'

Joy shook her head. 'We were poor. My father had nothing of value that I know of.'

'Maybe something that would have been important to someone? A document, for example, like a letter . . . or a will?'

Joy looked straight back at him — a classic liar's tactic, Shepherd noted — and shook her head again.

'Did Ruth perhaps want something that belonged to your father? Did you ever see her looking for something in his bedroom?'

'All I know is that last night I went to bed just like I have every night since I've been here . . . looking after him. I gave him his medication before I went to bed, and he told me . . .' She dragged out a hand from under Vicki's and clapped it over her mouth.

'What did he tell you?' Shepherd's nerves were on edge. She was about to say something important.

'He told me that he wanted to die.' She pulled her other hand away from Vicki, got up and walked to the sink. Leaning over it, she said, 'You don't need to look for Ruth.'

'Why not?'

'Because she always said she was going to leave after he died. I just didn't realise she meant straight away.'

'So,' Shepherd chose his words carefully, 'you're saying she knew he was dead before she left?'

Joy turned around to face him, closed her eyes and shook her head slightly. Shepherd interpreted it to mean 'I don't know.'

'Was Ruth angry or upset last night?'

Joy took a glass from the cupboard and filled it with water. She spoke carefully. Too damn carefully for Shepherd's liking. 'Our father's very ill. He's dying. Of course Ruth's upset. We're both upset.' She took a sip of water, then looked out of the kitchen window before speaking again. 'I mean, he *was* ill, has . . . died.'

Shepherd watched, slightly disturbed. She almost seemed to be relishing the taste of past tense.

He wrote in his notebook, *JH glad father is dead?*

'Is she what you might call an angry person?'

'What?' She turned from the window and looked at him. 'Oh no, Ruth is definitely not an angry person.'

Shepherd said nothing, waiting. He'd learnt this trick from Ron.

After a few seconds, Joy said, 'You think Ruth killed my father then packed up and left in the middle of the night?' She shook her head rapidly, and burst into tears.

Vicki jumped up and put a large arm around her shoulder, while Shepherd added to his notes. *JH's grief not convincing. Practised liar?*

He looked up to see Joy staring at him, and they locked eyes for a second before he wrote another note.

JH put belt around GH's neck?

47

JOY AND RUTH

December 1960

Before Joy and Mark went to Thursday's Bible Study, their mother gave Mark a shilling, and told them to buy a copy of the *Blackhunt Gazette*. Because of the two public holidays for Christmas and Boxing Day the paper had come out on Wednesday instead of Monday, and she didn't want to make another trip into town.

When they got off the bus, Joy told Mark she'd go to the news agency. Her heart was thumping as she read the headline blaring 'Missing Child Baffles Police'. Despite being overcome with sadness and fear, she couldn't help but notice that the headline was wrong. The police weren't baffled by *Wendy*, they were baffled by what had happened to her. And why on earth couldn't they use her name?

Under the headline was a blurry black-and-white image of Wendy's smiling face, chopped out of the annual school photograph, and enlarged. She was barely recognisable as the nine-year-old girl Joy had seen only a few days ago.

Joy had been so sure that Wendy would be found, mainly because that was what everyone said would happen, even Ruth.

'They'll find her any day now,' Ruth said as Joy lay on her bed at night, unable to sleep, unable to get Wendy's face out of her mind. Last night, after the two policemen had left with their folder full of fingerprints, Joy's mother told her children not to worry about Wendy, that Sergeant Bell would arrive with good news tomorrow because Wendy had probably just wandered off and fallen down a gully. Their father repeated that they were all to pray for Wendy, but Joy hadn't needed her father to remind her. Hadn't she been praying non-stop for her?

Despite everyone's prayers, the newspaper report filling the whole front page made it clear that police were no closer to finding Wendy, with or without the one doll her mother now said was also missing. Wendy had simply disappeared. Apparently lots of people had already come forward, claiming to have seen her in various towns and cities, but, according to the paper, Sergeant Bell was 'confident that none of these sightings warrants further investigation'. He went on to say that 'I, personally, will never give up looking for Wendy until she is found.' Detectives and uniformed police from Melbourne had arrived in Blackhunt and were searching the Boscombe house and farm, walking in rows of four along Wishart Road, the surrounding roads, and the lane that ran down to Kingfisher Primary. They had questioned anyone who'd been out and about that day, and everyone working in the shops and petrol station, but, echoing the headline, they were baffled. Hundreds of locals had joined the search, though not Joy's father, because he was praying with the Boscombes.

Tears trickled from Joy's eyes as she read that 'Police now suspect that the nine-year-old schoolgirl has been abducted'. And that the police and the Boscombes were pleading with the abductor to release Wendy and allow her to come home, to return her safe and sound to her distraught family.

Joy didn't want to keep reading, but when she got to the bottom of the front page and read 'Continued on page 4', she couldn't stop herself from turning to page 4, where she saw, with horror, a large photo of Wendy's dolls lying in the mud where Mrs Boscombe had found them. She shut the paper quickly and handed it to Mark.

Mark read the front page while they walked to Church, but did not turn to page 4. Instead, he said, 'Abducted. Just like that. I don't know what you reckon, but I reckon it's someone from Mildura who . . .'

While Mark put forward a theory as to who and how and why, Joy walked beside him shaking with fear, remembering Ruth's whispered words: 'Our father is responsible for what happened to Wendy.' After a couple of sentences, Mark saw how distressed she was and muttered, 'But I'm probably completely wrong. She'll probably turn up today.' They walked the rest of the way in silence, and Joy knew he wouldn't talk to her about Wendy again.

At the beginning of Bible Study, Mr Jones led them in a prayer asking God in all His mercy to bring Wendy back to her home safe and well, or if 'tragedy has befallen Your child', that she had already been 'gathered by angels and delivered into Your blessèd eternal garden'.

Joy cried silently, and Felicity put her arm around her.

Mr Jones gave them a list of passages from the Bible to read, and stayed with them for the whole time. All the passages spoke about kindness and love and forgiveness and children, and Joy knew Mr Jones had spent time finding these passages. The three of them read in silence, tears dripping from Joy's eyes onto her Bible's thin pink-edged pages. Mr Jones did not ask them to discuss what they had read, and after about half an hour, he suggested they stop reading and spend some time praying.

Joy prayed fervently. *Please, please God, look after Wendy. Please God, please.*

Then Mr Jones said it was time for him to give the benediction. 'May the grace of our Lord Jesus Christ guide and protect His children, especially His beloved child Wendy . . .'

Joy and Felicity burst into tears and Mr Jones patted their shoulders awkwardly. 'Don't worry, girls, I'm sure the police will find Wendy soon. The Lord is protecting her, wherever she is, just as He's protecting you.'

Joy nodded and tried to stop crying. It was all very well for Mr Jones to be sure that God was looking after Wendy, but who was looking after Joy Henderson?

48

JOY AND SHEPHERD

February 1983

> HENDERSON, George. A kind and loving family man and Christian. Always ready with a smile and a joke. One of God's angels in disguise. Condolences to the family. Conrad and Iris Waddell

As he's scrawling in his little policeman's notebook, I realise I'm going to have to tell him about Ruth, otherwise who knows what the hell he'll do? Plus of course I need to tell him about finding Wendy's doll in the chest, but I'm not going to do that yet. The police might say the doll by itself proves nothing, even if it does have my father's fingerprints on it. What Shepherd needs is Wendy's body.

The first problem with telling him about Ruth is that we don't talk about Ruth's accident. In fact, I've never discussed Ruth or her accident with anyone, except once with my mother when I was eleven. She was feeding the chooks — the Ruths — and I was standing behind the gate, as I'd been told to, when I blurted out the question she must have known I was going to ask one day. And so she answered me. In short, tight sentences that I've never forgotten.

'It' had happened before I was born. 'It' had been a terrible accident, and nothing could be done, then or now. The best thing to do, she'd said, the only thing to do, was to carry on as if 'it' had never happened. And that meant never asking her about it again, and never mentioning it to anyone, inside the family or out.

Then she'd walked away, pushing the wheelbarrow ahead of her. Down to the bottom of the bull paddock, digging out thistles with a mattock. Until just before tea, she was a bobbing blotch of blue and dark green, out of reach. Sometimes completely out of sight when the angle of the grey rain was just so.

So, as instructed, I pretended that the accident had never happened. I never asked any more questions, and never mentioned it again. Just like everyone else. I pretended that Ruth was a normal sister, but I lost count of how many times I wondered why God would let such a terrible thing happen to her.

And here I am now, with Vicki's great walloping body draped all over me, while Shepherd's waiting for me to confess to killing my father. I can sense he's desperate. Not that it matters. Because soon it will all be over.

I look up and he's watching me. I return his gaze, like any innocent person would. He scribbles some more.

'You think Ruth killed my father,' I'm careful to stay calm, 'then packed up and left in the middle of the night?' The eels are writhing, and I shake my head. And then the tears come. Good old Vicki throws an arm around me, while Shepherd studies me closely.

The sweat is dripping off me and I uncurl myself from Vicki and walk over to switch on the fan. 'Everyone in the area loves him.'

I'm assuming that Shepherd knows that my father is — was — the region's pillar extraordinaire, so there's no need to go into detail. I turn to face him again and let more tears slip out of my eyes.

Vicki leans over to him and speaks quietly, but of course I hear every word. 'Do you have to do this now? I mean, I know you need to find out what happened, but she's obviously distraught.'

He's clearly infuriated with Vicki, and there doesn't seem to be much love lost between them. That's good.

He says to no one in particular, therefore to both of us, 'The first twelve hours are the most crucial, even if they are the most painful.' Then, obviously to me, 'So . . . Ruth? Do you think she would be capable of hurting someone — specifically, your father?' I walk back to the table because I want to be close to this man.

I want to smell his desperation, so I can stay in control. I can't tell him about the doll's head — not yet, anyway. One thing at a time. Vicki follows me, and we both sit down. Shepherd leans toward me and raises his eyebrows a little, waiting for me to answer.

'Believe me, Detective,' I have mastered my quivering voice now, 'Ruth is definitely not capable of hurting anyone, including my father.'

Of course, I do not tell him about the argument we had. Or that Ruth was hysterical when I stormed out of the kitchen to go to bed last night. Or that as I shut my bedroom door she threatened to kill our now-dead father.

49

GWEN AND GEORGE

December 1948

Just before she fell down the steps and hit the cracked path, Gwen noticed the first bright-red slivers of hundreds of poppy heads about to explode into flowers. Each one was worth an extra half shilling in a posy or wreath.

When she hit the path, hundreds of slivers of bright-red pain shot through her.

Before she opened her eyes, the smell of the hospital alerted her. Both hands flew to her stomach, and she breathed out with relief when she felt the bulge still enormous and tight.

'Mrs Henderson?'

Gwen kept her eyes shut. She was going to pretend to be asleep until time wound itself back to before the fall. Before she became pregnant with this baby. Before she became pregnant with Mark. Before she walked down the aisle in that borrowed dress. Before the end of that dance. And then, right there, at that point, she was just going to push time a little to the left. *No, thank you*, she was going to say, and then she was going to walk back to Jean and her friends huddled together, watching and giggling.

'Mrs Henderson, are you awake?'

She swallowed and opened her eyes a little. A white chook, big-busted and bossy-looking, was frowning down at her. Gwen sighed, and as she breathed in, the baby kicked and a shard of pain crackled through her body, making her wince and open her eyes wide.

The nurse smiled, sat down on the chair and took Gwen's hand. 'You're in hospital, Mrs Henderson. You fell. Do you remember? Down the back steps at your home. Your husband found you and called the doctor.' Gwen wondered why she was speaking to her as if she was a deaf child. 'You're going to be alright.'

Suddenly Gwen remembered what had happened. 'Mark? What's happened to Mark?'

'Mark's fine. It's not him you need worry about.' Her voice changed. 'Mrs Henderson, I have good news and unfortunately some . . . very sad news.'

'What?' Gwen's voice trembled like the *gypsophila paniculata* that she had just started using in wedding bouquets. It grew so freely, robustly self-seeding like the poppies would, and produced the most delicate little white puffs of flowers, which hovered in the air like hummingbirds. No wonder every bride was asking for baby's breath now. 'The baby's still alive, I felt him kicking.'

The nurse was kind, but her words were like rose thorns. Gwen did not understand the medical terms, but 'one tiny dear soul', along with 'a sad difficult labour ahead', were all too clear.

By the time the nurse left the room, Gwen had all but forgotten the 'good' news.

50

JOY AND RUTH

December 1960

Mark handed over the paper to their mother, and she read the front page and sighed. 'Poor Wendy. I'm sure they'll find her soon. I'm sure she'll be safe and well.'

Joy nodded miserably, as her mother turned to the death notices and said quietly, 'Let's hope there's a good one today.'

Later that afternoon, when Joy was scrubbing the laundry trough, she heard a car come down the driveway, and opened the back door to find Miss Boyle standing there.

Miss Boyle had lived with her bachelor uncle for years (Joy had no idea how many, but because Miss Boyle was so old it was probably a hundred) before he had tragically died (also, Joy assumed, many years ago). Even though it was a tragedy, Miss Boyle happily related the story of his death whenever she had the chance, always ending it with, 'But the dear man left behind a lovely life insurance policy, so my money worries are over.'

Joy liked Miss Boyle, but over the years, when she'd been sitting silently listening to people who'd forgotten she was even there, she heard nasty rumours about Miss Boyle and her uncle. That her family had sent her away to live with him because she'd refused to marry any suitable suitors; that she was his daughter from a sinful woman who had died; that she was (and here the rumourmonger would look this way and that way and then whisper) 'nothing but a whore'. It seemed each new rumour was nastier than the last one. Neither Ruth nor Joy knew what a 'hoar' was and nor could they find the word in the little green dictionary, but they did know it must be something terrible.

Whichever rumour was or was not true, the uncle had indeed left his farm and his life insurance policy to Miss Boyle. Instead of selling up and moving back to the city, where she'd grown up, she'd sold the cows her uncle had milked every single day of his life (even his last one) and had the rusty dairy pulled down. Then she'd paid men to put up fences to divide her paddocks into much smaller paddocks, each separated by a narrow strip of no-man's land, and install new easy-swing gates. According to Joy's father, 'the final insult' was a fancy brass nameplate she'd attached to her front fence declaring to visitors that they had arrived at Green Haven Fields. The following week, an advertisement had appeared in the *Blackhunt Gazette*, saying that anyone could, for a 'very reasonable rate', now keep their bull in one of the small paddocks at Green Haven Fields.

Joy could imagine how tight and bitter her father's voice was when he'd read the advertisement to her mother. But despite the indignation, many farmers, including Joy's father, paid that very reasonable rate to keep their bull at Green Haven Fields, because it meant they could now use their bull paddock for cows. Joy thought it was a clever idea because all Miss Boyle had to do was collect rent and keep the fences and gates in good condition, while each farmer paid just one-sixth of the cost of leasing a whole paddock while gaining back one whole paddock on their own farm.

However, according to her father, Miss Boyle lived 'a little too handsomely, if you ask me' and should go back to the city, where she could buy all the fancy-dancy clothes and hats she wanted and not wave her lucky money in their faces every day like it was all due to her brains and not her uncle's hard work and misplaced generosity. According to her father, all that money could be used by missionaries to convert heathens, and someone (presumably a man) should turn Green Haven Fields back into a real farm again because it wasn't right for a spinster to have 'men come and go all week'.

Joy looked forward to Miss Boyle's irregular visits to collect her parents' lease money. She'd arrive unannounced, never on the same day or at the same time, and always with a story to tell about someone. She seemed to be completely oblivious of God's rules about swearing, blaspheming, alcohol and women being demure {a white handkerchief neatly pressed into a small square}, even in front of Joy's father. And of course, when she swore or blasphemed or said something inappropriate, Joy's father just smiled and joked and was as nice as lemon meringue pie to her.

If Miss Boyle didn't arrive with half a bottle of red wine ('Thought we could knock this off together, Gwenny?'), she'd content herself with a cup of tea and a sultana slice. She'd sit in Joy's father's upholstered chair at the Laminex table and begin to tell one of her stories — about someone's hair turning a 'bloody awful green' after she asked the hairdresser to make it blonde, or how so-and-so had lost their goddamn wallet that had been stuffed with pound notes for his son's twenty-first birthday present — 'Or so he says, but we all know, don't we, George, where the slimy bastard would have been all afternoon?', or how the grandson of what's-his-name had had a car crash, run into a damn tree up on Ripplecreek Road, so he couldn't blame anyone else this time, but the stinking insurance company refused to pay out because they claimed he wasn't wearing his glasses. 'What I want to know is, how the hell would they know if he was wearing his bloody glasses or not? They wouldn't, would they? I mean, let's face it, he probably wasn't,' she snorted with laughter, 'cos he doesn't reckon he's got a chance in hell of pulling a girl if he has to wear those milk bottles, but how would they know, eh? Speaking of bottles, who's going to help me finish this one?' And she'd merrily wave the wine bottle.

Joy's mother's eyebrows would remain steadfastly raised throughout, a smile fixed on her face, and at the end of each story, she'd let out an 'Aa-ha', which Joy thought Miss Boyle was meant to interpret as a laugh. Joy thought her stories were always funny, even if she did swear and blaspheme her way through them.

Joy's parents, of course, politely refused the wine, because it was one of the Devil's temptations. 'Oh, not tonight, thanks, Miss Boyle [they never called her by any other name, to remind her, Joy assumed, that she was supposed to be married, supposed to be normal, supposed to move back to the city and fade into obscurity], I'm afraid we've just had a huge dessert,' 'Oh, my stomach's just not feeling the best after that stew,' 'We're just about to head into town, but you go right ahead, Miss Boyle.'

Miss Boyle would smile and pass the bottle to Joy's mother, who could do nothing but politely fill a glass for their bull's landlady, as her father, smiling politely, stirred his cup of tea loudly.

Joy never knew if Miss Boyle behaved this way in front of her parents because she didn't know how much it offended them, or precisely because she did know. But Joy enjoyed Miss Boyle's stories immensely, along with her open, breezy ways. The house was more cheerful and alive while Miss Boyle was there.

But today, she only wanted to talk about Wendy's disappearance. 'Gwenny, are you as speechless with fear and sadness for the poor girl as I am? And her parents — what must they be going through? I haven't had the heart to go round and ask them for rent money. I mean, how could I? I think I'd break down on the doorstep, and then they'd be comforting me, wouldn't they? It's too, too sad, isn't it? Just a cup of tea, this morning, thanks Gwenny. And Ron Bell is beside himself, while the young whippersnapper he's got with him makes you depressed just looking at him. Between you and me, I'm wondering if *he* didn't have something to do with the poor girl's disappearance. I mean, nothing like this ever happened till he arrived, did it, and don't you think he has a face like a three-horned bull that can't find a cow? Apparently he's obsessed with some sort of strange jigsaw puzzle. Graeme Whittaker saw him leaning over it in the station a few weeks back when he took his son in to get his Ls, and the man was damning this and damning that, like the sun hadn't come up that day. Very suspicious, I think. And he doesn't fit in exactly, does he? Apart from anything, he should be out catching Wendy's murderer, not playing with puzzles. Do you think there's something wrong with him? True as God, I'm just speechless about the whole thing, Gwenny.'

Despite feeling ill about Wendy, Joy found herself smiling. 'Speechless'? The woman never stopped talking. And despite asking 'Gwenny' all of those questions, it was clear she didn't want Joy's mother to actually answer any of them.

But more than anything, Joy just wanted everyone to stop talking about Wendy Boscombe, because whenever they did, she wanted to curl up in a ball and cry.

Her mother put down a cup of tea in front of Miss Boyle, and shook her head. 'He seemed nice enough when he was here last night.'

'Did he?' She took a sip of her tea and screwed up her face like she'd taken a bite of a lemon. Looking at Joy sitting at the other end of the table, she waved her teaspoon at the sugar bowl just out of her reach. 'Well, that just goes to show you, doesn't it, Gwenny? Anyone who has something to hide can be nice when they want to be, eh?'

As Joy got up and handed the sugar bowl to Miss Boyle, she wondered what Shepherd could possibly be hiding. And Miss Boyle too, for that matter.

51

JOY AND SHEPHERD

February 1983

> HENDERSON, George. The Lord is my shepherd; I shall not want. He maketh me to lie down in green pastures: he leadeth me beside the still waters. He restoreth my soul. Though I walk through the valley of the shadow of death, I will fear no evil. Condolences to the family, Reverend Alistair Braithwaite

'So, can you tell me who might have wanted to kill your father?'

Joy shook her head. 'I told you, I haven't lived here for years. And everyone for miles around loved him.'

'They did,' Vicki piped up. 'It's going to be a large and very sad funeral.'

Shepherd ignored her. He wished he'd sent her back to town, but when he'd arrived at the farm she'd come out to the driveway to have a 'confidential discussion' with him. They'd met once before when Ian Duncan, who he used to play squash with, had also died in his bed. His poor wife had called Shepherd when she'd found him and even though there were no suspicious circumstances, he'd said he'd come out, and told Vera to call Ian's doctor. Vicki, along with her grin and overly familiar ways, had arrived not two minutes after Shepherd.

She was harmless but damn annoying. This morning she'd told him she could conduct post-mortems, so it had seemed like a good idea for her to stay. Now he wasn't so sure.

He *was*, however, sure that Joy was no sorrier about her father's death than the cows in the paddock were. Those tears had been pathetic. He was convinced that Joy was adept at lying, but her claim that Ruth was incapable of hurting anyone had the dreaded ring of truth. Given the neatness of the abandoned bedroom, he was pretty sure Ruth *had* fled of her own accord. Still, he would have to find her and get her side of the story.

There would be neighbours to talk to as well. Unfortunately, that meant talking to the Boscombes. He'd leave that for as long as possible.

But all in good time. Right now, he thought that if he played his cards right, Joy would confess. Then he wouldn't even have to question the neighbours. Or search for Ruth — once she heard that her sister had been arrested, she'd be banging at the doors of the station.

Years ago, Ron and he would talk about what it would be like to solve a real crime. Ron would say, 'It's just like doing one of those tricky jigsaw puzzles.' They'd both yearned for a real crime to solve, but every time the door of the station opened, it was another bored parent with another pimply teenager booked in for their L-plates. When Shepherd had been there three months, Ron arrived late, as usual, and emptied the contents of a rectangular white box onto the spare desk. Shepherd picked up the box and read '1000-Piece jigsaw puzzle for Geniuses. Contents: 1100 Double-sided Pieces.'

'Thought we'd practise our problem-solving skills,' Ron said, spreading out the 1100 pieces with gusto. 'We've got to work out which pieces we need and which ones are red herrings and can be thrown away. Every piece has two sides, and there's no picture on the lid to help us. Let's get cracking.'

For weeks they'd worked on that damn jigsaw puzzle in between licence tests and the occasional bingle or Saturday-night burn-out. After a few days Shepherd was frustrated, but Ron wouldn't let him give up. 'You wouldn't give up halfway through a criminal investigation, son. Who knows when we'll have a real crime to solve, only to find our brains have become as hard and sticky as the clay in a dried-up dam, and just as full of rubbish?'

Then, on the morning of 30 December 1960, three days after Wendy disappeared, Shepherd arrived at the station to find Ron there early for the first and last time, and the top of the spare desk clean. Neither of them ever mentioned the puzzle again.

Now Shepherd had to arrange the pieces of a different puzzle. George's pieces. Joy's pieces. Ruth's pieces. He had met George only a few times (church and bowls and old-time dances not being Shepherd's style), knew that he and Ron would have interviewed him after Wendy had gone missing, and that everyone — then and now — thought that George Henderson was a model citizen. The last time Shepherd had spoken to Neil Boscombe, George had still been regularly visiting Neil and Vi to pray for Wendy. Shepherd was glad he didn't know George well, so he could remain impartial while investigating his death. Joy and Ruth had both left home a long time ago, so he was going to have to collect and examine their very unfamiliar pieces. And he was sure that, just like that puzzle, every damn piece would have at least two sides. He already knew Joy was jealous of her sister and appeared far from upset that her father was dead. Maybe there was a significant event from her childhood that would shine some light on the events of the past twelve hours? Wendy Boscombe's disappearance must have had an effect on Joy, since she'd lived so close to Wendy and was about her age.

Shepherd thought back to Joy's father's persistent praying with the Boscombes.

Or maybe it was all to do with a recent argument she'd had with the deceased, or her sister.

All he had to do was collect the right pieces and put them into place.

When he'd graduated from the academy twenty-four years ago, he'd jumped at the chance to go to Blackhunt. All that space, green rolling hills, and easy-going country people with chooks and pigs and horses and cows and ducks and sheep to keep them busy and content. It would be one long holiday, where everyone knew and liked everyone else, including him.

But people hadn't been so easy-going. Most were scared of losing what little they had, whether they were farmers or the owners of the dozen businesses clustered together in the small town's depressing strip of shops. Everybody relied on good weather (lots of rain in winter and lots of sun in summer) and decent milk prices, but every year the weather and the prices got worse, farmers were paid less and less for their milk, and the price of everything else went up and up.

Shepherd quickly realised he'd never get to know everyone. The town's official population was only 897, but the region's was 10,792, spread across about 4000 square miles. Who could possibly know 10,000 people? A few stood out, for sure. Shopkeepers he bought from; the young lads who'd never pass the test for L-plates no matter how many times they tried; people of note like the rotating mayors and pushy councillors, along with people like George Henderson, who he knew more by reputation — the kind who joined every committee and liked reading their name in the local paper.

But most farmers and their families kept their personal difficulties to themselves and pretended not to see those of others. Whatever few pennies were not swallowed up by bills were savagely saved in readiness for the next disaster. If it wasn't the cost of maintaining miles of fencing on each farm, it was vet bills, and the price of food, and leaking rooves, and another baby, and the constant rain, and, and, and. Shepherd quickly stopped asking 'How are things?'

Despite the fact that every story he'd heard about country living didn't seem at all relevant in Blackhunt, in the early days Shepherd had enjoyed the easy policing and the community's unquestioning respect, and his sergeant, who insisted that he drop the 'sir' and call him Ron unless there were others around.

And then Wendy Boscombe disappeared, and things weren't so easy.

Twenty-plus years had gone by, and Wendy was still missing, presumed murdered. The locals' confidence in him and Ron had dwindled and although they kept searching, they never found any new leads or clues that could explain what had happened to Wendy. Despite his calm exterior, Shepherd felt more and more useless as the years passed. Just a few months ago, as he'd been idly flicking through her files again, he'd realised with a pang of horror that he too was caught in whatever had trapped the town and its surrounding farms in misery and despair.

And here he was now, in a farmhouse near the Boscombes' place, where another serious crime had taken place. The blood in his veins was heating up. Joy Henderson was definitely hiding something. But how much — and what? He could sense her fear, and was suspicious of how alert she was. But he wasn't going to try to get a confession out of her just yet. He needed to get things straight, ask some more questions, put some more pieces of the puzzle together.

'Okay, Miss Henderson, I think I have everything I need from you for the moment.' He snapped shut his notebook and gave her the smile Ron had perfected. Reassuring but authoritative. The 'you'll be alright, if I find out what I want to know' smile. 'I'll go and question the neighbours, see if they saw or heard anything, then I'll get back to you.'

He turned to Vicki, wanting to make sure that she didn't stay with Joy. 'Right, Doctor, I'm sure you've done everything you can here. Must have a clinic full of patients waiting for you.'

Vicki took the hint and jumped up too.

As Joy thanked them through what Shepherd was sure were more crocodile tears, he noticed that her forehead was sweaty and her hands were shaking.

Good, he thought. I have her right where I want her.

52

JOY AND RUTH

December 1960

Joy was scared. For Wendy. For her father. For herself. She wished the long holidays were over and she was at high school, away from her father's anger and endless discussions about Wendy Boscombe and the whole terrible thing.

'I know you're worried about Wendy,' said Ruth. 'But I'm sure everything will be fine.'

'Do you think they'll find her?' Joy asked.

'I don't know,' said Ruth, frowning. Then she smiled at Joy and said in a much lighter voice, 'But remember, even when someone is dead on Earth, they're alive in Heaven. Just like Jesus. So being dead is actually the best thing that can happen to a Christian. Don't you think?'

'I don't know. I . . .'

'Well, I'll tell you something *I* know — you can't mope around like this, thinking about nothing but Wendy, Wendy, Wendy. Let's talk about happy things. Guess what the most wonderful thing in Heaven is?' Ruth didn't even wait for Joy to try to answer. 'It's The Infinite Library.'

Joy's frown disappeared. 'The Infinite Library?'

Ruth was smiling now, and her smile was so wide that her birthmark looked like a huge purple balloon about to explode. 'It's the most amazing place on Earth — I mean, Heaven — because it has every book that has ever been written, is being written, and ever will be written for all of eternity. The walls are covered in bookshelves that grow longer and higher every day, and God has to keep adding new rooms.'

Joy felt her shoulders relax as she breathed in Ruth's words. She pictured The Infinite Library with its endless mahogany shelves and corridors and wings and storeys — and stories, she thought with a smile.

Every book ever written? That meant it would have the very first book ever written. She wondered what it was called. And what it looked like, what it was made of, and if it was in English? And if it wasn't in English, how would she be able to read it when she got to Heaven? Surely God would make sure that you could read every language once you got to Heaven, so everyone could read every book, including that very first one. It would be kept locked in a special cabinet with guards standing beside it, proudly protecting it for eternity. But no, there wouldn't be any guards *proudly* protecting it because there was no pride in Heaven, since it was one of the Seven Deadly Sins. And of course you wouldn't even need guards because no one would steal anything in Heaven. There would be a long queue of people politely lining up to look at the very first ever book, because surely you couldn't borrow it, even in Heaven where everything was perfect. There would be hundreds, thousands, millions of people queuing to see such an important book. And another line of millions of people waiting to read the first ever Bible. And the first encyclopaedia. And — Joy sighed at this delicious thought — the first dictionary.

'Yes,' continued Ruth. 'And you can find any book you want at any time because right at the front of The Infinite Library is The Infinite Catalogue.'

Joy sighed again. Because of her accident, Ruth had never been able to go to the shops to get Joy a birthday or Christmas present, but this year she had given Joy the best present in the world . . . the knowledge that one day, after Joy died, she would be able to visit The Infinite Library. If she made it to Heaven.

And this meant that right now, this very second, Wendy Boscombe might be in The Infinite Library, reading whatever book she wanted to.

53

JOY AND SHEPHERD

February 1983

> HENDERSON, George. A warm and hard-working man. Sincere condolences to the family. Graeme Plummer and family

Shepherd was sitting on a chintz-upholstered lounge chair sipping from the cup of tea Barbara Larsen had made for him, thinking that you couldn't go anywhere round here without having a damn cup of tea, no matter how hot it was outside. And this dark little lounge room was even more stifling than the Henderson kitchen. He was sure he and Ron would have interviewed the Larsens after Wendy's disappearance, but he didn't remember that encounter any more than any of the others, so he made a mental note to check the files later.

Colin Larsen was sitting on a dining chair he'd turned to face Shepherd, his right leg jiggling up and down as his eyes flitted back and forth to a dark tabby cat asleep on a pile of rags next to the fireplace. Shepherd had already made Barbara bristle by asking if there was a Mr Larsen. When she said tightly, 'Not anymore,' he decided to keep her on side and ask Vicki about Colin's condition later (it seemed that every home in the damn district had their own strange jigsaw puzzle).

For now, he was hoping to collect from the Larsens another piece of the Henderson puzzle. Joy, he knew, was withholding something — or a lot of somethings — and the Larsens might be able to give him one or two of them, particularly about missing Ruth. And while Shepherd suspected Joy had put that belt — now sitting on his passenger seat in an evidence bag — around her father's neck, suspicion wasn't evidence. 'Cross your I's, and dot your T's,' Ron had always said, as if it was funny, while he was leaning over Shepherd's shoulder to make sure he was filling out the hundredth driver's licence form properly. So as soon as he got back to the station, Shepherd was going to dust the belt for fingerprints, though he suspected that whoever had used it to squeeze the life out of George Henderson would have made sure not to leave any. He'd dust the bottles of pills, too — also sitting on the passenger seat in an evidence bag. It would take a few days for the fingerprint bureau in Melbourne to get back to him, and in the meantime he was hoping to put together enough other pieces to arrest the guilty party.

'So he finally died?' Barbara sighed, perhaps a tad melodramatically. 'Poor George. I shouldn't say this, but I suppose Joy will be relieved. Their relationship was . . . difficult.'

'Really?' said Shepherd. He put the cup of tea down on the little polished wood table beside the chintz chair, pulled out his notebook and made a quick note while Mrs Larsen kept talking.

'I guess it doesn't matter now. Eventually Joy escaped, of course. To be honest, I wonder why she came back.'

She glanced at Colin. His leg was still jiggling up and down, and he was still watching the cat who was audibly wheezing.

Shepherd underlined the word 'escaped' in his notes, and looked up with his neutral face on, imagining Ron's advice. *Don't say anything just yet, son. She'll keep talking. A good cop is a good listener. A silent listener.*

'Silent listener.' Why did that ring a bell? And why was it ringing right now?

'He was a lovely man. To everyone, as I'm sure you know.'

Shepherd nodded. *Yet someone murdered him.* 'So why did Joy have to . . .' Shepherd made a point of glancing at his notes, 'I think the word you used was "escape"?'

'Oh,' said Barbara, looking a little flustered. 'I'm sure I don't know.'

I'm sure you do. Shepherd smiled and waited.

'Well, I don't want to speak ill of the dead,' Barbara continued.

'Of course not.'

'And I never heard or saw anything. It was just an impression really. His children were so quiet, so . . . obedient. Even when they were teenagers.' She took a sip of her tea and Shepherd waited. 'Which was strange, even back then.'

Colin got up from his chair, knelt down next to the cat, and stroked its head slowly.

'Lots of children are shy,' Shepherd said. It was time to up the ante a little. 'Now . . . you said George was a lovely man . . . to everyone.' He took a sip of tea, wishing it was lemon cordial and ice cubes.

'Oh, yes. He was.'

'He was,' echoed Colin. 'But not to his children.' The cat lifted its chin, and Colin's hand slid around to scratch its neck. Shepherd was reminded of the belt around George's neck, and wondered if Colin was always so tender.

'What do you mean, Colin?'

Colin looked from side to side as if to make sure no one else was listening, while he stroked the cat down the length of its old back. 'He was nasty.'

'Colin!' said Barbara. 'You don't know that.'

'Nasty to his children.'

So Ruth had a reason to dislike her father too, thought Shepherd. Which Joy had lied about.

Barbara spoke quickly. 'What I don't understand is why the police are involved. George has been sick for so long. Surely it's no surprise that he died.' She held out a plate of dry shortbread and Shepherd reluctantly took a piece. He was so fed up with the bland, poverty-induced cooking he'd endured for twenty years.

'Yes, well that's the . . . unfortunate part.' He looked at the triangle of shortbread. 'You see, Mr Henderson was found — Joy found him, actually — with a belt around his neck.' He watched both of their reactions carefully.

'*What?*' Barbara virtually shouted the word.

Protesting too much? thought Shepherd.

'That's terrible. Terrible.' She sat down, still holding out the plate of shortbread, her face drained of colour.

That's hard to fake, he thought.

Colin had squeezed his eyes shut as if he refused to believe what Shepherd had just said.

'Yes, it is.' Shepherd bit on the shortbread, clamping it in his teeth and pulling down with his hand to break a piece off in his mouth. He took a swig of tea to soften it.

The phone in the hallway rang, and Barbara glanced at her watch. 'Sorry, I have to get this. It's important.' She kissed Colin's forehead as she walked into the hallway.

Colin leant close to the cat and looked at Shepherd. 'He's called Runty. Because he was the runt of the litter. They said the only thing to do was put him down, but my mother said we'd have him.' Colin smiled down at Runty, then at Shepherd. He's slept on my bed every night. For fourteen years.'

Runty opened his yellow eyes and stretched out a single paw to touch Colin's knee.

'He's my friend. But he's going to be dead soon.' Colin wiped his nose on his sleeve, first one nostril, then the other. 'He can't breathe properly anymore. And he can't really walk much either.' Shepherd gave Colin a sympathetic grimace and continued asking him about the Hendersons. He spoke calmly, quietly. 'Was Mr Henderson mean to Ruth?'

Colin shook his head. 'No, not Ruth.' He picked up Runty gently, and Shepherd could hear the cat purring, even though it was still wheezing. It was obviously very sick.

'Colin?' Shepherd said gently. 'We don't know where Ruth is. We're very worried about her.'

'You don't know where Ruth is?' he said, surprised.

'No.' The expression on Colin's face made him ask the next question carefully and firmly. 'Do you know where Ruth is, Colin?'

Still caressing Runty, Colin nodded.

Now we're getting somewhere, Shepherd thought. Maybe I was wrong about Joy.

Suddenly he heard Barbara speaking loudly — too loudly — on the phone. 'I don't care what you *think*.' And she obviously also didn't care what Shepherd heard. Or maybe she wanted to make sure he did hear. 'He's staying here with me. Him *and* the cat.'

Shepherd turned back to look at Colin, who had buried his face in the cat's back.

'Colin,' said Shepherd, pleasantly but still firmly. He had to stay calm. 'Is Ruth alive?'

Colin looked up and shook his head. Quickly. 'Ruth is . . . dead.'

Shepherd was suddenly hyper-alert. What the hell was going on here? 'Are you sure?'

Colin put his hands over his eyes and started sobbing. 'It was an accident. But she's in heaven now.'

Shepherd's mind was in overdrive. This is what he wanted. A quick confession and wrap-up. Seems he *had* been wrong about Joy. Never mind. He'd be able to tie up the loose ends today and get a decent night's sleep. And no judge would imprison Colin. He'd probably be institutionalised, but not imprisoned, as such. And Barbara would be able to visit him whenever she wanted to. 'I said I don't care.' Barbara's voice was like steel. 'You're not taking him away from this house or the cat, do you hear? I'm going to look after him until someone buries me.' Probably not, thought Shepherd, feeling sorry for her.

'A terrible accident,' Colin repeated, still hiding behind his hands.

Shepherd took another bite of the hard shortbread, as blood pumped into his brain. He manoeuvred the lump of shortbread to one cheek, and forced himself to speak softly. 'Colin, can you take me to Ruth?'

Colin looked up and nodded, tears rolling down his cheeks. One hand reached out and patted the cat, slowly, agonisingly, as if he was scared of hurting it. Or as if he knew that once he went with Shepherd, he would never be returning, never be able to pat it again.

'Now?' Shepherd said gently. He knew that, particularly if the offender had acted hastily or the attack really had been an accident, the victim might still be alive. Time was of the essence. He put down his cup of tea and the rest of the shortbread on the little table, relieved he wouldn't have to take another bite, and stood up.

'Yes,' said Colin, also standing up. 'I can take you to Ruth.'

'Let's go then.'

Colin said again, 'It was an accident.'

They walked into the hallway, where Barbara was spitting out words like they were sticks of kindling. 'I've looked after him all these years, and no one's said anything. Where were you all when I really needed help twenty years ago?'

'Excuse me, Mrs Larsen.'

Barbara whipped her head around and snapped at him. 'What?'

'Colin is coming with me.' Shepherd put on his impassive face. 'He's going to . . .' it was such a useful phrase,'. . . help us with our inquiries.'

Shepherd was not surprised when Colin told him to turn left towards the Henderson farm when they reached the road. But when he slowed down at the bottom of the hill to turn into the Henderson driveway, Colin said, 'No, not here. A long way to go yet, keep going.'

After another ten minutes of driving in silence, Shepherd became more curious — and more concerned, as he wondered where Colin might have put Ruth. A sudden thought nearly made him brake. Could Colin also have killed Wendy Boscombe all those years ago?

'Colin,' he said, deliberately calmly, and wishing he'd asked this question before. 'Can you tell me where Ruth is, to save you giving me directions while we drive?'

'Yes,' said Colin. 'Do you know Blackhunt cemetery?'

54

GEORGE AND GWEN

January 1949

When Gwen and the baby arrived home, the garden was an explosion of red poppies. But Gwen could not look at them. Dully, she asked George how he had coped. He told her that Barbara had come down early each morning with food, and had looked after Mark all day while he and Colin milked and worked on the farm.

Gwen nodded, not comprehending this side of Barbara, not comprehending anything.

Later that afternoon, when she was sitting on the couch feeling numb, with the baby asleep in the bassinet at her feet, there was a knock at the back door. She moaned and pulled herself off the couch.

'Hello, Gwen.' Colin looked straight at her.

'Hello, Colin.' She tried half a smile. He followed her inside and sat on the couch beside her. She wondered what he was doing. The milking didn't start for another half-hour, and he always went straight down to the dairy.

Neither of them said anything. Colin simply waited.

Then Gwen pointed to the baby. 'This is Joy.'

'Yes.' And he leant down and stroked her cheek. 'Hello, Joy.' Then he looked at Gwen. 'How are you, Gwen?'

Such a simple question. One that nobody had asked her. The few people who had visited her in hospital had avoided mentioning the only thing she wanted to talk about, and they had all been too distant, or too cheerful. 'Best to just look on the bright side, love,' from the woman in the next bed. 'She's beautiful, Gwen,' from Arnold. 'Absolutely beautiful,' from Marilyn. 'God works in mysterious ways,' from Reverend Braithwaite. 'We have to carry on as if it never happened,' from George.

But Colin had simply looked at her and asked the question.

Something had died inside her, yet she could not cry. She looked at Colin and knew he would listen. And he did, occasionally repeating a phrase when she faltered. When she finished, it was he who was crying, and she who had to do the comforting.

'It was an accident, Colin. Just a terrible accident.'

Through his tears, Colin repeated her words. 'A terrible accident.'

'And Ruth is in heaven now,' said Gwen.

'Ruth is in heaven,' said Colin, so sadly that Gwen wanted to wrap her arms around him.

They sat there, together. In silence. Even the baby in the bassinet at their feet stayed silent.

When it was five minutes to four o'clock, Colin stood up. 'I have to help George do the milking now.'

'Yes,' said Gwen. 'Thank you, Colin.'

55

JOY AND RUTH

February 1983

> HENDERSON, George. A kind and honourable man who loved God, his church, and his community. Deep condolences to the family. Kenneth Jones

Now that Shepherd and Vicki have left, I can think more clearly and get things sorted, but I can't stop thinking about Ruth. It looks like she really has gone. Forever. And now the real tears roll out of my eyes, as I think back to that wet Saturday afternoon, smack-bang in the middle of my last year of primary school.

I was watching my mother push a wheelbarrow full of thistles into the chook pen for the twelve Ruths, while I held the gate closed, my rubber boots chugged into the mud.

'Come on, Ruthies, come on,' my mother clucked.

'Mum . . .' The question came rolling out of my mouth of its own accord. 'Why do you call them all Ruth?' Eleven years of hearing her doing this, and it was only then, at that very minute, I'd ever thought it odd. That's the way it is when you're a child. You accept everything. Until you don't.

I thought she hadn't heard me because she went to the back of the pen and threw out the thistles with her bare hands. Nothing hurt her hands: not thistles, nor the tips of the wire that she stabbed into flowers, not even the cold of a bitter winter.

When she came back out and went into the little lean-to where we kept a 44-gallon drum full of chook pellets, I started again. 'Mum, why do you—'

'I heard you,' she said. She picked up the large scoop, swung it into the drum and we both watched the excess pellets cascade over the side. Then she walked back into the pen and scattered the pellets over the thistles in a long, wide arc.

I didn't know whether she'd answer me or not, so I just had to wait.

After she hung up the scoop, she rested the backs of her hands on her hips and said, 'You want to know why I call them all Ruth?'

'Yes, please.' I don't know why, but suddenly I was sorry I'd asked.

She stared across the bull paddock, over the dam and into the grey distance, then sniffed.

'A long time ago, I . . . had another baby.' She looked down at the empty wheelbarrow in front of her and sniffed again. I remember hoping that she wasn't getting a cold. She was never sick. Who would look after us if she was sick? Or died? 'A baby called Ruth.'

'Another baby?'

She licked her lips. 'Yes. But she died.'

'What do you mean *died*? How?'

She lifted up the handles of the wheelbarrow. 'It was . . . before you were born. It was an accident. Nothing could be done. A terrible accident. She died . . .' My mother swallowed. 'Before she was born. A stillborn baby.'

I was only eleven, and the words *stillborn baby* sounded like a sin. Words that would be whispered by a pointed-nose spinster with swollen veins in her legs and a pinched heart, words that would then be whispered by others, words that would scuttle around country roads faster than mice in a plague, until everyone knew about the terrible sin.

Her words echo in my head to this day, especially *before you were born*. I would have had a big sister.

'I fell, you see,' my mother continued. 'Down the concrete steps at the back door.'

I saw the rain was running down her cheeks, but I waited, listening silently. I was good at that.

'I was expecting, and I didn't have long to go. And if you . . . slip . . . when you don't have long to go, you can't stop yourself from falling.'

She looked at me then, but I said nothing.

'Everyone knows that.' Now her voice wasn't its usual beige, but ice-blue. 'Luckily, your father was right there. Right behind me. Or Ruth might not have been the only one to die.'

She didn't have to say anything else. I knew. 'He pushed you, didn't he? That's how baby Ruth died.'

She should have protested straight away, but she didn't. She took half a second too long to say, 'No! No, no. He rang the doctor, saved my life. But when I woke up in hospital, baby Ruth, well, she . . .'

'Was dead,' I said. And in the base of my neck, a bubble of intense purple loathing exploded and spread through my body.

She lifted up the handles of the wheelbarrow. 'It was an accident, Joy. I slipped, that's all. And we have to carry on as if it never happened.' She frowned. 'You must never mention this to anyone. Especially your father. He'd be too upset. And never to anyone outside the family. No one.'

I stood there, my cold fingers linked through the wire that held all the living Ruths captive, while she walked away, pushing the wheelbarrow ahead of her. Down to the bull paddock, to dig out more thistles with a mattock. Until just before tea, she was a bobbing blotch of blue and dark green, out of reach. Sometimes completely out of sight when the angle of the grey rain was just so.

I locked the gate of the chook pen, and looked at the Ruths eating the thistles and pellets. There had been dozens and dozens of Ruths beheaded, cooked and eaten, and now I knew there had been another Ruth, the first Ruth. My sister. I didn't believe for a second that it had been an accident, that she'd slipped, and that it was 'lucky' my father had been right there.

But I wasn't stupid, and I knew I had to do as she'd said and never mention 'the accident' to anyone.

But that loathing snaking along my veins? Well, that would never disappear, and I knew that one day I was going to make him suffer for what he did to Ruth.

When I went inside, my sister's murderer was sitting at the table, waiting for his afternoon tea, which I would have to make, because my mother was digging out thistles. As I filled the kettle, I stole a quick look at dead Ruth's murderer, and the purple loathing spread.

I placed two pieces of lemon slice on a plate and carried it to the table. Then poured the boiling water into the pot, my hand shaking, as I told myself over and over, *careful, careful.* He was watching me, like he always did. Waiting for me to make a mistake. But even while I was concentrating, I couldn't stop thinking about baby Ruth. How beautiful she would be, and how she would give me presents for my birthday, like bookmarks, or even books.

Poor baby Ruth. Who never had a first birthday, let alone an eleventh one like I'd had.

I poured milk into his cup, thinking that a dead unborn baby would be milk-white, soft and creamy. Not like the slimy dead calves the vet pulled out of cows with rope. They were stiff and cold and had angles everywhere. Baby Ruth looked sweet and soft in our mother, although I saw her struggling to get food from the cord, struggling to breathe, struggling to escape from the yelling and banging that penetrated our mother's stomach. Struggling to grow legs and feet, arms and hands, a soul. And eventually giving up the struggle. All this, in the exact place where I had grown and struggled and pushed for breath and life and mud and chooks and cows and rain and fear. And books. And the word images that exploded in my head. And I could not decide whether the unborn Ruth or the unborn Joy had made the right decision.

'Come on!' he growled. 'I haven't got all day!'

I turned the teapot back and forth, to speed up the brewing, then began pouring. It was too weak.

'Useless,' he spat.

I remember that as I spun the pot around and around, I wondered how they had known baby Ruth was dead. Now I was worried the tea was too strong. I poured it into a clean cup and carried it to the table. *Careful, careful.*

'Hurry up!'

I jumped, and a splosh of tea leapt out of the cup into the saucer. He watched me get another saucer. *Please God, help me to be more careful. For thine is the kingdom, the power and the glory . . .*

'Here you are, Dad.'

For ever and ever, Amen.

'Mmmh.'

I stood at the sink, waiting for him to finish his tea and biscuits, all the while thinking about Ruth, Ruth, Ruth.

Finally, he scraped back his chair on the lino and left, and I cleaned up.

If only Ruth had not died inside our mother, I thought, I would have a big sister to look up to, someone to help me with homework, to follow to the chook shed to collect the eggs, while I skipped behind her, throwing her questions. Ruth would pretend to be annoyed and turn around, saying, 'Joy, if you ask me one more question about the moon, honestly, I will simply scream!' And we would both laugh.

A big sister who would solve all my problems . . . who I could cling to when his rage exploded.

But later, while I was waxing eggs so they would keep through winter, I realised how silly I'd been. I would never have been laughing with Ruth or clinging to her, because if dead baby Ruth had lived, our parents would never have made me. It would have been Ruth waxing the eggs, Ruth making our father afternoon tea, Ruth doing everything. And, unlike me, she would do everything perfectly.

The truth was that I was nothing more than Ruth's replacement. And a poor, ugly one at that. No wonder my father hated me. That night, curled up in bed, I pictured the doctors taking dead baby Ruth out of my mother and throwing her into a rubbish tank like the one we had in the paddock, where they put all the diseased and rotting bits that people didn't want anymore, like amputated legs, burst appendices, infected tonsils, frostbitten toes and fingers. Sometimes they had to pull out a leg or a hand and push it back in at a different angle, before lighting the twisted piece of paper and throwing it in after the useless body bits and dead babies.

But even in the middle of such wild imaginings, I forced myself to imagine baby Ruth in Heaven, each day growing stronger and healthier.

Under the blankets, I shivered. It was always freezing in our house. It made me think that it would be nicer in Hell, where it was hot and there was no rain. And whenever I thought that, I quickly prayed for forgiveness.

If only Ruth was here, I thought. If only the strong, healthy, beautiful Ruth was here. If only God would send her to save me, like He had sent His son to save mankind.

And I whispered into the cold air, 'Ruth, I wish you weren't dead. I wish you were here.'

Ruth. The name was sleek and smooth, and its image was a long shiny silver slide. Unlike my own stubby name, which sounded like a spit of contempt. I especially hated its image — a short rusty rasp.

'Ruth,' I whispered again. 'Are you in Heaven?'

I opened my eyes, and in the darkness I saw Ruth standing in front of me. Her face had soft features and blue eyes like our father's, and a small nose dotted with brown freckles as if our mother had shaken some nutmeg across it. She had long, graceful hands, and was wearing a white cotton dress with a belt that sat comfortably around her thin waist. I could even tell she was wearing a bra. And that she never got cold. She was so neat and petite and no-nonsense that I thought she could have been in an ad for vacuum cleaners.

Except for a purple birthmark that covered the left corner of her mouth and her left cheek, and spread up over her left eye and under her hair. But I knew that if you looked at just the right side of her face, you'd never see the birthmark and you'd think she was an angel from Heaven.

'Ruth?' I said. 'What are you doing here?'

'I'm here to save you.' She smiled and her birthmark bulged. Her voice was like tissue paper crackling, and the birthmark moved in time with her lips. She spoke calmly and confidently, and inside my poor angry fearful stomach, the sticky black eels shivered and shrank. Just a little. But it was enough.

Then she told me all about Heaven, where it was always sunny and people laughed all day. There was enough food for everyone, the bedrooms didn't have cold draughts, and the lino didn't screech. God and Jesus were on their thrones, and the Holy Spirit was everywhere, spreading love and happiness. No one was allowed to hit or belt children, and if they did they were sent to Hell, where it was dark and hot and full of eternal misery, just like Reverend Braithwaite said.

'Are there books in Heaven?'

Ruth looked momentarily annoyed. 'Of course there are, but I'm not here to talk about books. I'm here because of our father . . . our father who *aren't* in Heaven.'

I remember thinking what a clever twist of words that was. 'Our father who killed me,' continued Ruth, her voice now like silk {whipped cream}. 'It's going to take time, but I promise you, we'll get our revenge.'

I wanted to hug Ruth, my wonderful never-born sister from Heaven, even though, of course, I couldn't. But I did remind her to speak quietly so our parents couldn't hear us talking. Not that *she* had to worry about being caught or punished. She would never have to fear our father, or his belt. Or even Hell. Not now, and not when she died, because she had already died and gone straight to Heaven.

For the first time in my life, I went to sleep feeling loved and a little less scared.

* * *

I wipe my tears away. I can't get sentimental about anything, even Ruth. I have things to do, things to stay on top of. And when I'm next with Shepherd and want to convince him I'm mourning my father, I'll remember what my father did to my mother and my sister.

I take a moment. And wonder if I did the right thing all those years ago by bringing Ruth into my life. But of course, back then, when I was eleven and scared, I didn't know what she would make me do.

56

JOY AND RUTH

December 1960

Four days after Wendy disappeared, Joy was on her way into the kitchen with the eggs, when she heard her mother and father talking quietly. She stopped, sure that they were talking about Wendy.

'This is terrible. I never thought anything like this would ever happen around here,' said her mother. 'We'll have to tell the children.'

'Of course you will,' Joy's father said. 'Everyone will be talking about it. Even if we wanted to keep it from them, we couldn't.'

Had Wendy been found?

'They'll be so upset,' said her mother. 'Especially Joy.'

'I'm sure they'll get over it, Gwen.'

Joy heard the screech of lino as her father pushed back his chair to leave. She opened the door and saw him grab a packet of glacé pineapple from the hamper Miss Boyle had given them for Christmas. She always gave them an enormous hamper, full of all sorts of goodies that Joy's mother loved.

After he left, she and her mother did the dishes. Joy knew her mother was going to tell her the news about Wendy — and that it was not good. But her mother remained silent. Maybe she was waiting until lunch time, when Mark would be back from the Wallaces', who bred ferrets. Her father had made Mark walk around there to pay for the new ferrets they were going to deliver next week. Joy knew it was his punishment for confessing to something he hadn't done.

When Joy had dried and put away the last cup, her mother scrubbed the draining board far more vigorously than was necessary as she said, 'I have something to tell you.'

'Is it about Wendy?' Joy's voice was small and scared, the eels in her stomach tense and alert. 'Have they found her?'

'Oh,' said her mother. 'No, they haven't, but I'm sure they will — and I'm sure she'll be fine.'

Joy nodded miserably.

'No, what I need to tell you is that, well, Mr Larsen . . . Mr and Mrs Larsen . . . are leaving.'

'What?' This was not at all what she had expected. *They can't leave. Mr Larsen has to bring chocolates and ring Beryl and make you laugh.*

'Don't say "what". You know it annoys your father.' She scrubbed the inside of the sink. 'They're moving. Back to the city.' Joy knew it was because of Beryl, but thought that her mother didn't want to tell her this. She waited silently for more information. 'I don't know how to tell you this, and you probably won't understand. But since everyone will be talking about it, even if we wanted to keep it from you, we couldn't. It appears that . . . Mr and Mrs Larsen are going to . . . divorce. And Mr Larsen is going to . . . marry someone else.'

Divorce? That was a terrible sin. Wasn't it?

Joy suspected that her mother was going to stop there, but she had to find out if it was because of Beryl. So, risking a sharp retort to mind her own business, she asked another question.

'Why?'

Her mother sat down at the table and, to Joy's surprise, gestured for her to sit down too, as she tore open a packet of glacé fruit. 'Mr Larsen is a lot older than me — and your father. And a long time ago — about the time I was born — he was courting a young woman. In those days, that meant he spent Sunday afternoons at her place, in the parlour with her family.' She sighed, and took a bite of pineapple.

'Everything was different back then. Mr Larsen courted Beryl [*I knew it!* thought Joy] for about a year. Sometimes he took her mother chocolates [*Of course!*]. And he and Beryl met in the park on Saturday afternoons too. Eventually Mr Larsen decided he wanted to marry Beryl.' Joy's mother took out a glacé fig and pushed the pack towards Joy, who found a cherry and popped it in her mouth.

'So why didn't he?'

'All I know is that he went to her house to ask her father for permission one day when Beryl was away visiting relatives. Mr Larsen explained that he had a good job at the bank then said, "And I've come to ask for your daughter's hand in marriage." Her father said, "Well, good luck to you." Mr Larsen shook hands with him, thanked him and left.' Joy's mother put the rest of the glacé fig into her mouth. 'That was how it was back then.'

'So did he marry Beryl?'

'Well, two days later a note arrived from her father saying that he was going to announce the engagement in *The Argus* the following week.' Joy's mother ripped back more of the cellophane from Miss Boyle's hamper, opened a tin of candied peanuts and poured some into her hand.

'And what happened?' asked Joy.

'The day the announcement was going to be in *The Argus*, Mr Larsen's boss went out and bought the paper, gathered everyone around and read the engagement notice to them: "It is with great pleasure . . . blah blah blah . . . pleased to announce the engagement of their daughter, Barbara Eliza, to Mr Robert Larsen."'

'What?' said Joy.

'Yes,' said her mother. 'Barbara.'

'But what about Beryl?'

'Mr Larsen realised that when he'd met with Beryl's father that day, her father had hurried the conversation along, and neither of them had ever actually called Beryl by name.'

'But surely Mr Larsen must have told Beryl's father that he'd made a mistake?'

'No. It would have been too humiliating for Barbara. And Beryl. To say nothing of the humiliation both sets of parents would have felt if he'd upped and married Beryl after that. It was a mess, and poor old Rob— Mr Larsen, was too nice to make a fuss.'

'So he *married* Barbara?'

'Yes, he married Mrs Larsen.'

'But . . . why? That's not fair.'

Joy's mother tilted her head to one side and gave a little shrug. 'No, but that's what happened. And Beryl . . . Well, she never married.'

Her mother put more of the candied peanuts in her mouth. 'I suppose Barbara hoped that Mr Larsen would eventually love her.' She shrugged again. 'Maybe they did grow to love each other. Despite what those books you read might say, marriage hasn't always been about love, you know. Not then, not now, not ever. And nobody can know what goes on in another family.'

'So why are they leaving?' asked Joy.

'Because,' Joy's mother sighed heavily, 'Mr Larsen has cancer. He doesn't have long to live. He and Beryl are moving to Melbourne, where he'll have better treatment.'

'What about Mrs Larsen? And Colin?' said Joy.

'Well, the *story* is that they're all moving — together — to Melbourne. But obviously that's not what's happening. I'm sure Colin will still want to see his father and . . . be with him when he dies, but . . .' Joy's mother paused. 'All I know is that the Hall Committee is having a farewell for them.' Then she hmphed and said, 'It's the most ridiculous thing I've ever heard.'

57

JOY AND SHEPHERD

February 1983

> HENDERSON, George. After a long illness, George has gone to our Lord's music hall. May the piano never drown out your guitar again. From your fellow band-members, Maurice (Johnnie B. Bad), Allan, John and Bert

'Morning, Shep.'

Shepherd was unlocking the station and turned around to see Vicki grinning behind him.

'What do you want?'

'I have something to show you,' she said, going in ahead of him. She lifted up the hinged end of the counter, made a beeline for Shepherd's office and sat in front of his desk, fanning herself with a manila folder.

Annoyed at the way she'd made herself at home, to say nothing of her giving him a nickname when they hardly knew one another, Shepherd sat in his chair on the other side of the desk and looked at her with raised eyebrows. 'Well?'

She stopped fanning, pulled out two sheets of paper, slapped them down on the desk, and resumed fanning. 'I decided to do a bit of my own investigating.'

The top piece of paper was a medical record from 1963, with the name 'HENDERSON, Joy' written across the top. Someone (Vicki?) had circled with red pen a file-note made by a Dr Merriweather: 'Scars on back, upper arms and upper legs. Probable cause: accident with boiling water.'

He slid it to one side to look at the second sheet of paper. It was another medical record, this time from July 1960, for 'HENDERSON, Mark'. It also had a circled file-note, written by a Dr Neighbour, which read: 'Evidence of extensive corporal punishment. According to father, long history of delinquency.'

'Where did you get these?' Obviously Vicki had breached confidentiality obligations in looking at these records, to say nothing of her showing them to him.

'I'll pretend you didn't ask me that, Shep. That way, I won't have to tell you a lie.' She stopped fanning for a second and leant in, grinning. 'Or, even worse, the truth.'

Shepherd glared at her, and shook his head.

'Good, eh?' said Vicki. 'Well, not good that those poor children were beaten half to death by their father, but good that I . . . stumbled across these records. The thing is, because they were seen by different doctors, no one ever bothered to put one and one together to get five.'

'What?'

'That two children with the same father were both victims of extreme abuse. They were both beaten so badly they had wounds and scars that doctors noticed *and* recorded. This was in the early sixties, Shep, way before mandatory reporting. Back then, everyone thought a beating now and then was okay. Hell, some people still do. But what that man did to those kids went way beyond the occasional backhand.'

'Wait, slow down. Who the hell is Mark Henderson?'

'Joy's brother.'

'Brother? I don't know about any damn brother.'

'I thought that might be the case,' said Vicki, smiling as if oblivious to Shepherd's frustration. 'And here's why.' With an annoying flourish, she slapped a third sheet of paper on the desk, her hand splayed across the page.

He had to pull it out from under her hand. It was another note from Mark's medical file, and Shepherd couldn't believe what he read: *24/01/61 Missing.*

'Missing? What happened to him?' This family was too much.

Fathers and sisters and brothers missing and murdered and — 'Seems he just ran away, Shep.' She almost looked disappointed.

'Packed a few clothes, emptied his bank account and disappeared. No one ever heard from him again. Someone thought he'd gone to Hobart, and the police down there spent about five minutes searching for him, but he was sixteen. Nothing criminal or suspicious about his leaving home. Especially because,' she looked at him pointedly, 'everyone knew the father beat the hell out of them.'

'How do you know all this when I don't? You didn't even live here then.'

'Oh, you know,' she said, turning her head towards the window. 'You hear things. From people. One of whom may or may not be called Alison Bell, who may or may not have been married to a police officer you knew.'

Shepherd shook his head again, looked down at the date and grimaced. 'Uh. That's why I don't remember.'

Vicki nodded sympathetically. 'Alison—'

'Let me guess. She told you. I was on compassionate leave.'

'She said your father had died.'

'But why didn't Ron tell me about this when I got back?' Vicki shrugged.

'What?' said Shepherd sarcastically. 'There's something you don't know?'

She looked apologetic. 'Well, Alison wasn't sure . . .'

'It's alright.' He grimaced. 'I was . . . a bit obsessed with the whole Wendy Boscombe thing, and when I got back about a month later, Ron told me that Headquarters had said we were to both "move on". The detectives from Melbourne were convinced that Wendy was either dead by then, or a long way from Blackhunt. There was nothing to go on. No clues, no ransom note, no sightings — apart from crackpots. Wendy had just disappeared.' Shepherd rubbed his forehead. It sounded pathetic when he put it into words like that, because neither he nor Ron had ever really given up. But it just hadn't made sense to go round and round in circles with no evidence, any more than it had made sense to keep working on that ridiculous jigsaw puzzle.

Dammit, now he would have to find Mark Henderson. He racked his brain, trying to remember more about interviewing the Hendersons after Wendy's disappearance. But it was impossible to recall every single member of every damn family on those depressing farms they'd visited. And, back then, Shepherd didn't really know George from a can of WD-40. He'd have to look them up in his file. He'd been so intent on finding Joy guilty that he wasn't doing his homework properly. He could kick himself — and this damn Henderson family.

He turned to Vicki. 'Alright, I'll dig out Mark's fingerprints and contact Headquarters in Melbourne to see if they have anything on him. But right now I want to talk to Joy Henderson again. Whatever all the homicide shows on telly might want you to believe, most crimes are pretty straightforward. Find the person with a motive and an opportunity, who was there at the time of the crime, and you have your guilty party. And right now Joy Henderson ticks all those boxes. Especially given the lies she told me about Ruth. I won't even have to find Mark if I can get her to confess. She doesn't seem exactly grief-stricken about her father's death.'

'Shep, the man brutalised his children. So badly one of them ran away. And you told me that Barbara said Joy had "escaped"? *Escaped*, Shep. As if she was a prisoner.'

'She did. But what about his standing in the community? He was always at church, always helping people, wasn't he?' Shepherd picked up Joy's file-note again. 'And it says here her scars were the result of an accident . . .'

'It says *probable cause*, Shep, *probable cause*. I can tell you right now, that coward Merriweather, rest his soul, wrote that to cover his own lazy arse. He probably went to the same church as George Henderson. And, by the way, who has boiling water poured over their . . .' She grabbed the sheet of paper from him and read, 'Back, upper arms and upper legs in an *accident*?'

Shepherd held up his hand. 'Alright. But if anything, you've confirmed Joy's motive — revenge. So thank you for your stolen intelligence, Vicki, which I will keep for evidence.'

'You can't be serious, Shep? I'm telling you, the man was a monster.' She pointed to the pieces of paper Shepherd was pulling into a neat pile. 'Look at what he did to her, to both of them.'

'I said, "Alright", Vicki. Yes, it was terrible what he did to her all those years ago. But I have to deal with what *she* did to *him* three nights ago.' He was kicking himself again — he *should* have already looked at the notes about the Henderson family in Wendy Boscombe's bulging files. But Joy was the guilty one, not him. To start with, she hadn't told him she had a brother, much less a brother who was missing. Nor had she told him the truth about Ruth. And who knows what else? She was as slippery as an angry eel, and he was sure she'd murdered her father with that belt.

'You want to know what I think?' Vicki's loud voice was annoying.

'No, but let me guess. You think I should let her get away with killing her father because he beat her. Well, that's not how the law works, Vicki. And by the way, will you finish the damn autopsy, so I know — officially — that the man was strangled in his sleep with his own belt? It's been three days and you still—'

'All done, Shep.' Vicki smacked the manila folder down onto the desk and opened it, revealing the front cover of her autopsy report. 'But you won't like it. He died from an overdose.'

'What? But the belt?'

'It must have been put around his neck after he died.'

'Damn.' He rubbed the middle finger of one hand over his brow. 'Alright, so she didn't kill him with the belt, so she must have killed him with the medication, right?'

Vicki looked sceptical. 'You think Joy gave him an overdose, then put the belt around his neck? Get real, Shep. Why would she do that? It would just point to her being guilty, wouldn't it?'

'Or . . .' But the idea that had been fluttering at the edges of Shepherd's brain vanished. 'Alright, what's your theory? You may as well spit it out, since I know you're going to tell me whether I ask for it or not.'

'Well, I think he killed himself.' She picked up her doctor's bag and looked at her watch. 'Sorry, I have to go and—'

'What?' Shepherd screwed up his face. 'What do you mean, he killed himself?'

'It happens more often than you'd think, Shep. Only a few days of life left, if that long; medication sitting on a table beside you; endless excruciating pain; nothing to live for. We never know if it's deliberate or accidental.'

'Accidental?' He loosened his tie. This woman was so damn annoying.

Vicki sighed and sat down again. 'Look, think about it. You wake up in pain, so you take some painkillers, go back to sleep, wake up again and take some more, even though you have no idea how much time has gone by. Do that a few times and, depending on what tablets you're throwing down, you're not *going* to wake up to take any more.' She shrugged. 'At least you don't die in pain.' She grimaced. 'Which nobody wants to do. So, George Henderson definitely died from swallowing too many pills, but I can't tell you what was going on in his mind when he swallowed them.'

'Or if someone else gave them to him, forced him to swallow them.'

'You mean Joy?'

'Yes. Of course I mean Joy.'

'You can't be sure, though, can you?'

'But the whole Ruth thing. She tried to make us believe that her sister did it. She practically told us that Ruth killed him.'

'I don't think so, Shep.'

'What are you talking about? First of all she made sure she was defending Ruth, trying to convince us that Ruth hadn't killed him, and then . . .' He rubbed his forehead again and shook his head. 'Look, she's playing damn mind games with me. With us. Don't think she hasn't pulled you into all of this.'

'But, Shep, she knew you'd find out about Ruth once you went looking for her, or spoke to the neighbours, or anyone. That it would only be a matter of time.'

'So it doesn't make sense.'

'It does if she's . . . maybe, insane.' Vicki looked positively pleased at the prospect. 'Or . . . damaged.'

'She's not insane, believe me.' His voice was tight, adamant. 'And she can hardly plead self-defence. George wasn't about to hurt her while he was in bed, dying. For god's sake, he could scarcely lift a cup to his mouth.' He looked straight at her. 'According to you, anyway. Which therefore makes it very unlikely that he gave himself an overdose.'

'Mmm. You'd be surprised what dying people can do when they have their mind fixed on something. Especially if that something is their own death. But I hear what you're saying, Shep. So, no, she can't plead self-defence. But think about what she had to put up with when she was a kid.'

Shepherd opened his mouth to repeat that the past had nothing to do with what Joy had done three nights ago, but Vicki kept talking.

'I once met a man in his fifties who was still scared of his father. The father was in hospital, bed-ridden, unconscious most of the time, and incontinent. Have I ever mentioned what a godsend adult disposables are, Shep? You must get them when the time comes. Anyway, he should have been put into a home, but everyone thought he'd be dead before the bureaucrats could line up their signatures. Of course, he proved them wrong and lingered for weeks. One day, I was on my way to the hospital, when some idiot crossed the road right in front of me. I only just braked in time. When I got out to give him a piece of my mind, you could have knocked me over with one of those file-notes in your hand. It was like I was looking at his old man thirty years before. So I offered him a ride to the hospital. He was a looker, I can tell you.'

'And your point is?'

'Well, on the way, this man starts trembling. The hospital was at the top of a hill, and you had to go up a winding road that—'

'Vicki!' Shepherd tapped the face of his watch.

'So he's trembling — visibly — and I ask him if he's alright, and he says, "Whatever you do, don't leave me alone with him." Those were his exact words. Verbatim, Shep. So I tell him that his father's harmless, whatever he's done to him in the past was just that — in the past.'

'My point exactly,' said Shepherd. 'Whatever George did or did not do to Joy twenty years ago—'

'Listen, Shep.' Vicki stood up, leant over and spread her plump hands on his desk. 'This man was still terrified of his father. He looked at me and repeated, "Don't. Leave. Me. Alone with that man." I rest my case.' And she sat back down, arms folded.

'Hell, Vicki. He was probably scared he'd do what Joy did — wreak revenge and kill the damn bastard.'

'Shep, Shep, Shep,' said Vicki. 'Don't you get it? This guy's mind was *infected* with what his father had done to him. It doesn't make him mad, but it does make him damaged. He was in his fifties and he was still scared of his father, and he hadn't seen him for nearly thirty years. Joy's only in her thirties.'

'It doesn't change the fact that . . .' He shook his head in frustration as the phone rang, and he picked up the handset. Vicki watched his face turn red before he finally said, 'I'll get back to you, Miss Henderson.'

He hung up and exploded. 'Jesus Christ! Now she wants the damn belt back. Why would she want the belt back, Vicki? Tell me what's going on in her "damaged" mind, for God's sake. There's certainly no lack of audacity. And since I'm sure I was the first person you told that the belt isn't the murder weapon, how is it that she knows I have no reason to hang on to it?'

'I'm not a psychologist, Shep,' said Vicki. 'Were her fingerprints on the belt?'

Shepherd shook his head. 'It's too old and cracked. So no decent prints worth sending to Melbourne. I've sent the prints on the pill bottles, but when they tell me Joy's prints are on them, that's not going to prove anything.' He sighed. 'But please don't tell me you think George put the belt around his own neck?'

'No. It's intriguing though, isn't it? Makes me think there's something else that we need to find out about the Hendersons, Shep. Meanwhile, since the belt isn't a murder weapon, you could give it to her, couldn't you? See what happens?'

'Maybe. But even if it's not the murder weapon, I'm still sure she killed him.'

'Then why don't you arrest her?'

'Because I don't have any proof, do I? Not now you've told me she didn't strangle him with the damn belt.' He stared at her annoyingly cheery face.

'I rest my case. Again.'

'Mmph. And what if George's prints aren't on any of the bottles of pills? In my book that would be proof that Joy gave him every damn pill he swallowed that night.'

'I'm willing to bet his prints will be all over them, Shep,' said Vicki. 'Meanwhile, I have patients to see.' And she stood up to go. He watched her head towards the door, then put the manila folder on his desk and picked up the evidence bag containing the belt. He'd follow Vicki's advice and give it back to Joy, but only so he could somehow make her tell him what happened on the last night of her father's life.

58

JOY AND RUTH

New Year's Day 1961

Mrs Felicity was laughing as she cut five enormous pieces out of her huge chocolate birthday cake.

Joy could still not believe that they were going to eat cake before lunch 'just for fun', which was Barry's approach to almost everything. And that they were going to use small forks to eat it, but only after Barry and Mr Felicity had come back into the dining room with some more presents for Mrs Felicity.

'Joy, dear, Felicity said your mother has a floristry business, but it's not the one in town, is it?'

Joy didn't think of her mother's work as a business. She shook her head. 'She does everything in one of the rooms at home.' She hoped that made it sound like they had a large house too. 'And she grows most of her own flowers.'

'Oh dear, and I gave you those roses for her. Now I'm worried she must have thought I was being terribly rude.' But Mrs Felicity didn't look at all worried, and kept on talking. 'What does she grow?'

'Everything, really. Roses, camellias, poppies, gypsophila . . .'

'Gyp-what?' Felicity asked.

'They're plants that have clouds of tiny white flowers on really fine stems so it looks like snow and—'

'Wait right there!' yelled Felicity, disappearing outside. She came back holding a tiny white kitten whose front paws were resting on Felicity's chin. 'Joy, meet Snowy,' said Felicity. 'Snowy, this is Joy, my best friend.'

Joy barely registered the words 'best friend' because Mrs Felicity started talking again. 'Oh, Joy, listen to this, you'll die laughing.'

At riding school the day before, one of the other girls had brought along a box of kittens, asking people to please, please take one. Felicity had picked out Snowy because she was all white. Back home, Felicity hid Snowy under her jumper and walked into the kitchen, thinking about how to tell Mrs Felicity about Snowy. What she didn't know was that Snowy's little tail was hanging down from under her jumper in full view. Mrs Felicity asked her daughter if they'd had elephants at riding school that day, and when Felicity looked puzzled and said 'No', Mrs Felicity said, 'What about giraffes?' Felicity said 'No' again, then Mrs Felicity said, 'Lions? Tigers?', trying not to laugh while Felicity shook her head and Snowy shook her tail. Then Mrs Felicity pointed at Snowy's tail and Felicity looked down to see it swishing back and forth, and they both started laughing. Felicity pulled Snowy out, and they gave her some warm milk in a little white saucer.

As they told Joy the story, laughing and interrupting each other to make it funnier, Joy stared at them. Finally, Mrs Felicity stopped laughing and said, 'What's wrong, dear?'

All Joy could say was, 'But what did Mr Felicity do?'

Felicity said, 'Laugh, of course!' finishing her sentence with, in Joy's mind, a large pink exclamation mark.

Felicity carried Snowy out to the kitchen and Joy patted her as she ate cold roast chicken from the saucer that was now permanently on the kitchen floor. When they had lunch,

Felicity fed her titbits from her plate, even though Mr and Mrs Felicity kept saying, 'Today is the last day she eats in the dining room, Felicity.' While the Felicities ate, talked and laughed, Joy couldn't stop thinking about what her father would do if she brought home a kitten.

He would throw it into a hessian bag, tie a knot in the bag, and carry it over to the dam, rubber boots swishing through the long grass that was to be next year's hay, banging the Dutch hoe on the ground to frighten away the snakes. He would make Joy go with him so she would learn a lesson from her selfish actions. Then at the top of the bank he'd push the bag into her hands and make her throw it into the dam as far as she could and watch it splash and then sink. He'd ignore the crying, and curse the waste of time.

And the next day at school, Joy would tell Denise Pollard that 'Tiger' loved being with her family, loved the attention and affection he received. She'd make up stories for two weeks, telling Denise that she played with Tiger every night with a ball of wool, that he came running up to her purring when she arrived home, that he slept on her bed, that he was growing every day, and that they'd even got the vet to give him some shots when he came to pull out Speckle's stuck calf. And then, after two weeks, she would say Tiger had disappeared, maybe a fox got him, maybe he ate some rat poison. And she would pretend to be upset, which would be easy because she would just have to remember how she'd felt when her father had made her fling the crying, meowing bag into the dam. Denise would say she could have one from the next litter, and Joy would have to say, *Thank you, that's very kind, but I'm too upset to have another one.* And she would be, too.

That's what Joy's father would do.

* * *

After lunch, they played charades. Mrs Felicity gasped when Joy said she had never heard of the game, and said, 'You'll love it, dear. It's right down your alley.'

After three rounds, when the girls had won, Barry pretended to be upset. 'It's not fair — two against three. You have to bring your brother with you next time, Joy, and then we'll see who wins.' Sitting in the Felicities' lounge room, with its solid wood furniture, intensely patterned rug and shelves full of books, Joy realised that this was the family that had been hiding in the mist all these years. And they had at last found her. The only difference between this and her fantasy was that she always had to go back to her real home.

That night she dreamt she put her meowing father into a hessian bag, tied it up tightly and threw it into the dam, afterwards wiping her hands like Pontius Pilate.

When she woke, drowning in guilt, Ruth whispered, 'It's okay, I promise. One day we'll kill him. Not yet, but one day.'

59

JOY AND SHEPHERD

February 1983

> HENDERSON, George. A sad farewell to a highly respected member of our committee, who worked tirelessly to share his knowledge and love of gardens. He will be sadly missed by so many people. Sincere condolences to the family. Blackhunt Shire Council

Shepherd put the brown-paper evidence bag on the table, annoyed at how dark it was in the kitchen with the blinds pulled down. Joy was making a pot of tea. He could sense her nerves, her desperation.

Or maybe it was his own desperation.

'So . . .Vicki assures me this did not kill him. But you already knew that.' He watched her, as she filled the kettle with water and turned it on, looking for a twitch at the side of her mouth, a dart of the eyes, a barely perceptible swallow, something, anything to confirm his suspicions. 'What I really want to know is *when* did you know the belt didn't kill him?

After you spoke to Vicki today? When you found him? Or when you put it around his neck?'

'Would you like some shortbread?'

Shepherd ignored her. 'There are two things I want you to know. First, I know you killed your father — if not with the damn belt, then with painkillers. And second, although I haven't been able to prove it yet, I will.'

As Joy put a plate of shortbreads on the table, she said, 'You'll never be able to prove it, Detective, because I didn't kill him.'

He reached for a shortbread, hoping they weren't Mrs Larsen's. 'Well, it wasn't Ruth who killed him, was it?' Damn. He hadn't meant to say that. But why hold back?

She got out two cups and saucers, and walked to the fridge. 'Milk? Sugar?'

'So I obviously can't arrest *her*.'

'I can have the belt, can't I? Since it isn't a *murder* weapon?'

He decided to play the same game of ignoring the issue at hand. 'Milk, one sugar, thanks.'

As she poured milk into both cups, he saw she was trembling. She was afraid of him. Or of something. He remembered Vicki's story about the fifty-year-old afraid of his dying father. But Joy's father was already dead, so it couldn't be that. *Is it because she's guilty?* He watched her place a horrible pink tea-cosy over the pot, turn off the power point the kettle was plugged into, return the milk to the fridge and concentrate on swinging the teapot back and forth on the bench, her hands trembling the whole time.

She poured some tea into one cup, looking intently at the brown liquid as it came out of the spout, then set the pot back down on the bench and resumed swinging. He waited and watched. He was going to be patient. And calm. And silent.

Because he had a feeling she was going to crack.

She poured some more tea, scrutinised it and, presumably satisfied that it was strong enough, filled both cups. She carried one to the table, and set it down in front of him. Then, in separate trips, she carried over the sugar bowl, her own cup of tea and a spoon for him. He knew he was watching a tense ritual.

When she sat down, he took a sip and decided it was time to take control. 'Look, Joy, why don't you just tell me what happened?'

Joy took a sip as if they were taking turns. 'Odd, isn't it, how people say you should drink tea to cool down? Completely defies logic, doesn't it?'

Now Shepherd was annoyed with himself. He'd driven all this way, on the pretext of returning the belt, to force the truth out of her and here they were drinking tea together like a couple of old cows chewing cud.

'The truth, Joy.'

She put her cup down. 'I think he killed himself.'

'Mmm.' Shepherd pursed his lips as if he was seriously considering this possibility; as if Vicki hadn't already suggested it.

They sat in silence, sipping tea. He could wait. Patience and silence . . . these were to be his most finely honed tools.

He even took a piece of shortbread. It was definitely one of Mrs Larsen's. Joy sat at the other side of the table, sipping tea, but not eating, not talking. Obviously trying to mess with him.

Well, it wasn't going to work. If he played his cards right, examined and positioned the jigsaw pieces carefully, he knew he'd get a confession out of her.

But as they continued to drink in silence, Shepherd felt himself getting angrier. The clinks of the teacups being put back in the saucers after each sip were infuriating and seemed to be getting louder. And it was getting hotter in the stifling kitchen. There was a fan by the fireplace, but it was turned off. It was as if she had designed the whole scene like a weird little diorama to unsettle him. When their eyes met for a second as he snapped off another piece of his shortbread, she had the audacity to half-smile at him.

He sipped his tea, and looked around the room as if he was totally comfortable, cool and in control. Joy, in turn, seemed obsessed with invisible crumbs on the table.

When she stacked the empty cups and saucers, he noticed she was no longer trembling. Did she think she had fooled him? Did she honestly think she could commit murder, then calmly sit there and say, 'I think he killed himself,' and clam up?

Dammit. He wasn't going to pussy-foot around anymore. He was going to have it out with her — properly. He was sick of her clever lies and polite distractions like cups of tea and shortbread. It was time to change tack.

He banged his palm on the table, and shouted, 'That's not good enough, Joy! You don't get to sit there calmly and claim that he killed himself, not when you killed him, while he was lying there, helpless, in his' — he pushed back his chair to stand up, and it screeched on the old lino — 'room!'

Halfway to the sink, Joy swung around, audibly sucking in the air, her eyes large and wild. The dishes smashed onto the floor.

'What are you doing?' she screamed, dropping to her knees and scraping the pieces together with her bare hands.

As Shepherd walked over to where she was kneeling, the pent-up torment of Wendy Boscombe's disappearance, Ron's death, Headquarters' apathy, the town's smallness, the region's poverty, George Henderson's swollen lips, and the hard tasteless shortbread burst out of his lungs into the hot dark air. And now the shouting was not contrived. 'Tell me the truth, Joy. I want to know why and how you killed your father.'

She looked at him with loathing. 'Why won't you believe me?' She had tears in her eyes. Her words, strong and hot, assaulted him, and it felt as if the walls of the dark house were closing in on them. 'What else do you need to know? Why can't you leave me alone? You don't understand anything.'

Shepherd thought quickly. He'd read about this. Hysteria that culminates in a confession. Sometimes the offender slithers out an admission to a lesser crime to confuse and deceive the police — or even themselves — but eventually the truth bubbles to the surface.

He knelt down to help her, their faces a foot apart. 'Well, why don't you tell me, Joy Henderson?' He wasn't yelling, but his voice was hard. 'What don't I understand?'

'Every night,' she whispered, and then stopped. She took a breath, closed her eyes, and continued in a whisper so small that Shepherd had to lean in. 'Every night, he sat in that chair, where you were sitting, and if we broke one of his thousands of rules, especially if the vet's bill was too big, or the butter factory's cheque too small, or the eel stew not to his liking . . . he got angry with us, like you just did. He'd bang the table, scrape back his chair and shout "Room," like you just did. And that sound . . . that sound.' She let out two sobs.

Shepherd waited.

She took another breath and looked at him. 'You have no idea what he did to us. Oh, I can show you what he did to us, physically.'

She pulled one collar of her long-sleeved shirt down her arm, ripping the shirt, and exposing her shoulder and upper arm. He kept his face composed but was horrified at the thick red strips of raised flesh creeping over the top of her shoulder and under her loose bra strap, wrapping themselves around the top of her arm like the tentacles of a red octopus. She bent over so her head touched her knees, and pulled up her shirt from the waist, revealing the lower half of her back. He forced himself to look at more strips of red, scarred flesh.

She straightened her back and pulled up the collar of the torn shirt, holding it in place with her left arm. He didn't know what to say, and he could tell she was contemptuous of him for this.

'Sometimes,' she continued, looking him straight in the eye, 'he'd keep us waiting for over an hour. Of course, we weren't allowed to do anything while we waited — that was part of the punishment, the long terrible wait — but one night I started reading *Rebecca*. I only made that mistake once.'

Shepherd did not want to know what her father had done to her for breaking the rule.

'Once, screaming with fear, I told him that it was the Devil making him do this. The words slipped out before I could pull them back. I instantly regretted it, but it was too late.' She sighed. 'And I always prayed. *Please, please, please God, don't let him do this to me. Make him stop. Please, please, please.* Always a selfish prayer. Always a sinner.'

Shepherd felt ill.

Joy continued, as if mesmerised, as if he wasn't there.

'The worst part was not knowing where the first one would strike — across the top of the back, or the middle, or the buttocks, or the thighs. But once the . . . tension . . . was broken, you just had to get through the next fourteen. Then he'd leave without saying anything. I'd thank God — literally — that it was over, and blot up the blood with an old towel, which hurt like hell. When I got into bed,' she lifted her chin a little, 'Ruth would whisper soothing words to me.'

Using her hands, she scraped some more broken pieces of crockery towards the saucer. 'But that wasn't the worst of it.'

Shepherd swallowed, not believing it could get worse.

'Afterwards, just a few feet away, on the other side of the wall, I could hear him playing his guitar, always the same song first. I'd be lying in bed, ashamed, scared, bleeding, and you know what he'd be singing?'

Shepherd could only shake his head.

'"You Are My Sunshine".'

Shepherd knew the song and could practically hear it coming through the walls of the house as they sat there, the tune suddenly eerie.

'That's what he did to us. Physically.'

Somehow Shepherd knew that her next words would be unforgettable.

'But you'll never understand what he did to us up here.' She pushed her index finger into the side of her head. Slowly. Three times. 'You want to know why he killed himself? Why my oh-so-holy and much-loved father committed suicide?'

And horrified though he was, into Shepherd's mind came the disturbing thought, *she's rehearsed this*.

She leant further forward, so their heads were too close. He felt heat throbbing between them. He stayed still, did not flinch, did not back away. He would let her roll. All the way to a confession.

'They'll say it was because the physical pain was more than he could bear — and it was bad. But he killed himself because I wouldn't do it for him.'

'What do you mean?'

'He asked me to give him all the painkillers, and I said no. I wasn't going to do what he wanted ever again. "Get me more Passiona, let the tea brew longer, throw the kitten in the dam, sit still, be quiet, ask for forgiveness." God, you have no idea what that does to a child. All topped off with his belt. I will never forget what he did to us — his children — and I will never forgive him. Never forget, never forgive, that's my motto.'

The vitriol was like fire in Shepherd's face.

'You got one thing right — I wanted to kill the bastard . . .' Here it comes, thought Shepherd. The confession.

'. . . but not if he wanted to die. I wasn't his silent listener anymore.'

She was good, he had to give her that.

Suddenly she sat back on her heels, the tips of her fingers spread across her forehead. 'I've just realised something. The bastard killed himself so that you'd think I killed him. So I'd go to jail for murdering him. It was the ultimate punishment for disobeying him, refusing to kill him. He's unbelievable.'

Shepherd frowned. The man was definitely a monster, so she could be right. Or she could be lying. The problem was, he couldn't decide. For all he knew, this might be an enormous elaborately planned performance to convince him of her innocence.

'But the belt? How do you explain the belt?' He was raising his voice at her, despite his plan to stay calm.

She tilted her head to one side, as if she was just working everything out.

Shepherd knew he couldn't yell at her again, but the frustration and uncertainty were excruciating. He had been so sure that arriving with the belt — the non-murder weapon — he'd be able to cajole the truth out of her. But suddenly he wasn't so sure.

He looked up and saw the blank wall above the table where they'd just had their cups of tea. A blank wall with a small clean rectangle.

And he remembered.

It was so long ago, and he'd been such a novice when he and Ron had visited and revisited every farmhouse within a fifty-mile radius of Wendy Boscombe's neatly lined-up dolls. Ron had asked the questions while Shepherd wrote the answers and jotted down relevant observations: anything odd like a furtive glance between family members, someone who wouldn't look them in the eye, someone who was overly friendly and cooperative.

And that wall-hanging had struck the diligent Constable Shepherd as very odd. He should be looking at it now, right where that clean rectangle was. Slowly, his memory of that one image unlocked other memories. A girl who had been so quiet, it had been unnerving. An older boy. Quiet, too. Their compliant, perplexed mother, and the father who had definitely been overly friendly and cooperative.

Staring at the blank rectangle now, he was pretty sure he had copied down the wall-hanging's awkwardly embroidered words. He'd assumed they were meant to be reassuring, but even then he'd shuddered at the thought of growing up with that sinister message literally hanging over you.

Christ is the head of this house
The unseen guest at every meal
The silent listener to every conversation

And what had Joy just said? *I wasn't his silent listener anymore.*

60

GEORGE AND GWEN

January 1949

Every day the tension in Gwen's head became more unbearable. Her neck and shoulders and chest were constantly taut as she waited for George's fury to explode again. Fury that would be followed by a hit or kick or slam, signalling the start of it all again. About six weeks after baby Ruth's burial, Gwen began to understand that something had shifted, but still she knew that to let down her guard would be reckless. And while she should have been relieved at the shift, the fear pressed in on her until her exhausted brain felt like it was covered with a thick grainy layer of wet concrete, slowly hardening. Or was that her heart? She couldn't tell anymore.

George was right, of course. Mark *was* a difficult child, and if George didn't discipline him, just as he himself had been, if he didn't take matters in hand, the boy would get worse and grow up to be a delinquent. George told her, as her great-aunt had, that children needed to be taught how to behave, and he certainly knew more about that than she did. When he screamed at Mark, the tension in her head hardened that layer of wet concrete a little more, and robbed her of access to words of protest. All she could do was mumble some unconvincing pleas.

By the time he hit Mark for the first time, the concrete had set into an impenetrable wall, and not even the pleas could get past that wall. Besides, it was just a slap, and if anything, Mark had deserved it because he'd been disobedient. It was for his own good. Surely.

When George appeared with the belt in his hand for the first time, she convinced herself that she did not know what he was going to do, and went to her workroom, where she wired and taped roses, twirled ribbons, and made neat records in the accounting book. And as she lay in bed that night, thinking of that dance in Willshire hundreds of years ago and the ever-narrowing road she had been on since then, she was too numb and scared to admit the truth — that she was relieved it hadn't been her at the end of his belt.

* * *

Meanwhile, Joy lay in her bassinet, watching and hearing how her family was to be. When Mark's mustard-yellow fear and red screams penetrated her tiny brain, her right hand moved up to her face, and her fingers ran along little raised lumps of the purple birthmark that covered the right side of her face. The lumps would disappear before she was one, but the birthmark would stay with her until she died.

And her left hand reached out to touch her other half. Her twin sister who had been beside her for eight and a half months.

But her hand reached into emptiness. Joy was alone.

61

JOY AND SHEPHERD

February 1983

> HENDERSON, George. With much gratitude, and sincere sympathy to the family. Clarice Johnson

Shepherd's knees were getting sore, but he didn't want to break the moment by moving.

'You're right — he couldn't strangle himself with the belt,' Joy said. 'It's time to tell you the truth, I suppose.'

Yes! thought Shepherd. *This is it.*

'Every night, for as long as I can remember, I've dreamt about killing him. Over the years, I must have dreamt of a thousand ways of doing it. Chopping off his head, pouring migraine pills down his throat, trapping him in the dairy and letting the cows trample him to death.' She looked directly at Shepherd. 'Because, as he once told you and your boss, no one could hear if you were screaming your lungs out in the dairy. Or, for that matter, in your bedroom.'

Shepherd was both horrified and exultant. *She's about to confess. At last.* He just wished that his knees weren't crying out in pain.

'Half the time, when I woke up I didn't know if it had been a dream or if I'd actually managed to kill him, but of course he was always still alive. Things just got worse and worse, and one day — the day before Wendy disappeared — I thought he was going to kill me. Then, when she did disappear, all anyone could talk about was keeping children safe, protecting them from the "monster". But no one cared about what the monster called George Henderson was doing to his own children.' She looked at him. 'And don't tell me that nobody knew, because everyone knew.'

Shepherd felt like she was accusing him of wilful neglect. And those medical file-notes and Joy's scars made him feel very uncomfortable. Weren't police officers supposed to protect people — especially children? Of course, until Vicki had shown him the notes, he hadn't known what had gone on in this farmhouse, but had Ron? Vicki had said everyone knew why Mark had run away, so presumably that included Ron. And they'd all just ignored it because George was an Elder in the bloody church.

'I often wondered,' she continued, 'if he was capable of . . .'

She didn't finish the sentence, but Shepherd knew she was about to say 'killing Wendy'.

Could George have had anything to do with Wendy's disappearance? Or was Joy deliberately distracting him?

She continued talking. 'After every dream, Ruth was right there, whispering that one day it wouldn't be a dream. One day we would . . .' She sighed. 'When I was sixteen, I left. And the dreams stopped. Just like that. The first night away, I couldn't believe it. And the second night, in Darwin, instead of dreaming about killing my father, I dreamt about finding Mark.'

She looked at Shepherd, and grimaced. 'So I rang every Henderson in every phone book in Australia that had an M as a first or second initial. But not one of them was Mark. Then I thought he must have left the country, so I moved to England, and kept searching. Wherever I went, I got a phone connected, and never had an unlisted number . . . hoping that Mark was looking for me, too. Every day, I hoped it would be the day he'd ring, or that I'd somehow bump into him, both of us drawn to the same place at the same time. How stupid is that?

'But the years rolled by,' she started sobbing again, 'more and more of them, and it never happened. Eventually I gave up and came back to Australia. I hadn't been here a month when Vicki did what I was hoping Mark would do. She rang Directory Assistance, got my phone number and called me. Asked me if I'd come and look after my sick father. What could I say? Maybe she'd somehow find Mark too and we'd both come back. I guess I thought I might also get an apology from my father if he was dying. Or, who knows, perhaps just forgive him.'

Or kill him, thought Shepherd. *You just said, 'Never forget, never forgive.'*

'As soon as I walked into the kitchen, I saw Ruth. That was a surprise. I hadn't seen her since I left, which made sense, I suppose. If it hadn't been for Ruth, I would have died of fear or madness when I was living here. She was the only one who understood me. Anyway, the day Vicki rang me, the dreams about killing my father started again. They were so vivid, it was alarming. And once I came back, things were worse than ever. I even saw my mother one day — in the chook shed. And Wendy in the driveway. So I suppose I was having . . . some difficulties.'

Joy looked down to where a tiny sliver of saucer had forced its way under one of her fingernails. A small ball of blood had formed, so she pressed the finger against the sleeve of her torn shirt.

'The night after Vicki rang, I dreamt I found the belt and wrapped it around his neck, and pulled and pulled until I squeezed every ounce of air from his lungs and every ounce of viciousness from his blood. He was awake but paralysed, so he couldn't stop me. I dreamt one version or another of that dream every night until . . .'

Shepherd's knees were about to crack into pieces. He noticed that somehow Joy was sitting comfortably on the floor. He had to move, but it would break the spell. He just wasn't sure who was weaving the spell and who was trapped in it.

'I made up my mind to stop dreaming about it, and kill him.' Shepherd inhaled quickly. *Yes, yes, yes.*

'So on Friday night, when I knew he'd be asleep, I walked into his room and I looked for that belt — that's why there were clothes all over the floor,' she took a breath, 'and when I found it, I walked over to where he was lying so I could strangle the bastard.

'But I hung it back up on the nail and went back to bed.' What game was she playing now?

Joy stood up, stepped over the broken crockery, and sat on the couch. Shepherd followed her, his knees heaving with relief. He was now convinced that she was telling the truth.

Or that she wasn't.

He almost laughed as he imagined telling Vicki that the encounter had resulted in two such bleedingly obvious and mutually exclusive statements.

Vicki had told him George Henderson's funeral was going to be the biggest in the area since some mayor's daughter had died ages ago. And, like a seasoned detective, Shepherd had read all the death notices in case an unusual name or a cryptic message turned up. But the notices only confirmed what a pillar of the community, he'd been — generous, devout, hard-working, admired.

Then there were Joy's scars. And the medical records Vicki had 'stumbled across'. And Colin's quiet assertion that George was mean, and Barbara's use of the word *escape*. Shepherd thought again of the jigsaw puzzle he and Ron had started before Wendy disappeared. With each piece having two sides, if you could ever actually finish the damn thing, there'd be two complete pictures, only one of which you could ever see, because the reverse picture was, of course, hidden from view.

If there were two sides to George, maybe Vicki was right about how he died. Maybe it was suicide. Or an accident.

'The next morning, Ruth was gone,' said Joy. 'I was relieved, but devastated. Because she said all the things I couldn't, or wouldn't, say or admit to myself, but she also never shut up. I got sick of her, I *wanted* her gone, and the second my father was dead, I didn't need her anymore.'

Shepherd nodded. Ruth was the other side of Joy.

'So,' Joy said, 'there are two things you must have realised by now. First, the day my father died was the happiest day of my life. Second, because he *wanted* to die, I wanted him to live. But, I did get up in the middle of the night, I did creep into his room, and I . . .'

Shepherd held her eyes. *Come on. Just confess. You'll feel much better.*

'No more lies,' she said, looking down and swallowing.

I knew it.

'I did creep into his room,' she repeated, 'and I did get the belt, but I didn't hang it back up on the nail. I was going to thrash his body with it, tear his flesh, make him bleed like he had done to us so many times, but I couldn't bring myself to do it, to be that *cruel*, that *violent* — apart from the fact that he would have woken up, even with all those pills. So I slipped the tail of the belt under the back of his neck, pulled it around and fed it through the buckle, then I pulled it as hard as I could. I had to do *something*, I had to physically do *something* to get a large, angry knot of revenge out of my system. It was stupid, of course, but,' she lifted her chin and raised her voice, 'it felt good. And I'm glad I did it.'

Shepherd breathed out. She'd confessed to the lesser of the two wrongs inflicted on George Henderson that night, just as he'd thought she might.

She continued, quietly now. 'But I didn't know he was already dead.'

Shepherd didn't believe her for a second. And in the next second, he did.

'So, I suppose I'm guilty of . . . what? Attempted murder?'

Shepherd shook his head. As far as he knew, what she had done wasn't even a crime . . . certainly not one that was worth dragging her into court for.

Just like a few days ago, two scenarios presented themselves to him.

Scenario one: Joy was telling the truth and George had accidentally or deliberately overdosed himself and then she'd tried to strangle him to death. In which case, that was the end of it. Mystery solved. Or to be precise, no mystery *to* be solved.

Scenario two: Joy *had* killed him with the painkillers, then put the belt around his neck, all the while planning to eventually confess to attempting to murder him after he was dead, and thus convince everyone that she *hadn't* killed him with the painkillers. Because, as Vicki had so annoyingly said, why would Joy put the belt around his neck after she'd already killed him?

The second scenario was a maddening circular argument that Shepherd couldn't get his head around, especially not while his knees were still burning and the memory of her scars was making him wince. But if he was ever going to eliminate — or prove — scenario two, it had to be by establishing facts, not by playing Joy's games.

'So, when you put the belt around his neck, didn't you wonder why he didn't wake up and struggle?'

'I thought the drugs were keeping him asleep. He had so many of those pills, and I didn't even know what they were all for.' She shrugged. 'Whenever I gave him drugs, he slept. For hours. I just followed Vicki's instructions.'

She got up, pulled out a brush and shovel from a cupboard and swept up the broken crockery. 'The weird thing is, I always thought that if I did kill him, I would want him to *know* that I was killing him. I was going to whisper, "I'm getting revenge. For everything you did to me, to Mark, to Ruth, to our mother." But when he told me he *wanted* to die,

I decided I didn't want him to know that I was doing his bidding. Even so, while I was pulling that belt around his neck, I wanted him to wake up and beg for mercy, wanted him to know that I was dishing out justice as well as getting revenge. As it turned out, neither of us got what we wanted. He had to kill himself because he didn't think I would, and I didn't get my revenge because the bastard was already dead.'

Shepherd was frozen. God, there was something strange about this damn house, this hot dark room, and this woman with her deep red scars and cold dark secrets.

'So, no, he didn't gasp or fight,' she said, tipping the crockery into the bin.

Shepherd was annoyed, confused. He just didn't know whether to believe everything Joy was telling him. But there was no witness, no murder weapon and no other evidence. Even Vicki had made it clear that she would have to testify that George Henderson could have taken those tablets accidentally or deliberately.

Joy Henderson had beaten him. She was going to get away with murder.

62

JOY AND RUTH

January 1961

'Mrs Felicity, can I ask you something?'

'Of course, dear.'

They were washing dishes while Felicity was out at the stables with Mr Felicity, and Joy knew it was now or never. 'When different people look at the same word, do they get the same picture in their heads, or do they get different pictures?'

'Mmm,' said Mrs Felicity. 'Do you mean does everyone see an elephant when they read the word *elephant*?'

'No-o.' Joy hesitated. 'When I see the word *elephant*, I see a thick brown, battered book with curled-up pages.' Mrs Felicity looked up from the pot she was scrubbing, and Joy could tell she was intrigued, so she continued. 'But sometimes it's not a picture. Sometimes it can be a feeling. Like when I read *butterfly*, I have that feeling you get when you think that one day you are actually going to die.'

Mrs Felicity raised her eyebrows at that one.

'Is there something wrong with me?'

'Well, Joy, I don't see any pictures when I see words, although I might think about what an elephant, or whatever it is, looks like. And I don't get feelings either. Not even when I see the word for something beautiful like a butterfly. I think you just have a very special . . . understanding of words.'

'What do you mean?'

'Well, some people can compose songs in their heads, like Beethoven, and others can imagine strange places and people that don't exist, so they write stories like *Dr Jekyll and Mr Hyde*. And I've read about people who have what they call "coloured hearing". They see colours when they hear certain words and numbers, or when they're listening to music. You must have something like that. But instead of seeing colours, you see whole pictures.'

As Joy listened, the eels shrank a little.

'Are there other words that you have images for?'

'There are hundreds! One of my favourites is *blurb*. It's a swing in a playground, at least fifty feet high. Because it ends where it starts, but takes you somewhere you've never been before.'

Mrs Felicity tilted her head, and said, 'Yes, I can see that.'

'Can you? It's amazing, isn't it?'

'What else?'

'Another of my favourites is *sliver*. It's shimmering drops of blood. And *nonchalant* — a duke lying on a couch. Don't you think?'

'Oh, I like that one. Keep going.'

'Okay. Well, *nectar* is an archway made of silk, and *sub-lime* is a soft, round lump of Christmas cake icing tucked into your cheek and melting; *turgid* is a muddy sponge, *topiary* is a room full of furniture that's all upside down, and *whet* — the one with the h — is a sword coming down so fast it makes a swish in the air. *Exoskeleton* is a line of angry mountains.' The words tumbled out quickly and wildly. Mrs Felicity wasn't laughing at her, so she continued. 'And then there are words like *perfect*, which you can rearrange to make another word that you can put right after it . . . like *perfect prefect*, which is crisp loneliness, and *latent talent*, which is a blue balloon sailing in a sky of exactly the same blue but you can just see the movement of the balloon if you know what to look for. And,' Joy hesitated, but she felt she just had to tell someone, 'then there are words like *Devil*, full of other words that mean almost the same thing, like *evil* and *veil* and *lied* and *die*. And ones that just sound wrong. You know, like *catapult* . . .'

'Catapult sounds wrong?'

'Yes. It's clumsy and jerky, but it should be slender and arched like something flying through the air, shouldn't it? Although at least it's quick and punchy.'

Mrs Felicity nodded, as Joy kept talking. 'And it's not just the words I *like*. There are words that make me angry or scared or sad, and have horrible images. When I asked Mr Plummer at school if we all had the same images, he laughed at me.'

'Well,' said Mrs Felicity, 'maybe he just doesn't understand that your brain works a little differently. Imagine if our brains were all the same. There'd be nothing to talk about and there'd be no Beethovens or Monets, no Marie Curies or Virginia Woolfs.'

She put the pot on the draining board and Joy picked it up to dry it.

'So, have you written these down somewhere, Joy?'

'No. Why?'

'Well, I think you should. Wait here.' She dried her hands and walked out of the kitchen.

When she came back, she handed Joy a notebook. But not one like Joy's parents used to write letters to the bank. This had a deep-brown hard cover with strange lettering all over it that reminded Joy of the tins at the back of the supermarket. Its pages were thick and creamy and covered with faint dotted lines to write on.

'Write them down in here. All the words you love — and all the words that are ugly, or make you angry or scared — and write down their images, too.'

Joy looked at the book in her hands, worried that she would leave dirty marks on such a beautiful thing. 'And then what?'

'And then what?' Mrs Felicity's voice was loud and excited. 'Then you will be a different person, Joy, and who knows what will happen after that?'

63

JOY AND SHEPHERD

February 1983

> HENDERSON, George. A hard-working member of our community who will be sadly missed. Sincere condolences to the family. Kingfisher Primary School

Shepherd might just leave me alone now. I'm pretty sure I've finally convinced him that I didn't kill my father. Plus I have the belt.

There's not much more to do, except clear out the house and go to the dam to see if it has actually dried up.

I order two skips, which they say will arrive tomorrow at six in the morning, and spend the rest of the evening and night thinking about how all of this might work out.

The next morning I'm up before the skips arrive so I can get most of it done before it gets too hot. I work methodically through the back porch, bathroom and laundry. None of them have much in them, and it's easy to carry or drag everything out and throw it all in the first of the two skips now lined up in the driveway, although the Dutch hoe in the cupboard in the back porch objects loudly.

The whole time I'm carrying and tossing, I'm thinking that very soon I'll be able to tell Shepherd about the doll in the chest, and my father's confession. I think I've worked out what I need to do, but if I'm wrong, all I'll be able to give Shepherd is the doll. If I'm right, then I'll be able to give him Wendy's body as well.

When I step into my mother's workroom, I wonder if I should keep something from there, but nothing's of use to anyone who isn't a florist. It only takes two trips and the room is bare.

When I open Mark's door, I pause again. He needs to know that our father is dead. I'll start searching for him again tomorrow. I'll hire a detective, put ads in every newspaper in the country. I won't stop until I find him and can tell him everything.

I step into his room and decide that I'm not going to keep pausing every time I walk into a room full of memories. I have to be ruthless.

Ruthless, fatherless, motherless. But not brotherless.

I'm surprised at how easy it is to lift and push and drag boxes of rubbish and disassembled furniture, now that it's over and I'm going to find Mark.

In two hours, I get through his room, my room, the kitchen, the good room. The only thing I haven't thrown out is the evidence bag sitting on the kitchen bench, the belt still coiled up inside.

Now there's just *his* bedroom. I avoid looking in the dressing table's dark mirror and walk over to the wardrobe to pull out the nail I found that night, the one with the magenta screams hanging off it. I put it beside the evidence bag, return to the bedroom and pull open the first of the wide drawers under the mirror.

When I see that it's empty, I assume these two drawers were my mother's and he just threw all of her things into the rubbish tank.

I expect that the second one will be empty too, but when I yank it open, something slides forward from the back. It's a square wooden box the woodwork teacher gave me on my first day at Blackhunt High School. For a split second back then, I thought it was a present from the school, but the teacher explained that Mark had wanted to make something special for his mother in the last few weeks of school, during the end-of-year activities. Mark hadn't quite finished the box ('It just needs to be lacquered'), so the woodwork teacher had happily locked it in the storeroom for the holidays. But of course Mark hadn't returned.

I sit on the bed, thinking how pleased Mark will be when I tell him that I gave it to Mum and she kept it till she died. And he'll be as surprised as I am that our father didn't throw it away. Maybe he didn't see it when he got rid of Mum's clothes, or didn't know that Mark had made it.

Looking at my mother's empty drawers, I think about how empty she must have been after both Mark and I left. A rush of guilt bangs into my stomach because I never once contacted her, and she died not knowing if I was even still alive. When I was in the train the day I escaped, I told myself that she was as bad as our father for never rescuing us from him, but that was just so I didn't have to feel guilty. With no family, no money and no choices, she was as trapped as her children were.

I decide that after the skips are gone, I'm going to go to the cemetery and say sorry.

I shake the box and hear something light moving back and forth inside. I slip the brass latch out of its hook and pull up the lid. Inside, there are lots of little rectangles of newspaper. I tip a few into my palm, then pick one. It's the death notice from Aunty Rose for Uncle Bill. There's a yellowed bit of sticky tape across the top so I turn it over and read another death notice.

> HENDERSON, William. Brother to George, brother-in-law to Gwen, uncle to Mark, Ruth and

Joy. He fought bravely to defend our nation. May the Lord bless thee

Three lines. Not even 'loved' brother or 'loved' uncle. Even I know it should read 'May the Lord bless thee *and keep thee*' but that would have meant paying for another line. I pick up four more and speed-read them. Two death notices for people I've never heard of, and then one that brings tears to my eyes.

LARSEN, Robert. A kind Christian neighbour, whose smile will always be remembered. George and Gwen Henderson

I'm cross that my parents didn't add my name to this one, and that there's no date so I don't know when Mr Larsen died. But I suppose it doesn't matter now.

I pick up another. It's not that I'm interested in them, I'm just resting before I unscrew the mirror and pull apart the other big pieces of furniture in here.

The next one is not a death notice, but it's still short and to the point.

HENDERSON, George and Gwen announce the safe arrival of Mark George on 31 July. Thanks to Dr Merriweather

I read the lines of Times Roman again, and suddenly I don't know who I'm angrier with — my dead father or my runaway brother. I tear the little notice in half, and in half again, and let the pieces fall on to the grey carpet.

All those people in this box are in the past, including Mark. I slam the lid back down, push the latch into place and throw the box on the bed. It bounces off the mattress onto the floor, out of sight.

I carry out the contents of the first of my father's drawers, sweating in the heat and cursing that I thought emptying the house myself would be cathartic or something. I should have just paid someone.

After I've emptied all his drawers, I can't pretend not to care anymore. I retrieve the box and tip its contents onto the empty bed where my father died. It doesn't take long to find the one I'm looking for.

> HENDERSON, Gwen. Loving wife of George, loving mother to Mark, Ruth and Joy. You were always my sunshine.

How dare he? How dare he refer to that song as if our family and their marriage was overflowing with sunshine and love? God, I hate that song.

My fingers keep trawling through the little pieces of newspaper, discarding the irrelevant ones, looking for the other one I've always wondered about.

And there it is. HENDERSON, Ruth Poppy. I read it quickly.

But there's a mistake. A serious mistake.

The words on the tiny rectangle of paper blur, so I squeeze my eyes to get rid of the tears, and try to work this out. There's no year on it. Why don't they include the date — at least the year — on these things?

My mind is trying to race through mud. I think about what my mother told me the day I asked her, *Why are all the chooks called Ruth?*

The heat and the sweat and the smell of my father's death are making me ill, but I force myself to read the impossible words again.

> HENDERSON, Ruth Poppy. Beloved daughter of George and Gwen, little sister to Mark, twin sister to Joy. In our arms for seconds, in God's for eternity.

Twin sister? No, no, no. Ruth wasn't my twin. The accident — her *murder* — was before I was born. The only reason I was conceived and born was because Ruth died. What the hell is going on here?

64

JOY AND RUTH

January 1961

'What's that?' asked her mother, pointing at the brown-paper bag under Joy's arm.

'Oh,' said Joy. 'Just some homework for Bible Studies.' How easily the lies slipped out these days.

When Joy took the notebook out of the brown-paper bag Mrs Felicity had given her, Ruth was excited.

'You'll have to hide it. We don't want him finding it. Or even our mother.'

They looked around the sparse room, and Joy said, 'In the second drawer, under my old jumper?'

Ruth nodded. Now that she had her new mustard jumper, the book would be safe hidden under the old one.

That night after tea, Joy pulled out the notebook and placed it on her desk. She felt the pages yearning to be filled with her special words and descriptions of their images.

She turned to the second page and picked up her blue pen, already knowing the first word she wanted to write. But as the pen was about to touch the paper, she decided that she needed to practise so she didn't spoil the beautiful notebook. She pulled out her old maths exercise book, and on the inside of the back cover wrote *blurb* over and over until she thought it was a little bit like Mr Plummer's alphabet across the top of the blackboard. It was still messy and clumsy, and she knew her father would shake his head at it, as he always did when he saw her handwriting. Sometimes he hissed.

Ruth whispered from the bed, 'What would he know about words and their images? And besides, he'll never see this.'

Joy pulled the brown notebook towards her, and wrote *blurb*. She took a breath, and leaving a little space, wrote a description of the word's image. She looked at it and sighed.

'The handwriting doesn't matter, Joy. Keep going.'

Joy nodded, and leaving a blank line, she wrote *turgid*. She took another deep breath, ready to write the description, when Ruth said, 'It's like you're writing your own dictionary.'

Joy filled a whole page with fifteen words and their definitions before she put down the pen and walked around the room a little bit.

'It's good,' said Ruth. 'Really good.'

Joy went back to the desk, and read what she had written, and felt . . . what was it? Ruth whispered in her ear, 'Dark Strawberry Cream chocolate', and the strange sensation that Joy had felt eating Mr Larsen's chocolate, when she believed he was the Devil, surged up and down her spine.

She turned the page and began to write *nectar*.

Without warning, the door opened sharply, and as she jumped, a line of ink shot out from the C.

His face red, he shouted, 'What are you doing? Get to bed. Now!'

The eels were hissing. What if he saw the notebook? She pushed it under her Bible, but it didn't completely cover it. 'Sorry, Dad. I was doing something for Bible St—'

'I don't care if you're writing to the Queen. Get into bed. Do you think we're made of money? Or are *you* planning on paying the electricity bill? You're a filthy, selfish sinner. What are you?'

'A filthy, selfish sinner.'

'Get to bed.'

As she walked towards her bed, grateful that she had already put on her pyjamas, he slapped her face.

The light was snapped off, the door slammed shut. She let out a sigh of relief. She got into bed, placed the back of her hand against her hot cheek and squeezed her eyes shut. She would have to wait until the morning to hide the notebook. To be heard creeping around now would be unforgivable. She also wanted to erase that errant line of ink. And *errant* {a set of stone stairs in a wild overgrown garden} would be the next word she would write in her dictionary.

She thought of some of the other wonderful words she'd add, like *particular* {a newly sharpened pencil}, *surgeon* {a perfectly vertical cliff}, *sleek* {a gold ribbon}, *probably* {a rubber ball bouncing down a wooden stairway}. She would never ever run out of words.

Lying there, she thought about how she would normally be drenched with shame from the stinging of her cheek and the thumping in her chest. But the thumping had almost gone, and the eels in her stomach were still. In the darkness, she realised that she still felt like Dark Strawberry Cream chocolate.

A different person, just like Mrs Felicity had said.

65

JOY AND SHEPHERD

February 1983

> HENDERSON, George. A community man who had a good and kind heart. Sincere condolences to the family. Alison Bell

'Before you were born.' I *know* they were my mother's words.

And then the penny drops. It isn't a mistake on Ruth's death notice, it's a mistake I made in assuming that my mother meant *years* before I was born, not minutes or seconds.

Another penny drops . . . it could have been *me* who was killed that day instead of Ruth. And if it had been me who died, then Ruth would have lived and been named Joy and the dead me would have been named Ruth. So, who's to say I'm not Ruth? Ruth *and* Joy.

And there's the anger again. Why the hell didn't they tell me?

Why all the secrets?

I stuff all the little rectangles back into the box because the only place they belong is in the skip, when I notice there's some thick cream paper lining the bottom. More secrets? I prise it out with a fingernail, sit back down on the bed and unfold three documents. The first is a letter addressed to my father, dated 17 March 1940 and on letterhead that says 'Federal Directorate of Recruiting and Mobilisation, Allied Land Headquarters'. There's a lot of bureaucratic beating about the bush, but the message is clear enough, even though I know nothing about World War II recruitment. Apparently, being a 'young Australian male', my father began three months of mandatory military training but was discharged before he finished it. According to the letter, the Directorate was 'taking appropriate measures to exclude unsuitables from the Services which includes persons demonstrating Manic Depressive, Delusional and Confusional states or other Mental Abnormalities'.

There are more bureaucratic banalities, and then a signature above the name Xavier P. Taylor, Consulting Physician, Psychological Section, Australian Imperial Force.

This is not exactly what I'd call good news. I read the second sheet.

It's another letter from the Directorate, dated 22 February 1942, explaining that 'as a consequence of The Hon. John Curtin MP Prime Minister of Australia invoking the *Defence Act 1903* in order to protect the rights and liberties of all Australians, it is now a requirement for all Australian men aged 18–35 and all single men aged 36–45 to join the Citizen Military Forces. Consequently, Mr George Joshua Henderson (DOB 18 April 1906) is to report to Puckapunyal Military Base on Monday the 31st of August 1942, at 8.30 a.m. sharp.' The final paragraph states 'this correspondence countermands any and all previous orders the addressee has received pertaining to active participation in mandatory service to defend the Commonwealth of Australia'.

A thud of sympathy whacks me in the chest. Not for my father, but for his brother whose stumps had frightened me when I was young.

The third sheet is my parents' wedding certificate. I have never seen it before, but I have always known the date:

Saturday, 22 August 1942. Aunty Rose once told me about their 'whirlwind romance', and how 'absolutely smitten' my father was with my mother, even booking the church for their wedding before he proposed. And now I know why.

I take Ruth's death notice, the letters and the marriage certificate out to the kitchen bench and put the evidence bag on top of them. At least I'll be able to tell Mark the whole story.

I'm carrying another load of my father's clothes out to the second skip when Shepherd's car pulls up ten yards behind it. What the hell does he want now? I'm not inviting him inside. Apart from not wanting to indulge him again, there's nothing left in the kitchen, not even that revolting pink tea-cosy, which I can see sticking out from under the broken crockery I dropped on the floor yesterday.

He stands behind his open car door, arms folded across the top of it. Jesus, does he think he's in some cop show?

'Joy,' he says flatly.

'Detective,' I say just as flatly, with my arms full of my father's white underpants, singlets and socks.

'I've been thinking.' He's squinting in the sun, looking a bit . . . well, vulnerable. My heart slows down a little.

'Oh yeah?'

'Yes. About you and your father's death — which I still think was a murder. Let's see.' He steps out from behind the car door and walks towards me. 'You had motive, tick. Opportunity, tick. You were at the scene of the crime at the time of the crime, tick, tick, tick.' He holds up a thumb and two fingers one by one. 'Jesus, you even admit that you went into his room to kill him. And that is one damn big tick, Joy Henderson.'

He shakes his head, takes a breath, and keeps going. 'But it seems that he was already dead, so you didn't kill him, even though you tried to. And Vicki will testify that he wanted to die, didn't want to face all that pain, and actually asked her to give him a whole bottle of pills or a quick injection. And when she wouldn't, because the woman apparently does have some professional ethics, he begged her to find his children so he could kill himself at home without any medical busybody do-gooders to prevent him or rescue him.' He sighs. 'Of course, you know all this.'

I try not to react. I actually didn't know any of that. Vicki did give me a hell of a lot of tablets for him, but who was I to question her about them? Hell, I was too worried that *she'd* be the one questioning *me* about how many he was having.

The lump of clothes in my arms is getting heavy and I want him to hurry up so I can take apart the rest of the furniture, chuck it all in here and leave this place. For ever and ever, Amen.

Should I tell him about my father's confession now, and show him the doll? Would it be enough? I don't think so. Maybe it would convince him to make a thorough search of the farm, and if my theory is correct, he'd find Wendy. Then he'd have the confession, the doll, *and* the body. And surely that would be enough? Surely he'd have to come to the inevitable conclusion that my father killed Wendy?

I open my mouth to tell him about the doll, but he starts up again.

'So his death certificate will read "self-inflicted unintentional death caused by administration of excessive prescription medication". And there you have it. Officially, he killed himself accidentally, so no one will even suspect that it was suicide. Let alone murder.'

I nod. 'He told me twice that he wanted me to kill him. I just didn't think he'd do it to himself after I'd said I wasn't going to.'

Shepherd continues as if I haven't said anything. 'Still, you put that belt around his neck, allegedly not knowing he was dead, and never wondered why he didn't struggle.'

I stare at him. 'We went through all of this yesterday.' The thing is, of course, that he can't let go. I've won and he can't stand it.

'I'll tell you another thing that's been bothering me, Joy Henderson,' he says, and I sigh, audibly. 'Why didn't you take the belt off? It did muddy the waters somewhat, didn't it?'

I shrug. He's right. It did indeed muddy the waters. 'Well, once I'd done it, I realised how stupid I'd been, but if I'd taken it off, there would have been marks on his neck anyway, so you would have been asking some pretty difficult questions one way or the other.'

'And as you probably guessed, the belt's too old and cracked to get any decent fingerprints from it.'

I toss my father's underwear into the skip on top of the contents of the old bureau. The five broken frosted glasses glint in the sun. I wish I'd kept two of them — one for me, one for Mark.

'I don't know what you want me to say. I'm never going to confess to my father's murder,' I reach in, wondering if even one of the glasses might be intact, 'because I didn't kill him.'

They're all broken, so I turn around to look at Shepherd, who just can't stop talking, goading me.

'Well, you would say that, wouldn't you? Whether you were guilty or innocent.'

We're standing in the sun facing each other, like two duelling gunmen in the wild wild west. Each waiting for the other to have a fatal lapse of concentration.

'You know,' he goes on, 'I asked the Larsens about Ruth, and Colin — through tears — told me she was dead. At first, I thought he'd killed her — and maybe even your father. Especially when he said he knew where she was. He even agreed to take me to her, and gave what I thought was a final farewell pat to his sick old cat. So, we got in the car and I followed his directions, trying to stay calm, hoping your poor missing sister was still alive and I could rescue her, and suddenly wondering if Colin had also killed Wendy Boscombe all those years ago, and I'd find two bodies wherever he was taking me. When he told me we were going to the cemetery, I thought, *oh God, he's buried her in a freshly dug grave*, but no. What a fool I was, running around chasing the proverbial wild goose, while you were fine-tuning your story.'

'Why didn't you tell me that you knew?'

'This may come as a surprise to you, Joy Henderson, but I'm under no obligation to tell you anything. You're the one under investigation.' He wipes sweat from his face. 'Colin said that Ruth's death was an accident, that your mother slipped—'

'Yes, that's right.' I interrupt him quickly, because he doesn't need to know any more than this, otherwise who knows what he'll start thinking? I was relieved he'd stopped bugging me about Ruth, and now that I know why, it's one thing I can stop worrying about. I'm still getting my head around the fact that she's my twin; that it might have been me who died, and Ruth who lived, or that maybe it was Ruth who lived — that I am actually Ruth. My brain is having trouble coping with this, and I don't need Shepherd trying to psycho-analyse everything in 50-degree heat.

'So you see, Joy, I am left to conclude that you lied to me about Ruth so you could send me off on that wild goose chase, distract me from the truth. But you had to know that I'd find out.'

'I didn't lie. I told you and Vicki that when I first arrived back at the farm, I saw Ruth for the first time in years, and that's true. And I told you that I hadn't seen her that morning — also true. Vicki was the one who told you that Ruth had "disappeared, gone". I even told you that she wasn't an angry person. Splitting hairs, maybe, but not once did I lie to you. I was very careful. I just didn't tell you everything.' Like my mother 'not-telling' my father about the price of the contact for our school books all those years ago. I make a half-grimace, to let him know that I recognise that my claim of not lying is perhaps open to interpretation.

'That's not the slightest bit funny.'

I really want to stop this conversation, so maybe I need to start one about the doll's head lying in the chest twenty yards away from us. In retrospect, maybe I should have told him yesterday when we were having our little *tête-à-tête*, but at what point could I have interrupted him and said, 'By the way, I forgot to tell you, I know where Wendy Boscombe's doll is'?

I'm dithering because I'd really rather see if my theory is correct before I get to the doll. I want all the loose ends tied up. Most of all, I want the Boscombes to have some peace. I know they'll be heartbroken when Shepherd tells them that my father killed Wendy, but they'll also be relieved that their ordeal is over — Mrs Boscombe said so herself to Vicki.

It's so unbearably hot, I'm wondering whether it's all worth it. It's not like there'll ever be a court case. But then I hear Ruth whispering, 'Justice and revenge, Joy. Never forget, never forgive. It could have been you . . . it was you . . . who died when our mother slipped. I am Joy, and you are Ruth.' Another timely, and frankly overdue, reminder to stay focused.

Shepherd starts talking again. He just won't give up, for crying out loud.

'Did you — do you — want me to believe you're mad? Talking to your dead sister? Dreaming of murdering your father since you were twelve years old? So that even if I *could* prove you killed him, a jury wouldn't find you guilty?'

'What's mad, Detective?'

He gives a single upward nod, and even though that should be the end of it, and he should now get in his car and leave me alone, he keeps talking. 'So, what now?'

'What now? I get rid of all this,' I wave one arm backwards towards the skips, 'and . . .'

There's a pause, and we both wipe sweat from our foreheads. Maybe now's the time for me to say *I found something curious in the shed over there*, but he starts asking more questions.

'So why did you even come back? He was going to die, and he couldn't hurt you anymore. If you'd just stayed away, there wouldn't have been any questions about the why or how. Or who.'

'I've told you already. In case Vicki found Mark too. Besides, I told Vicki I'd take care of him.'

He half-laughs. 'And that's what you did. Take care of him, didn't you? But not exactly in the way Vicki meant.'

'Yes, I did — take *care* of him.' It's ridiculous to be having this conversation in such rotting heat. The taut skin of my scars is smarting, and I still have to check the dam.

'Right.' He nods, then looks at the skips as though he's seeing them for the first time. 'I guess there's a lot to get rid of.'

'Yep.' I wipe my forehead again and come out with the perfect cue for him to leave. 'There's always a lot to get rid of.'

66

JOY AND RUTH

January 1961

'Gently,' whispered Ruth.

Joy picked up the eraser and placed her left index and middle fingers either side of the C to hold the paper firmly. She rubbed as gently as she could over the errant line. When the line was faint, Joy decided it would have to do because she didn't want to tear the paper. Ruth was leaning over her shoulder. 'I think that will do. You don't want to tear the paper,' she said, and her birthmark swelled as she smiled. 'Finish *nectar* and then just two more words. We don't want a repeat of last night.'

Joy had spent the whole day suppressing a torrent of wild desire and pleasure, the eels in her stomach all but drowning in an imagined ocean of Dark Strawberry Cream chocolate every time she thought about her dictionary. She wondered if she could tell Mark about the dictionary without him laughing — and if he saw word images too. If anyone was going to, surely it would be her own brother?

She finished *nectar* and then thought about what the next two words should be. Images of Wendy swirled in her mind, and with them came the words *jealousy* {a red imp dancing on a copy of the Bible} and *fear* {a cold metal knife}. She let the words and images engulf her.

'He won't be back from his Elders Session for another half-hour,' she said. 'I have time to do one more thing.'

She turned to the inside cover, which had a marbled pattern of different shades of browns and cream. In the top third, there was a small rectangle of white with a thin dark border.

'A title,' said Ruth.

'Yes.' Joy picked up her pen and held it above the white rectangle, hesitating. 'But it's so pristine. I don't want to ruin it. It's like . . . a newborn baby.'

Ruth scoffed. 'You know what happens to newborn babies, Joy? Some of them die, so they never get a chance to be "ruined". And the lucky ones who don't die, they quickly learn there's nothing *pristine* about life — it's full of vomit, cancer, migraines, scars, warts, poverty, eels, wars, hunger, measles, pimples, constipation, rotting teeth, bruises, chicken pox.' She took a breath. 'And let's not forget hatred, lies, fear, secrets, jealousy, anger . . . and beltings.'

'See?' said Joy. 'It's better to stay pristine and die than go through all that.'

'That's easy for you to say. I wish—'

'No. No, you don't,' hissed Joy, throwing down her pen. 'You don't know what it's like to be slapped and yelled at, to be scared every second of every day, to be belted till you're bleeding and lumps of flesh are dropping off you. I wish I was dead. I wish I was in Heaven with Wendy Boscombe — or even Hell. Anywhere *he* wasn't.'

Ruth did not say anything, while Joy fought off memories of the Felicities, and Wendy Boscombe's smile, and high school in a few weeks, and how Mark had tried to protect her when the ferrets had escaped, and books . . . the thousands of books waiting for her to read over the years that stretched ahead of her.

'Alright, alright,' she muttered. 'I'll put a title in the rectangle.' She thought for a moment, then picked up her pen. 'This is the best I can think of.' She pressed down hard on the inside cover so it sat flat on her desk, and wrote as neatly as she could.

'Maybe we'll think of a better title later,' said Ruth as she read what Joy had written:

My Beautiful Images by Joy Henderson

'But it's okay, isn't it?' Joy asked Ruth.

Ruth nodded and said, 'Better to be imperfect than non-existent.'

67

JOY AND SHEPHERD

February 1983

> HENDERSON, George. A kind neighbour who took good care of us. Barbara and Colin Larsen

Shepherd walked back to his car, then turned around. Joy was standing beside the skip full of her dead father's belongings, watching him. He hesitated.

'Come on, Detective,' she said, as if talking in the long heat was sapping her strength. 'I want to get this done, and even you must be sick of these conversations.'

'I am.' He sighed. 'I have one more thing I have to do. I don't *want* to, but I have to.'

'Oh Jesus. You're not arresting me after all, are you?' He leant into the car and pulled out an A4 envelope.

Joy raised her eyebrows. 'Is this how arrests are made in real life? Delivered in an envelope?'

Shepherd gave a small shake of his head. 'I have something you need to see,' he said, and took a few steps towards her, cursing the damn sun, cursing the truth. He ran a hand across the sharp fold at the top of the envelope. 'It was the fingerprints. I would never have been sure if we hadn't got his fingerprints all those years ago.'

Joy frowned at the mention of the word *fingerprints*. 'Ah, you found out that my father's fingerprints were on the bottle of painkillers, so you're now willing to agree that he killed himself. Or because my fingerprints were too, you're still convinced that I killed him.'

'If your fingerprints *hadn't* been all over that bottle, I would have been even more suspicious than I was. If that was possible. But I'm not talking about that. I'm talking about Mark.'

'You think Mark killed my father? That's completely ridiculous.'

'Will you just listen for once? I'm saying that I went looking for him.' He held the envelope out in front of him. An olive branch of sorts, he thought.

'What?'

'It occurred to me — for a split second — that he *might* have come back and murdered your father, since he had just as much reason as . . . well, as you did. Do you remember when we came and got the fingerprints of everyone in your family after Wendy Boscombe disappeared?'

'Of course I do.'

'After Vicki told me there was a brother who'd gone missing, I thought he might be on record somewhere and I could find out where he was living. But I couldn't locate him anywhere in Australia — and we have a lot more at our disposal than phonebooks. Of course, he could have moved overseas, but there was no record of him leaving the country either, so I contacted my new friends in the fingerprint bureau. And they found a match.'

'What? You're not messing with me, are you? This isn't some weird psychological game you're playing, is it?' Her voice was sharp, desperate.

Shepherd shook his head, feeling miserable. But also slightly annoyed by her accusation. She was the one who'd been playing psychological games.

'Where is he? Is he in Melbourne? Have you spoken to him?'

'Joy—' began Shepherd.

'I knew I'd find him one day. Does he know our father's dead? I've got to tell him he's dead and buried. Actually, dead and burnt. Or will be soon.'

She stepped forward, arm outstretched. The distance closed between them, and the envelope moved from his hand to hers. Like an exchange of spies on Glienicke Bridge, he thought, except he doubted he'd get anything in exchange.

He had to tell her before she opened it.

He grasped her wrist. 'Wait.'

'What are you doing?' She pulled her wrist away and started to tear the envelope open.

'Joy, he's dead.'

She scoffed at him, 'Don't be stupid. He's not dead. He ran away. It's my father who's dead. And my mother and Ruth, but not Mark.'

Shepherd knew he was talking quickly, but each word seemed to ooze out of his mouth like mud. 'He died in a car accident.'

'No, he didn't. He ran away.' But her voice was crackling, broken.

Shepherd looked at the gravel. And said nothing.

'I don't believe you,' said Joy. 'This is a trick. You're trying to trick me into saying something so that . . .' Her voice trailed off.

Shepherd shook his head.

She swallowed and whispered, 'When?'

'A long time ago — 1966. In Darwin.'

'No, no, no. He wasn't in Darwin then. *I* was there then, and he wasn't. I checked. I was there' — her voice was getting hot and loud and slow — 'and he wasn't.'

'He changed his name. To Mark Harrison.'

'No, he wouldn't do that. How could I find him if he changed his name?'

Shepherd found himself looking at the damn gravel again. 'So what's in here?' Joy's voice was quiet. He looked up and saw her holding out the envelope as if she wanted him to take it back again.

'It's a copy of his . . .' Shepherd took a breath. 'Death certificate. And a newspaper article about the car crash. I'm sorry. I really am.' She banged the side of the skip with her fist. 'This is all your fault. Why did you have to tell me? Did you think it would make me tell you I killed my father? Make me think I had nothing to live for? Well, you're wrong.'

Why did every conversation with this woman end with up with one or both of them yelling?

'I was going to keep looking for him!' she screamed. 'I don't want to know that he's *dead*. I don't want to know, you hear me?' She threw the envelope at him, but it twisted in the air and fell awkwardly, landing on the gravel at her feet.

Shepherd didn't know what to say.

'Go away,' she shouted. 'Get in your fucking police car and leave me alone!'

'No,' he said quietly. 'You're coming with me.'

68

JOY AND RUTH

January 1961

The room Felicity and Joy sat in after Bible Study was now overflowing with coats and hats and scarves and umbrellas. And when Joy poked her head into the kitchen at one end of the hall, she saw at least twenty CWA women fussing over plates of sandwiches and slices, loading scones with jam and whipped cream, filling two enormous electric urns with water, bustling and clucking over items in pie warmers, and pretending to protest loudly when yet another plate was carried in. It seemed like everyone within a hundred-mile radius had come to farewell Mr and Mrs Larsen. Joy guessed that most of them probably didn't even know the Larsens, but had come to gawp at the couple who were getting divorced, and pretending they weren't.

It was the first event in the hall since Wendy Boscombe had disappeared, because Joy's father had insisted they cancel the New Year's Eve dance out of respect for the Boscombes.

Her father's band, Johnnie's 50-50 Good Time Band, was on stage tuning instruments, but her father wasn't playing with them tonight because he was MC. Right now, he was standing at the door directing each woman to take her plate of food to the kitchen, and each man to put two shillings in the tin to help pay for the band and the Larsens' farewell present.

Joy had gone to dances like this at Blackhunt Hall all her life. Whenever anyone got engaged, or turned twenty-one, or moved away, or celebrated a twenty-fifth wedding anniversary, the CWA and Hall Committee swung into frenetic activity and arranged a dance.

Every dance was exactly like the one before it. The people, the music, the MC, the present, the speeches, the food. Everything. Except for the guests of honour.

The official start time was 7.30 pm, but people began arriving half an hour before that so they could get the best park, or the best chair for supper, or the best view of others as they came in. At 7.30 on the dot, her father got up on stage, picked up the microphone to welcome everyone and make a joke. Everyone laughed and clapped, then the bandleader, Johnnie B. Bad (whose real name was Maurice Parsons) announced the first dance, which was always a waltz 'to get everyone warmed up'. For an hour, the band played familiar tunes, until a break when the CWA women brought them out a cup of tea and a plate of biscuits, while everyone else talked about the weather and the mud until the band struck up the next song.

The guests of honour usually pretended to try to sneak in at the end of the break, but Joy's father always spotted them and announced their arrival over the microphone so everyone could clap them in. Then he'd make more jokes, saying something like 'Why so late, Fred, didn't you read the notice in the *Gazette*?', and everyone would laugh while the man shook his head, pretending to be confused, and the woman rolled her eyes and threw her hands up in the air as if to say, *you can never rely on a man*, making everyone laugh some more. Then her father would say, 'Well, we all know who wears the pants in this household,' and everyone would laugh again, even though they'd heard him say it a hundred times. Then Johnnie would grab the microphone back and announce the next dance.

It was always the same. Except tonight. When Mr and Mrs Larsen walked in, there was no fanfare, and Joy saw the 'happy couple' separate, as Mr Larsen walked towards the far end of the hall to greet people and Mrs Larsen made a beeline for the kitchen. Johnnie announced the next dance, and everyone stood up quickly so they could start dancing and avoid any more awkward moments.

Joy turned to her mother, and whispered, 'Mum, where's Colin?' She hoped he wasn't alone in their strange fairy-tale house. 'Mr and Mrs Boscombe are looking after him,' her mother replied quickly, walking onto the dance floor with her husband.

At 9.30 it was time for supper. The CWA women in the kitchen conducted the whole affair like air traffic controllers, directing teenage girls in and out with plates of sandwiches and cakes, and teenage boys — including Mark — in and out with enormous wicker baskets filled with cups and saucers and plates. They were followed by Hall Committee members carrying huge aluminium teapots, then more boys with jugs of milk and soup bowls full of sugar with teaspoons sticking out of them like the spines on an echidna.

When supper was over, Joy's father carried two chairs to the top of the hall and collected the farewell present from the cloakroom. He placed the chairs side by side with their backs to the stage and Johnnie handed him the microphone. Her father straightened his tie, coughed loudly into the microphone and called for attention. 'Good evening, everyone. I'd like to invite our guests of honour to come and take their place. Robert, Barbara.' As they clapped, he smiled the smile that people were so fond of, and Robert and Barbara sat down in the chairs. Robert was, as always, smiling and his eyes were twinkling. Joy thought Barbara's face looked like the smooth grey steel inside a milk can.

Joy's father began his speech. Joy hated this part of the night because he talked for too long and made horrible jokes, usually at the expense of the butter factory, the government and his wife. 'Well, here we are. Robert and Barbara, our good friends and neighbours, are leaving us to make a new life in Melbourne. And we're all here to say farewell. Don't the women look wonderful? You know, I used to think that make-up was a luxury, until Gwen ran out one day. I upped the housekeeping that week, I can tell you.' He looked from side to side of the hall with his mouth half-open in a silent laugh, as chuckles rumbled around the hall. 'Well, Barbara is a much-respected member of the community, and we will never forget the wonderful costumes she made for the Christmas concerts at Kingfisher Primary. And Robert has been a tireless worker as a member of the Hall Committee and the Kingfisher Parents Committee and . . .' On he went, extolling Robert's virtues, recounting some of the numerous times Robert had helped people, and telling funny stories about Robert's confusion with new-fangled things like televisions and fire 'distinguishers'.

It was a long speech, but even Joy had to admit it was warm and heartfelt, although she noticed he did not mention Barbara again.

Then came the present, wrapped in brown paper and string, which, regardless of the guests and the reason for the celebration, was always the same item.

'So, Robert and Barbara, we wish you all the best for your futures [Joy noticed the plural]. Please take good care of yourself [Joy noticed the singular] and those you love [Joy was sure he had never said this before], and accept this present as a token of our appreciation for all your work in our community.'

Some of the men called out, 'Speech, speech.'

Robert stood up, looking as if he was a calf only half out of its mother and not sure whether he wanted to keep coming. 'Well, I'm not used to so much tension.' Joy looked at Barbara sitting with her lips clasped together, studying her hands clasped together on her lap, and decided that Mr Larsen had said the 'wrong' word deliberately. 'Thank you for your kind words, George, and all those antidotes, and this lovely present, which we're delighted to expect. I'm touched by how many people are here, and . . . sad to be saying goodbye to so many good people. But times change even if you . . .'

Robert stopped, and there was silence.

This had never happened before. Usually Johnnie had to yell, 'Just open the present!' to bring the guest of honour's over-long speech to an end. But three cavernous black seconds went by, when even Joy's father froze like a dragonfly caught in a winter puddle that had iced over. Finally, Johnnie remembered what he had to do. His shout wasn't as loud as normal, but everyone laughed on cue. Except Barbara.

Robert looked at the wrapped present beside him and said, 'Well, I certainly don't know what this can be.' Everyone laughed again. Except Barbara. He pulled at one of the tails of the string, then peeled off the brown paper and exclaimed with mock surprise, 'A floored lamp. [Joy wondered if he'd meant 'flawed'.] Who would have inspected that? Thank you, everyone, thank you.' And that was the sign for the band to begin playing 'For They Are Jolly Good Fellows' while everyone sang along. Then her father shouted 'Hip, hip' and everyone shouted 'Hooray!' After the third 'Hooray' her father clapped Mr Larsen on the shoulder while they shook hands.

Barbara stood up beside Robert, but instead of beginning the usual circuit around the hall to thank everyone, they walked towards the exit as if they'd earlier agreed that this is what they would do, Robert holding the lamp parallel to the floor with one hand. Joy saw her father pick up the brown paper and string, and stand watching the 'happy couple'. When they reached the exit, he called over his shoulder to the band, 'Another dance.'

Johnnie announced that the last dance, as always, would be a barn dance. Robert put the lamp down and turned around. Barbara kept walking.

Joy hated the barn dance because after every four bars, the women were twirled from the man they'd been dancing with to the next one, so that every woman danced with every man and vice versa. That meant she had to dance with old men and pimply teenagers. And her father. She stood up to sneak into the kitchen, but Mr Jones intercepted her, holding out his hand. She shuddered inwardly but could do nothing but take his outstretched hand and walk with him to join the two circles of dancers.

A few minutes into the dance, she twirled into Mark's arms. They looked at each other awkwardly while they joined hands, then Mark said, 'I can't believe he's leaving.'

'He has to,' said Joy. 'He has to leave here to be happy.'

'Yes. I suppose so.'

They danced the next two bars in silence.

Three partners later, she twirled into Mr Larsen's arms. Holding one of his hands, she realised that it was scrawny, and she saw that his face was thin, even though he'd always been solid and large, like the friendly woodsmen in fairy tales. Did she only notice this now because she knew he was dying?

'Well, well, lass, it's my lucky night, obliviously. Not only because I received that lovely flawed lamp which was so unaccepted,' he winked at her, 'but because I get to dance with you.'

'Mr Larsen, please don't go. I want you to keep making your phone calls to Ber—' She clamped her free hand to her mouth.

'It's alright, lass. I'm sorry, but I have to leave because as I started to say in that terrible speech I couldn't even finish, you have to change sometimes. Even if it means hurting people. Or saying goodbye to people you'll miss, like you. And when you move to the city to go to university, you'll be making a big change too, and not one that everyone will want you to make, but one that you'll need to make. Just make sure you come and visit me . . .' he smiled just like a spy would, 'and Beryl. I'll make *you* a cup of tea for a change, but only if you bring the chocolate.'

Joy had tears in her eyes and all she could do was nod. By the time she was old enough to go to university (he sounded so sure that she would), Mr Larsen would be dead. Besides, she didn't know where he and Beryl would be living. Before she could ask, he twirled her to her next partner, Lachlan Stewart, who was covered with acne. While they were awkwardly avoiding each other's eyes, she imagined visiting Mr Larsen when she was eighteen and as composed and confident as Mrs Felicity. She knocked on the door of their cottage and a round smiling Beryl dressed in bright colourful clothes opened the door. 'Come in, dear. How lovely to see you again.' They had a bright, colourful house, and the kitchen had windowsills full of geraniums and tomatoes sitting in pots that Beryl had covered with mosaics. The pots were like Beryl — big, bold and colourful.

She followed Beryl into their bedroom, where Mr Larsen was lying under a pristine white blanket. Everything was bright, clean and cheerful. Joy sat down on a chair next to the floor lamp.

'Good afternoon, lass. Did you bring the chocolate?' He was grinning just like it was a Saturday afternoon and he was jiggling coins in his pocket.

'Dark Strawberry Cream,' she said, pulling it out of her bag. 'Like the time I thought you were the Devil.'

Even though his eyes had a thin grey curtain drawn across them, they were still twinkling. 'The Devil?'

'Yes. I thought you were leading us into temptation with the chocolate.'

'Well, I might be going to Hell, but I don't think I'm the Devil. Defiantly not smart enough for that particle job.'

They both laughed, and then Mr Larsen looked sad. 'I hope I'm not going to Hell.'

'You won't. I know you won't,' Joy cried.

'Well, we'll see soon enough, I guess. But one thing's for sure. If I get to Heaven, eventually you and I can spend a lot more time together. And who knows what flavour chocolate they'll have up there?'

'Dad says I'm going to Hell. And that he'll be pained because Mark and I won't be with him in Heaven.'

'That's even less of a surprise than the floor lamp. Well, you'll work it out, I'm sure. Now, enough doom and groom. How's university? What do you want to be when you finish?'

'I want to write dictionaries.'

'Well, I can't think of anyone better suited to that job.'

Then Beryl came in and held one of his hands. 'Sorry to interrupt, Joy, but, Robert, you have to die now.'

'Yes, I know, love. Well, this is it, lass. This is my final day on Earth and I want to spend my last minutes with Beryl, just as I spent my last years with her. Leave the chocolate on the table here so I can have a little of it soon, and when I die I can look at it and think of you.'

Joy stood up, tears streaming down her cheeks. 'Goodbye, Mr Larsen. Goodbye, Beryl.'

'I think you can call me Robert now, lass. And one last thing. Make sure your kitchen has a good fire extinguisher. Goodbye, Joy.'

The band stopped playing, and Joy realised she must have had five or six different partners since Lachlan Stewart.

People started saying goodbye, collecting their empty plates from the kitchen and their coats from the cloakroom, while the Hall Committee men began stacking chairs to put into the storage room.

She would never see Mr Larsen again.

She stood near her chair, trying to understand the Larsens' story and her sadness.

Her father walked up to collect her chair, a smile on his face, and placed a hand on her shoulder. He spoke quietly to her. 'What do you think you're doing standing there like Queen Muck? Get into the kitchen and make yourself useful.'

When she reached the doorway of the kitchen, she heard Mrs Johnson talking to the other CWA women as she wiped down the pie warmer. 'Anyway, *I* think he deserves a chance at happiness after all these years.'

'I don't know,' said Mrs Drake, washing cups and saucers in one of the deep sinks. 'I mean, he's *married* to Barbara.

Mind you, I would never have picked those two as sisters. Honestly, you could have knocked me over with a straw of hay.'

'It's Barbara I feel sorry for,' said Mrs Wallace, drying the cups and saucers as they came out of the soapy water. 'I don't know why she came tonight. You know she's decided to stay on the farm? It's Robert and Beryl who are going to Melbourne. How's she going to cope? Especially with Colin? How's she going to look after him, now that her husband and her sister are . . . ?' She stopped and sighed.

Joy was glad that Barbara and Colin were staying, even though Barbara was so mean. She pictured them in their pop-up fairy-tale house, with the tiny windows and doors shut as tight as a rabbit trap so no one could ever see in again. They were sitting in the kitchen alone and scared because Mr Larsen had taken the fire extinguisher. Joy would make sure she was extra nice to Colin when he came down to help them milk.

'She's a tough stick if ever there was one,' said Mrs Drake. 'Imagine going through everything she has all these years. Married to a man who wanted to marry your *sister*. You're right, Susan, it's Barbara we should feel sorry for.'

Joy had never thought about feeling sorry for Mrs Larsen. In fact, she had never thought about Mrs Larsen's feelings for even half a second. But Mrs Drake was right — what had it been like for Mrs Larsen, married to a man who loved her sister? Even if that man was Mr Larsen?

'Oh, yes,' said Mrs Wallace, dumping a tray onto the draining board. 'Still, they managed to keep it under their hats, didn't they? My Kevin said Robert told him they tried to do the right thing for years and years. But love won out, as they say. He said they mostly talked on the phone, although goodness only knows where Barbara was when they were talking to each other. And there couldn't have been too much funny business going on, or everyone would have noticed.'

'I bet there was *some* funny business,' said Mrs Johnson. 'Which means that while Beryl was getting money from all of us for the bull paddocks, she was getting a bit of something else from Robert, who doesn't even own a bull!'

Mrs Drake let out a disgusted 'Ugh', while a couple of the other women giggled, at exactly the same time as Joy let out an involuntary 'What?'

The women turned to look at her as if they were one massive cow with multiple heads.

Surely she had misheard. Miss Boyle couldn't be Beryl. Barbara was skinny, pious and tight-mouthed, and Miss Boyle was plump, blasphemous and boisterous. Besides, Mr Larsen always made 'trump' calls when he rang the mysterious Beryl, which meant she lived a long way away. Unless he said they were trump calls to trick Joy and her mother. Did her mother know all about this? Was that why Miss Boyle always gave them such a big Christmas hamper? Joy couldn't work it all out. Why didn't Mr Larsen just visit Beryl if she lived so close? Why telephone her? And who would name their child Beryl Boyle?

None of the women answered Joy. They all turned back to their tasks, except Mrs Drake who pointed to a pile of tea towels on the end of the long bench. There was an awkward silence as Joy started drying dishes, but after a few minutes the women began talking about this person's lemon cake and that person's sausage rolls. Clearly, they weren't going to gossip while Joy was there. As she picked up another plate to dry, Joy realised that, despite all their rules and prayers and punishments, adults had more secrets than she did.

69

JOY AND SHEPHERD

February 1983

> HENDERSON, George. A respected Elder of the Church and generous community member who gave so much. In God's garden at last. We're so very sorry, and hope you'll forgive us. Victor, Genevieve, Barry and Felicity Armstrong

It felt like time had stopped for Shepherd when Joy finally read the contents of the envelope, so he couldn't imagine what it was like for her.

At some point while they'd been standing in the Henderson driveway, he realised he couldn't just leave her there with the skips and the envelope and a house that was empty of everything but the smell of fear. The police station was too official and uncaring, and the town's one café was too depressing and completely wrong. So there they were in his kitchen with another damn pot of tea sitting between them.

'I was in Darwin — looking for him — when he died.' She stabbed the date of the newspaper clipping three times. 'Why the hell did he change his name?'

Shepherd shook his head, but they both knew why.

'I'm trying to remember . . . did I even see this article back then?'

Shepherd could see she was genuinely distressed. A very different Joy Henderson to the one who'd been sitting beside Vicki a few days ago with her dead father just two rooms away.

'There's no way I read this. The name would have jumped out at me. Wouldn't it?' She looked at Shepherd.

He nodded. 'I'm sure.'

'Why do they bury stories like this on page five?' She banged her fist on the table. 'It says he had no known relatives, but I was there. *I was there*.'

He poured the tea while she kept reading.

'I hate it when they say this: "The car ran off the road." It's not the car that runs off the road, is it? So did he . . . ?'

'His death certificate says it was an accident.' Shepherd couldn't stop himself from adding, 'But so does your father's.' He got some milk out of the fridge. 'For all we know, he could have been swerving to avoid an animal.'

'It says it was late at night, and out of town.' She looked at the tea in front of her. 'So, no one to hear him scream.'

Shepherd said nothing, and they both took a sip of tea.

Joy put her mug on the table and said, 'Vicki's an interesting person, isn't she?'

Shepherd let out a small laugh. 'Do you mean "annoying"? Yeah, well, her heart's in the right place.'

'I suppose.'

'What does that mean?'

'Well, having your heart in the right place isn't actually enough.'

'Isn't it?'

'Take my father. Everyone would say his heart was in the right place. But that's not even close to good enough.'

'Look, I would never defend what he did to you, but . . . he did do a lot of good in the community.'

She snorted. 'So?'

He walked over to a small desk piled high with folders and binders balancing precariously, and picked up the top one. He came back to the table, pulled at the press-stud on the flap, and spread out the pages he'd collected from the local paper. There were hundreds of death notices — all beginning with HENDERSON, George. 'Have you read these?'

'No, I haven't. And I don't want to. I know what they'll say — how wonderful he was, how pious he was, how kind he was. But I know the truth. And so do you now.'

They sat in silence again.

'I'm not going to his funeral, you know.'

'No?'

'No. Everyone will be grieving and carrying on, and what am I supposed to do? Pretend that he was the best father ever? Sob when they put their arms around me? I'm not going to do that. But I can't tell them the truth either.' She paused. 'So it's just better if I don't go.'

'Right,' said Shepherd. Talking of funerals always reminded him of putting his arm around his grieving mother while his father's coffin was being lowered into the ground, all the while thinking about Wendy Boscombe.

'Do you want to know what Ruth and I called him?' She didn't wait for his reply. 'Mr Hyde.'

Shepherd frowned an unspoken 'Why?'

'As in Dr Jekyll and Mr Hyde, ' Joy continued. 'The well-loved model citizen and the feared monster, both rolled up into one person. Pretty obvious parallel, wouldn't you say? So, no, I don't want to read what everyone has to say about him.'

'Fair enough. Well, I read all of them of course, paying particular attention to any that seemed to express a little too much sorrow, or not enough. Because murderers will sometimes do that kind of thing.' He paused. 'Even though I was pretty sure I knew what had happened.'

He spread out the pages on the table, and Joy could see a few circled in red pen.

'Like this one,' said Shepherd, picking up one of the pages. 'Which I thought was maybe too apologetic. "A respected Elder of the Church . . ." blah, blah, blah, usual stuff. Then "We're so very sorry, and hope you'll forgive us." Who says that in a death notice if they don't have a guilty conscience?'

Joy shrugged.

'Do you know these people? Victor, Genevieve, Barry and Felicity Armstrong?'

Joy grabbed the paper out of Shepherd's hand. 'I take it that's a yes?'

'It can't be,' she said. 'They're in Belgium. They wouldn't even know he's dead.'

'Who are they?'

'Felicity was a Friend of mine, with a capital F.' She paused. 'My only friend, actually. Her family was kind to me. I called them Mr and Mrs Felicity . . . it's a long story. But, according to the chemist in town, the father — Victor — died and the rest of them moved to Belgium. So I don't know what his name is even doing on the notice, or how they could possibly know about my father.'

'The chemist?'

'Yes. The Felicities, Mr and Mrs Armstrong, owned the chemist shop and the new owners told me that the previous owner died and the rest of the family moved to Belgium.'

Shepherd frowned. 'That's not right. The previous owners were Ian and Vera Duncan. Ian died in his sleep. Heart failure, according to Vicki. He was a great bloke. I used to play squash with him. And Vera didn't move to Belgium, she moved to Antwerp, a small town up in the Wimmera. She has family there.'

'But the chemist said Belgium. At least I think she did, or maybe she said Antwerp and I just assumed it was Belgium. I was upset — there was some horrible woman yelling and hitting her kid, who'd dropped her doll . . . which reminds me . . .'

Shepherd turned around, picked up the handset off the phone behind him and dialled.

'What are you doing?' Joy asked.

He swivelled back and held up his index finger.

'Afternoon, Derek, Shepherd here, Blackhunt Police. I need you to give me the name and address of someone who placed a death notice in the paper yesterday. For George Henderson. We're hoping they can . . . help us with our inquiries.' He put his hand over the mouthpiece and spoke to Joy. 'It's a very useful phrase.' He spoke into the mouthpiece again. 'Yep, I can wait.'

The silence was awkward. Joy got up and filled the kettle. She waited with her back to Shepherd while the water heated up.

'Victor and Genevieve Armstrong. Great. Got an address? And a phone number, please.' He wrote in the notebook in front of him. 'Thanks, Derek. Much appreciated.'

When Joy turned around, Shepherd saw that her whole body was trembling.

'Well, he's alive. And definitely not in Belgium.' He ripped off the top sheet of the notepad and held it out to her. 'South Australia, most probably a suburb in Adelaide, going by the phone number. So I'm guessing they didn't run over here and kill your father in the middle of the night.'

'Can I . . . ?' Joy pointed to the phone and Shepherd nodded. While she dialled, he walked into the lounge room and closed the door. He no longer had any idea whether she was innocent or guilty of George's murder or suicide or accidental death, or whatever the hell it was. He just had a strong sense that having lived with the daily fear of being thrashed and humiliated as a child, Joy had developed a secretive defence mechanism, which manifested itself as bravado.

It was definitely possible that Vicki was right and George Henderson had killed himself, accidentally or on purpose, and that Joy was innocent. But even if she was guilty and he arrested her, she would never be convicted. Assuming a jury ever heard the case, it would inevitably return a 'Not Guilty' verdict. Which was not the same as an 'Innocent' verdict . . . it was what Shepherd thought of as a 'Police Have Not Presented Sufficient Evidence of Guilt' verdict.

Shepherd realised it was over. For good. By letting her go, he was saving everyone's time and money, avoiding days of courtroom drama and expense. And more trauma for Joy. *Looks like I won't be solving a murder case any time soon,* he thought ruefully. *Not George's, and not Wendy's. Sorry, Ron. Sorry, Neil and Vi.*

When Joy came back into the lounge room, he jumped. God, she was supposed to be scared of him, not the other way around.

'I can't believe it. They want me to come over to Adelaide. Felicity's there, too.' She started to sob violently.

He pushed over a box of tissues and she blew her nose. 'I told them about Mark, and Mrs Felicity cried. Mr Felicity grabbed the phone and said to come straight away, that they'll take care of me until I get back on my feet.'

Shepherd gave one of his single upward nods. Joy looked around. 'It's time for me to go.'

'Yes, you should go.'

She stood up, and it took Shepherd a moment or two before he realised he'd have to drive her back to the farm.

In the car, Joy told him about how she'd been so in awe of the Felicities and how happy they'd been.

'I guess they'd have had their moments, too, though, don't you think?' said Shepherd. 'I mean, all families do.'

'I suppose so,' said Joy. 'But I never saw any. You know, I think they knew what was going on in our house — I even told Felicity once and she said she'd tell her parents, but they never did anything to save me. I worked out I had to do that on my own.'

When they got to the driveway, Shepherd stopped the car. 'I'll say goodbye here, then. And I guess you win.'

He put out his hand and they shook, holding on for a second too long as Joy said, 'It was never a competition, Detective. I just did what I had to do. And, believe me, I certainly didn't win. I've got the scars to prove it. Physical and mental.'

Shepherd's moral compass was swinging wildly, and it was all because of this damn Henderson family. He was still half-hoping for a confession, but he no longer knew what he'd do if she gave him one. Vicki and Joy were right — George Henderson had been a monster and had deserved to die, and suffer.

'Goodbye, Joy Henderson.'

'Goodbye, Senior Constable Shepherd.'

70

JOY AND RUTH

January 1961

Joy was still eating her stewed apples when she heard the screech on the lino as he pushed back his chair. Her head jerked up, at the same time as Mark's.

'Who's going to own up?'

The eels writhed. Own up to what? She ran through the day and couldn't think of anything she had done that could possibly have made him angry. It must have been Mark. Her sympathy was intense, but her relief more so.

Her mother carried the tomato sauce to the cupboard then walked out of the kitchen to go to her workroom, anticipating what would come.

'Does last Wednesday ring a bell?'

Wednesday. Joy thought they'd got away with it, and she knew Mark had too. She wondered how long their father had known and whether he had deliberately let them think they were safe.

On Wednesday afternoon, Mark had carried a box full of camellias into their mother's workroom while Joy was cleaning bloodstains from the laundry trough. On his way back past, he stopped and said, 'Hi. What are you up to?' Just like that. As if they were living in a normal house. As if they were a normal brother and sister. Maybe, thought Joy, it's because we're both in the same boat now, both equally terrified of the chair screeching on the lino and the screamed 'Room'.

'Just chores,' she said, standing up. 'Um, would you like to come to the Felicities with me tomorrow after Bible Study?' He nodded quickly, his face coming alive, then grimaced. 'No, I can't. He's already told me I have to help him fix the pump tomorrow afternoon. But I will next time. Unless I'm in Darwin.' And they both laughed. As if they were a normal family.

He leant against the wall next to the trough while she rinsed the sides of the trough and told him how she'd mimicked Mr Jones and Mr Felicity, and how it made the Felicities laugh even more than they usually did. Joy knew that Mark really wanted to go to the Felicities' house with her and laugh at her mimicking Mr Jones and Mr Felicity.

'Show me,' said Mark.

She put down the cleaning rag, pointed a finger at him and in a voice that perfectly matched their father's, said, 'What are you? I'll tell you what you are. A dirty, filthy sinner who's going to rot in Hell, that's what you are.'

'You're so good at that,' he said, laughing. 'You should be an actress. You really should.'

Joy felt her face heating up with embarrassment, then Mark said, 'Hey, come with me.' He walked ahead of her through the kitchen and into the good room without even hesitating. And she followed, despite the eels squirming.

'Look at this.' He opened a door of the bureau. 'Are you crazy?' Joy whispered.

'Don't worry. Dad's down in one of the back paddocks with a sick cow. He's waiting for the vet.'

'But Mum's in her room.'

'No, she's not. She's at the dam getting waterlilies. She won't be back for ages, and even if she comes back, I'll think of something.' Joy's heart lurched. Ever since Wendy had disappeared, her father had not let any of them go anywhere by themselves. Joy knew it wasn't just a shadowy abductor they had to be scared of. There were snakes everywhere now. What if her mother was bitten by a snake and collapsed and died? Stuck in the mud, like a cow? With no one to hear her screams? She'd have the Dutch hoe with her, but why hadn't she taken Joy with her as well? Joy could have kept an eye out for snakes while her mother leant over the water, eased the Dutch hoe over a flower and down into the water, yanked it to cut through the stem, then gently pulled it to the bank. Joy knew her mother would be trying to pick thirty or forty waterlilies as quickly as possible, and without bruising the flowers as she manoeuvred each one to the bank. She wouldn't be keeping an eye out for snakes that could sidle up and bite an unsuspecting person. If Joy was there, keeping an eye out, she could call, 'Snake, snake!' and save her mother's life.

She wanted to run after her, but she would feel stupid. Besides, she was enjoying being with Mark like this. He was reaching into the bureau, and Joy wanted to see what was so interesting. She sat down beside him as he pulled out an opaque bottle with a gold bottle-top and waved it in front of her face. She grabbed the bottom of it to hold it still so she could read the label.

Old Abbey
Cordialized Apricot Brandy

'So,' said Mark, 'who do you think's having brandy? Mum or Dad?'

'What?' Joy could not believe that her parents owned a bottle of brandy.

'It's got to be Dad. That's why he's so . . . that's why he does what he does.'

'Maybe it's from Miss Boyle.'

Mark raised his eyebrows, and Joy knew he hadn't thought of that. 'Maybe. But it's been opened, and it's not full. Someone's been drinking it.'

Joy stared at the bottle. It was impossible to imagine either of her parents drinking alcohol. They only drank tea and Passiona, and her father made sure that they knew that alcohol was the Devil's drink. But if he did drink brandy then Mark was right and it would explain why he became so enraged and out of control.

Except he never really was out of control. He exacted their punishments calmly, deliberately.

'How did you find it?' she whispered. Mark frowned. 'I just did, okay?'

Joy nodded. Every wall and floor of the house was infected with secrets and if Mark had discovered another one, Joy wasn't going to ask how or why. 'What are we going to do?'

'We're going to taste it.' He unscrewed the lid.

'No. You can't.'

'Yes, I can,' he said, lifting the open bottle. A strange odour wafted up her nose and reminded her of something, but she couldn't remember what. Something distant and aching and pleasant. 'If he can, then we can too. What's he gonna say? That it's a sin? Huh!' And he tilted back his head and poured the brandy into his mouth. As soon as the sharp liquid hit the back of his throat, he started coughing and spitting. 'Ugh — it's horrible.'

Instinctively Joy swung to one side to avoid the brandied spittle, and her shoulder slammed into the bureau. Although it looked like it was made of thick solid timber, it rocked backwards alarmingly, and Joy and Mark heard glasses clinking followed by a small smash. Joy pulled the door open and they both looked inside. At the wedding present from their father's parents. The delicate frosted glasses with a gold rim. The glasses that their father made a show of bringing out from the good room only at Christmas time. O come, all ye faithful.

One of them was lying on the top shelf, broken. Joy reached in carefully and pulled out a large piece that had gold grapes painted on it, and looked at the other much smaller pieces, all sharp and pointed.

It was the ferrets all over again.

'Jesus.' Mark's face was white. 'Okay. Don't panic. Let's get the pieces out. Quick.'

Joy didn't know which was worse — that the drops of brandy on the carpet looked like dark blood that had quickly soaked into the carpet, or that Mark had blasphemed again, or that they — no, she — had broken one of the glasses.

Trembling, she put her right hand in to pick up one piece at a time, placing each one into the palm of her left hand, scared of cutting herself on the fine sharp fragments, but more terrified that their parents would walk in. Mark was trying to mop up the brandy on the carpet with one sleeve of his jumper pulled down over his hand but it looked like he was spreading the stains, not removing them.

Looking at the pieces in her hand, she thought about how the glasses always reminded her of Passiona and Miss Boyle's hampers (there'd be no more of them) and shortbread and mince pies and Christmas cake.

Christmas cake.

'Mark, it's not him. He doesn't drink the brandy.'

'What? You think it's *Mum*?'

As she reached in to pick up another little sliver, it pierced her index finger under her nail. She gasped in pain as blood dripped out. 'Go get a towel,' he said, 'and the brush and shovel. Quick. Before they come back.'

She ran into her bedroom and wrapped her bleeding finger in one corner of the old towel she always used to blot up blood after he belted her, and got the brush and shovel from under the kitchen sink. Mark swept out the pieces of glass and tipped them into the towel Joy spread out on the carpet. Without needing Mark to tell her, she rolled up the towel, and ran down to the tank. She climbed to the top step and threw the towel and the pieces of glass into Hell's portal.

As she turned around, she could see the tiny figures of her father and the vet in one of the paddocks in the gully. He wouldn't be back for some time. She looked over at the dam, and saw her mother's head appear over the top of the dam's bank. She'd be at the house in fifteen minutes, maybe less, depending on how many waterlilies she was carrying. Joy sped back to the house.

Mark was scrubbing the carpet with some water and bicarbonate of soda, and looked up with alarm until he realised it was Joy. 'Alright. I've pulled the other glasses to the front. We never have more than two or three visitors at a time, so with a bit of luck he won't notice that they aren't all there. Not until we're both a long way away from here. In Darwin.' He smiled to reassure her, but she couldn't return the smile.

'Mum's on her way,' said Joy.

Mark closed the bureau door and looked at the carpet. The marks were barely visible now, but the smell hung in the air.

'Okay. I have to change, and clean my teeth to get rid of the smell. Don't let her come in here, not for a while.'

Joy nodded but she had no idea how she would do that if the phone rang or her mother wanted to go to her bedroom.

They walked out quickly and shut the door. As they were walking through the kitchen Mark said, 'We don't tell anyone. Ever. Right?'

'Of course not,' Joy said quickly. Except Ruth, of course. She told Ruth everything.

She ran to the back door while Mark went into the bathroom. All they could hope for was that the smell and the wet marks would be gone before either of her parents went into the good room, otherwise it would all be over.

She heard Mark come out of the bathroom, call out 'Okay' and go into his room. She wondered what he'd do with the jumper that smelt of brandy. *Please God, please.*

She went into her bedroom and opened the Bible on her desk. She was staring at the words when the door opened and she jumped.

'How do you know it's not him drinking the brandy?' Mark asked. 'I mean, I know Mum has it tough, but I don't think she'd drink alcohol. And if she did, why would she leave it in the cupboard like that?'

Joy hardly registered what Mark had said about their mother's life. 'Christmas cakes.'

'What?'

'Mum puts brandy in the Christmas cakes. It's in the recipe. She's crossed it out in the recipe book, but now I've smelt it in the bottle, I know that's what it is. Every year when we're making them, just before we put the dried fruit into the mix, she makes me go and see if there are any freshly laid eggs we can use. When I come back, there's always a strange smell in the kitchen, and before I can even ask her what the smell is, she always says she's just added more cinnamon and nutmeg. I had a feeling it wasn't, but I didn't know what else it could be. But it's definitely brandy.'

'Okay,' he said. 'Then why . . .'

They heard footsteps in the kitchen, and Mark changed his tone of voice and said, 'So we can talk about what else the twelve apostles did tomorrow on the way to Bible Study.'

Their father came in and looked at them suspiciously. He pointed at Mark. 'You. Down to the dairy to help Colin. The cows aren't standing around waiting for your lordship.' Mark nodded and as he walked towards the door, their father slapped his ear sharply.

Joy looked down at the Bible.

'And what do you think you're doing?' Her tongue sat on the roof of her mouth. 'Do you know what time it is?'

There was never a right answer to these questions. 'You should be peeling potatoes.'

She got up and walked out to the kitchen. *I wish you* were *a drunk who lost his temper when he was full of brandy. At least I'd understand why.*

* * *

That's what had happened last Wednesday, and now he was waiting for Mark or Joy to admit to it.

'So, Wednesday doesn't mean anything to either of you?'

Joy knew what was going to happen. She may as well just admit that she'd broken the glass and save Mark from a punishment, especially since he'd tried to save her after the ferrets escaped. But what reason could she give for being in the good room, and for knocking into the bureau? There was none.

He pushed his chair back further, the screech piercing her ears, her body already tingling in anticipation of what was about to happen.

When the red-hot shout of 'Room' exploded into the air, Joy felt her body ripple with defeat.

In her room, she took off her clothes and sat on her bed, her knees pulled up and her arms across her chest, her hands wrapped around her upper arms where scars were already forming. She knew her father had sat back down again and was calmly letting them wait in fear.

A minute or two later, she heard the screech on the lino again. *Please God, please don't let . . .* But she stopped. God was never going to answer her prayers. He just didn't care. And their mother wasn't going to come to their rescue either. She would be in her workroom, surrounded by ribbons and flowers and dead people's wreaths.

Joy heard him go to his bedroom and then to Mark's room. She lay down on her bed and pulled her pillow over her head. It didn't stop her from hearing the screams and sobs, but at least she felt like she wasn't eavesdropping. When she heard him stomping through the kitchen on his way to her room, she sat up quickly and straightened the pillow.

He entered the room. She stared at the floor. She did as she was told. As always.

Ruth closed her eyes and turned away.

She howled like a wild animal as the belt came down on her bare skin. She didn't try to hold back because she wanted him to know how much it hurt. The air was hot despite the cold outside, and even though her face was pushed into the bedspread, in her mind she could see him, panting and hissing and reciting the measured words as he raised his arm to bring the belt down again and again. She could see the red horns protruding from the top of his forehead, and the red spiked tail whipping back and forth, in perfect time with the swinging of the belt. She could see his yellow fangs and his black cavernous mouth. It opened wider and wider, until a thick silvery snake slid out and wrapped itself around his neck and chest, purring and licking his red skin.

After the eighth swish of the belt, she lifted her head violently as eel stew erupted from her mouth onto the bedspread. 'Stop it,' he yelled, and pushed the back of her head so her face fell into the mess.

She vomited again. And he stopped.

'You're disgusting.' He walked out, and as she lifted her face out of the vomit, she heard him walk into her mother's workroom and call out, 'Gwen, get in there and do something. She's been sick.'

Her mother came in and they silently pulled off her bedspread, then Joy wiped her mouth on a towel, and sipped from the glass of water her mother had brought in. Her mother rested her hand on Joy's shoulder, and said, 'You have to be more careful. Both of you. You mustn't upset him like that. Please. Just behave. *Please.*'

And through the wall, they could both hear the strumming of his guitar and the words of 'You Are My Sunshine'.

Later, Ruth whispered, 'It's going to be alright. I promise.'

And that night, in her dreams, it was alright. Joy crept into the kitchen, opened the cupboard, poured all the migraine pills into her palm, and hid behind the couch to see what would happen. He came into the kitchen, his eyes bloodshot and bulging, and his forehead throbbing and thumping, growing and shrinking, growing and shrinking, the red horns protruding from his forehead. He picked up the empty bottle and tried to tip out some pills, but there were none. He held it to his mouth and tipped back his head as if he was going to drink from it. But not one pill came out. He moaned loudly, and shook the upside-down bottle ferociously. Then he collapsed onto the kitchen floor, frothing at the mouth, and died. Joy came out of her hiding place, poured the pills back into the bottle, put the bottle back in the cupboard behind the cinnamon and bicarbonate of soda and went back to bed. In the morning, they would find him lying there and everyone would think he hadn't been able to get to his pills in time.

71

JOY AND SHEPHERD

February 1983

> HENDERSON, George. A kind and generous neighbour to my dear Robert for many years. May you rest in peace in God's many paddocks. Beryl Boyle

From the bottom of the driveway, I watch Shepherd do a three-point turn and head back to town, then I start trudging up to the house. I can smell smoke. I hate how the contents of that tank are always alight, always reminding me of the stench and misery of Hell. I'm trying to get the mess in my brain sorted out. Ruth was my twin and Mark's dead, but I've found the Felicities. Or to be precise, Shepherd found them for me. And he's letting me go.

I think I have Vicki to thank for that. Although I'm not sure why.

I walk past Mum's forty-two camellia bushes lining the driveway, the gaps between them filled by hundreds of bright-red poppies in full bloom, and think about all the flowers she planted and nurtured and picked and arranged. Her refuge.

Leaning down, I break off a poppy stem, which has some sub-stems and about seven flowers in bloom. We were never allowed to do that when I lived here because then it wouldn't grow any more flowers. I am suddenly full of aching sorrow for my mother, who grew so many flowers and worked so hard so we could have a bit more money. A mother I hardly knew in the midst of all the anger and fear that swirled around us. I'm sorry, Mum. Sorry for what he did to you, sorry that I left you, sorry there was no one here for you.

At least I had Ruth.

But who knows? Maybe Mum had Ruth too, in her own strange way. After all, she named all of the chooks Ruth, and that must have annoyed the hell out of my father. Was it a little act of revenge? A daily reminder of what he'd done? Especially whenever he chopped off the head of one of them? Maybe she even committed other tiny acts of revenge. For all I know, she was putting bicarb in his migraine tablets, too. I hope so.

Ruth Poppy Henderson. I hope Mum's buried next to her. When I finally get there, maybe even tomorrow, I'll surround their graves with poppy plants — hundreds of them.

The skips are still in the driveway. Everything's gone now, except the junk in the shed. And the doll's head.

Standing in front of the chest, I'm pleased with myself for not yet telling Shepherd about the doll's head. It will all make a lot more sense to him when I explain that after tossing away everything from the house, I decided to clean out the shed, starting with the chest, and discovered the doll. *You'll never believe what I've found.*

And then — soon — Shepherd will announce to the Boscombes and the whole region that my father killed Wendy, and everyone will know the truth: that the man was a monster and a killer. I'm sorry that he'll never be convicted and imprisoned, but his reputation will be ruined, and best of all, he *knew* that was going to happen. That's what they'd call a consoling thought.

For the first time in a long, long time, I want to believe in Hell, and that my father's right in the middle of it, screaming for mercy that he'll never receive.

I sift through memories of my childhood, searching for some happy ones. There are a few — the night we put contact on our books; being with the Felicities; writing down my favourite words and their images; making Mark laugh with my imitations of our father. But the strongest memories are of the belt. The belt that's still in the evidence bag on the kitchen bench, holding down all those documents I wanted to show Mark — the letters, the marriage certificate, Ruth's death notice. And the nail from the wardrobe sitting beside them all.

It's time to give those wheels of justice a good push.

The empty house is really giving me the creeps — it's lucky I don't believe in ghosts because there'd be a hell of a lot here.

I put the nail and the documents on the front seat of my car but take the evidence bag into the shed, pick up the ever-glinting axe — the one thing in FearWorld that never faded or deteriorated — and make my way to the blood-stained chopping block beside the empty chook pen. I hold the bag upside down and tip out the belt. It tries to slither away, so I stamp on it quickly, then pick it up and roll it around the buckle, like a snake coiled inside out. Very carefully, I set it down on the block.

It looks innocent, but believe me, looks can deceive.

An eye for an eye. Thanks to all those Bible Study classes, I know that's what it says in Exodus *and* Leviticus, so god was pretty adamant about it, wasn't he?

I lift the axe up high, then bring it down hard and fast before the belt can escape. Straight away, old blood starts seeping from the leather. Children's blood. It's thick, dull brown, and smells of fear. My father only ever used a single motion to kill a Ruth, but I'm not done yet. I bring the axe down again, and this time I hear Mark's screams of pain. They are red bolts of lightning. Mark. Mark. Mark. I swing the axe over and over, gasping and heaving, as pieces of belt bounce off the block in different directions, and scream after scream flies into the hot bright sky. As far as I'm concerned, my father killed Mark as well.

I scrape up the pieces of belt, put them back on the block and keep chopping. The blood is spurting out now, and the screams have merged into one long continuous howl. My arms are aching, but I keep chopping. My head is throbbing, but I keep chopping. My feet are swollen, but I keep chopping.

Now the blood from the belt is pulsing in time with my chopping, falling over the edge of the block like a waterfall smashing over a cliff. It spreads out around the base of the chopping block, and creeps over my shoes. Some dead white Ruth feathers float to the surface. The old blood spreads out further and further until the whole farm is covered with it, and the red screams have filled the sky, and people are wondering if this is the apocalypse.

Finally, when the belt is nothing but tiny pieces of bloodied leather, and my brain has calmed down, I sit on the dirt and push the axe handle away from me so it falls to the ground with a thud. That's when I see the triangular buckle still on top of the chopping block, glistening in the sun, calm and still, mocking me, confident of its immortality. I stand back up, centre it on the block, and pick up the axe again, holding the handle just behind the head with both hands. I lean in, so my head is right over it. The axe's blade is pointing straight up towards the screams that evaporated into the hot sky.

I bring the butt of the axe's head down in one short, sharp action, and hear the satisfying clash of metal against metal, before I feel hot pain in the corner of my jaw. I drop the axe and clamp both hands around the bottom of my face.

There's blood running down my wrists and my neck, mixing with the sweat. I'm scared to open my mouth in case the ricocheted axe has broken my jaw. I move my fingers back and forth along my jawline gently, gradually applying more pressure, until I am sure the bone is still in one piece. I open and close my mouth a little bit, then breathe out with relief — and anger at my own stupidity.

I pick up the axe once more and hold it so the blade is pointing to the sky again. As new blood drips from my face onto the old blood on the chopping block, I smash the butt onto the buckle again. This time I'm ready when it bounces off, and I move back quickly. I hit it again and again, each time avoiding the angry ricochet. And with each smash, the buckle lets out a high-pitched wail that reminds me of the kitten I owned for two hours.

I throw the axe into the dirt and look at the lump of metal on the block. It's still in one piece, but at least it's no longer recognisable.

That will have to do.

Back in the shed, I pull a hessian bag off one of the rusty nails, shake it, then stamp on it hard and methodically left to right, top to bottom, to kill any redbacks hiding in it, then turn it inside out to double-check. I carry it over to the chopping block, and throw all the pieces of belt into the bag, followed by the deformed buckle. I tie a knot in the top, hard and tight, so nothing can escape.

As I head to the undertaker's, I rehearse the conversation I've imagined many times now, relishing my favourite line: *This . . . is the last nail in his coffin.*

72

JOY AND RUTH

January 1961

'I'll never eat Christmas cake again.' The words were matter-of-fact, but Joy could see bubbles of red anger coming out of Mark's mouth as they stood at the end of the driveway to catch the bus to Bible Study.

'Me neither.'

She wanted to ask him why he didn't have his school bag with him and where he'd got that other bag from, but her back was hurting so much from last night's thrashing that she could hardly think and really didn't feel like talking. Maybe the Reverend had given the 'Young Adult Christians' a bag to use specially for their classes. Plus, she hated her father even more for ordering her — for no good reason — to come straight home after Bible Study without going to the Felicities.

When they were getting off the bus at Blackhunt, Mark bumped into her, and Joy turned around frowning, because she could tell he'd done it deliberately, but he looked straight at her and said, 'Sorry, Joy, I'm really sorry.' She was annoyed with him, but almost forgave him when he waved and smiled at her as she walked into the hall.

After Bible Study, when Felicity and Joy were hiding in the cloakroom, Joy said she didn't feel like mimicking anyone today, and that her father had said she had to go straight home. Felicity tried to cheer her up by telling her about Snowy's latest antics, but Joy didn't laugh, and sat looking at her shoes, picturing the welts on her back throbbing and growing and tightening into more scars.

'Come on, Joy, cheer up. It's not that bad,' said Felicity. 'I'm sure he'll let you come on Thursday.'

Joy looked at Felicity and wanted to feel angry with her, this girl who knew nothing of pain or shouts or screeching on lino. But it wasn't Felicity's fault, and she did at least invite Joy to her house and give her moments of happiness. And she was Joy's only Friend.

So in the little room of the hall where they usually laughed together, with the raw flesh of her back burning her, Joy told Felicity what her father did to her and Mark.

Felicity's outraged objections were like soothing cream on her soul. And then came what Joy was waiting for, the real reason she had told her friend about what her father did to her. Felicity said, 'I'm telling my parents. They'll make him stop.'

After the Felicities drove away, Joy stood in the Church porch waiting for Mark. After a few minutes the other students came out, but Mark was not with them.

When Reverend Braithwaite followed them, she asked him where Mark was. He shook his head and said, 'I was just about to ask you the same thing. We thought he must be ill.'

Scared that Mark would get into trouble again if the Reverend phoned her father, Joy laughed and said, 'Oh, that's right, he had to help Dad this morning. I'm so used to meeting him here, I forgot all about it.'

The Reverend insisted on walking Joy to the bus stop, and Joy knew it was because Wendy Boscombe was still missing and everyone was scared that whoever was responsible for her disappearance might take another child. Joy was worried that Mark would be at the bus stop so the Reverend would know she had been lying, but he wasn't there either. As there were other adults waiting, the Reverend said goodbye and walked back to the Church. Joy looked up and down the street nervously, having decided that Mark must have wagged Bible Study and would turn up any second to catch the bus home with her.

But he didn't.

On the way home, she looked out of the bus at the grey rain while the eels hissed in her stomach. She tried to recapture the feeling she had when she was writing down her favourite words and their images so that the eels would drown in Dark Strawberry Cream chocolate, but she couldn't stop worrying about Mark.

Maybe their father had arrived at the Church just after Joy went into Bible Study and had taken Mark back to the farm to help him fix fences? That seemed unlikely, but what other explanation was there?

What if there *was* a murderer living in Blackhunt and he had abducted and killed Mark? An even worse idea crept into her mind: what if Mark had wagged Bible Study, and their father had somehow found out, and Mark was on his bed, right now, naked and shivering, being belted not fifteen times, but fifty? Or a hundred? Being belted, literally, to death?

By the time she was walking up the driveway, the eels were snaking their way up her throat, making it difficult for her to swallow. Twice she thought she heard Mark behind her and quickly turned around, but there was nothing but mud and drizzle. The empty driveway made her think of Wendy Boscombe's dolls and how Wendy had disappeared. Not into thin air, she thought grimly, but into thick mud.

But Mark wasn't a silly nine-year-old girl. He wouldn't vanish into thick mud the way Wendy had. And he was too smart to get caught if he'd decided to wag Bible Study. Maybe he had pretended to be sick and had somehow found a ride home, and was lying on his bed waiting to laugh at her because he'd got out of Bible Study. Or maybe he really *was* sick from last night's eel stew, like she'd been.

But when she went into his room, his bed was empty. She stood still, hoping that he would jump out of the old wooden wardrobe to scare her, as he once had years ago. After a few seconds, she yanked it open, expecting him to scream 'Boo!' and start laughing. She stuck her head inside, but all she could see were six empty hangers. With a heavy dark blue choking her, she walked over to his chest of drawers and pulled open his sock drawer, where he was allowed to keep his bank book. Her father made sure his children saved every penny of the £1 notes that Aunty Rose sent them for their birthdays, along with the £100 they'd inherited from their mother's great-aunt when she died soon after Joy was born. Last year, after Joy had handed over the £1 note from Aunty Rose to be put in her bank account, she asked Ruth why her father let them keep the money. Ruth raised her eyebrows before saying, 'But if he took it, it would be stealing, wouldn't it? And our holy father would never break one of the Ten Commandments, would he?'

Frantically, she pushed aside Mark's socks. The bank book was not there. And neither was the magnifying glass Aunty Rose had sent him for Christmas, or the little pocketbook of capital cities of the world that she had sent the Christmas before.

Joy spun around quickly. Everything looked the same, but everything was different.

The dark blue had filled up her entire body including her head, which felt like it was being squeezed in the vice on the shed's workbench.

She ran into her room.

'He's gone,' Ruth said quietly.

'No, he can't go. He can't go.'

Ruth shook her head. 'He had to.'

'Why didn't you stop him?'

'You know I couldn't do that,' said Ruth sadly.

So now Joy knew why he'd said 'sorry' as they got off the bus, why he'd had a different bag, and why he wasn't in Bible Study or waiting for her at the bus stop.

She had to tell her parents, so they could find him quickly. She screamed at Ruth, 'I have to tell them. I have to tell them.'

'Wait,' said Ruth quietly.

'What for?' screamed Joy.

'Give him as much time as possible,' said Ruth. 'He needs to do this. He needs to get away.'

Joy didn't know what to do. She stared at cool, calm Ruth, then sat at her desk, still and scared.

'Just wait a little longer,' Ruth said.

Joy shook her head quickly.

'He'll be better off away from here,' Ruth said.

'That's not true.'

'Let him go, Joy. He has to go. Just like Mr Larsen.'

Joy put her head on her desk and sobbed. Ruth's arms were around her, but they felt like gossamer {a dead angel's wings}.

'Go away,' she shouted to the images that were curdling her brain.

When the sobs finally stopped, she stood up, her face red and blotchy, and wiped her eyes and cheeks.

The sooner she told someone, the sooner they'd find him and bring him home and everything would go back to normal. He would be punished, of course. The worst punishment ever. He probably wouldn't be able to walk for days. She shuddered. But it would serve him right, abandoning her like this.

Could she do that to him?

'He'll find somewhere safe,' Ruth whispered. 'And, one day, when our father is dead, he'll come back.'

Joy turned to her perfect sister and hissed, 'He won't. I'll never see him again. It's alright for you. You didn't get thrashed half to death last night, did you?'

Ruth ignored Joy's accusations. 'If you don't give him enough time, they'll find him and he'll never forgive you. His life will be even worse.'

'But what about me?'

Her mind was racing. He must have caught a train to the city and then to the airport, so he would be on his way to Darwin by now. The police in Darwin could catch him when he got off the plane.

He said he'd take her with him. He *should* have taken her with him.

She stood up. She would follow Mark to Darwin. She would catch a train to Melbourne and a plane to Darwin. It wouldn't matter if she left Ruth behind. Their father didn't even yell at her. All because of the accident that no one was allowed to mention. 'Joy,' said Ruth softly, 'you can't get on a plane by yourself and fly to Darwin. Mark is sixteen, but you're only twelve. They'll drag you back. You have to stay. At least a bit longer.'

Joy hated how Ruth knew her every thought. 'Then I have to tell them he's gone.'

'Not yet. Give him some more time.'

She thought about what her father would do to Mark if he had to come home. And then she thought about what her father would do to her if he knew she hadn't told them immediately.

All she wanted was a normal, happy family. Was it so much to ask for? A normal family, without any missing children ruining everything? She pictured Mr Felicity pushing food back into his mouth with his fork while he was talking and laughing; Snowy eating roast chicken and purring on Felicity's knee; Barrington talking about books; and Mrs Felicity's enormous lemon meringue pies.

And she knew that Ruth was, for once, wrong. Mark could come back home and their father wouldn't belt him to death. Because Felicity was going to tell her parents, and they were going to make the beltings stop.

Ignoring Ruth's cry of 'Not yet, not yet' Joy raced out of the bedroom and into the back yard, shouting, 'Mum, Mum! Where are you? Mark's run away.'

73

JOY AND SHEPHERD

February 1983

> HENDERSON, George. A community-minded person who gave his all. Blackhunt will be sadder for his passing. Condolences to the family. Blackhunt Fire Brigade

Mr Dunne didn't disappoint me. Right down to shuddering when he picked up the hessian bag. As if he knew it held my father's belt — stained with children's blood and magenta screams.

Back at the house, there's not much more to do now.

The most important thing is to check the dam. The more I think about it, the more I'm sure it will have dried up, and if I'm right, everything is going to fall into place. If I'm wrong, then I'll come back and tell Shepherd about the doll's head. I'm not exactly looking forward to seeing what I suspect will be in full view there, but I know Shepherd will thank me for it.

Without the Dutch hoe to take with me, I pick up the axe again. Any snake that wants to have a go at me today is going to get its slimy little head smashed in quick smart.

But any snakes that might have been lazing around waiting for soft pink flesh to bite must have been frightened by the swishing of the axe through the long yellow grass, and the angry vibrations rolling down my body, through my stomping feet and into the earth.

When I get to the outer bank of the dam, its cracked dry clay reassures me that inside it's going to be dry, or close enough. Keeping a sharp eye out for snakes, I climb the bank, knowing that, along with everything else, I'm going to spot a hessian bag that has tiny bones in it.

I can hear him hissing at me, 'Throw it, damn you. Throw it.' And I can hear the kitten scratching at the hessian with its little white socks, and its squeaking promises of affection. I hear it squealing through the whole of its arced flight to the water, then the splash . . . then silence.

No wonder I hated him. No wonder I decided to kill him.

Decided to kill him, Detective, which does not mean that I did *kill him.*

Vicki's pills saw to that, as her autopsy proved.

At the top of the bank, I see that I am right. At the bottom of the cracked mud crater is a small, dirty puddle not three feet in diameter. I see the dinghy, lopsided, and am mildly surprised that the wood has not rotted away. Around the perimeter are bones and ribs connected to spines connected to long triangular skulls. The remains of thirsty cows that got caught in the sticky mud, panicked trying to pull themselves out, and fell, breaking their legs and drowning. I always felt so sorry for them.

I see lots of hessian bags and have no idea what's in any of them except the one with the kitten bones. I wonder what he disposed of in the others. Half a rusted tractor is lying on its side, the rest submerged beneath the dry clay; there are rusted pieces of machinery that I can't identify. I see six or seven mottled tractor tyres dotted around like giant aniseed rings. I see hundreds of dead dry waterlily stems and roots lying on the clay, limp and sad.

And I see the old rusted 44-gallon drum.

I walk onto the foot-wide ledge, then half-walk, half-slide down the sloping wall of the inside of the dam, which I guess is about twenty feet (not the 'fifty feet forever' my father told us), trying not to slip on the sticky clay. I'm still worried about snakes, although it's probably too hot for them to be out sunning themselves.

When I get to the drum, I shiver even though the temperature is abominable. I'm not sure I can do this, but I hear Ruth whispering in my ear: *justice and revenge*.

I put the axe down, sit beside the drum and, one by one, I unclick the five clips that hold the lid in place, and let it drop onto the cracked clay.

That was the easy bit. I lick my lips, curse the heat and look inside.

There, lying on the bottom of the drum, is a rock. And a pile of bones. Human bones. They are not large bones, not the bones of an adult, but the bones of a child.

Wendy Boscombe.

I can see Shepherd telling Wendy's grieving, but relieved, parents that the rock was used to weigh down the drum, so it would sink and disappear from sight. Forever and ever, Amen. Because no one in 1960 would have believed that any dam around here would ever dry up.

I am more horrified than I thought I would be, and a rush of vomit buckles my stomach and spurts out of my mouth.

Poor Wendy.

I wipe my mouth with the back of my hand. I'm tempted to scoop up a little of the brown water in the centre of the dam to wash the vomit from my chin, but I'm terrified there will be a snake resting in the small puddle.

I force myself to look inside the drum again. Force myself to look at what's left of poor Wendy Boscombe. Bones and a pair of yellow plastic sandals.

Then I stand up and pick up the glinting axe. *Justice and revenge.*

I walk back to the house quickly, swishing the axe ahead of me and remembering what happened when Bell and Shepherd questioned us all after Wendy disappeared.

First of all, my father said he didn't leave the farm, but then my mother unexpectedly spoke up and reminded him — in front of the police — that he *had* left the farm that day. My father laughed nervously and said, rolling his hands back and forth on the top of his chair, yes, he'd gone down the tractor lane to work on the back fences. The tractor lane that ran alongside the Boscombe farm. And then he said that he'd taken the tractor, not the van, because the van wasn't durable enough. Mark had washed the van, inside and out, that very evening, and I suspect Bell would have noticed the sparkling clean van parked not far from the glistening axe. My father claimed he hadn't seen any cars on Wishart Road, but then he changed his mind and said he had seen a blue car. But he couldn't provide any other details about it or anyone inside it. Then he made a point of telling Bell that he was going around to the Boscombes that very night to pray with them.

Did Shepherd note all of these things in his little police officer's notebook as he played detective? Would he reread his notes and think, 'Yes, George Henderson behaved very suspiciously that evening'?

Still, I doubt they ever suspected him. Ron Bell's judgement would have been clouded by my father's status as a pillar of the community and a longstanding Elder of the Church. And there was never any evidence to make them think he could have been responsible for Wendy's disappearance.

Well, there's no lack of evidence now. Wendy's bones are lying in the bottom of George Henderson's dam, and her doll's head is in the bottom of a chest in George Henderson's shed. With his fingerprints all over it.

Finally, it's time to tell Shepherd.

74

JOY AND RUTH

Australia Day 1961

Joy stayed in her room for two days while social workers, Sergeant Bell and Reverend Braithwaite came and went, came and went. Dr Neighbour even dropped in once, ripping off a prescription for Joy's mother. It was like being trapped under the surface of a large frozen dam. Joy couldn't eat, and she could barely talk. But in her bedroom she had her beautiful book of words and images, and Ruth.

It had only been a few weeks but Wendy's photo was no longer on the front page of the paper, or even on page 3 or page 5. She was old, sad news, replaced by the upcoming Agricultural Field Days, the first ever to be held in Blackhunt.

The whole family, or what was left of it, was dumbstruck. Her mother's eyes were red on the inside and blue-brown on the outside. Her father's whole face was permanently red.

Colin did the twice-daily milkings by himself. He still brought up some of Maisie's milk each morning, but Joy noticed it was only half a bucket now because Mark wasn't around to drink three glasses at every meal and more in between.

On the night that Mark ran away, Sergeant Bell came around and questioned them each, alone, in the good room. 'Do you have any idea where he might be?' Bell asked Joy gently.

Joy looked up at him through her swollen eyes. She and Ruth had known that the police would ask this question, knew the answer that must be given. Joy swallowed and nodded. But so cracked was her voice, so tiny was the space where her heart had been, and so full of eels was her throat, that Bell had to ask her to repeat her answer.

She coughed to find her voice again, wiped her eyes, and spoke a little more strongly and loudly. 'Yes,' she said, sniffing through tears. 'I know where he'll be.' She felt bad, she felt like the worst sinner in Hell, like Judas, but she and Ruth had agreed. She sobbed again, and the words came out in little bursts. 'He always said,' she stopped and swallowed. Would she really say this? 'He always said he was going to go to . . .' Her voice was breaking again, so Sergeant Bell leant in to hear properly. 'He always wanted to go to . . . Hobart.' Then she sobbed uncontrollably.

Sergeant Bell patted her shoulder and said, 'Good girl.'

When she was back in her bedroom, she thought she would write down some more of her beautiful images, but even her favourite ones were limp and grey, like wet cardboard. She finally slept, dreaming of Mark lying on a sunny beach in Darwin, his magnifying glass, book of capital cities and bank book lying beside him. He whispered to her, 'I'm sorry, Joy.'

The next day, she left her room only to go to the kitchen to get lunch and tea. Each time, she picked up some of Mrs Larsen's egg and lettuce sandwiches that Colin had brought down, then walked back into her room like a ghost. Her father did not call her back or scream that she was ungrateful. But Reverend Braithwaite was there at lunchtime, and Sergeant Bell was there when she came out for tea, so there could be no yelling or shouting or punishing. Besides, her father seemed defeated.

As she placed some sandwiches onto a plate, Sergeant Bell stood up to leave, saying, 'The thing is, George . . . Gwen, because Mark's sixteen, and he's run aw— left home of his own volition, we can't open a search or an investigation. I've notified them in Hobart, but they don't have the time to go looking for runaway teenagers, I'm afraid. Still, a friend of mine down there said he'd keep half an ear open for Mark's name.'

'Half an ear?' spluttered Joy's father.

'I know, George, but there just aren't the resources — or, to be honest, the need — for anything more.' He paused. 'Look, I haven't mentioned Mark's . . . adventure to anyone. Don't see any need to spread gossip and rumours. In fact, the only people who know are those social workers, the doc, and the Rev., and I've reminded them about their confidentiality obligations. If I were you, George, I'd be telling everyone that he's headed off to the big smoke for work, and no one ever need be the wiser.'

Her father stared at Bell, who pursed his lips then said, 'I won't even tell young Shepherd. He's away at his father's funeral, plus he's upset enough about poor Wendy, so no point in getting him more riled up, particularly as it's obvious there's no foul play. Just a young kid who's decided Blackhunt isn't big enough for him. That's the story I'd be telling, if I were you. No shame in that, George. Nothing at all for you, or your family, to be ashamed of.'

But Joy knew her father *was* ashamed, that his reputation meant everything to him. So she was not surprised when he pulled out the letter from Blackhunt High School, asking him to let Mark stay at school because of his excellent academic and sporting records, and tossed it in the fireplace, right then and there, in front of Sergeant Bell and the rest of his family. Once it was nothing but ash, he turned and looked at his family. 'That person's name is never to be mentioned in this house again.'

When Joy heard her parents go to bed on the second night after Mark had left, she pulled out *My Beautiful Images* again and the words and pictures flowed out of her like water from a burst dam, bubbling with hate and anger. Words like *belt, hot, death, hell, heaven, eels, axe, scars, yell, fury, lies, fear, mud, trapped, Satan, ferrets, father, Church, drown, rain, kill.* And the images conjured up by these words were wild and bizarre. Images of black skies and deep oceans, of imps and other strange creatures in Hell, of tongues and horns, of volcanoes and exploding suns, of twisted bodies and screaming skeletons, of witches and headless dolls, of hissing eels and snakes, of dead babies and dead calves, of barbed wire and chopping blocks, of black gloves and red smoke, of broken glass and blood.

Each one reeked of anger and hopelessness and darkness, and while she could hardly believe what was coming out of her head and her hand as the writing hurtled down the page, she knew that she had to let these images break through the membrane because behind the membrane was an infinite menacing darkness that she could not control. Her father did not come in and shout at her to turn out her light, so she kept writing, writing, writing.

When her hand was aching and her head was throbbing, she put down the pen and flicked backwards through the book, stunned that she had filled over twenty pages with her scrawl. When she reached the first page, she scoffed at how she had tried to write so neatly that first night, and how upset she had been when her father had frightened her as she was writing *nectar*. She let the first page fall from her thumb, to reveal the inside cover where she had written the title: *My Beautiful Images*.

She flattened down the inside cover, as she had that night decades ago, but barely two weeks ago really, and sucking in a long, determined breath, picked up her red pen. Breathing heavily, she crossed out all three of the stupid, docile words, pushing harder and harder until the letters were completely buried. Then she wrote a new title across the whole of the first page, in large, angry red letters, going over and over the newly written letters until they were thick and strong and engraved into the page for eternity. Ruth smiled her approval.

A Sinner's Dictionary
by Joy Henderson

Much better. She turned back to her last entry and continued writing, this time with the red pen. There seemed to be no end to the words and images exploding out of her head and making her angry and hot and alive. Forget Dark Strawberry Cream, now she felt like she was a dark raging flame of anger, as the eels shrank into a corner of her stomach, scared, lying low.

And as the darkness grew deeper and spread through her veins like the Devil himself, she knew they would never find Mark Henderson.

Or Wendy Boscombe.

75

JOY AND SHEPHERD

February 1983

> HENDERSON, George. God keeps close those who are special to Him. One of our earliest customers, and a real gentleman. Arnold and Marilyn Paterson

Sitting on the floor of the good room beside the phone, I think I can see small stains of the brandy that Mark spat out twenty years ago and maybe a tiny shard of glass, but I'm probably imagining things, and I certainly can't afford to let my imagination get out of control. Not now.

I call Directory Assistance, cursing that I threw the tele-index into one of the skips, and get them to put me through to Blackhunt Police before I change my mind. Shepherd gave me the Felicities; I'm giving him Wendy. Or, to be precise, Wendy's bones, and the person I know is responsible for Wendy's death. It's a fair exchange. And it's justice.

While the phone rings, I rehearse what I'm going to say. When it goes to voicemail, I'm momentarily put off balance, but leave what I'm sure is a coherent and persuasive message. Back to Directory Assistance again so I can talk to the ever-sympathetic Derek at *Blackhunt Gazette*. To be fair, he's much more sincere this time.

Still sitting on the brandy-stained carpet, I go through everything again in case I've made a terrible mistake. I don't think I have, but what if I've remembered some conversations or events incorrectly? I've read somewhere that our brains rewrite memories to protect us from hating ourselves. That each time we remember an event or a conversation, we remember ourselves in a slightly better light. And you do it over and over, until instead of remembering that you were speechless with fear in an interview, you remember that you were confident and articulate. Or that you were the person who helped the elderly man who fell over, not the person who walked around him in a hurry to get home on time to watch your favourite TV show. And that's what you'll tell your friends, because you'll actually think it's the truth.

So I'm a little bit concerned that my memory might be flawed, but the more I think about it, the more I'm sure that I remember everything clearly. Every one of my father's words and actions that day, along with his every thrash of that belt.

Time to leave.

When I get in the car, the letters and marriage certificate — documents I'll never be able to show Mark now — are sobbing on the passenger seat. Ruth's death notice, I observe wryly, is silent. I may as well burn them. That way it really will be over.

I collect a box of matches from the shed and walk down to the rubbish tank. At the top of the wooden steps, I stare into what I once thought was the portal to Hell. Decades of accumulated ash and rubbish are piled so high there's only about 20 centimetres left at the top. I twist the sheets of paper into a single taper, light one end of it, and toss it over.

It feels good.

In fact, it feels so good that I pull out another match, light it, carefully tuck the unlit end back in, and drop the box into the tank. When I'm a couple of steps down, I hear the remaining forty-eight red tips hiss one after the other like a chorus of angry snakes.

Back in the car, the steering wheel is scorching hot and I'm suddenly yearning for rain and mud again. Who'd have thought? Turning out of the driveway to go to the Boscombes' house, it dawns on me that I might have to testify, or whatever it is you do when the police are trying to prove that a dead man killed a nine-year-old girl twenty-three years ago. So maybe I won't be going to Adelaide just yet.

Before I've reached the Larsen driveway, I notice the wind's picked up, and it's really strong. Hot and strong.

Fifteen minutes later, when I turn off Bullock Road to cut through to Wishart Road, I smell smoke. And something tells me I shouldn't have lit one match and thrown it into the tank, let alone fifty of them.

76

JOY AND SHEPHERD

February 1983

> HENDERSON, George. A kind man whose compassion and prayers were unmatched. Heartfelt sympathy to the family. Neil and Viola Boscombe

Jealousy, Shepherd thought wryly as he drove away from the Henderson farm, twists a sharp knife in your guts.

Joy would soon be on her way to Adelaide to the Felicities, while he would be forever feeling like a cow stuck in mud at the edge of a dam. Wendy Boscombe's disappearance would haunt him forever, and now so would George Henderson's 'accidental, self-inflicted' overdose.

When he got back to the station, he tried to distract himself from the Hendersons and Wendy Boscombe by completing some paperwork and tidying his desk. But the more he tried to push them all from his mind, the more he felt the need to focus on them. Right now, he was missing Ron a lot, and wanted someone to tell him he'd done the right thing in letting Joy and her memories and scars go to Adelaide.

Finally, as he stood up to put the last sheet of paper in the filing cabinet, wondering if that was smoke he could smell, he decided to ring Vicki. Half-smiling to himself, he imagined her saying, 'Shep, you have no evidence, so of course you had to let her go. And even though I'm a doctor — Hippocratic oath and everything — let's face it, he deserved to die a long, slow, painful death.'

As Shepherd walked back to his desk, the phone rang, and he sighed and dragged over the appointment book for driving tests. But it was a familiar voice on the other end.

'Alex — it's Nev Potter from Blackhunt Fire Station.'

'What's up, Nev?'

'You've probably heard this on the radio, but there are massive fires burning over in South Australia and I don't know if you can smell it already, but the wind's blowing a dump of smoke and ash this way. Nothing to worry about right now, but we're staying alert.'

'Ah! That's what I could smell when I got back to the station. So nothing local that we—?'

'Hang on a minute.'

Shepherd could hear him talking to someone else in the station.

He drummed his fingers impatiently. It seemed to take forever. 'Okay, just had a comms. Johnson's Road. Units are on their way. I'll let you know if we need you, but it should be alright.' Shepherd pushed down the phone's spring-button to ring Vicki, but instead of hearing the dial tone when he lifted his finger, he heard the long beeps that told him he had a message. He dialled 101 and listened, not sure that he wasn't dreaming.

She was breathing heavily and talking way too fast for him to understand everything the first time, although he caught the words *Wendy Boscombe* loud and clear. Before he'd even worked out what was going on, a mechanical voice began. 'To listen to this message ag—'

He knew the drill all too well, and pressed 2, this time prepared for the rush of words, scribbling what he could catch in his notebook. He still couldn't understand everything, and was annoyed that she'd been disconnected for some reason before she finished the last sentence.

He played it again, filling in the gaps in his notebook. He listened one more time, checking that he'd transcribed the message correctly in his notebook: 'Shepherd, it's me. Meet me at the Boscombes as soon as you can. My father, he's a murderer. Wendy Boscombe's doll is in his chest in the shed, and Wendy's in the damn—'

'What the hell?' He slammed the notebook down onto his desk. 'Wendy's in the damn *what*, Joy Henderson?'

He stared down at his notebook, thinking rapidly.

Could she be telling the truth? Was Wendy's disappearance finally going to be solved, thanks to Joy Henderson — the person who Shepherd still suspected had murdered her own father?

77

JOY AND RUTH

February 1961

There were only two days to go before Joy started high school, and her pile of books had been placed into Mark's bag, his name on the inside crossed out with thick black permanent marker, and replaced with hers. His Form 5 books, including *Pride and Prejudice*, had been taken to the school's second-hand bookstore.

After Sunday School that morning, Felicity told Joy that she had told her parents about the beltings and she was sure they'd talk to her father and make him stop. Joy told her he hadn't belted her since Mark had left. 'See?' said Felicity, smiling with pride.

Joy wasn't sure though. Maybe Felicity was right, or maybe it was simply because Mark had run away and her father was still in shock.

She had not been to Bible Study or visited the Felicities since Mark had left, and although she sometimes wondered how she could ever face Felicity's parents again, she knew that one day at Sunday School, in a few weeks or maybe a few months, she would say to Felicity, 'Can I come to your house today?' and Mr Felicity would ask her father, like he had the first time, and her father would dare not refuse. But until then, she wanted to stay home and keep writing.

She had nearly filled her book and didn't know what she would do when she got to the last page. On the nights that she couldn't write in it, she felt unsettled and incomplete, as if her bones were out of alignment. Sometimes she thought it was the only thing keeping her from acting out one of her dreams and actually killing her father. Or herself.

Sometimes she just sat and read the words and descriptions, which was almost as good as writing them.

In bed she wondered what Mark was doing in sunny Darwin, and consoled herself with the thought that his last words to her were 'I'm sorry.'

Sometimes, in the dark, she heard his screams from his empty room.

When she wasn't thinking about Mark, she was thinking about poor Wendy. People had stopped talking about her, but Joy was still worried. One night, Ruth said, 'I don't think they're ever going to find Wendy.' Joy had sighed and said, 'I think you're right. If they were ever going to find her, they would have by now, surely?'

Reading the words she had scrawled in that red-hot fury after Mark had left, Joy felt as if the world was split into two, like Dr Jekyll — one side, where she lived, dark and menacing; the other side, where the Felicities and now Mark lived, sunny and cheerful. One day she would escape and find Mark. She closed the book and held it to her chest, her arms making a large X across its chocolate and cream cover.

When her bedroom door opened, she looked up to see her father standing in the doorway. He was thinner and his face was grey. Looking at his red eyes, Joy knew something was about to change. Her stomach lurched and a surge of emotion rose from where the eels lay waiting, up through her chest and head, a tenderness that sprang from what she now shared with her father — a deep, sad loss. Years of useless anger and fear to bring them to this.

He's going to tell me he loves me. That he's sorry, that the days of the belt are over.

And then, in a moment bursting with orange and yellow sparks, she realised he was going to tell her that the police had found Mark! *He's about to walk into the bedroom, a big grin on his face.*

All is forgiven and the good glasses have been filled with Passiona.

A pink ripple of anticipation made the hairs on her arms tremble, as his mouth opened. But the words that came out were not what she had expected. He pointed at the book held against her chest and said quietly, 'What is that?'

* * *

When the last swish of the belt had cut through the air, he smashed the book against her left cheek then waved it in the air, venom dripping from his teeth. 'I'm burning this piece of filth, do you hear? From now on, the only book you'll be holding in this house is the Bible.' He turned off the light and slammed the door behind him.

She sat in the dark, eyes squeezed shut, blood seeping down her chin and into the space between her gum and the inside of her cheek. She would plead with him when he came home. *Beat me all you want, but please give me back my dictionary.* She would do anything he wanted. Anything.

A little black curl of an idea crept into her head. *If you give it back to me, I'll tell you where Mark is.*

But Ruth whispered, 'No, you can't do that.'

Joy knew she was right. Apart from anything, she would have to admit that she had lied when she'd said he would be in Hobart.

She heard the back door slam. He was walking down to the rubbish tank. Climbing up the old wooden steps. Throwing her book over the rim to land on years of accumulated rubbish — mouldy orange peel, rusted soup cans,

Ruth carcasses, eels' and rats' heads, rags and ash. Lighting a twisted length of newspaper and tossing it in. She would wait until he was in bed, then run outside and rescue it. The rain would stop it from catching fire and it would be sitting there, wet and afraid, waiting for her, calling out to her in the night like Wendy's dolls. Even if the ink smudged and the pages fell apart, she wouldn't care. She had to rescue it. She would even jump into the damp smouldering stench pit if she had to.

Please God, please don't let . . .

'Why are you praying?' came Ruth's voice, sharp like broken glass. 'When was the last time God answered one of your prayers? It's gone forever, Joy. He's burnt it, and you can't rescue it.'

The flames from the burning twist of newspaper were spreading out, hungrily, eagerly. One of them licked the edges of the sinner's dictionary, and Joy watched it transform into the Devil, hot and evil. He jumped on top of her creation, laughing and dancing, a long red finger curling with glee as he beckoned other flames to come dance, come destroy. The other flames, in the shape of orange imps, jumped towards him. The Devil leapt off and heaved back the cover to reveal the title scrawled on the inside: *A Sinner's Dictionary*. Like children blowing out candles on a birthday cake, they flung back their heads, bent forward and blew flames from their mouths. Black letters smouldered and floated from the page. Then the imps turned to the first page, and laughing at Joy's descriptions of the images, they opened their mouths, sucked in the red air and got ready to blow out flames to ignite the pages.

'Stop!' A thunderous voice boomed from above, and the imps scuttled to one side of the tank.

'It's Him!' one of them whispered, and they huddled together tightly.

But the Devil stood his ground, looked up and spoke in an equally thunderous voice. 'Lord, we were only helping your servant, George Henderson, destroy the sinner's dictionary. Only doing what you would want us to do, Master of the Universe.'

'That. Is. A. Lie. Restore the book.'

The imps looked at the Devil for guidance, but he was cowering, his arms wrapped around his head.

'Now!' thundered God.

The imps ran back to the book and smoothed the pages with their red hands, trying to stop the letters lifting off and evaporating.

'It's too late, Lord,' said one of them.

'Too late,' the others echoed, and they ran to where the Devil was whimpering.

There was a loud explosion as a bolt of lightning erupted from the sky, and the Devil and the imps melted into a single red lump of wax.

'Excellent,' boomed the voice from the sky.

'It's not excellent!' Joy screamed. 'My book is destroyed, and my father is still belting me, and Mark's gone. Why do you allow these things to happen?'

'You don't understand, Joy.' God's voice was still booming. 'It isn't easy being God.'

'That doesn't make sense. You're supposed to be omniscient and omnipresent and omnipotent.'

'But there are so many people, and so many sinners. So many sins and so many prayers.' It sounded like a schoolyard rhyme that, just six weeks ago, she and Wendy might have skipped to in the schoolyard.

A huge black knot started to unravel in Joy's head. If god (no longer deserving of a capital G) was omni-everything, why did he create Earth filled with people with free will, if he knew that billions of them would go to Hell? Why not just let everyone live in Heaven right from the beginning of the universe? And why order everyone to worship him when surely that was Pride, which was a Deadly Sin? There seemed to be so many flaws in the stories she'd been told, mostly their startling and suddenly obvious lack of logic.

'You're not omniscient, are you?' she said quietly. 'Or omnipotent, or omnipresent. You're not omni-anything. In fact, you're *not*.'

God's mouth opened to protest, but there was silence.

Joy lay in the dark silence, letting the black knot continue to unravel. That very morning in church (no longer deserving of a capital C), they had all echoed like sheep, 'Blessèd are the meek, for they shall inherit the earth.' Thinking about it now, Joy's soul exploded with contempt. The meek Joy Hendersons of the world weren't going to inherit the earth. They were the people who were trampled on and broken precisely *because* they were meek. And god, via the reverend (no longer deserving of a capital R), urged, insisted, *commanded* they remain meek, promising them non-existent rewards for being meek, while protecting the reign of the *un*-meek, the George Hendersons of the world.

But this particular meek person had had enough of the trickery, the deception, the duplicity. Joy Henderson was going to fight back. Not like a boxer coming out of the corner at the beginning of round one. Oh no, that would be fatal while her father had the power and the strength and the law behind him. No, she would pit duplicity against itself. She would become, outwardly, the most modest, the most pious, the most compliant person, while inwardly, the real Joy would become the most devious, the most irreligious, the most duplicitous. While the reverend shouted lies from the pulpit, she would put on a smile so saintly it would fool the Devil. And her father. In fact, she would outdo her father's duplicity.

If no one was coming to her rescue, and she couldn't escape to Darwin to join Mark for another four years, she would find a way to survive behind her barbed-wire prison.

Let her father come home. Let him pull her out of bed and pull off her clothes and belt her till her back and buttocks and thighs bled.

She was going to take . . . A violent image burst through the membrane in her head. It was a hot red ball rolling down a hill, getting larger and hotter, larger and hotter.

She was going to take revenge.

PART FOUR

78

JOY AND SHEPHERD

February 1983

> HENDERSON, George. Respected member of our Parents and Teachers Association for many years. Our thoughts are with his family. Principal and Staff, Blackhunt High School

Shepherd read the transcription of Joy's telephone call over and over. For all he knew, she was playing more games. But on the other hand, he'd just let her go, so why would she complicate matters even further?

He walked into the back room and once more dragged open the filing cabinet that contained nothing but suspension files full of folders that he and Ron had compiled after Wendy disappeared. He'd spent — wasted? — hours poring over the files at random, examining photographs of Wendy's dolls, Wendy's bedroom, the driveway; and rereading interviews with hundreds of locals, always willing a clue — just one tiny damn clue — to leap out.

But Wendy might as well have disappeared into a black hole that day.

Quickly, conscious of the time that was slipping by since Joy had rung, Shepherd pulled out the suspension file labelled Local Interviews A–H, and the file with HENDERSON George across the top. He opened it and reread every line, this time with Joy's breathless words ringing in his ears. *My father's a murderer.*

According to the file, George Henderson was working near the Boscombe farm at the time of Wendy's disappearance. He claimed that he'd been on his tractor, which meant, as both Ron and he had agreed, it would have been impossible for him to abduct Wendy. But both of them had also noticed that his van was newly washed. George said that he hadn't seen any other person or vehicles on Wishart Road, but then changed his mind and claimed to have seen a dark-blue car. But he couldn't provide any more specifics about said vehicle.

And, Shepherd now knew, George Henderson had a history of perpetrating horrendous violence against children.

Now he really did need to ring Vicki.

'It's Shepherd. I need you to take a drive with me to the Boscombes. I'll explain why on the way.'

He sat and waited for her, drumming his fingers on his desk. Damn the Hendersons, and damn Vicki, who said she'd be five minutes.

Finally she pushed open the door, flashing her grin. 'Can you believe what they're saying about the fires in South Australia? There's ash falling on Melbourne already, and it sounds like we'll get it too.'

They walked out of the station to be assailed by the ferocious heat, high winds and the pungent smell of smoke. Shepherd was suddenly exhausted. Images of Joy, George with the belt around his neck, Ruth's grave, and Wendy and her dolls were swirling in his head and he couldn't work out any of it. He leant against the wall and ran a hand over his forehead.

Vicki looked at him, took the keys from his other hand and got in the driver's seat. God, she was annoying. But he walked around to the passenger side without protesting. Besides, it wasn't as if Headquarters cared about what he did or didn't do.

'It usually takes me about forty minutes to get there,' said Shepherd. 'Do you know a quicker route?'

'Ha. I may not have lived here as long as you, but I know the back roads like the inside of Mrs J's warts.' She grinned at him; he didn't smile back.

'What's up?' she asked.

'There's a fire on Johnson's Road.'

Vicki's face dropped. 'Hell. It said on the radio all the fires were in South Australia.'

They were silent while Vicki drove down the main street to head out of town. As she turned onto a dirt road that led towards the Boscombe farm, she said, 'So, why are we visiting the Boscombes?'

'Joy Henderson rang and told me to meet her there. Claims her father killed Wendy.'

'What?' Vicki stared at Shepherd, astonishment written all over her face.

Shepherd nodded grimly. 'And she claims to have *found* Wendy. And the doll.'

'Jesus,' said Vicki quietly. Then she looked over at Shepherd again. 'What doll?'

'One of Wendy's dolls went missing when she disappeared.' Shepherd realised he would have to tell her the whole damn story. 'The Boscombes moved here from Mildura when Wendy was six. Wanted to get away from the heat. Liked the cold, apparently, and the green rolling hills.'

Vicki let out a sarcastic 'Mmm.'

'Wendy had an older half-sister in Mildura, who had a toddler Wendy was fond of. But down here Wendy was alone.'

'I can relate to that.'

'Really?' For some reason, Shepherd had assumed Vicki came from a large boisterous family. 'So Neil — always one to go overboard — decided to make her a big family of dolls. He wrapped rags around some old fence posts, Viola made dresses for them, and Neil painted faces on them. Not that he was any Vermeer.' Vicki threw him a look of surprise. 'I'm not a complete philistine, you know,' Shepherd said. 'Anyway, the eyes were crooked, and the mouths were big red grins.' Shepherd grinned himself. 'A bit like yours.'

'Mmm, hilarious.' But she was obviously listening intently. 'Go on.'

'Wendy was outside playing with her dolls when she disappeared, but one of them was missing, so we assumed that if we found Wendy, we'd find the doll . . . and vice versa.'

Vicki stuck out her bottom lip and nodded.

'We let it be known that "a doll" was missing, but we never released a description of it. Because the one that went missing was different to the others — Neil hadn't made it. The half-sister had sent it from Mildura. So, if anyone said they'd seen Wendy and the doll, or even confessed to taking her — there are some weirdos out there, believe me — we could ask "Was her doll with her? Can you describe it?" Pretty standard stuff. And a few weirdos did come forward, including a psychic who claimed Wendy was living in a town somewhere in Czechoslovakia. And you know what? Every one of those crazies who came forward said, yes, they'd seen the doll, but not one person came close to accurately describing it. Every one of them described a doll like the ones Neil had made for her because there were photographs of them in the newspapers.'

Vicki turned down a road Shepherd didn't know. 'And Joy's found it?'

'So she says. After I dropped her off. Which reminds me. Mark Henderson's dead. Car accident, years ago, in Darwin. Damn — she left his death certificate at my place.' Vicki's raised eyebrows asked the obvious question. 'Long story, but, yes, she was in my flat. Let's just say your concern for her welfare got to me. And I don't know, alright? I don't know if she killed her father or not, but — and I know this will make you happy — I can't charge her. No evidence, remember? Thanks to you.'

Vicki said nothing.

'Anyway, after I dropped her off, she called me. But it was while Nev Potter was telling me about the smoke coming over from South Australia and the fire on Johnson's Road, so she left a message.'

'Saying?'

'That her father killed Wendy, and she'd found the doll — and Wendy.'

Vicki frowned and made yet another 'mmm'.

'What does that noise mean? Are you suggesting that Joy Henderson is a liar?'

Vicki shrugged. 'We're all liars, Shep. It's not a question of *whether* we lie or not, it's a question of *what* lies we choose to tell. And to whom.'

Shepherd did his upward nod, wondering what lies Vicki chose to tell.

She swung him a glance and kept talking. 'So, we're meeting her at the Boscombes' house?'

'Yes.'

'And George Henderson killed Wendy?'

'That's what she said.' He looked at her. 'But she could be lying, of course.'

They were both silent again until they reached Wishart Road and turned right. Vicki didn't wait for Shepherd to yell 'Quick!' before she pushed down hard on the accelerator.

Even though they were still hundreds of yards away, they could see the brick chimney standing like a lone soldier staring with disbelief at a bloody battlefield. Still red-hot in places, the chimney looked like it could crumble any minute into the surrounding debris. The corrugated tin roof had collapsed around it and the house's walls were completely gone. Even from the road, they could see large household items smouldering and pieces of ash floating in the hot air. Four firefighters were dousing everything. As the police car turned into the driveway, all Shepherd could think of were the dolls and the pram that he'd seen there twenty years ago lying in puddles of mud.

'Christ,' muttered Shepherd. 'I hope they got out.'

One of the firefighters walked towards them, his gloved hand raised to stop them coming any closer.

Shepherd and Vicki pulled up, got out, and Shepherd went into autopilot.

'Alex Shepherd, Blackhunt Police,' he called out. He pointed with his thumb to Vicki. 'Local doc. I need to talk to the residents of this house. Do you know where they are?'

The firefighter waited until he was close to them before answering. 'Husband's badly burnt, we got here just in time. Ambo's already taken him to hospital. Seems his missus had left for town just before the fire got here. We're not yet sure where she is. Look, I know you're police, but the trees,' he motioned to the black forms lining the driveway, 'they're still dangerous. And there might be other fires. You need to leave the area, sir.'

'Right. Thanks,' said Shepherd. 'We'll let you get on and do your job. But can you drop in to the station later? I want to know what's gone on here.'

'Will do. By the way, this isn't the only place that's been burnt. Another unit's just radio'd to say George Henderson's place over the rise has gone too, and the Larsens next to it. Given the way the wind's been blowing all afternoon, my guess is it's the same fire and it started at the Hendersons'.'

Shepherd felt ill. 'Do you think it was an accident, or could it have been lit deliberately?'

'Too early to say. You'd like to think there's no such thing, but the reality is . . .' He shook his head. 'If it started at George's place, I guess it was a power line or something. Shame he died. He was a good bloke, did a lot around here. I'll be going to his funeral, along with hundreds of others, no doubt.'

When they reached the top of the driveway, Vicki looked at Shepherd with her finger poised over the blinker. He nodded, and she turned right instead of left. On both sides of the road, black trees were smouldering and they could see that the fire had come this way.

'Where the hell do you think Joy is?'

'I don't know, Shep. If she's got any sense, she's miles away. It's Mrs B I'm worried about.'

They weren't two miles from the Boscombe farm when they turned a corner and Vicki slammed on the brakes.

Five metres ahead of them was another car, but it was a charred, distorted shell. They both got out and ran towards it, hoping, but not really believing, that whoever had been inside had escaped.

Shepherd was first to reach the car, even though it took decades. He pulled open the door, burning his hand and cursing.

He peered into the cabin then reeled back in horror, stumbling away from the car. He leant over and vomited, and collapsed onto the ground. He'd never seen a charred body before, had no idea it would look like something from Hell. Vicki looked inside, then walked over to him, face stony still. He knew that she'd seen plenty of dead bodies before, but guessed that the sight of this one was going to stay with her for a long time.

He put his hand on the hot black dirt, and realised that he had never even known that dirt could burn.

79

JOY AND RUTH

1961–64

With Ruth's fervent encouragement, Joy began her small acts of revenge under the guise of piety.

The first thing to do was fix the tablets. As Ruth suggested, she tipped out a capsule from the brown bottle hiding behind the bicarbonate of soda box and examined it. Then she gently rotated the two halves in opposite directions, poured the white powder down the sink and refilled it with two pinches of bicarb. Putting the two halves back together was difficult, until she worked out she could pinch one so it would slip into the other half. She repeated this with two more capsules, then went back to the laundry. When her parents arrived home, she was pegging up wet towels on the wire stretched across the back yard. Over the next few weeks, she replaced the powder of one or two capsules whenever she had the chance. She could even tell which ones she'd already tampered with because of the small tell-tale dimple on the pinched half.

Ruth had many more ideas, but they agreed that, before attempting them, Joy had to perfect her outer self. Slowly, so as not to arouse suspicion, she became an increasingly devout, modest and obedient Christian. If she wasn't praying fervently within his hearing (for Wendy and all the heathens in Africa), reciting grace sincerely, or singing strongly — but not too loudly — in Church, she was obeying his every word. This included reading the Bible over and over, memorising verses so that she could mouth along with Reverend Braithwaite (she even reinstated the capital R). As she had predicted, it was easy to convince her father that his command to read only the Bible, and his years of religious indoctrination and punishments, had paid off. Her duplicity was, Ruth told her, brilliant.

It was nearly winter when they felt it was safe for Joy to continue tampering with more of his pills. And when he next had a migraine, she happily took him his dimpled tablets. It was, as Ruth had said, all so easy.

As the months and years unrolled like barbed-wire fencing, it didn't matter to her that she developed breasts, bled from her dark birth canal, and carried disgusting Kotex pads wrapped in newspapers to the putrid rubbish tank. It didn't matter to her that the rain and chores were endless, that anyone observing her would have declared her life one long brown misery. It didn't matter to her that school became little more than an interruption of the acts of revenge that she and Ruth devised together, and Joy executed. The only thing that mattered was that he was deceived.

But despite her pious and demure exterior, she could not escape his rage. The punishments continued, and the welts and scars became as tight and raised and purple-red as Ruth's birthmark.

Flower beds had to be weeded and mulched, but don't dare leave some weeds behind, or pull out a plant your mother was cultivating. Camellias and roses and waratahs and gypsophila and tulips and poppies and carnations and chrysanthemums had to be gently picked and laid in boxes to be carried to the workroom, but don't dare bruise any of them. Summer fruit had to be picked and washed and peeled and boiled and bottled, but don't dare spoil a piece. Eggs were to be collected and waxed for winter and cooked for your father's breakfast, but don't dare drop one. Because the hovering Christ knew if you broke any of the rules, and woe betide you if you were that stupid or careless.

But although her father continued to punish Joy, each little act of revenge tasted sweeter than the last; even better than Dark Strawberry Cream chocolate.

One evening, nursing her bleeding and broken skin, Joy wondered why he hadn't listened to Mr Felicity, who by now must have spoken to him and told him to stop. Could Mr Felicity have decided to stay silent? Surely not, because that would make him nearly as bad as her father.

Easing herself into bed, she thought about how it wasn't just the Larsens who hid the interior of their house, of their lives. Everyone was like that. Even the Felicities only showed you what they wanted you to see. There was that blurb from the book Mr Felicity had written, the one that mentioned his 'personal struggles'. And the tail end of an argument she'd overheard when she was about to open their library door one Sunday afternoon.

'He wouldn't listen to me in a thousand years,' she'd heard Mrs Felicity say angrily.

'And what would you have *me* say? He's a good Christian, Gen. The Lord will guide him.'

'Well, the Lord hasn't done a very good job of guiding him so far.'

Even through the library door, Joy had felt the anger rippling in the silent air until Mr Felicity said, 'I trust you're praying for forgiveness and guidance yourself right now.'

'What I meant was that he's not *following* the Lord's guidance.'

When she told Ruth about the conversation, Ruth said, 'They were talking about our father, you know.'

'No, they weren't,' said Joy.

'Oh, right. Who were they talking about then?' said Ruth in her silky smooth voice.

'I don't know. But it wasn't our father.'

* * *

When Joy was fifteen and hanging out her blood-stained sheets one morning after he had punished her for not cleaning the bathroom thoroughly enough, she wondered how old she had to be before he would decide that it was wrong for him to see her naked body bent over the side of the bed, let alone assault it. Later, Ruth whispered, 'You know, he never punishes you when you have your period.' Presumably, her trips to the rubbish tank with the bundles of newspaper told him that she was bleeding and made him leave her alone. Ruth smiled and said, 'It's such a shame that it's going to last so long this month. And every month from now on.'

While most of Ruth's ideas were designed to annoy and inconvenience him, her idea to destroy the photos was purely to feed their thirst for vengeance. Joy felt no compunction as she opened the old photo album filled with grainy photos of weddings and babies, mostly of people now dead, the corners barely held in place by little paper triangles stuck to the thick black pages. Her parents' wedding photo filled the front page. With her gravelly pen eraser, Joy gently rubbed over her father's face, smudging his features just a little so that no one would think it was anything but regrettable deterioration. Ruth whispered, 'That's perfect.'

A few weeks later, Joy erased one of his eyes almost completely, along with some of the background and some of his shoes, so it looked like the deterioration was random. And then she turned the page and rubbed out some of the little ancient wedding photo of her father's parents, and the formal photograph of him with his parents and Uncle Bill, making sure not to damage Uncle Bill. She turned to the page with the baby photos of her, Ruth and Mark. She held the eraser on her own baby face . . . but enough was enough.

She would not use her eraser on those innocent faces, not even her own.

Over the next three years Joy damaged every photo in that album, except the baby photos. One day, worried that her father would think it was suspicious that all of Uncle Bill's images were intact, she took the eraser to his face, whispering 'Sorry' as his schoolboy grin disappeared, like his adult legs.

Nervously, she unscrewed and lifted out the hand pump from the 44-gallon drum of diesel they kept beside the tractor, poured a bucket of water into it, and screwed the pump back tightly. It was two weeks before the tractor failed to start, but it was worth it because he was in a paddock near Wishart Road and had to walk back in the drizzle.

Success spurred them on, and they didn't mind waiting days, weeks or months to see the result of their work, especially because then there was no need to feign surprise.

Because he loved passionfruit on top of pavlova, she poured undiluted weedkiller onto the base of the passionfruit vine and topped up the container with water. She too loved the fruit, but it was a price she was prepared to pay.

She removed a string from the spare set he kept in his guitar case, and carried it, twirled up in her pocket, down to the rubbish tank with one of her wads of newspaper. Then, gagging from the stench, climbed up the wooden steps and threw it in. For a second, the eels slithered over each other because he was tall enough to look over the edge of the tank and see it lying there, impervious to the flames, but she doubted he'd ever bother to peer in that closely. One night, months later while they were having tea, he said he'd rung Alfred from Alfred's Music Store in Tallangung and told him to fire the useless lad who worked there. She felt sorry for the pimply-faced teenager, but couldn't be distracted by any consequences of her actions.

She snipped through three stitches on one side of the handle on his Elders Session case, and after several weeks, just when she thought she might have to snip some more, the handle finally broke off. The case hit the ground and burst open, his Bible and notepad falling into the mud. Joy's outpouring of despair and her gentle but ineffective attempts to wipe the mud from the pink-edged tissue paper of his Bible were, Ruth later said, commendable.

Ideas for insidious {a slinking rat with long fangs} revenge kept popping into Ruth's head, and the more pious and obedient Joy was, the more opportunities she had to execute them, and the more devious Ruth's ideas became.

From the pinpricks of revenge — such as snipping a tiny hole, just like a moth-hole, in the back of his favourite jumper — to the grand tortures — such as the bicarbonate of soda in his pills — Ruth thought of every single one, and Joy willingly executed them. Ruth, who had no scars and had never screamed into a bedspread or bled into sheets, wanted revenge as much as Joy. And she was remarkably ingenious when it came to devising ways to make him suffer.

Carrying out Ruth's most daring idea, Joy sank the little dinghy he'd just bought to make it easier to catch eels and to pick the waterlilies that were too far away to reach with the Dutch hoe. In the dark of night, she drilled ten holes in the dinghy with his battery drill, pushed the dinghy out into the water and watched it sink as she walked back and forth from the dam to the tractor lane about twenty times, flattening the grass in erratic paths.

Then she picked up a sheet of rusty corrugated iron that was lying on the bank, dragged it over to the tractor lane to make it look like someone had dragged the dingy there, then carried it back to the dam. Walking tentatively onto the narrow ledge, hoping the water wasn't deeper than the tops of her rubber boots, she held the sheet vertically over the deep water and let it drop. She and Ruth were sure that everyone would believe some rogues had stolen the dinghy.

But the next day, when there were only 147 days until she was sixteen and no one could make her stay, Joy walked into the kitchen after school to find him sitting at the table. He stared at her, and she knew that he had discovered what she had done at the dam. As she looked at his twisted red face, she felt her whole outer body begin to fragment and fall away, revealing her red-hot evil self. It was all over. He would kill her. She knew this as well as she knew the Ten Commandments.

Instead, he groaned and put his head on his arms. 'Need pills.'

The door to the good room was open and she could hear her mother taking an order on the phone.

She smiled and said softly, demurely, 'I'll get them for you.' She tipped some of the blue tablets into her hand and carefully selected two that had little dimples.

It was three days before her father got out of bed and two more before he went over to the dam to catch some eels and found that the boat was missing. Infuriated, he rang the police. Sergeant Bell came out, examined the now not-so-flattened grass and concluded that a person or persons unknown had stolen the boat. He claimed he did some investigating, but the boat's disappearance remained a mystery. Just like Wendy Boscombe's.

80

JOY AND SHEPHERD

February 1983

> HENDERSON, George. A hard-working farmer who took good care of his family and his animals. Condolences to the family. Fred and Jinny Pollard and family

Over the next few days, the press ran nothing but stories of the dozens of devastating fires that had swept across South Australia and Victoria. In the middle of a terrible heatwave, most of them were caused by lightning or spontaneous combustion, and fanned by strong winds, but some were lit deliberately and others were due to foolish acts such as throwing cigarette butts out of car windows and lighting open incinerators.

Blackhunt's fire, which destroyed farms along Bullock and Wishart roads, was one of the first to start in the state. The one on Johnson's Road had been a false alarm, Clarice Johnson having assumed the worst when she'd smelt the smoke from South Australia. But there were many others who had not been so lucky. The front pages of newspapers bled with images of black skeletons of houses and sheds, charred cattle lying stiff in black paddocks, and distraught children and adults clutching belongings — an egg whisk, a teddy bear, a photo of a dead puppy — that had somehow survived whichever particular fire had wreaked havoc on their lives.

Each image was tattooed into Shepherd's brain, but it was the occupant of that lone car on Wishart Road that filled his nightmares when he managed to get to his flat and sleep for a few hours. Nightmares where he saw her trapped in the car as flames roared around, the heat and smoke catching up, even with the accelerator pressed to the floor. When he woke, he felt as if he could still smell the burnt flesh and see her hands fused to the steering wheel, her head lifted towards the sky, and her mouth opened in a perpetual scream.

Kneeling beside him on the hot dirt and in the eerie silence, Vicki had quietly said, 'Maybe she was praying for forgiveness.'

Shep had lifted his head from his hands and spat out, 'Forgiveness for what, Vicki?'

* * *

Waking after his first full night's sleep, after the fires had finally burnt out or been put out, he looked at his watch, read 8.40, and wondered if it was morning or evening. When he heard noises in his kitchen, he opened the door sharply, in no mood for petty burglars.

'Morning,' said Vicki. 'Tea or coffee?' He stared at her.

'Coffee, then,' she said.

'Tea,' he said, and sat down at the table with his head in his hands. Now that he had time to think again, his mind returned to Joy and her message. In the middle of the chaos of the last few days, Nev had told him that the Henderson house was nothing but ash and debris, so presumably the chest with Wendy's doll had been destroyed, as well as whatever Wendy's remains had been in. And Joy would never be able to provide him with any further details.

On the table in front of him, Vicki had spread out the weekend newspapers: *The Sun* and the *Blackhunt Gazette*'s 'Special Bushfire Edition'.

He stared numbly at the black-and-white photos of one family's tragedy, which filled *The Sun*'s front page. Four children whose mother had burnt to death, their father in intensive care in Melbourne, and the brick chimney that, like the Boscombes', was all that remained of their home. Eerily, the girl in the photo reminded Shepherd of Wendy Boscombe because she was holding a doll similar to Wendy's missing doll. He started to read the story, but stopped before he even finished the first sentence, overcome with sorrow.

Vicki put tea and a toasted sandwich on the table, and turned over pages of the *Blackhunt Gazette* until the death notices were staring up at them. Shep shook his head, and pushed the paper aside. He took a bite of the sandwich, hot tomato scalding his tongue.

'There's one you need to read, Shep,' said Vicki. Reluctantly, he looked at the notice Vicki was pointing to.

> HENDERSON, Mark. Beloved and brave brother of Ruth and Joy. Too many years apart, too many unshared moments. May the sun always shine for you.

He read it again, thinking of all the questions that would remain unanswered.

He read the next notice. And the one under that. And the next one. All for different people. They weren't even arranged alphabetically. So much chaos in just a couple of days. Even though he knew many of the people who'd placed the notices, there were many he'd never heard of. He thought back to the naive constable of twenty-three years ago who'd assumed he'd soon know everyone in the region. He took another bite of the sandwich, barely registering the burning tomato on his tongue.

He stopped chewing when he read the two death notices starting with LARSEN.

> LARSEN, Barbara. The most loving and most loved mother in the world. RIP.

And the one under it.

> LARSEN, Runty. The most loving and the most loved cat in the world. RIP.

Shepherd rubbed the fingers of one hand on his forehead, remembering how Colin had patted the wheezing cat before going off with him to show him where Ruth was buried.

Vicki grimaced. 'Apparently, Barbara and Colin both got out of the house when they saw the flames coming, then Barbara went back in to . . .' she sighed loudly, 'save his cat. When she came back out, with the cat in her arms, a branch fell on top of her and killed both of them. The worst part of all of this is that the house somehow survived. They would have all survived if they'd just stayed in the house. Not that they could have known that, of course.'

'Jesus. So where's Colin?'

'He was in hospital overnight, but physically he's fine so they let him out.' Vicki grimaced again. 'They need the beds.'

'But where is he?'

'He's gone back home and—'

'What? He can't stay there by himself.'

'Viola Boscombe's there with him. She's moved in for the time being, since she doesn't have anywhere to live. And Neil will join them when he gets out of hospital. She said they'll look after him for as long as they can, that the three of them have lost people they love, that they need each other. They'll rebuild and he can live with them in their new house.'

'I guess that's a win-win, if you can have such a thing after such bloody horrible events.' Shepherd wiped his brow. 'All these death notices. They're like pins being stabbed into a gaping wound.'

Vicki shook her head. 'No, Shep, it's not making the pain worse, just acknowledging it, releasing it.'

He looked at her, unsettled by the fact that she was not being flippant for once. 'So who ever acknowledged Joy Henderson's pain? Or Mark's? Ruth's or Gwen's?'

Vicki shook her head. 'I don't know, Shep. Maybe you did. Maybe in letting her go, you acknowledged what that whole family had been through.'

'And George? I know he was a bastard, but I keep wondering what pain he must have lived with to be the man he was?'

'That's something we'll never know, Shep. But if,' and she lowered her voice, 'and I'm talking theoretically, of course, if his medical file accidentally landed on your desk, and you accidentally opened it, and you accidentally saw that he had a history of delusion and had been prescribed medication for depression for decades—'

'Jesus, Vicki. Do you make a habit of breaching patient confidentiality?'

'Absolutely not, Shep. So I promise,' she smacked her right hand on her heart, and looked as solemn as a gravestone, 'that George Henderson's file will never end up on your desk, accidentally or otherwise, and that I will never reveal to you or anyone else that he had delusions and depression.' She paused. 'Or did not. Whatever the truth may be.'

Shepherd sighed. 'Alright, I guess that partly explains it, but there must be plenty of people who have depression who don't go around beating their kids, leaving their bodies and minds scarred like that. To say nothing of murdering their neighbours' kid.'

Maybe, thought Shepherd, in letting Joy go, I have acknowledged her pain. And I should leave it at that. He just wished he could somehow do something about the phone message Joy had left him.

'Joy said she found Wendy and the doll, Vicki. I want to know what she found and where.'

'How are you going to do that?'

'I'm going to go out to the farm.'

Vicki shook her head. 'It's a pile of ashes, Shep. There's nothing to find.'

Shepherd picked up his keys, and turned to her. 'Are you coming or not?'

81

JOY AND SHEPHERD

February 1983

> HENDERSON, George. A magnificent contributor to our Club and community whose tireless work will be sadly missed. Blackhunt Rotary Club

'Joy wasn't lying,' Shepherd whispered.

He took out his handkerchief, draped it over a pen, then inserted the pen into the hole where the doll's head would have been joined to the body, and lifted it out of the chest.

'So this is Wendy's doll?' said Vicki. 'Or at least its head.'

Shepherd nodded. He carried the head back to his car and dropped it into an evidence bag.

'Jesus, Shep, I was sure it was going to be Wendy's skeleton in there. Not just that creepy doll's head.' Vicki was shouting from the shed, peering into the twisted and partially melted chest that they'd had to force open with the jemmy in the boot of Shepherd's car.

Shepherd was beside her again. 'Well, we'll fingerprint it, of course, see if anything comes up, but I'm not optimistic. To be quite honest, since I've not done much but issue licences for years, I'm not sure how long fingerprints last on anything.'

'But since I've done much more than just write prescriptions for antibiotics for years, I do,' said Vicki, looking smug and folding her arms across her chest triumphantly.

Shepherd waited for her to continue, then snapped, 'So, are you going to tell me?'

'Before I moved to Blackhunt, I had a job in—'

'Vicki! I mean, are you going to tell me if there'll still be fingerprints on the doll's damn head?'

'Ah. Well, the answer to that is yes. Porcelain's a very easy surface to lift prints from, and there will most certainly be fingerprints of anyone who handled this doll, even if it was twenty years ago. Unless they were wearing gloves. Mmm, I say "anyone", but Wendy's might not show up because she was young and children's prints fade very quickly. But we don't need Wendy's, do we?'

'No. Okay. That's good.' Shepherd sniffed, looked around the shed again, then turned back to Vicki. 'Alright, tell me what you did that means you know all this stuff?'

'A bit of this, bit of that, Shep. Mostly forensic pathology and helping out the coroner.'

'Oh. Right,' said Shepherd, feeling a bit outranked.

'So, what now?' said Vicki, aware of Shepherd's awkwardness.

'Apart from getting the doll's head checked for fingerprints, I don't know. What I really wanted to do was find Wendy, or what's left of her. Joy definitely said she'd found her,' he looked at the devastation around them, 'but anything big enough to hide a body has been destroyed.'

'True,' Vicki said. 'You know, they're pretty sure the fire started in a rubbish tank in the front paddock. What if Joy tried to burn something that proved George had killed Wendy?'

'But she wouldn't burn evidence — she'd want to *keep* it to prove what George had done. Besides, she said she'd found Wendy.'

'Right. Take me through the phone message again.'

Shepherd sighed. 'She told me to meet her at the Boscombes' because she'd found the doll in the chest and knew her father had killed Wendy.'

'So she didn't say she'd *found* Wendy, just that she knew George had killed her.'

'Yes, she did say she'd found her,' said Shepherd. 'She said, "Meet me at the Boscombes, my father killed Wendy, I've found the doll in the chest, and Wendy in something."'

'Okay, that's pretty definite. In what, though?'

'I don't know, because we were disconnected. The fire must have destroyed the phone line. Let's head back into town and see if there are fingerprints on that doll.'

They got in the car and started down the driveway. Vicki was staring at the paddocks that rolled away from where the farmhouse had been.

'Shep.' Her face was alert. 'I don't think you were disconnected because of the fire.'

'We must have been. That's why I didn't hear the end of the sentence.'

'No. Because if the fire started before she left the house, Joy would have known about it — she would have smelt it, probably seen it if she was out in the shed discovering the doll's head — or Wendy. She wouldn't have rung you with a fire bearing down on the house. She would have been getting away as fast as she could. The fire had to have started after she left the house.'

'Mmm, I guess.' God, she was annoying. Especially when she was right.

'So, let's assume Joy found Wendy, called you to tell you where she was, but hung up on you before she finished telling you. Why would she do that?'

'I don't know, Vicki.'

'Did you hear even the first letter of what she was going to say?'

'No, not even the first damn letter. I've listened to that message over and over. And read it at least fifty times.'

'Read it?'

'Yes — I wrote it down in my notebook.'

'Where's your notebook?'

'Here,' he said. He took one hand off the wheel, pulled the little spiral notebook out of the top pocket of his shirt, and handed it to her. 'The page with the bottom corner turned up.'

She read it silently, then looked away, back to the notebook, and back out the window.

'Shep, stop!' she yelled.

Shepherd braked violently, and the car skidded in the loose gravel. 'What the hell, Vicki?'

'Shep, look out your window. What do you see?'

'Ash, Vicki. Burnt paddocks and lots of ash. Just what you'd expect after a fire.'

'Exactly. Now take a look out my window. What do you see?' Shepherd shrugged. 'Dry paddocks. And . . . no ash. So what?'

'The fire obviously went that way,' she pointed past Shepherd at the black hills that swept up to the Larsen farm and beyond, 'but not that way,' and she pointed to the unburnt paddocks on the other side of the house.

'I repeat . . . so what?'

'Listen to this.' She read from his notebook, '"Wendy Boscombe's doll is in his chest in the shed, and Wendy's in the damn dot-dot-dot." See what's over there,' Vicki turned and looked out of her window, 'in the distance? You *did* hear her last word, Shep. Joy Henderson was telling you that Wendy was in *the dam*, Shep, not the damn-with-an-n *something*.' She flashed her infuriating grin. 'I don't recall Joy Henderson ever using the word *damn*; you, on the other hand, use it all the *damn* time.'

Her grin turned to a wry smile. 'Joy found Wendy Boscombe in the dam, and since the fire didn't go anywhere near the dam, I bet she's still there.'

82

SHEPHERD

February 1983

> HENDERSON, Joy. Loved daughter of George (dec.) and Gwen (dec.), loved sister of Mark (dec.) and Ruth (dec.). With much sadness, Alex Shepherd

Shepherd handed Vicki a piece of paper. He'd drafted the wording four times before finally typing it on the official form she was now reading.

> SUMMARY OF REPORT OF INVESTIGATION
> Date: Wednesday 16 February 1983
> Brief Description: Investigation into the disappearance and suspected murder of Wendy Kathleen Boscombe (DOB 4 November 1951), aged nine at the time of her disappearance on 27 December 1960.
>
> Established Facts:-
> The human bones found in a 44-gallon drum in the dam on the property of George Henderson

(dec.) were those of the victim, Wendy Boscombe. Plastic sandals, also found in the drum, have been described by the victim's parents as the same colour and size as those the victim was wearing when she disappeared. Although damage to the upper back of the victim's skull indicates the victim suffered a blow to the skull, Forensics reports that it was most likely not the cause of death, but, because the shape of the blow matches the arc of the drum, may have been sustained while the victim, possibly unconscious or already deceased, was being placed into the drum.

On 11 February 1983 at 14:38, Joy Henderson (dec.), daughter of George Henderson, telephoned Blackhunt Police Station from the Henderson property, leaving a message claiming that her father was responsible for the victim's death, and that the victim was in the dam, where Senior Constable Alex Shepherd and Dr Victoria Cooper subsequently found the victim's skeleton. Miss Henderson further claimed that she had found the victim's missing doll in her father's chest 'in the shed', the head of which Senior Constable Shepherd and Dr Cooper subsequently found in a chest on the Henderson property, which, according to many locals, George Henderson always kept locked because of the alleged value of the tools in said chest.

The fire destroyed most of George Henderson's property, including the shed housing the chest, before Senior Constable Shepherd could investigate Miss Henderson's allegations; however, the doll's head was intact. Forensics report that although bushfires burn at more than 1400°F, porcelain (of which the doll's head is made) can withstand temperatures of over 2000°F, thereby confirming that the doll's head could have been in the chest before the fire came through.

Testimony from the victim's parents, and a photograph of the victim's missing doll, lead police to believe that the head is from the missing doll, which is distinguishable because of a missing left eye. Police do not have a theory as to why the doll's head was taken from the child, nor what happened to the rest of the doll.

Forensics found faint fingerprints on the doll's head that they were able to identify as George Henderson's. As expected, the victim's fingerprints were not on the doll's head, due to the fact that children's fingerprints fade faster than those of adults as a result of a difference in the amount and types of oil in children's skin. There were no other fingerprints on the doll's head.

Joy Henderson died in a bushfire on the same day that she made her allegations, before police were able to interview her. Unfortunately, she did not provide a possible motive for, nor modus operandi of, her father's alleged actions.

Evidence of George Henderson's propensity for violence:-

Numerous local citizens reported that they believe George Henderson was violent to Mrs Gwen Henderson (dec.), his wife of 38 years. According to witness statements, Mrs Henderson frequently wore thick foundation on her face, neck and arms, but rarely any other make-up. Several local women say they 'all knew' that Mrs Henderson was covering bruises her husband had caused. Furthermore, one of the Hendersons' next-door neighbours, Mr Colin Larsen, said that Gwen Henderson told him George Henderson had pushed her down their back steps when she was eight months' pregnant. This hearsay statement cannot be verified, and hospital records show the stillbirth was 'the result of an accidental fall'.

Numerous local citizens and George Henderson's sister-in-law (Mrs Rosemary Henderson) have — without exception — confirmed, all initially with considerable reluctance, that it was 'common knowledge' that George Henderson inflicted severe corporal punishment on his children.

Miss Henderson revealed physical evidence (numerous scars on her shoulders and back) to Senior Constable Shepherd during an interview at the Henderson farm on Wednesday 9 February. She claimed the scars were the result of frequent and vicious beltings perpetrated by her father when she was a child.

In addition:-

- A medical record dated 14 July 1960 states that Master Mark Henderson (deceased son of George Henderson and brother to Joy Henderson) presented with severe scarring on the torso and limbs as a child of fifteen.
- A medical record dated 29 September 1963 states that Miss Henderson presented with severe scarring on the torso and limbs as a child of fourteen.

Neither doctor reported the alleged violence to authorities, mandatory reporting not yet having been legislated. The investigating officer came into possession of these medical files via an anonymous delivery.

There are no reports of George Henderson perpetrating violence or showing violent tendencies of any kind outside the family home. All local citizens interviewed reported that he was an exemplary and highly regarded member of the community (as confirmed by over seven hundred death notices in the local paper), and the minister of the church of which he was an Elder, Reverend Alistair Braithwaite, spoke highly of his spiritual integrity and sincerity.

Conclusion:-
Material forensic evidence (in the form of Wendy Boscombe's skeleton in the 44-gallon drum on George Henderson's property, and George Henderson's fingerprints on the head of the missing doll on George Henderson's property), and George Henderson's history of violence towards children strongly indicate that George Henderson was likely responsible for the murder of Wendy Boscombe, and the subsequent disposal of her body in the dam on his property.

Recommendations:-
That, given that the alleged offender is deceased and the likelihood of other evidence coming to light is minimal due to the fire that destroyed both the Henderson and Boscombe premises and outlying sheds, the investigation into the disappearance and murder of Wendy Kathleen Boscombe be closed.

That records show that on Tuesday 27 December 1960, George Joshua Henderson, for reasons unknown, and by means unknown, deliberately or accidentally killed Wendy Kathleen Boscombe and subsequently concealed her body and the head of her doll in order to escape detection.

Vicki handed it back to him with a nod. 'That should make the people of Blackhunt rethink their pillar of all things good. That, and the story on the front of yesterday's *Gazette*.'

'Yes,' said Shepherd, not sounding convinced.

'What's that supposed to mean?' said Vicki.

'I feel like there's still one piece of the puzzle missing.'

'If you're still regretting not arresting Joy, we've been through this. You didn't have evidence.'

Shepherd threw Vicki a look she interpreted to mean 'That's your fault,' then said, 'No, it's something else, something niggling at the edge of my brain that I can't quite grab. It's to do with Joy and that phone message she left.' He felt like the cogs in his head were in mud again, and the slow whirring was driving him mad.

He walked over to the Wendy Boscombe filing cabinet, and pulled out the file labelled HENDERSON, Joy.

He sat down to read and Vicki went to make tea.

When she came back with the pot, Shepherd had bits of paper spread out, with various words highlighted in pink and orange.

'Any luck?' asked Vicki.

'I think . . . I'm not sure . . . but I think Joy knew all along that George had killed Wendy. And that she came back to make him confess, or at least to suffer. I think she finally thought she could confront him, tell him what she knew. So I agree with you, Vicki, that she *was* telling the truth — she didn't want George dead, because she wanted him to be punished for killing Wendy. But he died, and then—'

'Whoa, wait,' said Vicki, 'go back. What makes you think she knew George had killed Wendy?'

'On the day that Wendy went missing and Ron and I were at the Henderson farm, I asked Joy to tell me about Wendy. She said, and I quote,' he read from a file-note in front of him, '"She *had* a half-sister." Past tense.'

'I don't know what you're getting at—'

'And then she said, and I quote again, "Who *has*" — note the present tense — "*has* a baby." Because the half-sister was, probably still is, alive.'

Vicki shook her head. 'So? Joy was, what? Eleven? Twelve? And she mixed up her tenses after she'd just found out a friend had disappeared. Or you wrote it down incorrectly.'

'No, I didn't.' He looked down at the file-note again. 'In fact, I specifically asked her why she'd used the past tense when she was talking about Wendy.'

'And what did she say?'

Shepherd read from his notes. '"I guess because I don't go to that school anymore."'

'Seems reasonable.'

'Maybe. There's something else too. When I took that damn belt back to her the other day, and she was telling me what it was like when she was a child, how scared she was, she said things got worse and worse . . . until one day she thought he was going to kill her. And that day was the day before Wendy Boscombe disappeared. George was obviously having difficulty controlling his anger.'

'There are a lot of assumptions in all of this,' said Vicki, but her eyes told him she was taking him seriously.

'Perhaps, but here's the clincher. Here's what's really been gnawing away up here,' he tapped the side of his head. 'How the hell did Joy know where to find Wendy? What was she doing over at the dam anyway? And, more to the point, how did she know it was *Wendy* in the drum? Okay, the bones are small, but for all she knows it could have been a child who died a hundred years ago. Or two months ago.'

Vicki opened her mouth to say something, but Shepherd held up his index finger. 'And the final bit of the puzzle — no one knew what Wendy's missing doll looked like, but when Joy opened that chest, it seems she knew exactly what she was looking at.'

'So you're saying the only reason she knew all these things *and* talked about Wendy in the past tense . . .'

'Is, yes, if she saw George kill Wendy — or at least get rid of her body and hide the doll's head.'

'God, that's bloody horrible, Shep. No wonder she was scared of him.'

Shepherd was reading his notes again. 'It says here Joy went over to the dam that day to pick waterlilies for her mother. She must have seen George putting Wendy in the drum and pushing her over the edge.'

Vicki looked horrified.

'When Ron and I were at the Henderson farm,' continued Shepherd, 'it was pretty clear she was very scared. We just assumed she was upset about her friend disappearing, but when Ron took George outside to tell him that we were sure Wendy had been abducted,' he looked at his notes again, 'Joy asked me if Ron was arresting her father. As I said, I thought she was frightened, but in hindsight, and now we've got Wendy's doll and her bones, well . . . let's face it, it's not exactly the first thing a twelve-year-old would think of, is it? Unless she knew there was a good reason for us to arrest him.'

Vicki frowned. 'But why would she wait all these years before telling anyone?'

'I'm guessing she thought he'd kill her too if she said anything. So she keeps quiet, and leaves home as soon as she can, planning to stay away forever — like Mark. Then you ring and say her dad's dying, so she thinks now is her chance to finally get justice for Wendy. I'm also guessing she had a frank conversation or two with him about it, and maybe he swallowed all those tablets to kill himself, because — another guess — she'd threatened to turn him over to the police.'

'The whole thing's too awful,' said Vicki. 'But I think you're right, Shep.'

Shepherd returned the sheets of paper to their folder, while Vicki poured the tea.

'So, you're the local hero now.'

'Not sure about that. I didn't do anything really, since Joy told me what to find and where to find it. Still, I feel like I've finally earnt my stripes here.' He stapled the summary to the ten sheets of the full report, and slid the pages into an A4 envelope.

Vicki smiled. 'What you did was never give up, Shep. What you did was go searching for the doll and Wendy, even when the place was nothing but ashes. And I think Blackhunt's pretty pleased with that. And your superiors should be too. So, do you still want to go to the bastard's funeral?'

'Yep, I want to see just how many people turn up.'

* * *

The now elderly but stalwart Reverend Braithwaite looked down at the people who had come to pay their last respects to George Henderson. The Reverend was only too aware that they were seated in the church where George Henderson had been the longest-serving Elder, and that it stood next to the hall where, for decades, that same man had smiled and joked and consoled people as if he were one of God's perfect angels.

The past twenty-four hours had been difficult for the Reverend. Over lunch the previous day, he had read the front page of the local newspaper with disbelief, then rung Shepherd to verify the journalist's claims. He spent the remainder of the day in his study, drafting and redrafting the service for George Henderson's funeral and praying for guidance. He put down his pen close to midnight, still unsure if the words and Bible verses he'd chosen were entirely appropriate. And then this morning, he had hastily rewritten the service, keeping only the psalms unchanged because it would be too unsettling for the organist and choir. Now, even as he walked to the pulpit, he realised he'd been too hasty, perhaps too disturbed by the grainy black-and-white image of the smiling but now definitely deceased Wendy Boscombe. The opening he'd rewritten was most certainly inappropriate but it was too late, because his tangled brain could not think of another, and he was frankly stunned by how many people were sitting in the pews.

He lifted his arms to the high-arched ceiling, and the cavern of the church was filled by his crackling voice, no longer the thunder it had been when Joy had sat in the front pew terrified of her father, the Devil and the threat of eternal damnation.

'"Holy is He! The King in His might loves justice. You have established equity; you have executed justice and righteousness."' He paused, concerned about what the congregation would think of his choice of words, but continued. '"For day and night, your hand was heavy upon me; my strength was dried up as by the heat of summer."'

Shepherd and Vicki threw shocked glances at each other, wondering what was going to come next. They had arrived early and, hoping to be both respectful of the mourners and inconspicuous, had sat in a pew towards the back of the church.

But they could not have been more conspicuous if they'd been dripping with Wendy Boscombe's blood. Apart from Reverend Braithwaite, they were the only people in the church. Not even the organist had turned up to George Henderson's funeral.

As he read from his notes, Reverend Braithwaite wondered just how many scones and lemon slices he and his wife could eat over the next few days, before mentally crossing out 90 per cent of the service, and walking away from the pulpit after just ten minutes.

83

JOY AND WENDY

Tuesday 27 December 1960

Joy carefully lifted up the Dutch hoe, held it out over the lily pad and gently slipped the head over a pure white waterlily. When it was about eighteen inches under the water, she quickly yanked it to cut the stem, slowly pulled the waterlily to the edge of the dam, then put it beside the others she'd collected.

'That's clever,' said a voice behind her.

Joy jumped with fright and winced as red pain shot from the welts her father had whipped into the back of her thighs and buttocks last night. How could she have been so stupid? How could she have let those revolting ferrets escape when she knew what he was capable of? Maybe she should have let Mark take the blame. Last night her time had finally come, and now the rest of her life would be punctuated by punishments.

She turned around, but not quickly because it hurt too much, and saw Wendy Boscombe standing three or four feet away, wearing a bright-yellow dress with a square neckline and yellow plastic sandals. She was smiling and pointing at the Dutch hoe.

My mother invented it. Not the Dutch hoe — you can buy them anywhere — but she invented a new way of using it to pick waterlilies for wreaths. She's very clever, you know. That's what Joy wanted to say, but she was scared that if she opened her mouth, she would actually say, *My father nearly killed me last night. He invented a new way of using a belt to punish his children. He's a murderer, you know.* So she didn't open her mouth, but gave Wendy a half-smile.

Wendy, still smiling, said, 'I walked through the paddocks. It's not that far really,' as if answering a question that Joy hadn't asked. 'We just got back from our beach holiday and I wanted to show you my new doll.' She held up a doll that would have been beautiful except that it had one eye missing. 'I left all my other dolls in our driveway, because they got muddy and dirty cos I slipped and the pram fell over. I pretended they were in a car accident and I lined them up like dead people, face down in the mud.' She laughed, but Joy didn't know what was funny. 'I don't care about them anymore. I have Jessica now.'

Joy didn't have one doll, let alone a handful, that she could just leave lying around in the mud after getting back from a beach holiday. She touched one painful buttock, knowing that she didn't want to even think about what her father would do to her if she did have dolls and left them lying around in the mud. The only toys she'd ever had were hand-me-downs from Mark, which had mostly been hand-me-downs from Colin. So even though the doll with the missing eye was ugly, Joy felt a tremor of shiny white jealousy right where a purple bubble of hatred lived at the back of her neck. All those dolls, and a father who didn't care what she did or didn't do with them.

'See, her face is made of porcy-lane. My dad said she's worth a fortune.'

'A fortune?' said Joy. Her father had tools that he said were worth a fortune and he kept them locked in a chest that he never ever opened. He didn't go around giving them to children to play with, so Joy didn't think that the ugly Jessica could be worth a fortune. But what did she know about dolls and such things? All she knew was that Wendy was lucky to have a doll with such a beautiful creamy lace dress and shiny black shoes, even if it was missing an eye. And to have smiling parents and a sister, even if she was a half-sister. And to have beach holidays and chocolate milkshakes.

'What was your milkshake like?'

'Which one?' asked Wendy, stroking the doll's silky cream dress. 'The one you had the other day, after school finished,' said Joy, wondering how often Wendy had milkshakes.

'It was delicious. Cold and frothy and very chocolatey,' said Wendy. 'Milkshakes are delicious, aren't they? Especially chocolate ones.'

Joy nodded. But she'd never had a milkshake. Her family didn't have money for luxuries, what with the government and the mud and the butter factory conspiring to make life difficult for them. She wondered why the Boscombes were rich and had money for milkshakes and holidays since their farm was the same size as the Hendersons' farm. Maybe because they only had one child?

'Do you want to play?' Wendy asked.

'Okay,' Joy said, pushing down her white annoyance at Wendy and all her milkshakes. 'But I have to pick eight more waterlilies first.'

While Joy picked the waterlilies and laid them down next to one another in the mud (a bit like Wendy's dolls, she thought), Wendy played with Jessica, pretending that she was the doll's mother and that they were sitting on a beach having a milkshake together. The Boscombes, Joy concluded, must be the only wealthy farmers for miles and miles and miles.

Each time Joy guided another waterlily to the bank, she glanced over at Wendy, who was pretending to slurp on a milkshake and talking to Jessica in a grown-up voice. 'What's your favourite milkshake, Jessica? Chocolate or strawberry, dear?' Just as Wendy's mother no doubt spoke to Wendy.

When Joy put the last waterlily next to the other twenty-four, she called out, 'Okay, I can play now.'

'Goody,' said Wendy, jumping up. 'Let's play hidey.'

'Hidey?' said Joy. She thought they were going to play with the doll. 'Don't you want to play with Jessica?'

'Nah, I want to play hidey,' and she put the doll beside Joy's waterlilies. 'You count to fifty and I'll hide. No peeking.'

'Alright.' Joy covered her eyes with her hands and faced the other way. 'One, two, three . . .' She counted quickly, not to be mean but because she knew she had to get the waterlilies to her mother and start doing the potatoes for tea. 'Seven-eight-nine . . .' She counted faster. She would get into trouble if the potatoes weren't cooked on time. 'Eighteennineteentwenty.' She lowered her voice, skipped twenty or so numbers, then said loudly, 'Fortyeightfortyninefifty. Here I come, ready or not,' and turned around.

Joy looked at all the rusted equipment and junk lying around the dam, as a ripple of yellow fear rolled through her. She didn't have time to play games. She had to get back to the house and do her chores. Why had she agreed to play hidey?

She couldn't see Wendy anywhere behind the piles of junk, but she was sure the nine-year-old was peeking through a tiny gap and could see Joy. Which meant that, as Joy approached, Wendy could just move around whichever pile she was hiding behind so she would stay out of sight and it would take forever to find her.

Joy felt the eels biting her stomach. 'Wendy, I don't have time to play. You have to come out. I have to go back home.'

But there was silence.

Joy walked away from the edge of the water to the top of the dam's bank, thinking that she would be able to see Wendy from there. But she couldn't. 'Wendeeeee, Wendeeeee! Where are you?' Still Wendy didn't answer her. 'Come on, Wendy,' she called out loudly. 'I have to go.' Now she was getting annoyed. Where was she? 'I have to go,' she called out more loudly. As she scanned the banks again, she saw a flash of yellow moving from behind a large tractor wheel on the other side of the dam, and disappear behind an old rusty 44-gallon drum. *A-ha,* thought Joy. *She's just crawled into the drum.*

She walked towards the tyre, getting crosser and crosser with Wendy for not coming out. Just because Wendy could have chocolate milkshakes whenever she wanted and throw away dolls like they were scraps of paper, and had a father who didn't belt her for letting out ferrets, that didn't mean she could ignore Joy when Joy told her she had to go home.

She doesn't know what it's like to have anything bad happen to her. She's so spoilt with her dolls and chocolate milkshakes and beach holidays.

A tiny bit of Joy decided she would creep up on Wendy and give her a fright. Just a little fright. Because life wasn't all chocolate milkshakes and porcy-lane dolls. It would do her good to have a little fright. Joy tiptoed towards the drum, breathing very lightly and quietly, so Wendy wouldn't hear her coming.

When she was about twenty feet from the huge tyre, she walked up the bank a few yards and then down towards the back of the drum. From there, she could see that the drum was angled so it was facing towards the water, and that its lid was lying in the mud right in front of the open drum.

She stood still, waiting for Wendy's arm to poke out and pull the lid up to hide herself completely. Because that's when Joy would jump and shout 'Found you!' and give her a huge fright.

As she took her first step back down the bank, a movement to her left drew her attention, but it was just an eel swimming in the shallow water at the edge of the dam. It wasn't a very big one, definitely not big enough to put in a stew. In fact, even though it was a fast swimmer, it looked like a baby eel — it was thin and hadn't grown fins yet. It was going to swim right past the front of the drum, and Joy wondered if Wendy would be frightened by the eel, because she was sure Wendy's family didn't kill and eat eels. In fact, she thought with a tiny hot-pink twinge of contempt, Wendy had probably never even seen an eel, let alone tasted one.

Unless you could get chocolate eel milkshakes. Oh yes, she'd probably had one of those.

Joy watched the eel wriggle through the shallow water. When it was about a foot away from the drum, her heart suddenly stopped. That was no eel. It was a snake. She could tell by the shape of its head. No wonder it didn't have fins. And it had stripes — like a tiger snake.

Joy stood still, wishing that she was holding the Dutch hoe, and wondering why her father always said, 'Take a stick or the hoe,' yet had never told her what to do with it if she saw a snake. But there was nothing to worry about. It was obviously a baby snake because it was so small and thin — and it was no doubt going to swim right past Wendy hiding in the drum.

Unless it was looking for somewhere to sleep. And had decided the drum was the perfect place.

As if reading Joy's mind, the snake curved its body and began to swim towards the edge of the dam, right where the drum was.

It's only a baby snake, thought Joy. It won't hurt her. And everyone always says that snakes are more afraid of people than people are of them. It's probably going to slither under the lid, not actually go into the drum.

Even so, I should call out to Wendy, warn her.

But that tremor of shiny white jealousy rippled out from the back of Joy's neck and spread through her body. *She doesn't know what it's like to have anything bad happen to her. Maybe being frightened by a baby snake will teach her a lesson. Just a little lesson. Just a tiny taste of something bad, so she knows what it feels like. Because it's not fair.*

The snake was wriggling out of the water not ten inches from the open end of the drum.

Now was the time for Joy to call out, *Wendy, watch out, there's a snake and it's coming towards you.*

But Joy's tongue was pressed against the roof of her mouth, and the words did not come.

The snake slithered a little closer. And still no words came out of Joy's mouth.

Then the baby snake lifted its head out of the water and flicked its tongue in and out. Joy knew it was using its tongue to smell, and wondered if it could smell flesh. Or fear. Or both.

And then Joy heard Mr Larsen's voice, one Saturday afternoon months ago, when he was sitting on the other side of the table telling Joy and her mother how Colin had killed a baby snake near the house because he knew that baby snakes were more dangerous than fully grown ones. Seeing Joy's look of surprise Mr Larsen had added, 'Well, lass, when a baby snake bites you, they just spit all of their poison into you, no matter what. While a grown-up snake, well, they know not to do that, to keep some for the next bite. If they use it all up, they're like a cow after she's been milked. But your baby snake, lass, she's not careful like that, cos she's not yet learnt she hasn't got a definite supply.' Joy had seen her mother's smile come and go in an instant when Mr Larsen said 'definite' instead of 'infinite'.

She should certainly warn Wendy now. *Wendy, watch out, there's a baby snake coming towards you.* She should say it now. Right now. Before it was too late.

What did her father always say? *Snakes love water. And children.* Joy watched the snake swim closer and closer to the drum's opening, and then her ripple of jealousy evaporated and was replaced with thick yellow fear.

Finally she opened her mouth — just as Wendy's smiling face and one hand appeared as she started to crawl out of the drum.

'Joy! Here I –'

And just as 'Snake!' at last burst from Joy's mouth, Wendy's hand pressed down on the middle of the baby snake's back.

Joy watched, frozen, as the snake's head reared up and Wendy looked down to see what her hand had touched. As she screamed and jerked back her hand, the snake darted forward, and sank its teeth into Wendy's exposed skin above the left corner of her dress's neckline.

Wendy screamed again and reared up, and Joy heard a thick red thud as she hit her head against the rim of the drum.

And suddenly Joy knew what she had to do with the Dutch hoe. She ran to where the waterlilies were lying, pain exploding with each step that pulled at the strips of her damaged flesh. She picked up the tool, crying out at the smarting in her legs and buttocks, and then, with the hoe raised high in the air, she took a deep breath and walked, quickly but quietly, back to the drum, so that she could take the snake by surprise. When she saw it about five feet from the drum, basking in the sun, she slowed down and took tiny silent steps towards it, until she brought down the hoe, fast and hard, and smashed it into the snake's head. She pulled the hoe back and saw that the snake was wounded but not dead, so she brought it down harder this time, crying out at the pain from her torn back as she stretched and bent. She took a step closer, repositioned the hoe in her hands so the blade was pointing straight down, and pushed it into the snake's flesh just behind its head. When she felt the blade hit mud, she let out a short cry of relief, but lifted the hoe again, knowing that a decapitated snake can still bite. She brought the blade of the hoe down again and again, until the head was a brown and white mass of skin and flesh and fangs, and then she attacked the still writhing body with the blade of the hoe, cutting it into ten, twenty, thirty million pieces, while she gagged and wept.

Finally, when she was sure that the snake was completely incapable of doing anything, she threw the hoe into the mud, sat down, and cried huge sobs of disgust and relief. She didn't know how long she'd been sitting there crying when she remembered Wendy. 'Wendy!' She spun around to see if Wendy was alright and saw her head face down in the shallow water.

'Wendeeeee!' Joy raced over to her, stepped into the water and knelt down to shake Wendy's shoulder.

She looked up into the hot air. 'Help! Help!'

But there was no one to see or hear them. 'Help!' she screamed again, louder than she had screamed even the night before when her father had thrashed her with his belt.

She shook Wendy again. But Wendy's head lay in the water, still and heavy. Joy stepped backwards out of the water.

Why wasn't Wendy saying anything? She couldn't be dead. It took forever for a snake bite to kill someone. Didn't it? How long had she taken to get the hoe and mash the snake? Five minutes? Ten minutes? And why had she then just sat in the mud crying?

Mr Larsen's words hammered inside her head. 'If you get bit on an arm or a leg, lass, you're going to be okay if you don't go running around like a bull that hasn't seen a cow in six months. But get bit on the chest . . .'

'Wendeeeee, Wendeeeee!'

But Wendy lay still and silent. Joy shook her shoulder again. 'Come on, come *on*, Wendy. I have to get back to the house. I have to get the potatoes on.'

She rolled Wendy over, thinking how small and light she was, and sat in the mud, not knowing what to do. As she dropped her head and squeezed her eyes tight in fear and despair, she heard the swish of air above her naked body as her father's belt came flying down to tear her flesh. Between her groans and sobs, she wished that Wendy and her dolls and milkshakes had never existed, that her father — not Wendy — was dead.

What would he do to her when he found out she had let Wendy get bitten by a snake? And then let her die?

She knew the answer. He would belt her until she was a writhing mass of blood and flesh like the snake she'd just mutilated, until the black, slimy eels burst from her stomach and slithered greedily over the pink and red pile that used to be Joy Henderson. Then he would throw her remains into the rubbish tank, where she would fall into Hell. He had already killed Ruth, beaten Mark into nothing more than thick mustard-yellow fear, and now he would kill her.

She sat in the mud howling, tears streaming down her face, and prayed. Please, God, please don't let Wendy be dead. Please forgive me. Please God. Don't let this happen. It was an accident, God, please. For thine is the kingdom, the power and the glory, forever and ever, please, God, please. Amen, Amen, Amen.

But she knew no one, not even God, would hear her howls or her prayers.

And then she heard Ruth whispering in her ear. *It's too late to save Wendy, but you can save yourself. There's no need to tell anyone. It was just an accident. Remember what our mother said? It's not lying to not-tell.*

Joy stopped sobbing, and lifted her head. She swallowed and nodded at Ruth's words. *We both know he'll kill you if you tell him.*

Which means he'll have killed both of us.

So with Ruth whispering instructions in her ear, Joy Henderson pushed Wendy Boscombe's thin little body back into the drum. Then she put in a large rock, pushed the lid onto the drum, and clicked the five clips, one by one, to fasten the lid.

With tears still pouring down her cheeks, she pushed the drum to roll it into the water. But it was heavy, the mud was thick, and her arms were trembling and weak. Remembering how she had closed the door under the house when she'd eavesdropped on Mr Larsen and Beryl, she sat behind the drum and pushed it with her legs, despite the skin at the back screaming with agony. The drum rolled a little and she heard the rock inside slide. She pushed again. And again. Until it rolled away from her over the muddy ledge.

She watched it bob in the water, and for a few horrible seconds she thought it would float, that the rock would not be heavy enough, or that the seal around the lid would be watertight, or that this was not the drum with the hole in it. But then, slowly, it began to sink — and then faster, so Joy knew the hole had gone below the surface and the drum was filling with water. She let out a huge single sob, and then cocked her head. Had she just heard a little bang from inside the drum? A groan? The word 'Joy'?

No, it was just the rock sliding inside the drum. Surely?

You're safe, whispered Ruth. *No one will ever find out.*

She and Ruth watched until the drum disappeared completely, and they knew it was sinking to the muddy, eel-infested bottom of the dam, fifty feet down. Joy stood up and walked over to the mashed flesh of the snake. Using the Dutch hoe, she pushed it all into the shallow water, and squashed it into the mud, where it couldn't be seen, and scraped more mud on top of it.

Quickly, said Ruth, *get the waterlilies into Mum's workroom, and start peeling the potatoes.*

Joy ran to where the waterlilies were sitting, and saw Jessica, a single eye staring up at her.

She picked up the ugly doll to throw it into the dam too, but Ruth stopped her just in time. *No. It won't sink.* The eels in Joy's stomach were on fire, and she was trembling. What was she going to do with the doll?

The tank. She would throw it into the tank and set it alight. She tapped the doll's 'porcy-lane' head with her knuckle. *It's like bone*, she thought, horrified. *The rest of it will burn, but not the head.* Which meant that if her father looked over the edge of the tank he might see it lying there.

Thinking, thinking, she gathered up the twenty-five waterlilies and stuck the doll in the middle of the stems where it couldn't be seen. At the shed, she saw her father must still be out fixing fences because the tractor was gone, so she laid the doll on the concrete floor, picked up the axe, and severed the doll's head with a single downward sweep of the sharp glistening blade.

Once she'd set the cotton body alight and dropped it into the rubbish tank, it quickly disintegrated into ashes.

That was the easy part.

Now all she had to do was hide the doll's head.

EPILOGUE

JOY AND RUTH

February 1983

> HENDERSON, George. Husband of Gwen (dec.), father of Mark (dec.), Ruth (dec.) and Joy.

I've been able to smell the smoke for a while, but now I can also hear a wild roar {a kaleidoscope full of crazily shaped pieces of glass}. A vibrant, perfect image.

I've never been so scared in all my life. Not when the ferrets escaped, not when Wendy died, not when I put the belt around his neck and pulled it as hard as I could.

There's nowhere to go. I can't outrun the fire, so now it really is all over. My biggest regret is that I won't get to see the Boscombes' reaction when they hear that my father killed Wendy. They'll have to hear it from Shepherd now. I just don't know if—

'Don't worry,' says Ruth. 'He'll find the doll. And Wendy.' I look around, surprised. 'I thought you'd gone forever.'

She shrugs. 'Couldn't let you go through this alone, could I?' It's only the second time we've been away from the house together. The first time, of course, was when we were at the dam with Wendy and her doll.

'You think Shepherd will work it out?' I say, although I know my lips aren't moving.

'Well, you were very clear about the doll being in the chest, and Wendy being in the dam.'

'So, the Boscombes can finally stop wondering what happened to Wendy. They'll have some peace. And be able to hold a proper funeral, with her bones in the coffin.'

Ruth nods. 'And I bet there'll be a lot more people at Wendy's funeral than his.'

'A shame Mum can't make the wreaths.'

The smoke is curling through the car now, and the hot roar, the crazy kaleidoscope, is catching up. I look at Ruth. 'What now?'

The birthmark stretches into smoothness, as she purses her lips together, thinking.

'Not much,' she says, looking at the flames speeding up the hill. 'A little bit of time to be grateful that we had each other, and Mark, and the Felicities.'

'They'll be sad.'

'Yes, but then again they didn't try to save us, did they? In the end, they were just like everyone else.'

The fact is, I've never been sure whether they did or didn't try to save us. Or if Felicity even told them what he was doing. But it doesn't matter now.

The ash-grey of the smoke rolls in, and I start coughing. As the smoke fills the car, time comes to a standstill, just as it always did when our father pushed back his chair on the lino.

My head is thumping, lungs screaming, trying to find oxygen, but just smoke, lungs full of it, brain crumbling, thousands of images bursting through membrane.

'It's okay,' says Ruth, her voice crackly and far away. 'Everyone knows he's a murderer, which is what we wanted. They might not ever have cared what he did to you and Mark, but they'll be appalled when they hear that he murdered Wendy. And Shepherd will never—'

I can't hear her properly anymore. My head is aching, and when I try to breathe . . .

But will Shepherd work it *all* out?

'Don't worry, he won't,' says another voice. Mark's in front of me, grinning, holding *A Sinner's Dictionary*, standing next to Ruth. The smoke has gone, and the three of us are in The Infinite Library, surrounded by shelves filled with books stretching into, well, infinity.

That's good. Ruth, Mark and me in The Infinite Library. I'm where I need to be now.

THE END

ACKNOWLEDGEMENTS

I have been privileged with a remarkably impressive team at Penguin Random House Australia, who have worked miracles with my manuscript. I will never be able to fully express my thanks to my publisher, Beverley Cousins, and my editor, Catherine Hill, two extraordinary people who worked enthusiastically and diligently with me on everything from concepts to commas, employing not only their vast set of skills but also their seemingly innate knowledge of how to make this novel work. I have learnt so much from you both, and enjoyed every minute of your company. Thank you to Claire Gatzen for your excellent proofreading skills; Justin Ractliffe for your behind-the-scenes support and management; Lou Ryan for your insight, energy and advice; members of the sales teams for your hard work and commitment; Tom Langshaw and your team for the brilliant audio work; Adam Laszczuk for the stunning cover; and Lucy Ballantyne and Emily Hindle for your outstanding energy, knowledge, enthusiasm and creativity. Everyone I have worked with at PRH has been talented, committed and fun . . . an author's dream team.

One Friday night in February 2019, the literary agent Jacinta di Mase read my manuscript on a plane, and a few minutes before midnight sent me an email that has changed my life. Among other unforgettable words was the phrase 'I want to sign you up', and so it all began. Thank you, Jacinta (and your team), for believing in my work and championing it so enthusiastically.

The manuscript only ever became more than a dream due to Antoni Jach and the writers in his MasterClasses. Thank you, Antoni, for the intellectual and creative challenges, and for 'being in my corner' since the first day we met. What you do for emerging writers is astounding. Endless thanks to the committed and generous MC and SG writers for your enthusiasm and for helping me hone many extracts (long live the QFL!). Special thanks to Nick Gadd, Moreno Giovannoni, Susan Hurley, Karen McKnight, Janine Mikosza, Ellie Nielson, Phillip Schemnitz, Jane Sullivan, Honeytree Thomas and Ailsa Wild. And especially to Marion Roberts for putting me on this 'pathway to publication'.

Gracias especiales, Marina Alamo, not only for your warm, intelligent friendship but also the bottomless teapot, newly sharpened pencils and 'a room of one's own' in Mexico for an entire month, where I penned many thousands of these words.

A great deal of the polishing of this novel was completed during a Varuna Residential Fellowship in January 2020. I wish to thank the Eleanor Dark Foundation, Vera Costello, Carol Major, Veechi Stuart and the incomparable Sheila Atkinson for making my time in that serene and inspiring environment special in many ways. And to my fellow residents — Paris Floyd, Ella Jeffery, Audrey Molloy, Vanessa O'Neill, Janet Saunders and Lucie Stevens — whose stunning work blew me away: thank you for the talks, the readings (wow!) and the ongoing friendships.

Thank you, Alex Davie (for your technical knowledge about fires and fire-fighting), Stacey Stewart (for your invaluable midwifery knowledge that gave birth to the truth about Ruth), Pam Cupper, Phil Taylor and Dr Xavier Fowler (for willingly being recruited as sources of information about

World War II and conscription), and Tracy Weir and Stuart Andrew (your advice about all things police-related helped me uphold the right). Any errors or omissions relating to these matters are mine.

Thank you, Adam Bartlett, Tony Birch, Karen Corbett, Sari Smith and Arnold Zable for your generosity of spirit and mind while I was studying creative writing at the University of Melbourne. Your wisdom and encouragement have kept me going and going for many years, and through many moments of self-doubt.

Thank you to the members of The Lovely Ladies Book Club for reading not one but two early drafts of the manuscript a year apart, and convincing me that intelligent readers such as yourselves might find something to enjoy in my novel. This is a strategy I highly recommend to all authors! Thank you, Viv Barrett, Belinda Bickerton, Deborah Burbidge, Sawsan Howard, Leena Johnson, Nicole Knothe, Lyn LoMoro, Deidre Ochoa, Shikha Parmar, Sarah Timms and Stephanie Wenlock.

Thank you, Kirsten Alexander, Liam Pieper, Jock Serong, Benjamin Stevenson and Jane Sullivan for kindly giving your time and sharp minds to read this novel ahead of publication — while I trembled. Your support for an unknown writer embodies the generous spirit of Australia's writing community.

Thank you for your unique support and contribution, Fotini Agrotis, Viv Barrett, Frances Brooks, Ken Chau, Lindy Cowan, Carmelina di Guglielmo, Anita di Mase, Liselle D'Souza, Quinn Eades, Eva Eden, Alicia Eldridge, Ali Fulcher, David Green, Foong Ling Kong, Lauren Marshall, Beatrice Matthews, Carol Middleton, Marilyn Miller, Sarah Monaghan, Bronte Seidel, Maha Sidaoui, Karyn Siegmann, David Smith, Shane Thomas, Natalie Vella (and Memoria Podcast), Robyn Wallace-Mitchell, Megan Walton, Deanne Weir, Carol Wulfsohn and Miriam Zolin.

To my magnificent plot 'maestras', Rosemary Bunnell, Prudence Davie, Tiffany Plummer and Ruth Shepherd, your brilliant minds have given this book some of its best twists and turns, and my gratitude runs deeper than the Hendersons' dam.

To my extra-special writing mates, I am eternally grateful for your ruthless edits, challenging questions and treasured friendships. Thank you from the bottom of my heart, Stella Glorie, Russ 'Red Pen' Hogan, Jane Leonard, Tiffany Plummer, J. P. Pomare, Glen Thomson and the Cs of the MYWC. (And don't worry, JP: free edits!)

And finally, because we always leave the best to last, infinite thanks to Alex and Prudence, and Ella and Xav, who have not only brought me infinite joy but have backed me all the way in this endeavour. Thank you for everything you have given me, especially the laughs (and the earrings).

Thank you for reading this book.

If you enjoyed it please leave feedback on Amazon or Goodreads, and if there is anything we missed or you have a question about, then please get in touch. We appreciate you choosing our book.

Founded in 2014 in Shoreditch, London, we at Joffe Books pride ourselves on our history of innovative publishing. We were thrilled to be shortlisted for Independent Publisher of the Year at the British Book Awards.

www.joffebooks.com

We're very grateful to eagle-eyed readers who take the time to contact us. Please send any errors you find to corrections@joffebooks.com. We'll get them fixed ASAP.

Printed in Great Britain
by Amazon

80254374R00253